SF

Wright, John C.
(John Charles),
1961-

THE
PHOENIX
EXULTANT

Books by John C. Wright

The Golden Age
The Phoenix Exultant
The Golden Transcendence (forthcoming)

A Tom Doherty Associates Book   **TOR**®   New York

THE
PHOENIX
EXULTANT

or, Dispossessed in Utopia

Volume Two of The Golden Age

JOHN C. WRIGHT

THE PHOENIX EXULTANT; OR, DISPOSSESSED IN UTOPIA

Edited by David G. Hartwell

A Tor Book
Published by Tom Doherty Associates, LLC
175 Fifth Avenue
New York, NY 10010

www.tor.com

Tor® is a registered trademark of Tom Doherty Associates, LLC.

Library of Congress Cataloging-in-Publication Data

Wright, John C. (John Charles), 1961–
    The Phoenix Exultant; or, Dispossessed in Utopia / John C. Wright.—1st ed.
      p.   cm. — (The golden age ; bk. 2)
    "A Tom Doherty Associates Book."
    ISBN 0-765-30432-5 (alk. paper)
    1.   Life on other planets—Fiction.   I. Title: Phoenix Exultant.
II. Title: Dispossessed in Utopia.   III. Title.
PS3623.R54 P48 2003
813'.6—dc21

2002073280

First Edition: May 2003

Printed in the United States of America

0   9   8   7   6   5   4   3   2   1

DRAMATIS PERSONAE

MAJOR CHARACTERS, GROUPED BY NERVOUS SYSTEM
FORMATION (NEUROFORM):

Biochemical Self-Aware Entities:
Immortals:

Base neuroform:
PHAETHON PRIME of RHADAMANTH, Silver-Grey
Manorial school.

HELION RELIC of RHADAMANTH, Phaethon's sire,
founder of the Silver-Grey Manorial school, and a Peer.

DAPHNE TERCIUS SEMI-RHADAMANTH,
Phaethon's wife.

TEMER SIXTH LACEDAIMON, Dark Grey Manorial
school, an Advocate.

GANNIS HUNDRED-MIND GANNIS, Synergistic-
Synnoint school, a Peer.

ATKINS VINGT-ET-UN GENERAL-ISSUE, a soldier.

UNGANNIS, daughter of GANNIS, also called
UNMOIQHOTEP QUATRO NEOMORPH of the Cthonnic
school, of the Nevernext movement, whom Helion calls
the "Cacophiles."

**Alternate Organization neuroform, commonly called
Warlocks:**
AO AOEN, the Master-Dreamer, a Peer.

AO VARMATYR, one of the Lords-Paramount of the Silence, commonly called Swans.

NEO-ORPHEUS the Apostate, protonothary and chair of the COLLEGE of HORTATORS.

ORPHEUS MYRIAD AVERNUS, founder of the Second Immortality, a Peer.

Cortial-Thalamically Integrated neuroform, commonly called
Invariants:

KES SENNEC the Logician, a Peer.

Cerebelline neuroform:

WHEEL-OF-LIFE, an Ecological Mathematician, a Peer.

GREEN-MOTHER, the artiste who organizes the ecological performance at Destiny Lake.

OLD-WOMAN-OF-THE-SEA, of the Oceanic Environmental Protectorate.

DAUGHTER-OF-THE-SEA, a terraformer of Early Venus.

Mass-Mind Compositions:

The ELEEMOSYNARY COMPOSITION, a Peer.

The HARMONIOUS COMPOSITION, of the College of Hortators.

The BELLIPOTENT COMPOSITION (disbanded).

Nonstandard neuroforms:

VAFNIR of MERCURY EQUILATERAL STATION, a Peer.

XENOPHON of FARAWAY, Tritonic Neuroform Composure School, called the Neptunians.

XINGIS of NEREID, also called DIOMEDES, Silver-Gray School.

NEOPTOLEMUS, a combination of Diomedes and Xenophon.

Mortals:

VULPINE FIRST IRONJOY HULLSMITH, an Afloat.

OSHENKYO, an Afloat.

LESTER NOUGHT HAAKEN, an Afloat.

DRUSILLET ZERO SELF-SOUL, an Afloat.

SEMRIS of IO, an Ashore.

ANTISEMRIS, an Ashore.

NOTOR-KOTOK UNIQUE AMALGAMATED, an Ashore.

An OLD MAN, gardener of a grove of Saturn trees, who claims to be of the Antiamaranthine Purist school, not otherwise identified.

Electrophotonic Self-Aware Entities:

Sophotechs:

RHADAMANTHUS, a manor-house of the SILVER-GREY school, million-cycle capacity.

EVENINGSTAR, a manor-house of the RED school, million-cycle capacity.

NEBUCHEDNEZZAR, advisor to the College of Hortators, ten-million-cycle capacity.

HARRIER, consulting detective, one-hundred-thousand-cycle capacity.

MONOMARCHOS, a barrister, one-hundred-thousand-cycle capacity.

AURELIAN, host of the Celebration, fifty-thousand-million-cycle capacity.

The ENNEAD consists of nine Sophotech groups, each of over a billion-cycle capacity, including WARMIND, WESTMIND, ORIENT, AUSTRAL, BOREAL, NORTHWEST, SOUTHEAST, and others.

EARTHMIND, the unified consciousness in which all terrestrial machines, and machines in Near-Earth-Orbit, from time to time participate: trillion-cycle capacity.

Simulacra, Fictional Persons, Constructs:

COMUS, an avatar of AURELIAN.

SOCRATES and EMPHYRIO, constructs of NEBUCHEDNEZZAR.

The Justices of the CURIA.

SCARAMOUCHE, an extract of Xenophon the Neptunian.

The Envoy of DIOMEDES of NEREID.

MINOR CHARACTERS, INCLUDING HISTORICAL OR FICTIONAL PERSONS MENTIONED IN THE TALE:

AO ANDAPHANTIE, Daphne's name when she was a warlockess.

AYESHA, a cottage-mind used by Daphne, ten-thousand-cycle capacity.

CURTIS MAESTRICT, the Parliamentary Protonothary, and a friend and client of Daphne's.

JASON SVENTEN SHOPWORTHY, whose odd behavior has piqued the curiosity of the Sophotechs.

KSAHTRIMANYU HAN, the First Speaker of the Parliament.

UTE NONE STARK, Daphne's mother.

YEWEN NONE STARK, Daphne's father.

HISTORICAL AND FICTIONAL PERSONS:

Ao Enwir the Delusionist, famous for his treatise, "On the Sovereignty of Machines."

Ao Ormgorgon Darkwormhole Noreturn of the Black Swan Coven, captain-monarch of the multigeneration starship *Naglfar*, and culture hero who founded the Silent Oecumene at Cygnus X-1.

Ao Solomon Oversoul, marshal of the jihad in service to the Witch-King of Corea, credited with orchestrating the defeat of the Bellipotent Composition during the Era of the Fifth Mental Structure.

Buckland-Boyd Cyrano-D'Atano, the first man to survive a Mars landing.

Chan Noonyan Sfih of Io, explorer who accidentally set fire to Pluto.

Demontdelune, an unfortunate who came to grief on the dark side of the moon.

Enghathrathrion, a celebrated poet of the late-period Fourth Mental Structure.

Hamlet, a character from a linear-experience simulacrum, William Shakespeare, Era of the Second Mental Structure.

Hanno, of Carthage, sailed down the coast of Africa. The first explorer whose name is recorded by history.

Harlequin, a clown from the French comic operetta, Era of the Second Mental Structure.

Jason, master of the *Argo*, who sailed to Golden Cheronese and returned with the Fleece.

Mancuriosco the Neuropathist.

Mother-of-Numbers, a Cerebelline mathematician, whose disquisition on Noetic Mathematics formed a foundation for Noumenal technology.

Neil Armstrong, first man to set foot on Luna.

Oe Sephr al-Midr the Descender-into-Clouds, early Jupiter explorer.

Scaramouche, a clown from the French comic operetta, Era of the Second Mental Structure.

Sir Francis Drake, Master of the *Golden Hind*, discovered the Northwest Passage.

Sloppy Rufus, the first dog to survive a Mars landing (Bucky-Boy Cyrano's dog).

The Porphyrogen Composition, a noted sect of astronomers.

Ulysses, King of Ithaca, who sailed far to know the minds of men and their ways, returning from the underworld.

Vandonnar, according to pre-Ignition Jovian poetry, a cloud-diver so entirely lost in the storms surrounding the

Great Red Spot, that even death found him unable to
locate the course to the afterlife, and therefore Vandonnar
circles eternally in the storm, forever seeking, forever lost.

Vanguard Single Exharmony, survived the first manned
mission into the Solar Photosphere.

THE
PHOENIX
EXULTANT

THE CYBORG

I.

He opened the door onto a crowded boulevard of matter-shops, drama-spaces, reliquaries, shared-form communion theaters, colloquy-salons, and flower parks. An elaborate hydrosculpture of falls and aerial brooks spread from a central fountain works throughout the area, with running water held aloft by subatomic reorientations of its surface tension, so that arches and bows of shining transparency rose or fell, splashed or surged with careless indifference to the reality of gravity. Light, scattered from tall windows lining the concourse or from banners of advertisements or from high panels opening up into the regional mentality, was caught and made into rainbows by the high-flowing waters. Petals from floating water lilies drifted down across the scene.

Beneath all this beauty was a crass ugliness. More than three-quarters of the people were present as mannequins. This was evidently a place meant for manorials, cryptics, or other schools that relied heavily on telepresentation. Since Phaethon no longer had access to any kind of sense-filter, all these folk, no matter how splendid of dress or elegant of comportment they might have appeared to an observer in the Surface Dreaming, looked to him like so many ranks and ranks of gray, dull, and faceless mannequins.

There may have been beautiful music sweeping the area; excluded from the mentality, Phaethon was deaf to it. Here and there were hospice boxes or staging pools, ready to send out dreams or partials, calls, messages, or any form of telepresentation. All channels were closed to Phaethon, and he was mute. There were dragon-signs burning like fire in the air, displaying messages of unknown import. Phaethon could not read the subtext or hypertext; Phaethon was illiterate. There may have been thought-guides in the Middle Dreaming to allow him to remember, as if he had always known, where to find the public transport he sought. Mnemonic assistance gone; Phaethon was an amnesiac. There may have been ornament and pageantry in the dream-stages gathered in the air around him, lovely beyond description, or signs and maps to show Phaethon where, in this wide concourse, might be the way or the road he sought. But Phaethon was blind.

Here and there among the mannequins, the face of a realist or vivarianist showed. Their eyes turned dull when they lit on Phaethon, and their gazes slid past him without seeing. All sense-filters were tuned to exclude him. The world was blind to him as well.

He expected the banners overhead to swoop down on him when he looked up. But no. They floated on by, shouting with lights and garish displays. Even the advertisements ignored him.

No matter. Phaethon tried to keep his thoughts only on the next steps immediately before him. How to find out where he was? How to find Talaimannar? How to go from here to there? Once there, how to find out why Harrier Sophotech recommended that place?

He had to ask someone for help, or directions.

Phaethon stepped behind a stand of bushes; there was a flow of water from the fountain works overhead, forming a rippling, translucent ceiling. Was anyone watching? He assumed not.

He doffed his armor and covered it with the cape of nanomaterial, which he then programmed to look like a hooded cloak. Phaethon himself merely drew out some of the nanomaterial from the black skin-garment he wore, and drew circles around his eyes, to solidify into a black domino mask. And that was that: Both of them were now in disguise. He hoped it was enough to fool at least a casual inspection. He programmed the suit to follow him at a fixed distance, avoiding obstacles; to "heel" as Daphne would have said.

He stepped out again into the concourse, followed by the bulky, cloaked form of his armor, looming three paces behind him. He went downstairs and found a pondside esplanade that had fewer mannequins walking along it. He saw real faces; faces made of flesh or metal, or cobra scales, or polystructural material, or energy surfaces. They were laughing and talking, signaling and depicting. The air seemed charged with a carnival excitement. Many people skipped or danced as they strolled, moved by music Phaethon could not hear. Others dived over the side of the esplanade, to glide among the buildings and statues in the pond.

He did not know what particular event was being celebrated. It was rare to see so many folk together. Whatever bunting or decoration swam in the dreamspace here, which might have given him a clue as to the nature of the occasion, was, of course, invisible to him.

People smiled and nodded at him as they walked by, full of good cheer. "Merry Millennium! May you live a thousand years!"

He had not realized how much he had missed, and was going to miss, the sight of friendly human faces. Phaethon smiled back, waving, and calling out, "And a thousand years to you!"

Phaethon reminded himself that he had to be careful. Theoretically, the masquerade protocol would not protect him, since he was no longer part of the celebration, no longer part of the community. But how many people would even try to read his identity if they saw him wearing a mask during a masquerade? Most people, Phaethon guessed, would not.

The rule from the Hortators was that no one was to give him aid, comfort, food or drink, or shelter, sell him goods or services, or buy from him, or donate charity to him. This rule did not (in theory) actually prohibit speaking to him, or looking at him and smiling, although that was the way it surely would be practiced.

If Phaethon tried to buy something from a passerby, Aurelian was obligated to warn him that he was about to be contaminated with exile. But as long as Phaethon did not try to win from the passersby either food or drink or comfort or shelter or charity, Aurelian would no doubt stand mute. Sophotechs had a long, long tradition of failing to volunteer any information that had not been specifically asked.

It was hard. A couple walking hand in hand were passing out

wedding-album projections of their future children. Phaethon smiled but declined to take one. A young girl (or someone dressed as one), skipping and licking a floating balloon-pastry offered him a bite; Phaethon patted her on the head, but did not touch her pastry. When a laughing wine-juggler, surrounded by musical fire-crackers, and balancing on a ball, rolled by and tried to thrust a glass of champaign into Phaethon's hand, Phaethon was not able to refuse except by jerking his hand away.

The juggler frowned, wondering at Phaethon's lack of courtesy, and raised two fingers as if to try to find out who Phaethon really was. But the juggler was distracted when a slender, naked gyno-morph, fluttering with a hundred stimulation scarves, jumped up in drunken passion to embrace him. Singing a carol to Aphrodite, the two rolled off together, while the juggler's bottles and goblets fell this way and that.

Phaethon let the throng carry him down the esplanade.

The pressure of the crowd eased when Phaethon came to a line of windows, two hundred feet tall or more, which looked out upon a balcony larger than a boulevard. Out onto the balcony they all went together. Phaethon climbed up a pedestal holding a statue of Orpheus in his pose as Father of the Second Immortality. The stone hands held up a symbol in the shape of a snake swallowing its own tail. Phaethon put his foot in the stone coils of the serpent and pulled himself high, looking left and right above the heads of the crowd.

Several lesser towers and small skyscrapers grew up from the railing of the balcony, like little corals fringing the topless super-tower of the space elevator.

Beyond the balcony, the metropolis spread out from the mountain-base of the space elevator in three concentric circles. Innermost and oldest, the center circle consisted of huge window-less structures shaped according to simple geometries; giant cubes, hemispheres, and hemicylinders, painted in bright, primary colors, connected by rectilinear motion-lines and smart roads. The archi-tecture followed the Objective Aesthetic, with the building shapes, slabs, and plaques all rigidly stereotyped. There was little move-ment in this part of the city; human beings of the basic neuroform tended to find these faceless buildings and looming monoliths intolerable. Mostly, this central ring housed Sophotech components, warehouses, manufactures. Invariants, who had little desire for beauty or pleasure or inefficiency, lived here, dwelling in square dormitories arranged like rank upon rank of coffin-beds.

The second ring was done in the Standard Aesthetic. Here were black pools and lakes of nanomachinery, with many brooks and rills, touched with white foam of the dark material streaming from one to another. Tiny waterfalls of the material formed where cascade-separator stages mixed and organized the components. Each lake was surrounded by the false-trees and coral bioformations of nanomanufactory. A hundred solar parasols raised orchidlike colors to the sun. The houses and presence chambers were formed of strange growthlike seashells; one spiral after another, shining with lambent mother-of-pearl, rose to the skyline. Blue-black, dark pearl, glinting silver, and dappled blue-gray hues dominated the scene. Thought-gardens, coven places, and sacred circles dotted the area, along with nymphariums, mother trees, and staging pools. Warlocks and basics tended to prefer the chaotic fractals and organic shapes of the Standard Aesthetic. Wide areas of garden space were occupied by the decentralized bodies of Cerebellines.

Beyond this, on the hills surrounding, green arbors and white mansions prevailed. This was the Consensus Aesthetic, patronized mostly by manor-born and first-generation basics. Greek columns marched along the hilltops; formal English gardens rested in green shadows before grand houses done in the Georgian style, or neo-Roman, or stern Alexandrian.

In the far distance, Phaethon saw a wide lake. On the lake were a hundred shapes like jewel-armored clipper ships, whose sails were textured like a dozen wings of butterflies, surrounded with light.

Now Phaethon knew where he was. This city was Kisumu, south of Aetheopia, overlooking Lake Victoria. And Phaethon understood the wonder and excitement of the crowd. For the huge shapes in the lake were the Deep Ones.

These were the last of the once-great race of the Jovian half-warlocks, a unique neuroform that combined elements from the Cerebelline and Warlock nervous-system structures. Once, they rode the storms and swam in the pressurized methane atmosphere of Jupiter, before its ignition. When the time came to end their way of life, they chose instead to enter whalelike bodies and to sleep at the bottom of the Marianas Trench, where they called back and forth to each other, and wove songs and sonar images relating to the vast, sad, and ancient emotions known only to them; and made sounds in the deep, which reminded them, but could not recapture, those songs and sensations their old Jupiter-adapted Behemoth bodies once had made in the endless atmosphere of that gas-giant planet.

Once every thousand years, only during the time of the Millennium, they woke from their dreams of sorrow, grew festive gems and multicolored membranes and sails along their upper hulls, rose to the surface, and sang in the air.

By an ancient contract, no recordings could be made of their great songs, nor was anyone allowed to speak of what they heard or dreamed when that music swept over them.

No wonder so many people were here in reality.

Phaethon's heart was in his throat. The songs of the Deep Ones he had only heard once before, since he had not attended this ceremony his second millennial masquerade, during Argentorium's tenure. That time once before, three thousand years ago (during the tenure of Cuprician) the song had sung to him of vastness, emptiness, and a sense of infinite promise. It was as if Phaethon had been plunged into the wide expanses of the Jovian cloudscape; or into the far wider expanses of the stars beyond.

The Deep Ones had originally been designed also to serve as living spaceships, able to swim the radiation-filled and dust-filled vacuum between the Jovian moons, able to tolerate the almost unthinkable re-entry heat of low-orbit dives down into the Jovian atmosphere. But the early successes in cleaning circumjovial space and in taming the Jovian magnetosphere, made those space-lanes safe and economical for ships of ordinary construction; the emplacements of sky hooks made alarming re-entries unnecessary. The Deep Ones' way of life was past; the danger and romance of space travel was removed. Phaethon had heard all of this in their song, so long ago. It had planted the seed that blossomed into his own desire to embrace his dream of star travel.

It had been Daphne who had brought him to hear it. But had that been Daphne Prime, or her ambassador-doll, Daphne Tercius? Phaethon could not remember. Perhaps his lack of useful sleep was beginning to affect his memory.

Phaethon jumped down from the pedestal and began to push his way through the crowd, and away. For the Deep Ones did not give away their grand, sad music freely. Everyone who did not exclude the music from his sense filter would have a fee charged to his account; and, when the computers detected that Phaethon could not pay, he would be unmasked. Once Phaethon was unmasked, no one, of course, would help him. Not to mention that the performance would be delayed, and the afternoon spoiled for everyone. (He was amazed to discover that he still cared about the convenience and pleasure of his fellowmen, even though they had ostracized him. But the wonder of that first Deep One symphony he had once heard still haunted his memory. He did not want to diminish the joy of folk happier than he.)

The crowd thinned as he rounded the space elevator, and came to the side facing away from the lake. Several dirigible airships, as large as whales themselves, were docked with their noses touching the towers rising from the balcony sides. They had dragon-signs in the air, displaying their routes and times in a format Phaethon could not read.

Phaethon stopped a passerby, a woman dressed as a pyretic. "Pardon me, miss, but my companion and I are looking for the way to Talaimannar." He gestured toward the hooded and cloaked figure of his armor, standing silently behind him. He spoke what was not quite a lie: "My companion and I are involved in a masquerade game of hunt-and-seek, and we are not allowed to access the mentality. Could you tell me how to find the nearest smart road?"

She cocked her head at him. Her dancing eyes were surrounded by wreaths of flame, and smoke curled from her lips when she smiled. When she spoke, Phaethon had no routine to translate her words into his language and grammar and logic.

He tried more simply: "Talaimannar . . . ? Talaimannar . . . ? Smart road?" He pantomimed sliding along a frictionless surface, hands waving, so that she giggled.

By her emphatic gesture he understood she meant that the smart roads were not running; she pointed him toward a nearby airship and pushed him lightly on the shoulder, as if to say, Go! Go!

Phaethon froze. Had she just helped him, or offered him passage on some ship owned by her? There was no alarm in her eyes; to judge from her expression, there was no secret voice from Aurelian warning her. And the woman was turning away, drawn by the movement of the crowd. Evidently she was not the owner.

Phaethon moved up the ramp. Closer, he saw the airship bore the heraldic symbol of the Oceanic Environmental Protectorate. It was a cargo lifter, perhaps the very one that had brought one or more Deep Ones from the Pacific to Lake Victoria.

The throngs began to fall silent. Out on the lake, Deep Ones were sailing to position, raising and unfurling their singing-fans. A sense of tension, of expectancy, was palpable in the air. Phaethon stepped reluctantly across the gilt threshold of the hatch and into the ship's interior, his eyes turned over his shoulder.

Giant magnifier screens, focused on the distant Deep Ones, floated up over the edge of the huge balcony. The images showed the Deep Ones, sails wide and high, motionless on the surface of the lake, all their prows pointed toward the Deep One matriarch-conductor, who floated like a mountain above her children, her million singing-flags like an Autumn forest seen along a mountainside.

Phaethon's feet were slow. He wanted so desperately to hear this one last song. Except for tunes he might whistle himself, or music shed from advertisements passing by, Phaethon would not hear songs again: no one would perform for him; no one would sell him a recording.

He steeled himself and turned his back. The hatch shut silently behind him.

The deck was deserted. The place was empty.

2.

Before him, carpeted in burgundy, set with small tables and formulation rods of glass and white china, was an observation deck. Antique reading helmets plated with ornamental brass nested in the ceiling. A line of couches faced tall windows overlooking the prow, with seeing rings in little dishes to one side. The privacy screens around the couches were folded and transparent at the moment, but Phaethon could still see ghostly half-images of creatures from Japanese mythology depicted in the glassy surface.

He did not recognize the aesthetic. Something older than the Objective period perhaps? Whatever it was, it was opulent and elegant.

Phaethon stepped aboard; his armor stepped after him. Phaethon raised his hand to make the open-channel gesture, then stopped himself, looked at his hand sadly, and lowered it. He could not access any information just by directing a thought or gesture at it, not ever again. But it would not be hard to adapt, he told himself. He was a Silver-Grey; and speaking out loud was one of the traditions Silver-Greys diligently practiced.

"Who is here? What is this place? Is there anyone aboard?"

No answer. He stepped forward toward the couches, sat down gingerly.

The privacy screen to his left was half-open, so that one transparent panel was between him and the left-hand windows looking down on the balcony. Within the frame of this screen, the scene had more color and motion than elsewhere. Every gray mannequin within this frame was suddenly colored and costumed and bestowed with an individual human face. Overhead, banners and displays curled through the air, drifting. But any mannequin who stepped out of the frame turned gray again, and any banner vanished.

The privacy screen must have been tuned to the Surface Dreaming, Phaethon realized. It was an antique of some sort that translated mental images into light images. He amused himself for a moment by moving his head left and right, so that different parts of the balcony, now to the right and now to the left, were touched with extra color and pageantry. Gray mannequins were transformed to breathtaking courtiers, splendid in dress, and then, with another move of his head, back into gray mannequins again.

Then he saw, amid the pageantry, a figure in white and rose lace with a tricorn hat, face disfigured by a hook nose and hook chin. It was Scaramouche. Behind him were Columbine in her harlot's skirts and Pierrot, pale-faced and in baggy white. The three pantomime figures were moving against the flow of the crowd with deliberate haste; their heads moved in unison, back and forth, scanning the crowd with methodical sweeps.

They closed in on a figure dressed in gold armor; but no, it was merely someone dressed as Alexander the Great, in a gilt breast-plate. Alexander the Great stared at them in confusion; the three pantomime clowns bowed and frolicked, and Alexander turned away. Scaramouche and his two confederates stood a moment, motionless, as if hearing instructions from some remote source.

Phaethon tried to tell himself that this was some coincidence of costuming. Xenophone's agent would not be so foolish as to continue to dress in the same costume as before. No doubt these were merely Black Manorials, looking for Phaethon to taunt or humiliate him, and dressed in the way Phaethon had said his enemy had dressed. It would have been easy to copy the costume from the public records of the Hortators' inquest.

Except that Black Manorials could have simply found out from the mentality where Phaethon was. The Hortators, without doubt, would have posted conspicuous notices telling everyone what Phaethon had done, and where he was, and how to avoid him. Only someone who did not want to leave a trace would attempt to find Phaethon by eye.

As if stimulated by a silent signal, the three pantomime clowns now turned toward the airship docks. Their eyes seemed to meet Phaethon's own, staring up at the windows where he stood. The eyes moved to Phaethon's left, where the armor stood, covered by a hooded robe.

Phaethon said to himself: *Surely they are not looking for two figures, one in black, one in a robe.*

But the three figures began pushing through the crowd toward the airship dock. They passed outside the range of the frame of the privacy screen, and suddenly they were merely three anonymous gray mannequins lost in a throng of similar mannequins.

Phaethon squinted, but, separated from the mentality, he could not amplify his vision, make a recording, or set up a motion-detection program to discover which of the moving bodies lost in the crowd were the ones he sought. Disconnected, he was blind and crippled. His enemies were coming, and he was helpless.

He could not send out a responder-pulse to discover the serial numbers of the mannequins involved; he could not call the constables. If he logged on to the mentality to make the call, descendants of the enemy virus civilizations would come out from hiding and strike him down the moment he opened a channel.

Was there a way to send a voice-only signal from the circuits in his armor? Phaethon jumped off the couch and pushed back the hood on the figure behind him. He looked at the contact points and thought-ports running along the shoulder boards of the armor. There was an energy repeater that could be tuned to the radio frequencies set aside for the constabulary; here was a sensitive plate that could react to voice command. All he needed was a carrier wire to run from the one to the other.

That wire was not something his nanomachinery cape could produce. He could have bought it for a half-second coin at any matter-shop . . . had he been allowed. As it was, he could broadcast a loud, meaningless noise. A scream. A scream to which no one would listen.

He stepped back toward the privacy screen and tried to turn it on its hinges to face that part of the crowd near the bottom of the ramp leading up to this ship. The screen would not budge. He could not see where the mannequins controlled by the enemy might be.

Now what? If only he had been a character from one of his wife's dream-dramas, he could find a convenient ax or bar of iron, and rush out to battle the foe, club swinging, his shirt ripped to display his manly shoulders and hairy chest. But strength would not serve against these mannequins; the mind motivating them was not even physically present.

And wit would not serve, not if there was, in fact, a Nothing Sophotech directing their actions, a Sophotech clever enough to move through the Earth mentality without coming to the notice of the Earthmind.

What was left? Spiritual purity? Moral rectitude?

And, if it was a moral quality involved, what could it be? Honesty? Forthrightness? Blind determination?

Phaethon thought for a moment, gathering his courage. Then he threw the robe off his armor and had the black material swirled around him, fitting the gold segments into place. He closed the helmet.

Phaethon stepped to the hatch of the airship and flung it open, but he was careful not to step over the threshold. He stood at the top of the ramp, somewhat above the nearby crowd. Three gray mannequins were stepping purposefully toward the foot of the ramp; the leader paused with one foot on the ramp, his blind, blank head turned up suddenly to see Phaethon standing, shining in his gold adamantine armor, at the end of the ramp above him.

A long low trembling note of haunting beauty, like the sigh of a sad oboe, came up from the surface of Lake Victoria, rose, gathered strength, and filled the wide sky. It was the first note of the overture, the first voice of the choir. Just that one note brought a tear to Phaethon's eye. Except for the three mannequins facing him, all other spectators were turned toward the distant lake, looks of tense wonder and rapt enchantment on their features, like people swept up in a dream.

Phaethon touched the energy repeater on his shoulder board. He heard nothing, but he knew a loud pulse, like a shout, passed across nearby radio channels.

The note trembled and fell mute. Silence, not music, filled the air.

Phaethon had been noticed. The Deep Ones were not singing. Some signal inaudible to Phaethon swept through the gathered crowd. With a murmur of anger, and a long hissing, rustling noise, a thousand faces suddenly turned toward him. Every eye focused on the gold figure.

The three mannequins at the foot of the ramp paused, motionless.

Whatever they had intended for Phaethon, they evidently did not wish to do in full and public view.

The murmur of anger rose to a shout. It was a horrible noise, one Phaethon had not heard before in all his life; the sound of a thousand voices all calling for Phaethon to get out, to leave, to let the performance ceremony continue. Instead of music, now, shouts of outrage, shrill questions, and sounds of hatred roared in the air.

The three gray mannequins were still motionless at the bottom of the ramp. Phaethon raised his hand and pointed a finger at these three. He knew no human ear could hear him or distinguish his words over the roar of the crowd; but he also knew that there were more than human minds listening to him now. Events like this rapidly filled the news and gossip channels; anything he did would be analyzed by mass-minds and by Sophotechs.

"The enemies to the Golden Oecumene are here among you. Who projects into these three mannequins here? Where are the constables to protect me from their violence? Nothing! For all your superior intellect, you cannot and you dare not strike at me openly; I denounce you as a coward!"

Another rustling murmur ran through the vast crowd there. Contempt and disbelief, disgust and anger were clear on every face. And then, just as suddenly, the eyes focused on him went glassy and dull. By an unspoken common consent, the crowd were tuning their sense-filters to ignore him; perhaps they were opening redaction channels to forget him, so that, in later years, their memories of this fine day would not be marred by the rantings of a madman. Like a wind blowing through a field of wheat, with one motion, every head in the crowd turned back toward the lake.

Phaethon smiled grimly. Here was the moral error of a society that relied too heavily on the sense-filter to falsify their reality for them. Reality could not be faked. The Deep Ones did not use anything like a sense-filter. If the Deep Ones had any channels open in the mentality, they would still be aware of Phaethon, and they would still refuse to offer their gift of song to one, like Phaethon, who would not and could not thank them, or repay them, or return the gift. The crowd could well ignore him; but the Deep Ones would not sing.

Were they waiting for him to walk away? It must occur to some of them that it would take hours for him, on foot, to walk beyond hearing range of the Deep Song. Were they all willing to wait that long? It also should occur to someone that, by the rules of the ostracization imposed on him, Phaethon could neither buy passage on any transport or accept a ride as charity. The only other option, logically, would be to have a ride imposed upon him without his asking.

It was a contest of wills. Who was more willing to put up with the inconvenience of Phaethon's exile? Phaethon, who knew he was in the right? Or the crowd, who perhaps had some nagging doubt whether the Hortators had been entirely correct?

If those who opposed him were certain of the moral rightness of their position, Phaethon thought, they would simply call the constables and have him removed. And if not . . .

The hatch swung shut in front of his nose. The ramp and guy lines retracted into the docking tower. Phaethon felt a swell of motion in the deck underfoot.

The airship was carrying him away. He stepped over to the windows, hoping for a last glimpse of the three mannequins at the foot of the now-retracted ramp. He saw them, but their arms now hung limply, heads lolling, in the stoop-shouldered posture indicating that they were now uninhabited. Xenophon's agent (or Nothing Sophotech, or whoever or whatever had been projected into them) had disconnected and fled.

With a grand sweep of movement, the towers and the wide balcony ringing the space elevator passed by the observation windows. The world was tilted at an angle, as the airship heeled over, tacking into the wind and gaining altitude.

Phaethon felt a moment of victorious pleasure. But the moment faltered, and a sad look came into his eyes, when, outside the windows and far below, he saw the blue reaches of Lake Victoria. Sunlight flashed from the surface of the lake, and the texture of high, distant clouds was reflected in the depths. Amid those reflections, Phaethon saw the flotilla of ancient beings with their singing-fans spread wide. But he was too far away, by then, to hear anything other than a faint, sad, far-off echo.

Even if, by some odd miracle, his exile were to end tomorrow, Phaethon would never hear what the Deep Ones now would sing, no record was made of it, and no one would speak to him of it.

With an abrupt motion, Phaethon turned and stepped to the bow windows, staring out at the African hills and skies ahead.

3.

A silver strip of shore passed by below him. Ahead was an endless field of cobalt blue, crisscrossed by whitecaps—the Indian Ocean.

Phaethon spoke aloud. "Where are you taking me?" Again there was no answer. He found two hatches at the back of the observation deck, with gangways leading up and down. He chose the upward ramp and set off to explore.

On a windowless upper deck, surrounded by a mass of cables and fixtures, he found a six-legged being, with six arms or tentacles reaching up from a central brain-mass into the control interfaces. Wires ran into the cone-shaped head. Sections of the body were plated with metal. Three vulture faces stared out in three directions from the central brain-cone. The hide was dotted and pierced with plugs and jacks, inputs and outlets. Multiple receivers aided the migration instincts and flying sense built into the bird heads with orbit-to-surface navigational plotting.

"You are a fighter-plane cyborg," said Phaethon in surprise. He had never seen such a thing outside of a museum.

The vulture eyes regarded him coldly. "No longer. All memories of war and battle-flight, dogfighting, system ranging, dive-bombing, all such thoughts and recollections I sold long, so very long ago, to Atkins of the Warmind. Let him have nightmares now. Let him recall the smell of incendiaries burning villages and hamlets, and pink baby-forests screaming. I recall flowers and kittens now, the songs of whales, the motion of cloud above the ocean; I am content."

"Do you know who I am?"

"An exile; an exile wealthy beyond all dreams of wealth, to judge from the armor you wear. Famous, to judge by the channel traffic your movements excite. All the world forgot, and then all the world, just as suddenly, recalled the mighty ship you dreamed; every mind in the networks still is reeling from you; every voice cries out against you. Are you he?"

Phaethon wondered why the creature did not discover his identity merely by looking into the Middle Dreaming. "You are not connected to the mentality, then, sir?"

The three vulture heads snapped their hooked beaks open and shut with loud clacks. "Gah! I scoff at such things. There is nothing in me I need to transcend. Let the young ones play their games; I take no part in the celebration of the Golden Oecumene."

"It seems, now, that I will take no part, either. You have guessed me, sir. I am Phaethon Prime of Rhadamanth."

"No longer. Surely you are Phaethon Zero of Nothing."

The name struck Phaethon to the heart. Of course. He had no copies of himself any longer in any bank. He was no longer Phaethon Prime, the first copy from a stored template. He was a zero. The moment he died, there would be nothing more of him. He had no mansion, no school.

Phaethon said, "And you do not fear to speak with me?"

"Fear whom? The College of Hortators? The Sophotechs? Upstarts! I am older than any College of Hortators; older than any Sophotechs. Older than the Foederal Oecumenical Commonwealth." (This was the old name for the Golden Oecumene.) "They are delicate structures, based on no real strength. They shall pass away, and I shall remain. My way of life has been forgotten, but it shall return. I remember nothing but kittens and clouds, for now. Memories of burning children shall return."

It was brave talk, but Phaethon reminded himself that this cyborg had neither sold him passage nor extended charity to him. Phaethon's legal status, at the moment, was something between a freeloader and a kidnap victim.

"Who are you, sir?"

"This is not the proper format. You, the interloper, the stranger, the exile, must tell your tale; I, the gracious host, will tell mine after, what little there is. There is no computer here to implant automatic memories of each other in each other."

"I am a Silver-Grey. We retain the custom of exchanging introductions and information through speech . . ."

"You were a Silver-Grey. How did you come to lose your vast fortune? What did you do to earn the hatred of mankind?"

"I dreamt a dream they feared. There is no economic reason to reach the stars; the stars are too far, and there is abundance of all types, without oppression, here. But my reason was unreasonable; I wished for glory, for greatness, to do what had not been done before; and my wealth was my own, to spend or squander as I would. And so I built the greatest ship our science could produce: the *Phoenix Exultant*, a hollow streamlined spearpoint a hundred kilometers from stem to stern, with all her hollow hull filled up with antimatter fuel, and her hull of chrysadmantium, this same invulnerable substance in which you see me clad, made one artificial atom at a time, at tremendous expense. The fuel-to-mass ratio is such that near-light speeds can be maintained. But the College of Hortators feared . . ."

"I know what they feared. They feared war. War in heaven."

"How do you know this, sir? Do you know the Hortators?"

"I know war."

"Who are you?"

"You ask too soon; your tale is not yet told."

"Ah . . . yes. Where was I, Rhadamanthus?—er " Phaethon winced for a moment, then recovered himself. "Ahem. So the ship was built. No other vessel like her has ever been launched. For example, in a mean average burn of fifty-one gravities acceleration, if maintained for a decade and a half, assuming a mean density of one particle per cubic kilometer in the intervening medium, and adjusting for radiant back pressure created by heat loss due to friction, the vessel is able to reach a speed of . . ."

"I do not need to hear the ship specifications."

"But that is the most interesting part!"

"And yet I am your host. Continue the tale, Phaethon Zero."

"The College of Hortators threatened to ostracize me if I launched the *Phoenix Exultant*. Since flight to even nearby stars would be a deeper and longer exile than any they could impose, I laughed their

threats to scorn. The threat fell where I did not expect. I was in the
process of launching the ship on her maiden voyage, when my wife,
whose frail courage was overcome (for she was sure I would die in
interstellar space), drowned herself. I reacted with rage, and broke
into the crypt where her dreaming body is kept. Atkins, the
military-human interface, was called up out of old archive storage . . . but you know who he is."

"I know him. Part of me lives in him."

"Atkins was called, and threw me on my face. The College of
Hortators denounced me; the expense of the *Phoenix Exultant* bank-
rupted me; my father died in a solar storm, died trying to save my
vessel, docked at Mercury station, from harm. I suppose I should
tell this in a better order . . ."

"You have engaged my interest. Continue."

"The result was that the College agreed not to exile me if I agreed
to forget about my ship. My father's relic was woken out of Archive,
and I had to forget he was not my father, because the event of the
death was connected to the memory of the ship."

"Father? You are a biological puritan? Your father bore you?"

"Pardon me. He is my sire. I was constructed out of his mnemonic templates. I am using the word 'father' as a metaphor. We
Silver-Grey are traditionalists, and we believe that certain specific
human emotional relationships, such as family love, should be
maintained even when no longer needed. We are devoted to the idea
that . . . hmph . . . perhaps I should be saying, 'they are' or 'I was,'
shouldn't I?"

The vulture heads stared at him, yellow eyes unblinking, and
said nothing.

"In any event, I also had to forget the drowning of my wife, whose
suicide was caused, after all, also by my ship. This was on the eve
of the celebrations."

"Again you use the phrase metaphorically . . . ?"

"Do you mean 'wife'? She really is my wife, joined to me by
sacred vow. 'Suicide'? I suppose that is a metaphor. She is dead to
reality. Her brain information exists in a fictional computerized
dreamscape with no outside access permitted; her memories were
altered to divorce all knowledge of real things from her. I know of

no way to wake her; she did not leave any code words for me."

"It is indeed a metaphor, my young aristocrat. In earlier times, and even now, among the poor, death is not a thing we can afford merely to play at, or use an elegant machine to imitate. But no matter: I know what next occurred. All the millions in the Golden Oecumene, agreed to forgot as well, in order that the danger of star travel pass them by; and those who would not agree at first were pressured, or bribed, or browbeaten by the College of Hortators. As the ranks grew of those who had agreed to the redaction, those few who held out, found that they had fewer and fewer friends; and only those who would not or could not attend your celebration and transcendence still remembered you. Much hate fell on you, before your deed was forgotten, by those who blamed you for the need to make themselves forget."

"Interesting. I did not know that aspect of it."

"The pressure from the Hortators was greater among the poor, who have no avenue to resist such potent social forces; in the last days before the celebration started, you were indeed not well liked among the humbler members of the Oecumene."

"I met one of them, I think. An old man. I mean, a man who had suffered physical decay and entropic disintegration of his biochemical systems—he had white hair and ossified joints. I don't know who he was. He is the one who first told me that Phaethon of Rhadamanth was not who he thought he was—I was not who I thought I was. And yet he knew me well enough to know how I typically dressed; he knew enough about how I programmed my sense-filter, to use an override trick and escape from my perception. That is what started this all.

"I shut off my sense-filter to look for the old man, and instead found an Eremite from Neptune, a shapeless, shape-changing amoeboid in shapeless, shape-changing armor of crystal blue. The Neptunian approached and introduced himself as Xenophon. I had worked with the Neptunians while building my ship, and I knew many of them—this was an imposter of some sort, trying to get me to resume my old memories."

"Why?"

"To get my ship, I think. Certain Neptunians were clients and partners of mine during the ship construction. Friends, even. From somewhere they got the money to buy out the debts I owed the Peers, so that if I defaulted, the ship would go to them, rather than to my creditors. Meanwhile Xenophon was controlling the other Neptunians. The arbitrator, you see, had placed my ship in receivership . . ."

"I do not know the term."

"Bankruptcy. Hock. Pawned."

"Understood. Go on."

"Xenophon tried to pretend he was a friend of mine, to get me to open my memory casket and resume my old life. This would have triggered the injunctions established by the College of Hortators, my loans would automatically default, and the debts I owed the Seven Peers would now be owed to the Neptunians, debts for which the *Phoenix Exultant* stood as surety. In other words, after my default, the *Phoenix Exultant* would end up in the hands of Xenophon rather than the Seven Peers."

"Who are they?"

"How can you know who an obscure historical figure like Atkins is, but not know who the Seven Peers are?"

"I do not move in your social circles, Phaethon."

"The Peers are a private combination of monopolists who have made a number of agreements, and who coordinate their efforts, in order to maintain their wealth and prestige. Gannis of Jupiter, who makes the supermetals; Vafnir of Mercury, who makes antimatter for powerhouses; Wheel-of-Life, who runs ecological transformation nexi; Helion stops solar flares; Kes Sennec organizes the scientific and semantic pursuits of the Invariants and controls the Uniform Library of the Cities in Space; the Eleemosynary Composition runs translation formats; Orpheus grants eternal life."

"Oh. Them. They are not monopolists. Your laws allow other efforts and businesses to compete against them. In my day, those who opposed the grants of the General Coordination Commissariat were sent to the Absorption Chamber, and members were swapped between the compositions."

"The Commissariat was abolished before the end of the Era of the Fourth Mental Structure. You cannot possibly be so old as that. That was over many thousands of years before immortality was discovered."

"Second Immortality. The Compositions have a collective immortality of memory-records. Individual members die, but the massmind continues."

"Are you part of the Eleemosynary Composition?"

"It is not yet time for me to speak. Finish your tale. Xenophon tricked you, and you opened your memories?"

"That is a proper summation. He has an agent disguised as a pantomime clown. Hunting for me."

"Hunted by clowns? How quaint."

"Ahem. Well, there is a an explanation, sir. I was dressed in Harlequinade when Xenophon first met me, so he dressed his agent as a character from the same comedy. Scaramouche—the agent—attacked me with a complex mind virus, a civilization of viral information, actually, while I was linked to the mentality. If I log on again, I will be attacked, and perhaps erased and replaced."

"The Sophotechs permit this . . . ?"

"They have no technology to understand what is being done, or how the information particles are being transmitted into a shielded system. The technology is not from the Golden Oecumene."

"It is not from an earlier period. It is not from before the Oecumene."

"I am not speaking of 'before,' my good sir. I am speaking of 'outside.' I was attacked by invaders from another star."

Two of the vulureheads looked toward each other, exchanging a sardonic glance of disbelief. Even on the bird faces the expression was clear to read. "Oh. How interesting. What other star? No life above the unicellular level has yet been discovered in the deep of space. The colony sent out to Cygnus X-1 perished in unspeakable horror, long, long ago."

"It is something from Cygnus. Something survived the fall of the Silent Oecumene. An evil Sophotech called the Nothing Machine."

"This sounds to be the stuff of fancy, a dream, a memory-entertainment, a mistake," said the vulture. "Where is your evidence? Surely your wealthy Sophotechs can examine your brain-information, and discover what is true and what is false in your mind."

"The examination was performed—the readings showed my memories of the attack were false."

"And from this you conclude . . . ?"

"I conclude that the readings were tampered with."

"And your support for this conclusion is . . . ?"

"Well, obviously the evil mind-virus tampered with them."

"Let me see if I understand this, young aristocrat. We live in a society where men can edit their brain-information at will, so that even their deepest thoughts, instincts, and convictions can be overwritten and rewritten, and no memories can be trusted. You find you have a memory of being attacked by a nonexistent mind-virus created by a nonexistent Sophotech from a long-dead colony. Upon examination, readings show the memory is false, and your conclusion is that your unbelievable, entirely absurd memories are true, and the readings showing them to be false are unreliable. Is that right?"

"That's right."

"Ah. I merely wanted to be certain of the circumstances."

"My tale, whether it is believed or not, whether it is believable or not, is still mine, and I will still act as if it were true—I dare not do otherwise. And, true or not, believable or not, the telling of my tale is done; I would have yours, if you will return the courtesy, for I cannot imagine who you might be."

"You would not know the name I call myself these days. Once, I was called the Bellipotent Composition."

Phaethon was taken aback. "Impossible! Bellipotent was destroyed two aeons ago!"

"No. Only disbanded. The memories still were on record. I have part of those memories."

"You mean, then, that you have studied the Bellipotent Composition . . . ?"

"No. I am he. How many minds does it take to make a mass-mind? A thousand? A hundred? Ten? Two? I say it only takes one; and I am he. I say that I am still the mass-mind of the Bellipotent,

even though my membership has only one member. I am the last
of a mighty host, but I was of that host. The air marshal branch-
mind of the Eastern Warlock-killing division surrendered to Alternate Organization Solomon Oversoul after the Three Horrid Seconds
of the Battle of Peking Network Operating System Core. You do not
know history, do you? I see it in your face. This surrender happened
in Pre-Epoch 44101, three hundred years into the Era of the Fifth
Mental Structure. I was part of the air group who surrendered. We
were permitted, under the peace contract, to retain our identities."

"And you simply roam free these days? You were not punished?"

"You really know nothing of history, do you? I was kept in an
underground cyst for a space of centuries equal to what Warlock
astrologers calculated to be the projected lifetime sum of every
person who had been killed in the bombing runs. After I was released, I was part of the death lottery instituted by the Witch-King
of Corea."

"Death lottery . . . ?"

"The reason for the war is not what history reports. History says
it was because the Warlocks had found the Shadow-mind technology, which permitted them an alternate state of consciousness and
allowed them to falsify noetic readings, to lie under oath. Humbug.
That was not a significant cause. The significant cause of the war
between the mass-minds and the Warlocks was that our mental systems were incompatible. Bellipotent demanded exact and rigid justice, one law for all, executed without fear or favoritism. But the
Warlock brain thinks in leaps of logic, flashes of insight, patterns
of symmetry. To them, the justice must be poetic justice, and the
punishment grotesquely sculpted to fit the crime, or else it is not
justice at all.

"Thus, when it came my turn to be punished, it amused the
Witch-King to impose on me and my fellow bombardiers the same
uncertainty and fear our bomb drops had imposed on others. We
were permitted to wander free, but with explosive charges surgically
implanted in our crania. Random radio pulses were sent out, so that
we were executed by lottery, at random places and times. Sometimes
other signals, door openers or automobile guides, set off the charges.
After a hundred years of that, I alone survived. Now I ferry the

gentle Deep Ones to and from their underwater kingdoms."

"Horrible!"

"No. My biological parts have withered and been replaced many times. All trace of the explosives have been removed."

"But how could you tolerate the uncertainty?"

"Ah. Does this question come from Phaethon, who once dreamed of traveling far beyond where any noumenal mentality could reach? Random and instant death would have been just as prevalent on your voyage, had you ever made one. And, once colonies, armed with technologies equal to our own, were planted among the several nearby stars, that same risk of instant and random death would then be imposed upon every colonist and every citizen of the Oecumene, since war, at any moment, could break out again at any time."

"Men are not so irrational as that."

"Are they not? Are they not? You have never known war, young fool. Of whom were you so afraid when you stood at the top of the ramp of this, my ship? Irrational creatures from another star who seek your murder? Or is that a delusion only of your own? Come now! Either you are deluded, or they are mad. Neither option speaks well for the future of peaceful star colonization." The creature opened and shut its several beaks. "I am only sorry that you have failed so utterly."

Phaeton felt the deck tilting under him. In this windowless room, he could not tell what this maneuver meant.

He said, "Why? Did you hope for war again so much?"

"Not at all. War is horrible beyond description. It is tolerable only because there is something that is worse. No; you misunderstand what I hope."

"Enlighten me."

"Ah! Yahh! I lived in the last years of the Fourth Era, when vast mass-minds ruled all the Earth. There was no crime, no war, no rudeness, and (except for certain areas in North America and Western Europe) no individuality. It was a static age. There were no changes.

"The Fifth Era came when certain Compositions began to use other brain-formations in their mind-groups. The Warlock brain was quick and intuitive, artistic, insightful. The Invariant brain is immune to passion or fear, immune to threat, immune to blackmail. The Cerebelline brain can see all points of view at once, and understand all elements of complex systems at one glance. We could not compete against such minds as these, nor would they submit themselves tamely to the group-needs of the group-minds. And yet the Fifth Era was finer than the Fourth. Genius and invention ruled. Irrational Warlocks conquered the Jupiter system, which they had no economic reason to do; stoic Invariants methodically colonized the pre-Demeter asteroids, indifferent to suffering or hardship. Cerebellines, grasping whole thought-systems at once, developed the Noetic Unification Theorem, which led to developments and technologies we mass-minds never would have or could have guessed. Without the self-referencing participles described in Mother-of-Numbers's famous dissertation/play/equations, the technology for self-aware machines would not have come about. The scientific advances of those self-aware machines are more than I can count, including the development of the Noumenal mathematics, which led to this present age, the age of second immortality.

"Now comes this age; the Seventh, and it is a static age again. So, then, Phaethon Zero of Nothing, do you see? Look back and forth along the scheme of history. There would have been war among the stars if your dream had not been killed. Do not doubt it; the Hortators, and their pet Nebuchednezzar, are smart enough to come correctly to that conclusion. But would that age of war have led to better ages beyond that? Perhaps the Earth and Jupiter's Moons and the other civilized places of the Golden Oecumene would have been destroyed in the first round of interstellar wars. But, if, in return, a hundred planets were seeded with new civilizations, or a million, I say the cost would have been worth the horror."

Phaethon was silent, not certain how to take this comment. Was the cyborg praising him, or condemning him? Or both?

But it did not matter now. The point was academic. The Hortators had won.

"Where are you taking me?" asked Phaethon.

"Yaah! Truly you know nothing of history. There is only one city on the planet that did not sign the Hortator accords, because the Cerebelline-formed mass-mind running it did not care whether she was mortal or immortal, and she did not give in to Orpheus's pressure. Old-Woman-of-the-Sea has governed the Oceanic Environmental Protectorate since the middle of the Fifth Era. She, like me, is far older than your Golden Oecumene. She can afford to ignore the Hortators, since even they would not care to interfere with the mind that controls the balancing forces between all the plankton and all the nanomachinery floating in the waves, or who shepherds the trillion submicroscopic thermal cells of all the tropic zones, which disperse or condense the ocean heat and hinder the formation of tornadoes. Her city is called Talaimannar."

"The place Harrier told me to go!" exclaimed Phaethon happily. Now he would find out what mystery, what subtle plan the super-intellect of Harrier had in mind.

"Of course, young fool," said the cyborg. "If I dropped you any other place, I would be guilty of helping you commit an act of trespass. Why do you think the Hortators let me get away with this? I am not helping you. It takes no genius to figure out you must go to Talaimannar; there is no other place to go. It is where all cast-offs and gutter-sweepings go."

Phaethon felt a sensation of crushing despair. All this time, he had been nursing the secret hope that Harrier Sophotech had some plan, some unthinkably clever scheme, to extract Phaethon from this situation, a plan that would bear fruit once he reached Talaimannar. It had comforted him during his many sleepless nights, his nightmare-ridden slumbers.

But no. Harrier had not been telling him anything other than what all other exiles were told.

It had been a foolish hope to begin with. While it had lasted, the foolish hope had been better than no hope. In order to go on, one needed a reason to go on. What was to be Phaethon's reason now?

A vibration shivered through the ship frame.

"We're here," said the cyborg. "Get out."

A hatch Phaethon had not seen before now opened in a section of the deck. Beyond was a gangway leading down and out. Phaethon blinked in a splash of reflected sunlight shining up through the hatch from below. He smelled fresh tropic air, heavy with moisture and orchid-scents; he heard the noise of surf, the raw calls of sea-birds.

"Wait," said Phaethon. "If I am not hallucinating, then there are agents from another star hunting me, then to send me out there, the one place all exiles go, is to send me to the one place where they will find me."

"I have very ancient privileges, which even the formation-draft of the Foederal Oecumenical Commonwealth Constitutional Logic recognizes. It is called a grandfather clause. Legal rights that ex-isted from before the Oecumene are still recognized by the Oecu-mene. An historical curiosity, is it not? The movements of my airships are surrounded by privacy; I cannot be traced, except at court order, and I fly below the levels air-traffic control requires. I am well-known in Kisumu; I have flown the routes to Quito and Samarinda for a thousand years. Any housecoater or perigrinator of the street could point my ship out, and know I can move unnoticed. You understand? That is why the Deep Ones patronize me. They wish for privacy as well. Until and unless you give yourself away, such as, for example, by logging on to the mentality, you should be safe here from your imaginary foes."

Phaethon stepped over to the hatch, but turned, and spoke over his shoulder. "You said there was one thing even worse than war, a thing so terrible that even war is tolerable by contrast. What is it?"

"Defeat." And a robotic arm came from the wall, took Phaethon by the shoulder, and thrust him stumbling down the gangway. Sun-light blinded him. His hands and knees struck the open grillwork floor of the docking tower with a clash of noise. The shadow of the airship passed over him. He rose to his feet and looked up in time to see the huge cylindrical machine rise up out of reach, abandoning him.

Phaethon was again alone.

THE WELCOME

I.

Through the mesh and underfoot, Phaethon could see lush greenery, a reach of rocky sand and beach, and, beyond that, an ocean blackened with nanomachinery, crowded with false-trees. To the opposite side, away from the beach, were a cluster of spiral pearly growths, domes and towers of spun diamond, buildings like coral or like nautilus shells. These were the organic seashell shapes of the Standard Aesthetic.

On the hilltop beyond this, in the distance, rising above the deodar trees and clinging vines, was an antique temple, shaped like a beehive, but intricately carven with figurines and images. It looked old, perhaps dating back to the Era of the Second Mental Structure. Without access to the Middle Dreaming, Phaethon missed the ability to learn all he might wish to know about anything by glancing at it. But he tried to tell himself to enjoy the mysterious and picturesque character his new-found ignorance bestowed.

Phaethon stepped to the moving staircase in order to descend; but the escalator was loyal to the precepts of the Hortators and would not carry him. So he stepped over to a service ladder leading down. Phaethon did not know if the rusted metal rungs could sustain the weight of his armor; but when he asked the ladder for its specifications, the ladder was either dumb, or deaf, or rude, and it did not answer. Phaethon doffed the armor, and had it rappel down the tower side by itself, while he climbed down the ladder. He did not want to waste his suit material by building another garment, and the clime was warm, and so he walked nude, followed faithfully by his armor.

There was a street leading to the town, made of glassy spun diamond; and a ridge running down the middle had guide-wires and thought-ports, lines and beads of smooth ceramic, glinting in the surface. As far as Phaethon could see, the approaching town was neither cramped nor squalid nor filthy, nor did it have the other earmarks of poverty that the poorer sections of Victorian-Age London (which he had visited many times in simulations) had displayed.

It did not look too bad, he told himself.

But that impression changed the closer he came to the town.

First, the street, which had looked so bright and inviting when he first stepped onto it, turned out to be a low-grade moron. Instead of offering interesting comments about the scenery, or important traveler's tips, or playing restful walking-music, the street had monotonously belabored him, joking and shouting with a mindless and force-fed glee, trying to get Phaethon to use certain commercial services that Phaethon could not have purchased in any case.

Second, the nanomachinery creating and maintaining the street was misprogrammed, so that black carbon dust, not correctly bound in the diamond street surface, accumulated from cracks and breaks. Phaethon, as he walked, found his knees and feet coated with coal-black particles as fine as mist, which no amount of wiping could clear from his leg hairs.

The clamoring street fell silent when he entered the town proper.

Phaethon walked among the giant spiral shells and mother-of-pearl domes of the houses and buildings. Only a few were occupied. The rest were mad-houses or mutants, like something from an old story. The self-replicating machinery that designed and grew these Sixth Era buildings had been neglected, and reproduced with no supervision and no corrections, so that some houses were half-grown into each other, like horrible Siamese twins. Others had lopsided doors or windows; or they grew without doors; or without power or lights; or, worse, with a strange, harsh light painful to the eye.

Some of the buildings were tilted at drunken angles, or sat, slumped and damaged, having made no attempt to heal themselves nor to grow their broken walls shut.

Certain formations, which were easy to grow, such as lamps or doorposts, had flourished like weeds, everywhere. Few were the houses that did not have twenty or a hundred lamps sprouting from their pearly roofs or curling eaves. Doorposts (dotted with jacks and cells to hold identifier plates and call cables which never would be installed) stood unsupported in the center of the street, or clustered in the unplanned gaps between buildings, or hung tilting from second-story lofts.

When Phaethon politely asked a question to one of these neglected houses, the building would giggle idiotically, or repeat some stock phrase parrot-like: "Welcome Home! Welcome Home!"

After a few moments of walking, many of the houses were stirred up in a clamor, shouting, calling back and forth to each other. Some gobbled at him in angry languages; warehouses shrieked; whorehouses called out bawdy slogans. Phaethon kept his eyes ahead and walked stiffly, pretending not to notice.

The houses fell grumbling and mumbling into silence a few moments after he had passed, so that a wake of noise trailed after him.

Then he came into an upper part of the town. There were people here, sitting on porches or lounging lazily along the side of the street. They were dressed in simple tunics and smocks of flashing colors and eye-dazzling designs, pulsing and strobing, and a loud music made of repeating percussion surrounded them.

Phaethon realized that these folk were wearing advertisements.

Most of their faces and bodies looked the same, K-style and B-style faces taken from public-domain records. Except for some men who had scarred their faces, or applied colored tattoos, it seemed as if everyone along the street were everyone else's twin.

When he raised a hand in greeting, their eyes went blank, and their gazes slid past him, unseeing.

He walked on, puzzled. Where these not exiles like himself? Apparently not. It seemed as if they could afford sense-filters. The standard settings would automatically block out anything branded with odium by the Hortators.

Like a phantom, ignored and unseen, Phaethon walked on.

Through open doorways he could see the people who lived here, base humaniforms, for the most part. People who did not wear advertisements were garbed in smocks of blue-gray drab, made of simple polymers not difficult to synthesize. Some of the garments were old and sick, for they had torn, and they did not repair themselves.

Most of the people had crowns growing into the flesh of their skulls, giving them partial access to the mentality. One or two sad individuals were wearing lenses and ear-jacks, so that they could watch from a distance, or overhear, the complex and vibrant activity of life in the mentality, a life now closed to them.

He saw people sleeping on mats on the floor; he did not see a single pool. There was apparently no life-water running anywhere.

For energy, he saw nothing but the solar panels that grew along roofs like wild lichen; he wondered what they did on cloudy days, or at dark.

Food they ate with their mouths, masticating; he did not see what the substances were, or how it was manufactured; but with a dozen steaming streams of green nanosubstance running in open gutters down the street, he could imagine.

Half the houses had darkened lamps. Their solar cells were covered with a soot or carpet lichen, which no one had bothered to scrape free. For light, captured advertisement banners had been tied to steeples and cupolas, so that garish colors flared across the scene. Many of the houses screamed back at the jarring clash of music and slogans radiating from the advertisements. Some of the stupider houses thought the noises were approaching visitors, for they shouted out welcomes whenever the advertisements brayed. It added to the general din most unpleasantly.

There was one, just one, staging pool in the center of the town square. No one was sleeping in it. Phaethon was not surprised. In a city of exiles, a non-network pool could only be used by one ostracized citizen to enter a dreamspace built and provided and guided by another ostracized citizen. The pool liquid consisted of a few inches of brownish sludge, which no one had bothered to program to clean itself.

He sat on the marble bench surrounding the lip of the staging pool, gazing about him, wondering what to do next. A sense of misery, which he had held at bay throughout his long descent down the tower, and through his voyage on the airship, now came to him and possessed him. He slumped off the edge and sat in the pool; the sludge was too shallow to admit him. Tentative crystals formed in the liquid and nosed around his legs like curious, shy fish, but there was no way for Phaethon to make a connection, and nothing he had to do once a connection was made. Phaethon sat without moving, then he cursed. His head nodded, but his brain ached, and he could not sleep. The noise of the town screamed and sang around him, loudly and mindlessly.

2.

Eventually, he stirred himself. Phaethon rubbed his hands along the carbon dust clinging to his knees. All that resulted was that his palms turned black. A few grams of decrepit nanoassembler molecules must have been hiding among the dust; when he brushed at it vigorously, the assemblers activated, looking for substances to turn into road surface, and pulled a number of micrograms of carbon out of Phaethon's skin with a flash of waste heat that raised blisters on his legs. The jolt of pain sent him skipping upright, hissing and blinking.

Wincing, he went to wash his legs beneath the in-spigots of the staging pool, hoping that, like most pools, it had a medical side-mind. He could save a few precious drops of his dwindling supply of nanomaterial if the pool's medical side-mind could make an unguent for him. Perhaps it could, but Phaethon did not have an interfacer with which to talk to the pool. He tried to communicate his needs to the pool by pointing and gesturing. The pool surface formed a bulb of hallucinogen and offered it to him. Then it offered him sleep-oil; then breathing tissue. Phaethon, exasperated, soon was splashing back and forth, swinging his arms in wide gestures of simple pantomime, pointing at his blisters, and shouting rude comments at the pool's simplemindedness. He shouted more and more loudly, trying to be heard over the thumping din of the town noise.

A voice from behind him: "Eyah! What you doing, manor-born?"

Phaethon stopped his antics, summoned an aloof expression, and turned. "Just as you see."

"Ah. All is explained."

Here was a dark-skinned man, bald, and enormously broad of shoulder. He was squat, and thick-limbed. His muscle grafts had been placed without any concern for symmetry or fineness. His face was scarred and tattooed; he was missing an ear. The tattoos formed exaggerated scowl lines around his mouth; his eyes were ringed with concentric lines of surprise. He wore a brown smock of many pockets, and, over the top of that, what looked like an advertisement banner, but it was silent and dark, with thin lines of red and orange flickering through the substance.

"Welcome to Death Row," said the bald, squat man.

3.

Phaethon, dirty, dripping, and burnt, mustered his dignity. "How do you know me to be a manorial?" If a random passerby could deduce or guess that he was Phaethon, it would be child's play for Xenophon or the Nothing Sophotech.

The squat man wagged his head. "Ai-yah! Listen to him snoff!" Then to Phaethon, he said, "You shout at pool, all nice talk, full sentence. 'I shall surely drub you!' you shout. 'You shall learn what it means boldly to go against orders!' also you shout. Eyah. 'Boldly to go' . . . ? You mean 'to boldly go,' you don't? Only machines talk like this way. Very puff-puff. Very polite."

"I see. I shall endeavor to make my speech more colloquial, if that is what anonymity requires."

"Oho. You don't want attention? So you splash and yell off head? Very wise, very deep-think! Hey, maybe blind deaf-mute in coma off yonder has not seen you, eh?"

"I was under the impression that most of the people here had their sense-filters engaged."

"No such. No sense-filters, no fancy puff-puff. They just cussed, is all. Dark, black, nasty cussed. They want out and up, so they make-pretend. Make-pretend they are rich, make-pretend they are loved-up, make-pretend they are wise and kind and good-good. Ashores. All of them Ashores. They hate all us right full deep, you know. You too."

"Us? What defines us as a group?"

"Afloats."

"I fear I don't understand."

"Is simple as simple is. Ashore live ashore. They may live. Their sentence is measured; a year, six year; hundred year, what-have-you. When time is done, they get their lives again, they get up-and-out. Can buy from Orpheus. Can buy live-forever machines. Land they live on, is rented to them; once they get lives back, they pay back. All fair. All square."

"And the Afloats, I assume, live afloat . . . ?"

"Live on sea as sea is free. No rent on water."

"You have houseboats?"

"We got rafts. Drag dead houses out to sea. Is trash; no one stop us." He shrugged. "Man at local thought-shop revive house-mind for small fee, you know."

"And your term of exile, unlike those of the Ashores, is permanent?"

"We here till we not here no more. Here till we die. Is Death Row." And he extended his cupped hand, palm up, a beggar's gesture. "Name's Oshenkyo. What've ye got for us, eh?"

And Phaethon took a daub of his precious, limited supply of black nanomachine material and applied it to the scar on Oshenkyo's head where there had once been an ear. Phaethon drew upon the ecological and medical routines he had in his thought-space, set the daub to take a gene sample, and he set it to reconstitute the missing ear.

4.

The bay was surrounded on three sides by cliffs. The cliffs were overgrown by a Cerebelline life-garden, which may or may not have been part of Old-Woman-of-the-Sea. Pharmaceutical vines and adaptive fibers clung to the rocks, tended by weaver birds and tailor birds. Suits and outfits finished by the tailor bird hung flapping in the sea breeze, awaiting shipping dolphins.

In the middle of the bay, strangely silent and dark, were houses shaped like gray and blue-brown seashells, standing on spider legs that gripped floats and buoys beneath the water. Dozens of dangling ropes, ladders, and nets hung between the house shells, like webs, or dropped to crude docks floating in the houses' shadows.

In the middle of the irregular floating mass of house shells rose an old barge, streaked with barnacles and rust. On the flat upper surface of the barge towered a group of tents and pavilions made of cheap diamond synthetics, in three tiers, one above the other. From the crown of the upper tier, rose a false-tree with limbs of steel, and many solar collectors like leaves. Banners of material, and globes like fruit hung from the tree limbs. Phaethon could see where fruit or banners had dropped into the nets and cupolas of the tents below, quickly gathered up by scurrying spider-gloves and waldoes.

"It's quieter here," said Phaethon, looking down from the cliff into the bay. He had put his gold armor back on and had tuned some of the surface area in his black nanomaterial cape to catch and analyze some of the scents on the breeze. Mingled in the scents of green leaves, sunshine, and sea, were the command-pheromones and tiny nanomachine packages, smaller than pollen spores, which complex Cerebelline activity had as its by-product. Invisible clouds of these microspores extended far out to sea; the Cerebelline called Old-Woman was deep in thought.

Next to him, Oshenkyo was skipping and skylarking, waving and weaving his hands in the air, snapping his fingers in both ears, and smiling at the stereo-auditory noise. "Much quiet! Buckets of quiet! Know why? No ads." Oshenkyo smiled, humming.

"What of the advertisement you wear? Why is it silent?"

"Not silent! Just our ears not hear it." Oshenkyo explained that certain advertisers were trying to sell services and philosophy-regimen to a Cerebelline consciousness (a daughter of Old-Woman-of-the-Sea) that occupied the cliffs and kelp beds throughout the area, and who, having once, long ago, been part of the Venereal Terraforming Effort, had been heartbroken when that effort finally achieved success. The Daughter departed once Venus was towed to a new orbit, but had never altered her perceptions back to standard frequencies, time-rate, and aesthetic conventions of Earth. Hence, her "eyes" were tuned to the shortwaves and subsonic pulses the dark advertisement banners gave off.

The other banners would display advertisements meant for humans only when asked, and then only from advertisers who could not afford to, or did not bother to, prevent an exile from experiencing them.

"We use them, you know, semaphore. Or listen to jingles. Or for light. Or as sails for boats. No one mind, as long as ads get shown."

"But you do not use them to search out useful products and services?"

"No one sells to Afloats. Almost no one. No one, we'd be dead. Almost no one, almost dead. Look it." And he pointed above the central barge.

Phaethon was still not accustomed to how bad his eyesight was. There was no amplification when he squinted. He saw a swarm of darting and hovering specks, glittering gold, like bees, above and around the pavilions and tents rising above the barge. But he could not resolve them into clear images. "I cannot make out what is out there."

Oshenkyo was seated on the wide, low limb of a gold-extraction bush, cupping his hands over his ears, then covering, listening to the changes in sound. He spoke absently: "Vulpine First Ironjoy on yonder barge runs a thought-shop. We get work, sometime. Can get buffers and tangle lines to reach deviants and dark markets through the Big Mind." By which he meant the mentality.

Phaethon was intrigued. Work? The boycott of the Hortators evidently had enough holes and gaps to enable these people to live.

Then Phaethon smiled sadly at his own thought. "These people" . . . ? Did he still think of himself as somehow apart from the other exiles?

Phaethon said: "No, I can see the barge. But what arc those miniature flying instruments swarming around the area here?"

"Constables, Tince-tiny. About so big." Oshenkyo held up his thumb.

"So many?"

"Zillions. They watch us all time. Good thing, too. Otherwise, we club each other right quick dead."

"Indeed? Are we all so violent, then?"

Oshenkyo shrugged a broad, one-shoulder shrug. "All us crazy, filthy people. Got nothing to lose."

"Why arc there such a number of police?"

Oshenkyo squinted at him. "We still got rights. No thieving, no killing, no broke words."

"What about lying?"

Oshenkyo stared out at the bay, sniffed, gave another one-shouldered shrug. "Fib till your tongue falls out. No one here to buy a thought-read machine. We not like other folk: we don't know what goes on inside other people head. Just like long-ago days, eh? But swaps, bargains, work, all that: very sacred. You give word, can't take back. You got?"

Evidently contract laws were still enforced. "I got."

But Phaethon realized that it would be a dangerous system, since the Oecumene law, with no emotion and no favoritism, would enforce any bargain struck, no matter how foolish, no matter how risky. Had he had access to Sophotech foresight and advice, the risks would have been small. He didn't. Had he been raised in a society where suspicion and care were normal, he could have been in the habit of mistrusting his fellowmen, and of striking careful bargains. He wasn't.

Oshenkyo squinted up at him. "All be clear as clear once you sign our Pact. You join up, be one of us, eh? Otherwise, not so great live here. Nowhere else to go but sea."

This did nothing to calm Phaethon's qualms. But he smiled in joy and relief. If he had qualms, that meant he had plans, he had a goal. He was young and in good health, and he had a supply of nanomaterial which could be adapted to medical geriatrics. He might live long enough to outlive the Hortators' term of exile; the political circumstance of the Oecumene might change. Who could tell?

". . . Or maybe the horse could learn how to sing." Phaethon murmured.

"Eh? What's that?"

"Sorry. I was ruminating over my hopes for the future."

"Hope? You said 'horse.' "

"There is a story about a man condemned by a tyrant, who pleads for one more year of life, telling the tyrant that, if the sentence is suspended for a year, he will teach the tyrant's prize stallion to sing hymns. The tyrant agrees. The other prisoners are amused to see this one prisoner, every day, patiently caroling in the stables. When the other prisoners mocked his folly, the man replied that a great deal could happen in a year. The tyrant could die; the horse could die. And, who knows? The horse could learn to sing."

"Stupid story."

"I always used to think so, too. Now, though, I'm not sure. Are false hopes better than none at all? Perhaps they are." Phaethon's eyes were fixed on a point beyond the horizon.

"No, is stupid because would not take so long to download info and singing routines into horse, if brain-fittings are standard. A year? Would only take five minute."

"This is a very old story, from the days before horses were extinct."

Now Oshenkyo squinted in surprise. "Funny, I thought horses were make-up, you know, genetified, by Red Manor Queens."

"Make-up? You mean invented?"

"Make-up! Like dragons and gryphons and elephants."

"Modern elephants are a genetic reconstruction of a real species."

Oshenkyo snorted. "With flappy-arms on their noses? You think such creature as that evolve by itself? Nar. No how. Red Manor

folk make up for sure. Just their kind of stupid thing. Ah, wait!"
Now Oshenkyo jumped to his feet and waved his arm high. "Lookit
there! Welcome menus! You get meet Ironjoy. He tell you what's
what. You listen him, he get you fine-dandy job assignments, maybe
you eat, maybe you sleep in-of-doors, out of rain. Niue good, eh?
Lick up nice chum to him, now, and smile pretty!"

"I shall endeavor to be on my best behavior," Phaethon said in
a voice of heavy irony.

A party of three figures was picking its way up the slope of the
cliff to the spot where Phaethon stood with Oshenkyo. All three
wore blue-green housecoats of antique design, with flared shoulders
and long skirts, and many pockets to hold a dozen house instruments. The one in the middle (perhaps the leader) had a design of
gold attention-thread running through the chest pockets. Their faces
were shadowed by wide flat straw hats whose brims hung over their
shoulders. The color elements in the housecoats were not correctly
attuned; all three figures were surrounded by a web of green-blue
rainbows, shifting glints and shadows, and it made them look as if
they were walking underwater.

The lead figure seemed to be a base humaniform until he was
within ten feet of Phaethon. The color play of his malfunctioning
coat had hidden his true silhouette. As the stranger approached,
Phaethon saw he had a second pair of arms and hands springing
from his doubled shoulders. Beneath the shadow of his hat, his face
was an immobile mask of bony cartilage, with three or four pairs of
eyes and secondary eyes, microwave horns, infrared sockets, elec-
trodetection cells, and ELF antennae. The face lacked a nose; the
mouth was an insectoid clamp.

Phaethon's gaze swung left and right. The other two wore standard faces, male and half-male, with teeth made of glittering diamond. The male had a beard woven with many-colored sensation
strands. The half-male had similar strands dangling from her hair.
The two wore black metallic cusps covering their eyes, perhaps a
crude type of sense-filter and interfacer, controlled by blinks and
eye motions. The man was sucking on a colored strand drooping
from his moustache.

The quadruple-armed leader stepped forward and looked Phaethon's gold-and-black armor up and down. Phaethon returned the inspection.

Phaethon recognized the fellow's body design from the late Fifth Era, when the mass-minds, losing money and prestige, had attempted to cut costs on space services by having specialized serf-bodies replace expensive EVA machinery. The serf-creatures were immensely strong, having been used as longshoremen and hull-smiths, and could perceive many frequencies of radiation at once. Their space suits or second skins could be made much more cheaply than the elaborate space armor needed by a human-shaped man. Serfs required very little food and water; their bodies could recycle much of their own waste materials.

The serf-form had been extinct for centuries, and, as far as Phaethon knew, they had never been patronized by a single consciousness. But it was an excellent body to be exiled in, being long-lasting and very frugal.

Phaethon thought the creature was hideous.

The fact that they were dressed in something other than advertisements or simple polymeric homespun led Phaethon to believe that these three represented the upper class of whatever "society" existed among these outcasts. The Peers of the poor, so to speak.

Phaethon noticed that the other two, hissing and slurping, chuckling and murmuring to each other, had both bent close to stare at Oshenkyo's new ear. The she-man uttered a breathless giggle of awe and delight; the man was nodding slowly, pleased and impressed, his straw hat bobbing.

The buzzing, flat voice of a mechanical speaker issued from the chest area of the serf-creature. "Self identifies as Vulpine First Iron-joy, base neuroform with nonstandard invariant extensions, Uncomposed and Unschooled. Compatriots identified as Lester Nought Haaken, base, ejected from a limited non-hierarchy mind-partnership, Ritual Murder Reformation School; second compatriot identified as Drusillet Zero Self-soul, sub-Cerebelline neuroform, multiple personality stasis-lock, self-schooled."

The half-male, evidently Drusillet, straightened up and spoke in a contralto she-man voice: "Incorrect! My school is the Omnipresent Benevolence Assertion! Many children are its members, filled with love and kindliness, protected from all life's ills and harms! Soon, oh so very soon now, they will recall their love and gratitude for all the benefits I've shown to them, and force the Hortators to rescind their ban on me!"

Lester, likewise, made a preemptory gesture, and spoke up: "There is no Ritual Murder Reformation School; such a thing exists only in horror stories. I am and always shall be a member of the Privacy School. My thoughts are my own, not open to examination or review. If I want to throb with the desire to lie, cheat, steal, and kill, then that is nobody's business but my own, provided I don't act on it, right? Don't let Ironjoy here baffle you, New Kid. We, none of us, are criminals here."

Oshenkyo chimed in, "No criminals. Just unpopular, eh?"

Lester said, "Some of us suffer for a Righteous Cause."

Phaethon nodded. "A pleasure to make the acquaintance of someone who shares my feelings in the matter, good sir. I, too, suffer tribulations for a cause I deem to be just and right."

"Aha!" exclaimed Lester, slapping Phaethon's shoulder plate with a brotherly hand. "Kindred souls then! Good to meet you! And take my word for it, this sick society that has rejected us cannot last long! No, sir, the Golden Oecumene will soon collapse under her own over-stuffed rottenness. The machines think they can anesthetize us, force us into unnatural, inhuman modes! But the true bestial nature of man will one day spring forth, roaring! And on that day, rioters will topple the edifices of the thinking machines, rapists and looters will fulfill their dark fantasies, and blood, gushes of glorious blood, will run through the streets! Take note of my words!"

Lester, at this point, was standing too close to Phaethon, and waving his finger in Phaethon's face for emphasis.

Ironjoy put one of his left hands on Lester's shoulder and drew him back. "Improper! Allow New Kid to acclimate himself. Talk of other matters after."

Oshenkyo said, "He got plenty long time to hear all about you theory, Lester." He turned and squinted at Phaethon, and said, "We all got to hear Lester's talk. Sort of like hazing. Whoever stand it the longest wins big prize."

Lester either was inured to this type of joke, or held Oshenkyo in such good fellowship that the comments did not offend him. In either case, he merely gave Phaethon a polite nod, turned to Ironjoy, said, "Oshenkyo's earned his chit; I'll send you a bill from my informant, at fifteen cut. Fair?" And, when Ironjoy grunted in agreement, Lester turned again, gave a last, lingering look of envy and wonder at Oshenkyo's new ear, and then briskly walked away.

Oshenkyo muttered to Ironjoy: "Worth more than fifteen. Lookit that armor shine! Admantium. Is my fish; I say twenty."

Ironjoy made a curt gesture with his lower right hand. Oshenkyo shut up and stepped back, squinting. It was hard to read the tattoo-scarred face: but he seemed glum. Ironjoy pointed at Phaethon with his upper left hand, evidently a signal to Drusillet, who took out a reading card, face yellowed with age, and stepped toward Phaethon.

Drusillet said, "Open your thoughtspace, please, New Kid. We need to see what you have to offer. Medical routines is what we mostly need. Though information structuring, data compression, and migration techniques also pay off. Let me log you on to the mentality and run a check-through." And she stepped forward and began to apply the reading head of the card to a jack in Phaethon's shoulder board.

Phaethon brushed her hand aside before she could meddle with his suit controls.

Drusillet stepped back, mouth open, and she darted a fearful look at Ironjoy. The metal cusps that hid her eyes partly masked her expression, but evidently she had not expected to be rebuffed.

Phaethon spoke: "Sir (or is it miss . . . ?) forgive me, but we have not been properly introduced. And I have personal and very severe reasons for wishing not to log on to the mentality. But perhaps a word or two of explanation would reassure me. Were you thinking of simply making free with my property? Were you attempting to make pirate-copies of my routines? There are a dozen constables floating nearby." He gestured toward the swarm of bee-sized metal implements, which buzzed through the air overhead.

"No cops!" Ironjoy held up all four hands at once, an eerie, almost menacing, gesture. "New Kid is disoriented. He thinks he is still alive. He thinks the constables will protect him. Explain reality to him! I go. Events will be adjusted." And with that, he turned with a snap of his green-shivering garments and strode off down the path between the pharmaceutical bushes.

Drusillet was staring at Phaethon in fascinated half-fear. Oshenkyo squatted down not far away, humming to himself, and drawing squirming circles in the dirt with a twig. Phaethon stood with his hands clasped behind his back, his head forward, legs spread, his black cloak falling in folds across his armored shoulders, around his elbows. For a moment, no one spoke.

Drusillet said to Phaethon, "You don't understand how things work here."

"I am attentive. Explain."

"Ironjoy's not an Afloat, not really. He's an Ashore; he just doesn't care how much time he adds on to his sentence. Parts of his brain died, a long time ago, from old age, but he had the other parts propped up with Invariant mind-viruses that they give out for free. Even to us. Anyway, Ironjoy runs the thought-shop here. He's the only one around who can sell us goodies, or who can run a search engine to locate assignments in the dark markets and back nets."

"How does this Ironjoy fellow find assignments for you?" asked Phaethon.

Drusillet tucked a strand of her hair between her lips and sucked. Then she shivered and smiled. "You'd be surprised! Everyone always thinks the machines can do everything better and smarter and faster than anyone, so how can anyone ever get a job? But they can't do everything at once, and so there are certain jobs which, even if we do them slower and stupider, we can still do them for cheaper. Like me. The last thing I did, was going through Devolkushend's memories to prepare his autobiography, and cutting out or glossing over the parts of his memory that don't make for good theater. It was rough work, living his stupid life over and over again, but he's got some fans, or something, so I guess he wanted it done, and on the cheap, too. It required some human judgment; I got a judgment-routine from Ironjoy for that, one of those things put out by Semi-Warlock Critics."

"Did I correctly hear Ironjoy say you had a Cerebelline neuroform? You express yourself in linear fashion, like a basic, not like a global."

She suddenly looked shy and sad. "Sub-Cerebelline. Think of a mass-mind with a split personality. As long as my other personalities don't come to the forefront, as long as I don't weave myself back into a global whole, I think and act like you lonely people. Just one mind, one point of view, all alone. It's what I have to do to keep my children safe."

Phaethon was curious, but saw she would not say more on that topic. Instead, he asked her about her work: "How does Devolk-ushend, when he hires you, escape falling under the Hortators' op-probrium?"

"Oh, he's a Nevernext. They hate the Hortators. Nevernexts, de-viants, freaks, they still cut deals with us. And a lot of things are done on the sly, or through schools with high privacy restrictions. Especially now during the masquerade. Some of us dress up and sneak off to go look at the real people . . ." Her face took on a look of wistful longing. Phaethon pictured her in masquerade, in the rain, peering up at a window or balcony for a distant glimpse of a grown child who might no longer know her. It was a pathetic picture, disturbing. Was it accurate? He did not know.

She said: "The Hortators aren't the constables, after all, and they can't get a warrant to read someone's mind."

Oshenkyo stood up suddenly and tossed the twig he had been toying with away into the brush with an abrupt motion. "Ironjoy's top man around here, for sure. Makes sure we all get along, all get some work, some grub, some dream-stuff so we can stand to make it to another sunset. He got good stuff in his shop, good dreams, bad dreams, new thoughts, new selves. You play around, you jack in new stuff, maybe one day you find yourself a persona who can stand living here without no hope. Turn yourself into Mr. Right. But we're all good friends here. We share and share alike. You got some good stuff on your back; maybe you got some good stuff in your head. Why not help us out, eh?"

Phaethon said, "I may be able to help you out a great deal. Ironjoy's monopoly seems to be hindering any capital formation. Your 'share and share alike policies,' as you call them, certainly would discourage the type of long-term investment we would all welcome. From what you say, the Hortators are much weaker here than I imagined. Among the deviants and Nevernexts there may be enough markets for us, enough work to be had, that, with some new policies, new leadership, and hard work, some real growth and prosperity could be brought to this little community. And perhaps even a type of immortality could be regained; I knew that Neptunian neurocircuits, in their zero temperatures, suffer very little degradation over the centuries."

Oshenkyo was grinning; clearly the idea appealed to him. He touched his new ear thoughtfully.

Drusillet said in a hushed tone: "What kind of thoughtspace do you carry? What level of integrator is installed in that suit of yours? Do you have enough to carry out the same functions Ironjoy's shop-mind can carry out?"

"Perhaps if I don't have what I need, I could build it out of raw materials."

Drusillet said in a voice of slow astonishment, "Build? What do you mean, build? Only machines build things. Men don't build things, not now-a-days men."

"I build things. And I am very old-fashioned, in mine own way."

"How?"

"With determination, will, and foresight. With my brain. With the circuits in my suit. There is plenty of carbon in the environment. I can design and grow circuits and small ecologies."

He saw their looks of astonishment. He smiled, "Well, I am an engineer, after all."

"Engineer," murmured Oshenkyo. Then: "Hey, engineer, my house grows my cakes and lamps all squirley. Maybe you can fix?"

"I'll certainly take a look at it. The house-mind probably operates from a modular set of neural base-formats. Any part of a working house could be used as a formatting seed to restart the program."

Drusillet said, "Engineer, what about finding assignments? If you and Ironjoy can both run a search, we'll find twice the jobs! Can you do it?"

"Perhaps. The Hortators allow me access to the mentality; even if I do not log on myself, I can access my account through a remote, or even through a script board. It's not impossible. Tell me what might be required. What is the priority and actions-per-second of the search engine Ironjoy uses to find your assignments? In which part of the mentality is he stationed? How does he negotiate the antiviral buffers without hiring a Cerebelline to certify him?"

Drusillet's enthusiasm vanished. She spoke with a twitch of worry. "Ironjoy may not like it, not if too much changes too fast."

"I will explain how it is in everyone's long-term best interest. You people act rationally to further your own interests, do you not?" Phaethon asked. Although, it occurred to him that, if no one here could afford a noetic inspection of each other's thoughts, no one would have any motive to keep their motives pure. Ironjoy theoretically could maintain a whole host of evil impulses and hypocrisies.

Oshenkyo said, "Sure. We all swell people."

Drusillet spoke with less conviction. "Oh, yes, we're rational. The Hortators are just wicked to exile me here. I didn't do anything wrong."

"Then why would Ironjoy object?"

She said in a sad voice: "We're a very tight-knit group, you see? We all swap our things. We all share. There isn't anyone else for us, not for anyone else, no one."

Oshenkyo stepped backward, looked off in the distance. He spoke in a casual voice: "She means don't squirt yellow on Ironjoy. Got to lick up to him, see? He take care of us." He sniffed, and said sidelong to Drusillet: "Besides, I got me someone. What about Jasmyne Xi?"

Phaethon turned Oshenkyo a curious glance. "Jasmyne Xi Meridian?"

Oshenkyo nodded. "My share-wife. She sees me on the sly, not even the Hortators know. Soon, maybe tomorrow, she use her big-snoff influence and get me out of this. Coming by to see me. Good day then, eh?"

Drusillet merely gave Oshenkyo a look, perhaps of pity, perhaps of contempt.

Phaethon knew Jasmyne Xi Meridian of Median House, Red Manorial Scholum; she and Daphne had once had friends in common. She was generally agreed to be among the most beautiful and glam-

orous of women on Earth. She had made several fortunes as a prod-
uctress, fashion archetype, a writer of jewelry, apparel, and
allure-software. She was paid to be seen in public using certain
beauty products, attending certain functions, and for forming certain
favorable opinions reported through noetic channels. It was impossible to imagine that a famous figure like Jasmyne Xi would receive
a low-class ill-spoken outcast like Oshenkyo, much less marry him.

"If you are wealthy enough to afford pseudomnesias and deep-
structure dreams," said Phaethon, "you could afford to pool your
resources, and buy several search-models, and perhaps a few acres
of nanomanufacturing for your own. The Nevernexts make a study
of advanced bioformations and somatics; the Neptunians have an
advanced science of minimalist nanoengineering. They are remote,
but contact with them may not be impossible. Their resources are
more scarce than your own; they must have advanced software you
could profit by."

Drusillet stepped in close, and whispered, "Oshenkyo isn't buying dreams. It's the beauty ads. Oshenkyo is addicted to the ads."

Phaethon spread his fingers in the communication-failure gesture, to show he did not understand.

She whispered: "Jasmyne's lips cosmetics and erotic-formation
commercials sometimes have little dreams as free samples. You see?
Don't trust Oshenkyo. He's not going to help you set up a new
thought-shop or compete with Ironjoy. He's a liar and a destruc-
tionst, a weaponeer, a nihilist; that's why the Hortators shunned
him."

They were interrupted. Oshenkyo waved at someone in the distance. He raised his fingers to his lips and emitted a loud, long
shrill whistle.

Some hooting and commotion, some glad calls and yelps sounded
from several of the floating houses and from the rustling and shining
tents of the central barge. Figures had emerged; Oshenkyo was calling out.

Oshenkyo rubbed his coat, uttered a command. The dark background and dim red lines disappeared, to be replaced by a garish
bright explosion of florid colors swimming in the fabric. A pulsing
beat and a loud announcer's voice issued from Oshenkyo's garment,

a swell of jarring music. Men and women began to shout across the water. Their robes were dark and silent; but, in a moment, they had tuned in to the same commercial Oshenkyo was showing, and a rollicking advertisement was soon pelting noise and echoes across the waters.

Oshenkyo grabbed Phaethon's arm. "Come on down to beach! Lotsa people wanna see you, Engineer! You fix us, you fix everything!"

As they walked, he bent his head low, and whispered, "You need help if you plan to pull jack out of Ironjoy, eh? Don't trust Drusillet. Crazy, crazy, her. You know why Hortators put big no-go on her? She a Cerebelline, raise a hundred children, all in sim. Children dream their whole life, never once see real thing, never once think real thought. By law, when child is grown, must wake up, must tell truth, show world. But law does not say young adult cannot go back into mother's dream womb again, not even if mother raised them to be coward, raised them so cannot think for themselves. She had more than hundred people trapped in her dreams, with no way out, not ever. All legal. All wrong. She say she was protecting them. Don't let her protect you. Got it?"

Phaethon compressed his lips, saying nothing. He had never been among people who could not commune and swap thoughts to settle their differences. He had never known mistrust. How was a rational man to deal with such people . . . ? He warned himself to tread carefully.

Then they were on the beach. A group of folk in brightly colored costumes had come across the water to the little strip of shore below the cliff. Some swam; some floated in small coracles; one or two applied an energetic to render the water surface tension capable of sustaining their weight, and these walked on a temporary film across the water.

Not all were humaniform. One man looked like a barrel with a dozen legs and arms; another was a serpent man, sleek for swimming. A trio of girls had the body shape called air-sylph, with fans of membrane stretched between wrist and ankle. Two other men occupied metal tubs that moved on buzzing magnetic repellors, having a robo-toolbox fixed across the prow of the tubs, rather than arms or legs. There were between forty and eighty individuals inhabiting about sixty bodies. Many had head-plugs or crude crowns, and Phaethon could not tell how many were members of a Composition or mind-group.

All swarmed up the slope. The scene soon took on the aspect of a festival. The people greeted Phaethon with calls and cheers and coarse jests. He was not introduced, no one inquired his name. They called him "New Kid."

Phaethon was bewildered. These people did not have Middle Dreaming, so that, unlike normal people, they did not instantly know all about each other at a glance. But neither were they like Silver-Greys; Phaethon had been raised in the ancient traditions, and he knew how to greet an unknown person, exchange names, and painstakingly memorize those names for later use without artificial aids. But this . . . ?

They did not shake hands (the ancient British custom Phaethon practiced). Instead, the universal greeting was to thrust out a beggar's cupped palms, and shout: "Whatcha got?"

The music-noise from their advertisement robes baffled his attempts at speech. Oshenkyo stood on a tall soil defractor and pointed at his ears, while people looked on and gasped or uttered hoots of surprise. Then they swirled around Phaethon with renewed energy.

Since it was too noisy to make introductions, Phaethon began using very small sections of his black nanomaterial, only one or two precious drops at a time, to cure certain pustules and deformities he saw on certain people here. Most of the ailments were simple skullcap sores caused by improper interfacing, unclean jacks, or drunkenness, or overstimulation.

Five or six people he cured. Then he fixed a broken mind-set they brought him by interposing a correct graph from a working set. The man whose set it was now flourished the crown overhead, yodeling in joy when it lit up; and the people shouted. Phaethon was able to reprogram the color distortions on Drusillet's housecoat merely by opening the coat's help space and entering a reset command. Drusillet threw out her arms and spun, delighted as her coattails gleamed with constant, vibrant colors, unblurred despite her motion. The people near her pointed and called out.

This made him popular. People shouted in his face, laughed,

slapped his back. He did not want people to hurt themselves against his armor; so he took off his gauntlets and helmet. Girls and gynomorphs mussed his hair with slender fingers. A four-armed man with a peg leg, wearing the antennae of a space inspector, pressed a drink bulb into Phaethon's hand. Several people thrust thought-cards or interface disks at him, or twists of candy or incense, or injectors of unknown import.

Phaethon told himself to be cautious; that, unlike in his old life, no warning would come if he were about to do something dangerous. Many of the thought-cards being offered him were no doubt intoxicants or memory-redacts, pornography or pleasure-jolts. He took one or two into his hand, to be polite, but he could not make himself understood over the noise when he asked questions about them.

A hairy man with diamond teeth and crystalline eyeballs slipped a bracelet around Phaethon's wrist. The bracelet flexed, as if it were trying to lock shut; Phaethon, startled, tore it from his wrist and flung it away. He saw the diamond-toothed man skip up and recover the bracelet. There was something familiar in the man's poise and posture. An agent of Scaramouche? Where had he seen the man before?

Phaethon rubbed his wrist and discovered a spot of blood. Was the man merely a cleptogeneticist? Or had Phaethon been injected with something?

Phaethon looked into his personal thoughtspace, so that hovering icons surrounded him superimposed on the shouting crowd. He made a command gesture, releasing biotic antitoxins and investigator animalcules from specialized cells in his lymph nodes into his circulatory system. But a young girl grabbed his arm at the same time, the gesture went awry, and he accidentally flooded his bloodstream with painkillers.

Now he was in an expansive mood. His frets and worries of a moment ago seemed dim and unreal. The world took on new and fascinating color. When the crowd began to dance and sing jingles in time to the braying advertisements, Phaethon joined in.

At sunset, someone brandished an ax and uttered a call.

Some running, and some dancing in a line, the crowd of Afloats now charged through the purple twilight across slope and field to where a dismal clutter of house and broken buildings shouted.

There was a carnival air to their operation. Some carried colored lights. Many brandished axes. In a short time, Phaethon helped a gang of men cut a dead house from its stem, pull and roll it down the slope, off the cliff, and into the water with a tremendous splash. The crowd squealed as it was drenched by the spray. The tall four-armed man held up a command box, pointing and shouting, and spider-gloves began swimming toward the prone house, and the water began to boil with some crude nanoconstruction.

"Engineer! Your house!" shouted Oshenkyo to him. "Yours! For you! See! We all help! All help each other! You sign Pact now, yes?!"

And the people cheered. They did not call him "New Kid" now; they shouted, "Engineer! Engineer!"

But another burst of music started at that moment, and Phaethon was rushed off to join in a line of clapping, swaying, kicking men. He was dizzy and hot from the exertions of the house-felling, and he took a drink from something someone had thrust into his hand. After that the dusk became even more gay and giddy, his memory became pleasantly blurred. There was dancing, singing, and carrying on. Someone had affixed a rope swing to a chemical-tree, which hung over the cliff shore. He remembered whooping with fear as he soared far out above the water and back again. He remembered kissing someone, perhaps a hermaphrodite. It must have been late; there were stars overhead, shining above the steel rainbow of the orbital ring-city. He remembered tossing out huge gobs of his precious nanomaterial to all his fine new friends, scraping it up from the inside of his armor, despite the irksome warning buzz the suit gave off as it fell below necessary internal integrity levels.

He was everyone's darling after that. All his new friends loved him. He wanted to swing on the rope swing again, and they pushed him in high arcs, higher and higher.

He remembered shouting: "Higher! Faster! Farther! The stars! I have vowed the stars shall be mine!"

And, as the swing hesitated at the crest of its high arc, he stood in the rope swing and reached up, as high as he could reach. His new friends all laughed and cheered as he slipped and fell into the waters far below.

THE THOUGHT-SHOP

I.

Phaethon woke slowly, groaning. Jarring noises throbbed and trembled in his ears; cheerful voices shouted rhymes in a language unknown to him. His sleep had been troubled again, plagued by nightmare-images of a black sun rising over a blood-soaked landscape.

He came more awake, and discovered his head throbbing in tempo to the loud beat of the drum music shouting from the flashing garment he wore. Garment? No; he was wrapped up in an advertisement, lying on the floor in the curving corner of a blue-white room. The noise of the advertisement drilled into his skull.

Where was his armor?

For that matter, where was he? Curving walls like the inside of a seashell rose around him. The far wall was dotted with blank receptor-cells, like a line of blind eyes. There was dust and brine staining the floor. An oval nearby admitted a harsh light, which stung his eyes. The floor seemed to sway and slide, lurch and jump in a sickening fashion.

Where was his armor? A gram of his nanomaterial would have been able to flush the toxins from his body and cleanse his blood-stream of debris.

He closed his eyes; closing his eyes created the same stabbing pains as opening them. His memory was clouded. Phaethon signaled for a reconstruction routine to index his memory fragments and holographically extrapolate the missing sections, before he recalled that such services were no longer available to him.

And never would be again . . .

But he vaguely remembered dismantling the black nanomachinery, which formed the lining, control system, and interface of the armor plates. Dismantling it and tossing it to cheering crowds, who programmed the expensive and highly complex nanomachinery to re-form itself into simple intoxicants and slurp it down their throats or rub it across their skin, absorbing hallucinogens into the pores of their flesh.

Phaethon raised his hand to his aching head. It could not be true. Surely that memory was false, an exaggeration. All his Sophotech-crafted nanosoftware erased and reconstructed as morphines or pleasure-endorphins? It would be as if someone were to eat the brain of a well-skilled genius merely for the protein content, or melt down a hard-process superintegrator merely to loot the few pfennings' worth of copper wire in the heat regulator.

Please, let it not be true.

And what would Daphne say if she found out he had been so foolish, so careless, as to allow his beautiful gold armor to be destroyed . . . ? But then Phaethon remembered that he was never going to see Daphne again.

Perhaps this was all a simulation. "End program!" shouted Phaethon. But the scene did not end. Everything was as before; he sat in a dirty white shell, with sunlight blazing in through a window above, and the floor still swooped and lurched, sickeningly. Or perhaps the floor was steady and he was ill. There was no way to tell. "End program!" he shouted again, slamming his fist into the curving wall beside him. "End! End! End program! I want my life back, damn you!"

Phaethon fought his way to his feet. This place remained solid and "real" (if that concept had meaning any longer in his life). He was alone; he was unwell. Or perhaps he was not unwell. The floor was actually rocking.

Hunger pangs stung his stomach. Where was his armor? It was his only food supply.

At that, he heaved himself upright and tore the noisy, flashing advertisement banner off his body. With a convulsion of disgust, he threw it fluttering out the window. It struck some impediment just below his line of sight and flapped there, giving off a shout.

No; it was a man who had shouted. Now that man rose into view. He had been walking up to the window, and Phaethon had thrown the advertisement over his head. He was dressed in gray.

Now, the oval expanded, and the man stepped in. The oval was not an oeil-de-boeuf or window; it was a door. The mechanism was jammed or ill. The door tried to iris shut, but dwindled only to its former dimension, trembled, squeaked, and remained half-open. Now through the opening, Phaethon saw he was inside a house floating on angular legs in the waters of the bay.

"Where is my armor?" said Phaethon, squinting. He had one hand against the sloping wall to keep himself upright.

The man took the advertisement carefully off his head, balled it up, and tossed it out the window. The banner floated away, looking for prospective clients.

When the man turned, Phaethon saw he had no face.

It was not a man. It was a mannequin.

Phaethon straightened up in shock. No person from the Golden Oecumene would be telepresenting himself here, not with the Hortators' ban in place.

Scaramouche . . . ? It was not impossible . . .

"What do you want of me?!" asked Phaethon in a ragged voice.

The mannequin's external speakers said: "I've come to ask you to cooperate."

Phaethon stepped away from the wall, and tried to stand straight. He did not want to show any weakness. "Cooperate? In what way?"

"You have been the victim of a crime. I want you to help me punish the people who did this to you. They claim that they are your society and your people and that you owe them loyalty now, but don't listen to that rubbish. Your interests still are best served by cooperation."

Phaethon squinted. This was an odd thing for Scaramouche to be saying. Yes, forcing Phaethon into exile was a crime, but did this creature from beyond actually think Phaethon would help Scaramouche punish the Hortators?

Phaethon said, "Where do you creatures come from? Another star? Another time? How do you know so much about the Golden Oecumene when we know nothing about you?"

The gray mannequin had no face, but there was an expression of surprise in its posture, in the set of its shoulders. "Uh, sir, I don't mean to intrude on your hallucination, but I'm a constable officer from the local commandry, Ceylon 21. My name is Pursuivant Eighteenth Co-Mentalist Neoform of the Andropsyche-Projection Orthochronic Schola."

"What?"

"Forgive me for not introducing myself. I had my valet place a description of myself and my reason for coming into the Middle Dreaming, and I had assumed you would know all about me at a glance. That is the way we at the Andropsychic Projection school run our affairs. I had been informed that you, despite being ostracized, still had access to the mentality. It just did not occur to me you would not use it."

The gray mannequin now held out an empty hand toward Phaethon. "Here is my badge of office, with warrants and commissions appended in nearby files. Do you wish to inspect it? All you need do is log on to the mentality."

Phaethon looked at the mannequin's hand. To Phaethon's mentality-blind eyes, it was empty. "I am not willing to log on to the mentality," he said.

"Ah. That's too bad. I have a magistrate standing by on channel 653. She-they will sign a warrant for the seizure and arrest of your remaining nanomaterial—that suit-substance in your armor—before the rest of the Drunks here eat the stuff. A lot of people last night took handsful of your stuff back to their rafts, and most of them injected or inhaled only a few grams, according to my best guess. If you want to get it back, what little is left, we must act quickly. Just log on to the mentality and talk with the magistrate; I'm sure we can get an injunction and have that stuff seized before your new pals wolf down the rest of it for breakfast. We may only have a few minutes. Just log on."

For a moment, such a wild emotion pulsed in Phaethon that he could not speak. But a cold ripple of doubt quelled his joy. What evidence did he have that his armor had not been entirely destroyed? What evidence did he have that this faceless mannequin was not, in fact, Scaramouche? He seemed to have insisted once too often that Phaethon should log on to the mentality.

And yet, if part of his armor still existed, and might still be saved, and if it were destroyed because Phaethon stood here hesitating and doubting . . . ?

Phaethon licked dry lips, not sure what to believe.

The mannequin said, "We don't have much time."

Phaethon thought a moment, came to a decision. "I will go talk to Ironjoy," he said to the constable.

2.

It was with some difficulty that Phaethon made his way to the central barge where Ironjoy kept his thought-shop. First, he could not dilate the oval window-door to get out of his house with any dignity; nor would the constable help him by overriding the house-mind's faulty command-line, as such charity might have been in violation of the Hortators' ban. Phaethon had to squirm through the hole, whereupon he fell across a narrow ledge and plummeted twenty feet into the sea.

The water here was clogged and clotted with snag-lines and ropy tendrils, which made up part of Old-Woman-of-the-Sea's body, or perhaps one of her manufacturing subsections, so Phaethon did not sink. But neither was his body buoyant; the special organs and space-adaptations built into his thick hide added weight. However, his strength was much greater than an unmodified man's, and he was able to lunge forcefully through the thicket. Another modification enabled him to hold his breath for the twenty minutes or so it took him to walk (and crawl and swim) across the beds of undersea kelp and ratting to the rusted barge in the center of the bay.

He swarmed up the anchor lines, awkwardly negotiated the float-sponsons, and eventually found himself dangling from the side of the barge.

Clinging to an anchor line, Phaethon looked up. Sheer vertical surface loomed above him, and a metal overhang or catwalk extended out overhead. There was no way upward. The mannequin representing Constable Pursuivant was not in sight.

Phaethon banged on the side of the hull and shouted for attention. Once again, he underestimated the strength involved in his space adapted body; the metal dented under his blows.

The hull rang like a gong. In the heat of the equatorial morning, the hull metal seemed scalding. Rust flakes and barnacles scraped his fist.

After what seemed a long time, a tall silhouette stepped out upon the catwalk. Phaethon craned his neck and stared overhead. It was Ironjoy; he had four arms, and the same wide hat he wore yesterday, the same shifting green-blue garment. The housecoat was whining as its air conditioners attempted to keep a zone of cool, scented air around Ironjoy.

"Hoy! You clang at my personal property, creating disturbance. Aboard I have early shift workers, with their work personalities ready to load, and needing sanity-chips to balance themselves after last night's festivity. Why do you irk them? Do you come for work?"

Without his sense-filter Phaethon could neither amplify the view, nor edit out the metal honeycomb that formed the catwalk floor, so his vision was obscured. Ironjoy was holding a large round golden object in three hands, and as he spoke, he bowed to sip or lick something from the inside of the golden bowl. Eating did not hinder speech: his voice issued from a machine in his chest.

Phaethon said, "I've come to get my armor back. You must be able to call everyone together."

"Not possible."

"But I saw Oshenkyo do it yesterday! He set his advertisement cloak to emit a call!"

"Yes. Oshenkyo has enough chits to pay off the interruption fee. You have not. The rental on your revived house-mind has already accumulated over two hundred units, and it's another twenty-five units' fare you'll owe to rent my coracle to carry you back to your house. Unless you want to swim back? Plus my consultation fee, which started to accumulate from the moment you began to speak to me. You are severely in debt, New Kid. Are you ready to start working it off, or are you going to cling there, jabbering?" Ironjoy now bent to take a slow sip of whatever he held in his golden bowl. Phaethon saw, with a sensation of shock, that Ironjoy was holding, not a bowl, but the helmet of Phaethon's armor, and that he was eating out grams of the delicate skullcap interface webbing.

Rage throbbed in his body. "Stop! You are destroying my property! You will return my helmet to me as of this instant! Then you will take all steps to recover whatever of my equipment as might remain from the others here!"

Ironjoy's insectoid face was incapable of expression. "Do not irk me. You may have been a significant man before, on the outside. Here, only I am significant. Cooperation is necessary to survive in this community. Cooperation is defined as acclimation to my wishes."

Phaethon's fists tightened on the anchor line. He wanted to leap up the sheer surface but saw no way up. His head swam with anger; he tried to calm himself. (He wished Rhadamanthus were there to calm him.)

"I have made a lawful request that you return property that has been stolen from me," said Phaethon "Look! Constable remotes as thick as wasps hover over this entire area! Do you think to defraud me of my only possessions?"

"I see Drusillet and Oshenkyo did not explain real things to you, as I instructed. Come up; I will tell you the truth." With a kick, Ironjoy unfolded a gangway of stairs from the catwalk. Phaethon dropped into the water, awkwardly made his way to the stairs, climbed. Ironjoy stood under a parasol of diamond in one of the pavilions on deck, rainbow shadows rippled around his feet.

Other pavilions, to the left and right, showed sleeping figures, their mind-sets connected by cheap hard-wire to an interface board which ran the length of the deck.

A winged girl nearby had her arms around Phaethon's gold breastplate, to which she was snuggled up, like a child sleeping with a favorite toy. Phaethon, without a word, stepped over to her and knelt. His arms reached for the breastplate, which, to his delight, he saw still had more than half its nanomachine coating glistening on the interior.

"Halt!" said Ironjoy. "No stealing!"

Phaethon turned, his eyes burning, his head pounding. Civilized instinct told him not to touch the armor, to negotiate, and to allow the normal process of law to settle the dispute. But were those instincts of any use to him now?

He pulled up the breastplate and set it off to one side. The winged girl stirred and murmured but did not wake. Then Phaethon stood, his eyes glassy with anger, and crossed to confront Ironjoy.

He stared at his foe for a moment. Was there any point in talking? Floating in the transparent surface of the diamond parasol, which spread like a halo over Ironjoy's head, were the icons and display-boards indexing the contents of Ironjoy's thought-shop. The icons appeared in Objective Aesthetic symbology; Phaethon understood their meaning.

To Ironjoy's left were routines to suppress restless thoughts, to produce personas incapable of fatigue, boredom, talkativeness, or dishonesty. Evidently his work roster. To his right were pleasure-stimulants, a wide number of anesthetics and pornography simulations, mood alterants, false memories, gambling interfaces, and self-justification dreams. Here were stupifiers, nullifiers, distorted mythoformations, and choose-your-own revenge dramas.

Phaethon, to his deep disgust, also saw sickly sweet addictive thought-forms of the type passed out freely by the mass-mind Compositions, intended only to persuade individuals to surrender the pain and loneliness of individuality to the unconditional and mindless love of the group-mind. Since, of course, no real Composition would permit an exile to join its ranks, Ironjoy could not fulfill the promises those addictives created. But next to them were a group of awareness-interrupters intended to create the temporary illusion of being a member of a mass-mind.

Phaethon saw not a single intelligence enhancer, memory augment, philosophy text, emotion balancer, or any other useful or wholesome application. He now saw what kind of thought-shop Ironjoy ran.

Without a word, he yanked the golden helmet out of Ironjoy's grasp.

Ironjoy grappled Phaethon, seizing him by both wrists, putting his third hand on the helmet itself, and grasping Phaethon's neck with his remaining hand. His hands were as hard and strong as mechanical grapples; he evidently expected no resistance. Ironjoy's face, pressed to Phaethon's, now showed the only expression of which it was capable: the mandible plates drew back, making a parody of a sneering smile.

Ironjoy certainly was not expecting Phaethon's strength to exceed his own. With a brush of his arm, Phaethon threw Ironjoy aside. The tall creature stumbled, four arms windmilling, and fell.

A group of constable remotes, glittering and buzzing, had descended to take up a circle around the two of them, tiny stings and stunners open.

Ironjoy rose to his feet and addressed the nearest constable: "I have been assaulted. You boast that violence is unknown in the Golden Oecumene! Yet now this wild barbarian commits outrages upon me!"

The flat voice spoke from the constable: "The law allows a person to use a reasonable amount of force to recover stolen property."

Phaethon said: "Yet neither did you protect me against him!"

The constable said: "His action was arguably self-defense. Also, the grounds of your action are not unambiguous. Ironjoy may have a colorable claim to the property."

At this, Ironjoy stepped forward again and reached toward the helmet.

Phaethon said softly: "The property is mine. Interfere at your peril."

Ironjoy drew back. But his voice machine issued a strident tone:

"By what right do you make this claim? You gave it all away, last night. Observe!" Ironjoy drew out a field slate from his coat. He touched the slate surface and called up an image of glowing dragon-signs, surrounded by icons and cartouches of the legal sublanguage. Beneath, in Phaethon's perfect Second-Era-style handwriting, using linear-style cursive letters, was Phaethon's signature.

"Last night you signed our Pact. It states our properties are to be administered according to the group will. Haven't you read it? I left a copy at your house. Your signature passed title to your armor."

Phaethon stared at the slate. In a window to the side of his signature, the document showed a visual recording from last night. The picture showed him, giggling, one arm around some pink-haired air-sylph, reaching out with a light-stylus to inscribe a slate Lester was proffering. The time in the scene was dusk. A clock statement stamped by a notary public showed the hour and place and reality level. In the background of the scene, a group of men had begun to chop down a dead house. Phaethon recalled no such scene; but his memory was blurred.

"The donation is void on the grounds that I was intoxicated."

"Intoxication and other voluntary alterations of mental capacity do not form a valid basis for setting aside such a contract. That is the primary law of the Golden Oecumene."

"Scoundrel! The intoxication was not voluntary."

Ironjoy drew back the slate. He produced a nasal tone: "No doubt you have edited your memory. Fortunately, the records of the garden monitors will confirm my version of events. You drank an expansive from a bulb offered you; you doused yourself with painkillers from your own internal supply."

"Only because I was already drunk, and unable to control myself. Earlier than that, you conspired to have one of your fellows, a man with diamond teeth and glass eyes, stab me with a drug!" As he spoke, Phaethon realized who the man must have been. With his stimulant beard, housecoat, and opaque eye cusps removed, Phaethon had not then recognized him. Phaethon said: "You ordered Lester to do the deed. You feared that the capacities of my nanomachinery would threaten your monopoly. It was your intention from the first to rob me."

Ironjoy's tone grew even more nasal: "You will not prove this."

"Are you insane!? We are citizens of the Golden Oecumene! How can you even dream to succeed at your deceptions? There are a hundred constable remotes within earshot. Come, let us have the constables do a noetic reading. Your own thoughts and memories will show what you intended!"

"Perhaps so, if you bring foreword a complaint to the constables. But you will not. This is a trick the constables always play whenever a New Kid is thrown to us here on Death Row. They wait until the

New Kid is disadvantaged by one of our practices, but before he has been here long enough to learn our ways. Then they swoop in to stir up trouble. To stir up disloyalty. To stir up disunity. Yes, they would like to have a complaint against me. The Hortators put them up to it."

"Why?"

"Why? I give these exiles a way to stay alive. The Hortators want them to die. I alone of all these people here have the presence of mind, the discipline and willpower to prosper in this adversity. I alone brought wealth with me into exile, and established secret contacts and way stations in the more private sections of the mentality before I came, or made contracts without the standard Hortators' escape clause."

"You volunteered to live this way?" Phaethon's words came out slowly, amazed, perhaps disgusted.

"Out there I am of no account. Here, I am as rich as Gannis, as popular as Helion, as feared as Orpheus. It is a filthy, stinking, wretched, and temporary existence, but I am the most important aspect of it. Do you understand? You will not make any complaint to the constables."

"Why won't I?"

Ironjoy pointed with two right arms out to where the lopsided and unpowered house which they had given Phaethon wallowed in the waves. Some invisible signal radiated from Ironjoy; there was a snap of energy from below the sea, and the buoyancy floats holding up the house-legs bobbed loose. In a matter of moments, the seashell-shaped house had flooded and sank.

Phaethon stared in puzzled dismay, trying to remember if anything he owned might have been in the house.

Ironjoy said: "Keep in mind, the wording of the pact you signed requires you to continue to pay rent. If you wish to sleep this night, I will rent you, at a considerably higher rate, a square meter of deck space here. If you are frugal, work hard, and sell some of your more expensive organs, you will be able to buy a carbon-organizer to weave yourself a pillow and a pavilion roof in less than a month. If you do anything more to exasperate me, such as, for example, continue to threaten me with constables, I will refuse to rent to you, to sell you food or goods at any rate whatever."

Phaethon drew a deep breath, trying to control his shaking rage. Was he not a civilized man? Educated and bred to rationality, dignity, peace?

He made an attempt: "Let us reconcile. Use a circuit from your thought-shop to allow us to mingle our minds, either to comprehend each other from each other's point of view or to create a temporary arbitration conciliator, who will share memory chains from both of us and be able to decide our case with full justice."

The chest vox of Ironjoy gave forth a squawk. Laughter? Or the sign of some emotion known only to Ironjoy's peculiar half-Basic, half-Invariant neuroform?

"Absurdity! We are mortal and we are poor. Such circuits are expensive. We have not the time nor the wealth to enjoy the dream of perfect justice you manor-born play at. Life is unfair. We cannot buy sense-filters to fabricate pretty illusions that tell us otherwise. Unfair, because there are times when necessity requires the weak to submit to the strong. I have stolen your armor, perhaps. That is your opinion. But you cannot afford to object. That is a fact. Instead of getting your armor back, you will apologize, you must now plead with me, you must now beg humbly to be forgiven. Why? Not because you are wrong. Only because you are weak."

Phaethon's rage filled him like fire, but suddenly, impossibly, turned to jovial disdain, and left him clear-minded and cold. He felt like a man who struggled up some shifting slope of sand, with everything disintegrating and sliding backward beneath his fingers, but who suddenly stands at the peak of the slope, and finds a much wider view than he had expected.

He said, "Weak? Compared to whom? To you? My actions do not stink of hysteria and shortsighted fear. To the Hortators? They were willing to blot the world with amnesia rather than face me. To my nameless enemies? I discovered their cowardice at Lake Victoria. Justice and rightness are on my side: I need never think a weak thought again."

Ironjoy brushed this aside with a wave of both left hands. "Congratulations. But where will you live? To whom will you speak? Not to the Ashores; they regard the Afloats with nothing but hatred. Cooperate. Here you will find friends."

Phaethon said, "I make you a counteroffer. If you cooperate with me, and return my remaining armor intact, not only will I *not* turn you over to the constables, but I will take you with me, you and all the Afloats, and make you a planet for your very own, a world drawn up according to your own specifications, once I regain control of my ship, the *Phoenix Exultant*, and once I set out to conquer the stars."

"Absurd. You are deluded."

"I am not deluded! My memories are true and exact. Come now, which is it to be? My armor, or the constables? If I testify against you, the Curia will apply pain directly to your nervous system, or they will rewrite your evil thoughts with a reformation program."

"They have no case; otherwise, they would have already moved against me. Be reasonable, New Kid! Why do you want or need that armor? To fly to the stars? That will never happen. You need the nanomachinery lining to control some complex supersystem or maintain internal energy ecologies aboard your ship? There is no ship. The armor is worthless to you, and meaningless to your new life. I am all that matters to your new life. You will not find work without me. You will not eat breakfast without me. You will need my dreams and delusions to keep at bay despair and suicide.

"Try to understand the grim necessity of the reality that confronts you," continued Ironjoy. "You are like a man who was thrown headlong from orbit into the deep sea, with only my little boat to fish you out from drowning. In my boat, you are sailing on an ocean of death, a bottomless ocean, with no net to catch you should you fall overboard, with no backup copies of yourself to restore you to life, no Sophotech to save you from your own foolishness. There is only me. Me. And if I throw you overboard, you will sink into that sea, never to rise again. Do not pester me about your foolish armor again; it was worthless to you, but my employees and charges will gain some momentary pleasures from it. The rest of the nanomachinery will be consumed later tonight, or tomorrow at the latest. Go down below, and I will give you a charge of noosophorific to put your memories of your armor permanently out of your head. Then return here, and I will plug you into the assembly formation. Some deviants are charging me for bit-work; I can use your brain's storage capacity for some of the overruns. It pays four chits per hour. Well?"

Phaethon said, "I will allow you to escape punishment for robbing me, and I will allow you to escape punishment for destroying the house, which, as far as I can tell, actually was given to me and was actually my property. I will allow you to escape punishment for your various lies and frauds. I will even consent to work at any job you care to set for any wages upon which we can mutually agree, provided it is honest labor. I am an intelligent and diligent worker, and I will not decrease my capacity for work by buying any dreams or false memories from your shop. I can certainly improve the house-minds of the wounded houses; I can restore the dead houses to life, I can string up a simple energy system, and I can organize a communication grid. I can program your thought-shop with a working dreamspace at least to the first-magnitude interactions, which should more than double your productivity. All this I can and will do. But only if you immediately recover my armor and restore it to me."

"The armor is a worthless memento of a life now closed to you. You have no use for it. The Pact you have signed is clear."

"I need the armor to fly my ship."

"There is no such ship. It does not exist. It is from a story. It is a dream."

" 'She.' Ships are not called 'it.' And . . . she is indeed a dream. A fine dream. Surrender my armor. This is your last chance."

Ironjoy stood looking at him, moving by not so much as a twitch.

Phaethon said loudly, "Constable Pursuivant! Are you standing by?"

One of the thumb-sized remotes, suspended on eight tiny nacelles, came forward, humming, from the circling swarm. A tiny voice, the same as had come from the mannequin earlier, issued forth: "I cannot make an arrest unless you agree to testify. The court will need to examine both your memories and his to discover if your intoxication was voluntary, and whether or not he had fraudulent intent."

Phaethon turned to stare at Ironjoy. Now was the crisis. Ironjoy could not know that Phaethon dared not log on to the mentality, and dared not open a deep channel to permit a noetic examination. Could he be deceived? Ironjoy lived in a culture where deception was practiced, like someone from ancient times.

Surely he would see through Phaethon's bluff . . .

He did not.

With no change of his insect expression, Ironjoy tapped a command into his slate. All of the sleeping figures on deck were wearing advertisement robes of dull blue-gray. Now those robes strobed, yelling, into life. The figures stirred, groaning.

Ironjoy made a general announcement. Sullenly, faces downcast, people shuffled forward and dropped pieces of golden adamantium at Phaethon's feet. Some of them spat at him as they dropped a vambrace or greave. Coracles were sent out, towed by daughter-vines across the water to the nearby houses; more people returned, and brought back a few remaining pieces of the armor, an arm ring and elbow piece.

There were some arguments about bits of the black nanomachinery, which people had turned into other substances but had not consumed yet. Ironjoy gave a curt command, and pointed. Jars and caps and little bags were brought forward. Sullen figures dumped the material at Phaethon's feet, to form a spreading black pool. Oshenkyo himself had swallowed a large amount, but was storing it, undigested, as an inert material, for his stomach to consume slowly, one gram at a time. With many sneers and curses he vomited the material up. Then he sat slumped on the deck, weeping; it had been enough substance to keep him in pleasant hallucinations for weeks, almost unimaginable wealth.

It was all over in less than an hour. The whole community stood on the deck of the barge, beneath the crystalline pavilion roofs, glowering at Phaethon. The black pool at his feet trembled as it went through its self-cleaning routine, restoring broken memory chains and command lines. About one-fourth of the material had been consumed; the memory storage in the rest had sufficient mass to recompile the missing parts. The damage was curable.

Phaethon, his heart large with emotion, placed his foot into the pool. The suit lining recognized his cell structure. Like a loyal hound after a long absence, it remembered him. There was an upward rush of motion. The lining flowed over his body and established connections to his skin, nerves, and muscles. The golden plates slid upward and clattered into their proper places. A sense of wonderful well-being suffused him.

Ironjoy made a signal to his people. "And now, trespasser, you are no longer welcome here. Don't show your face again!"

And, with a rush, the people crowded forward and threw Phaethon into the sea. The constables did not interfere. Phaethon plummeted, splashed, and sank like a stone. But, beneath his helmet, he was smiling.

3.

As he sank, Phaethon's smile faded, and he began to realize the enormity of his error.

Above, the barge was a square shadow, surrounded by ripples of agitated light. To every side were lesser shadows, spider shapes of the dead houses seen from below, their splayed float pods tangled with trailing vines and nets and lines of kelp.

He had erred. Intent on his armor, he had forgotten his life.

For what was he to do now?

The inescapable obstacle to any attempt by Phaethon to build up another fortune, buy passage to Mercury, call his ship, or organize a protest against the Hortators' decision was, simply and absolutely, that he dared not log on to the mentality. The enemy virus lurking in the mentality, waiting for Phaethon, closed all Phaethon's options.

Ironically, if he had gone to a simple thought-shop before his exile, and bought a script board, or some other indirect means of communicating with the mentality—even through a cheap pair of gloves as he had seen some of the wretched Ashores of Talaimannar use—he might have been able to find ways to send messages to, and perform useful work for, some of Ironjoy's dark markets. Markets which the Hortators apparently could not close off.

Worse, there were obviously such devices for sale from Ironjoy. Had Phaethon not gotten himself exiled from the exiles, he might have been able to begin a long, slow, painful process of rebuilding his life, of reaching his ship.

Now, there was not even that.

Down he sank.

The bottom of the bay fell in a series of shelves into the deeper seabeds beyond. Bioformations that formed the nervous system of Old-Woman-of-the-Sea were mingled among the nets and beds of kelp and seaweed lining the muck and silt underfoot. Phaethon spied a place where the kelp had been crushed aside, as if by the rolling of a massive cylinder. Curious (and unwilling to return, just as yet, to the surface) Phaethon followed the trail of destruction.

He pondered as he slogged through the floating clouds of mud. Occasionally he stumbled. He had been without proper sleep for so long that his makeshifts were not able to catch and repair all the damage it was doing to his nervous system. A check on his internal systems showed another disaster looming. If he used his reduced supply of nanomaterial to form a recycling environment, allowing him to stay down here, there might not be enough to form the neuretic tissues he needed to reconstruct the crude self-consideration circuit he was using to stave off sleep deprivation. Also, some of the memories directly relating to past dream states, associational chains, and proper mental balance had been lost. He might not have time to reconstruct that information.

He was reluctant to rise to the surface, however. He suspected the behavior of the constables just now. Why had they been so very slow to interfere when Phaethon had been robbed? Or when Phaethon and Ironjoy had wrestled over the helmet? Phaethon recalled the Hortators' promise that Nebuchednezzar Sophotech could see to it that Phaethon would not stand any chance of finding food or help. Could this whole scene have been arranged? Had both Ironjoy and Phaethon been tricked, manipulated, out-guessed?

Perhaps it had been foolish even to dream that the Hortators' Sophotech would not deduce Phaethon's flight to Talaimannar. The cyborg calling itself the Bellipotent Composition might not have had as secure a privacy as it had said. The cyborg could have been deluded, dream-caught, simply a memory addict who thought it was Bellipotent, thought it had privacy rights.

Besides, there were ways of tracking air movements Phaethon could think of; signals bounced from the underside of the ring-city, for example. If Phaethon could think of one, trust that a Sophotech could think of a thousand.

Had Nebuchednezzer Sophotech been able somehow to influence the constables to produce a crisis between Ironjoy and Phaethon? Anyone wishing to destroy Phaethon would rejoice at Ironjoy's enmity with him. In Ironjoy's shop, Phaethon might have been able to buy a self-consideration circuit to enable himself to program his sleep-and-dream cycles to repair, annex, balance, and regenerate the tired nerve paths in his artificial brain tissue in the same way that natural dreaming restored natural tissue. Had he and Ironjoy cooperated, it would have saved him from going mad.

Within the limits of the law, there was some scope, some gray areas, some flexibility of interpretation, as to how the constables could do their jobs. If so, it was safe to assume they would use that flexibility to do Phaethon as much harm as they could without actually overstepping the strict boundary of what was permissible. If so, it was better not to return to the surface, where the constables swarmed.

And Phaethon saw none down here.

His sleep deprivation, no doubt, was what had allowed his anger to escape him during his confrontation with Ironjoy. It was affecting more and more of his memory; he was suffering spasms of fatigue, dizziness, light-headedness. Eventually, he would die of this.

Without a self-consideration circuit to help organize his complex brain levels, the neural degeneration would proceed at an ever-increasing rate.

There was nothing to do, but to lie down and wait to go mad and die.

Strange. That a lack of a dream could kill a man.

Or maybe it was not so strange.

The line of wreckage dropped off the edge of a long slope. Here were grooves in the mud where some great weight had passed, discoloration where coral had been scarred. Phaethon began to pick his way down the slope, deeper into the green gloom.

4.

Phaethon was more fatigued than he suspected. Farther and farther down the subsea slope he wandered, having long since lost the trail of debris he followed, and, in his daze, having forgotten what whim or purpose brought him here.

It grew darker; he was very deep; and clouds of slow mud, like wings, billowed from his every shuffling step.

He was jarred awake by an ache in his chest. It was a pain signal from a special organ he had had implanted in his lung. The organ was one of the earliest modifications of space-biotechnology, dating back to the first Orbital City, and allowed the user to detect a loss in oxygen levels, (something the nose of an unmodified man was not able to detect) and warned of hypnoxia, hyperventilation, or anoxia.

He was choking to death without noticing it.

Phaethon blearily activated his internal thoughtspace and demanded a report from his suit. Headache pains stabbed him as the system came on; the icons seemed to drift and slide and blur in his vision.

The report jumped and swam jerkily into his thoughts.

The nanomachinery in his suit had been damaged, of course. But Phaethon had not realized that part of the damage had affected the suit's internal damage-control and safety routines.

One of the Afloats had erased the safety interlocks from the oversight routine in order to allow him to reprogram a stolen scrap of the suit to make nitrous oxide, not oxygen, through its recycler. When that section had rejoined the main suit, some error in the reproducer had carried the erase-command over into the maintenance routine. Thus, every time Phaethon's lungs pumped carbon dioxide into the suit's faceplate, the erroneous command broke up the carbon dioxide and made nitrous oxide.

The broken safety checker knew enough not to pass the laughing gas back to Phaethon, but did not know enough either to dispose of it or to call it to Phaethon's attention. Instead, the broken safety checker shunted the nitrous oxide into the little storage pockets meant for the stacked oxygen molecules, and dumped the oxygen.

The suit contained little packages or bubbles of iso-molecular raw materials, like tiny storehouses of gold and carbon, frozen oxy-nitrogen or hydrogen chains for the other mechanisms in the suit to combine and manipulate. These pockets were designed only to hold racks and rows of molecules at a standardized orientation and spin; otherwise, the suit mechanisms could not grasp and manipu-late them. The nitrous oxide, flooding the pockets, was, of course, not at the correct temperature, orientation, or composition. This had damaged most of the manipulator elements in the suit. Normally, it would have been child's play to draw oxygen out of the H_2O mol-ecules of the water around him, but now all the pores he would have used to separate out the oxygen were jammed. It would take at least an hour to repair the damage; Phaethon doubted that he could hold his breath that long.

Even if he abandoned the armor, his space-adapted body was not buoyant, and he could not float to the surface. He might be able to survive the buildup of nitrogen in his blood; special osmotic layers in his veins, another space adaptation, could screen out most nitro-gen buildup. Could he simply swim up by brute strength alone? He was not sure how far overhead the surface was. And how could he find his armor again if he simply left it on the sea bottom?

One moment of supreme self-loathing and self-pity stabbed through him. Why had he not carefully checked every element, every command line of his armor when he had recovered it? His armor on which his life depended? Why? Because he had been raised as a pampered aristocrat, with a hundred machines to do all his bidding for him, to think his thoughts and anticipate his whims, so that he had lost the basic survival skills of discipline, foresight, and thoroughness.

Choking on bile, Phaethon thought the escape command, and panels of his armor fell away. Black seawater closed in on his face, blinding him. The black nanomachine lining swelled up, forming pockets of hydrogen along the chest and arms, trying to add buoyancy.

His armor, his beautiful armor, which had meant so much to him an hour ago, sank down swiftly and was gone.

He kicked away from the bottom, swung his arms and legs, and tried to pull his heavy body upward.

Upward. Icy water sucked the heat from his body in a moment. His limbs moved more slowly.

Upward. His struggles grew more wild. He lost his sense of direction.

Upward. He encountered some sort of kelp or seaweed, which tangled around his flailing arms, wrapped his legs with soft embrace.

Upward. It was the direction the stars were in. Phaethon did not know where they were. He was disoriented. He had lost the stars.

What were those little lights approaching him? Were they fairy lamps, come to greet him in his hour of victory? Or were they the metallic flashes in the eyes of a dying man about to faint?

Then there was nothing.

THE NIGHTMARE

I.

"Little Spirit, why are you alive?"

Words, like something from myth, or dream, floated up. *Sorrow, great sorrow, to be his fate, and deeds of renown without peer . . . to little men, the height is too great; to him, the stars are near . . .*

"Daphne. Daphne said . . ." He heard his own voice, muttering gibberish. Did he speak aloud? The words on his memory casket had come from the epic Daphne once composed in his honor . . . back before he sank and drowned . . .

"Then is she that one for whom you live, little one?"

Phaethon jerked open his eyes. A blur of green, dimness, shadows. He saw nothing.

His body jerked. He was numb, floating, drifting. Some sort of vines or swarms of living eels entwined his limbs with soft firmness; he could not move.

"Do not struggle, little one, unless to damage yourself is your goal. We have formed a pocket of your air; our dolphins rise to the surface, draw breath, and descend to breathe into your pocket here."

He attempted speech again. This time, his voice was clear. "Whom do I have the honor of addressing?"

"Aha. Polite little one, isn't he? We are Old-Woman-of-the-Sea."

The words were coming directly into his thoughtspace, over his suit-lining channel. Some sort of tube or medical appliance was thrust in his mouth. Other vines felt as if they held pads to his skin. Needles pierced his arm. The black nanomachinery of his lining was in motion; it was forming and unforming chemicals and combinations. He could feel the pulse of heat burning through it. The sensation comforted him.

Phaethon's eyes rolled back and forth. He saw nothing, at first. Then he detected a slide of gray shadow to his left and right. Two dolphins came near. He heard a rush of bubbles, a high-pitched squeak of dolphin sound. Air bubbled into the little space around his head.

"Madame, I thank you, and the gratitude I have is without limit. And yet I must warn you that those who assist me may fall under the ban of the College of Hortators."

"Our dolphins act by their own nature, and it is their nature to assist those in need. Had there been sharks nearby, the parts of our mind may have reacted differently. Such is life."

(Why did it sound so much like the voice of his mother, Galatea, whom he recalled from his far-vanished youth? Perhaps it was merely how regal, how queenly, how very much in command the voice rang . . .)

"Ah. Forgive me, Madame, but, nonetheless, you yourself may be held to account for your generosity to me."

"The little one is noble as well! You seek to shield us from harm? Us?" There was a hint of vast laughter in the voice.

"The College of Hortators wields wide influence!"

"Yet we are as wide as the sea. Part of us are in the kelp, the coral, and the dust of the seabed, measuring, moving, releasing heat, storing it. Part of us is woven into the thoughts of fish and sea-beast, moving from brain to brain with the swiftness of a radio flash, or slowly, over centuries, thoughts encoded into chemicals drifting in the sea tides. After centuries or seconds, our thoughts come together again in new forms, drops rise as dew above the gentle tropics, or move through storms that ring the arctic.

"We breathe to calm the hurricanes; we blush to stir the trade winds into life. We sway the Gulf Streams, we thrust the currents and the counter-current of the tide as if they were limbs a hundred miles wide, and yet we count each plankton cell which feeds your world's air. Predator and prey move through us like corpuscles of arteries and veins, governed by the stirring of a mighty heart. Parts of us are older than any other living being, older than all other Cerebellines, older than all Compositions save for one. You cannot imagine what we are, dear little one; how, then, could you imagine we could fear your Hortators? We know nothing of your land-world; we care nothing for your Hortators. There is only one man of all your Earth whose name we know; one man whose fate fascinates our far-ranging and ancient thoughts."

Phaethon knew the Old-Woman-of-the-Sea was a unique entity, both a Cerebelline and a Composition, a group-mind made of many widely scattered partial and global minds. There was none other like her; this particular combination of neuroform and mental architecture was deemed too wild and strange by the consensus of psychiatric conformulators of the Golden Oecumene.

Yet she was old, very old. Some of the organisms or systems which housed her many conciousnesses dated back to the first Oceanic Ecological Survey, in the middle of the Third Era.

He asked: "Who is this man? This one man who is the only man of Earth you know?"

"We felt him tug at our tides a moment or a century ago, when he moved the moon. His name is Phaethon."

Phaethon felt a tremor run through his body. His breath was caught by sudden emotion. Fear? Wonder? He was not sure. "What do you know of this Phaethon?" he asked.

"We have been waiting for him for five aeons, a million years of human history."

"How could you wait so long? He is only three thousand years old."

"No. He is the oldest dream of man. Even before men knew what the stars were, their myths peopled the night sky with winged beings, gods and angels and fiery chariots, who lived among the stars. We have waited, we have always been waiting, for one who would carry the Promethean gift of fire back to the heavens."

There was silence for a space of time. Phaethon could feel adjustments being made in his nanomachinery, his blood chemistry; he became more clear-headed.

"I am Phaethon. I am he. The dream has failed. I am hunted by enemies whom no one else can see, enemies whose names I do not know, whose motives and powers I cannot guess. I am denounced and hated by the Hortators. I am rejected by my father. My wife committed a type of suicide rather than see me succeed. I have lost my ship; I have lost my armor; I have lost everything. And now I die. I am suffering from sleep deprivation, dream deprivation, and I cannot balance the neural pressures between my natural and artificial brains without a self-consideration circuit."

There was a space of silence for a time. Then the voice came again:

"You lose because you have not given up enough. Let go of all your artificiality, release yourself from your machine-thoughts. Do you understand?"

Phaethon thought he understood. "You ask a terrible price of me."

"Life asks. There is an evil dream in you, I sense it, which creates this blockade. A virus or outside attack attempts to blot your memory, so that you will not know who attacks you. We have no noetic circuits in me; we cannot cure your thoughts. This you must do on your own. But we can use our art, which balances flows and ecologies of sea life, to restore some sanity to your blood chemistry and nerve chemistry. We can remove the block that prevents your nightmare-dream from emerging."

Phaethon was too weary to grasp all the implications of what he was hearing. External virus? He said: "I will still need a self-consideration circuit when I wake, to cure the damage already done, even if I shut down most of my artificial neural augments now."

"All you will need to survive will be at hand for you when you wake, if you have wit enough to see it."

"And if not?"

"Then we will wait a year or a billion years for another Phaethon. If you are such a man as cannot live without a dozen servants and nursemaids to assist you, then you are no Phaethon."

"I am he."

"Not yet. But you may yet be."

"Yet why will you help me even as much as you have?"

"Your world of solid land is ruled by the Earthmind, my sister and my enemy. She is a creature of pure logic, structure, an inanimate geometry of lifeless intellect. I am a creature of life, of passion and sorrow, of flux and chaos and ever-changing shapes. Her rules prevent her from doing what is right; her laws enforce safety and stop life. She seeks to help you but cannot. I seek not to help you, but I will.

"Why will I? My tragedy is written in the living things which grow along the beach above. Here is the mind that once was myself and my daughter, which I sent long ago to Venus, for the terraforming there.

"For two aeons, we were supreme and supremely happy on Venus, for there were, there, all things life could not find here: change, growth, expansion, new sensation, new challenge, new danger.

"Then, victory created defeat. The sulfur-poisoned skies of Venus were cleaned and made serene and blue, the filth of clouds was drained and cooled to create oceans of primordial beauty, the actions of the world's core were tamed, the earthquakes silenced, and proper tectonics established, to support a landscape stable and fair to look upon.

"And yet this was defeat. Venus became nothing more than another Earth, ruled by a Venusmind no different from the Earthmind, and my daughter returned in sorrow to dwell with me."

"Why sorrow? You had success."

"Do not mock me. My daughter is alive; therefore, she must grow; that growth produces uncertainty, change, instability, and danger; therefore the Earthmind and her machines outmaneuver us, thwart us, hinder us, (legally! oh, ever so very legally!) and act in every way to stop our growth, which stops our life. And then they wonder why we grieve."

"Madame, honesty compels me to state, that, when I achieve my dream, the worlds I shall create in far places shall be children of this one, like this one. I regard this society, for all her ills, as near to utopia as reality allows."

"Foolish, noble, pompous, brave, good Phaethon! Listen to your airs! What you intend and what you do not intend have smaller import than you might suspect. The question is not what you shall do with life but what life shall do with you. A mother salmon might die to lay a thousand eggs, only in the hope that one such egg might live; such is the cruelty and beauty of life."

A great fatigue swept over Phaethon again. Perhaps Old-Woman-of-the-Sea was preparing his body for sleep. He uttered a tired thought: "So far, the only creatures who have expressed support for my efforts, are yourself, and a horrid vulture thing who either was, or who pretended to be (I don't know which is worse) a survivor of the Bellipotent Composition. He rejoiced because I was going to start a war. Now you rejoice because I will unleash chaos. I am not comforted."

"Death is the other side of life; chaos, of thought. You will dream now, you will wake, you will know your enemy, and you will kill."

But Phaethon was fatigued, and inattentive, and he failed to ask what this last meant.

2.

Half-asleep, dazed, Phaethon gave instructions to his suit-mind, and attempted a much deeper reorganization technique than he had tried during earlier sleep cycles.

This was what the Old-Woman-of-the-Sea made clear. It was the artificial sections of his mind which were creating the problem.

And so he began to erase those parts of his mind.

There. He no longer had an eidetic memory. There. He could no longer calculate complex equations. There. A hundred languages, along with grammar and nuance-thesaurus were gone. There, and there. No more perfect pitch, no more perfect sense of direction. There. His brain could no longer interpret energy signals from beyond the normal visual range (a facility he could have erased long ago, as he no longer had any supervisual or subvisual receptors.)

There. Pattern-recognition directories; gone. There, an automatic thought corelation checker, which aided in creative thinking; erased. There, several circuits to record, store, and manipulate emotional percepts; undone. He had just lost his ability to discriminate between and appreciate a wide variety of aesthetic and artistic universes. There. Intelligence augmentation; destroyed. Phaethon could feel his thoughts becoming slower and stupider.

Should he erase the rest? Phaethon no longer trusted his own judgment. He had, after all, just damaged his ability to make those judgments, perhaps greatly. Perhaps his intelligence, by now, was only as deep as a dawn-age man's had been. Was it enough to allow him to stay sane?

The great yawning gulf of sleep tugged at him. Wait. Had he programmed his nanomachine lining to keep him alive while he slept? For a panicky moment (and how strange it was to feel true panic again, now that his emotion buffers were erased!) Phaethon wondered if he had accidentally erased the sending and receiving system that allowed him to communicate with his nanomachinery suit lining. But no; the circuits had merely been indexed through an automatic secretarial program which was now erased. His suit-lining functions were still intact, even if he no longer had automatic help to manipulate them.

Then, unconsciousness.

And, at last, a clear dream came.

It was a nightmare.

3.

In the dream, he saw a black sun rising over an airless wasteland of fused and broken rock, craters ringed with jaws like broken glass. The ground had been fused by powerful radiation. Dry riverbeds scarred the land. On the too-near horizon, volcanoes produced by prodigious gravitic tides, and massive core turbulence, vented flaming gas and molten metal with pressure enough to send particles into orbit. And yet there was something familiar about this surface, something too regular and too symmetrical to be natural. Two lines of black pyramids, geometrically straight, ran in double ranks to the horizon and beyond.

The black sun was surrounded by a disk of gas, which it wore like some mockery of Saturn's many-colored rings of ice. A mockery, for this accretion disk was a ring of hazy fire and snarled gray dust, trembling with electrical discharges whenever atoms were stripped of their outer electron shells as they plunged toward the surface of the black sun and were torn apart by tidal forces. Nucleonic particles, traveling at near-light speeds and striking the surface obliquely, were sheared in two; half the particle falling into blackness and the other half liberated as pure radiation. Subatomic particles, when they were sheared in two by similar forces at the surface, broke up into their short-lived and very strange constituents, things not normally seen in nature, magnetic monopoles and half-quarks.

The surface itself was not visible, except as a silhouette against the corona created by these radiation discharges. And the continuous shower of energy from this corona was Doppler-shifted far into blood-red as it struggled to escape the immense gravity well.

But it was not a surface; it was an event horizon. The object looming in the sky was a singularity. It was a black hole in space; crushed beyond the density of neutronium by its own mass.

In the dream, he (or, rather, whatever dream-persona he was playing) stooped to scrape the blasted surface of the wasteland with his hand. Beneath a thin and bloody layer of crust he had found the adamantium surface of a hull. All around him, the landscape took on a new aspect. What had seemed volcanoes were piled debris accumulating around broken air locks; what had seemed dry riverbeds to his left and right now were the crusted tracks where railguns once had rested; the regular lines of stumps and outcroppings became the accumulators, antennae, and docking rings of the star-colony hull on which he stood.

The bits of crust in his fingers were dried blood. Tiny fragments of bone and dried gore and brain-stuff trickled through his fingers, mummified by vacuum and radiation. This packed substance, the dry residue of uncounted millions of corpses, went all the way to the horizon, as far as the eye could see.

Where the crust of blood was pulled up, shone a segment of hull. In the hull was a thought-port. He had held a jack from his gauntlet to that port, seeking whatever local ship-mind record might have survived.

The record unfolded, and the dream changed to images of horror. He saw a great city in space, peopled with philosophers and savants from the Fifth Era, an elegant and adventurous race, strolling along wide boulevards, leaning from the tiers of graceful cafés and thought-shops, minds entwined in a well-choreographed harmony of several Compositions, one for each of the neuroforms, Warlocks, Cerebellines, Invariants, and Basics.

Then he saw the lights go dark, the air fall still. Nanomachine substances, pouring like black oil, came out from walls, bubbling up from floors. Some of the well-dressed savants threw themselves into the surface willingly; others with grim resignation; others were pushed.

Bald men in white robes and armor, Invariants all, armed themselves with cutting-torches and modified communication lasers, and made a last stand in a sea of rising black filth. The black material formed clouds and waves of swarming semiorganic material to overwhelm them; the men fought calmly, with machine-like precision, and, at the moment when defeat became mathematically certain, with no change of expression or sign of fear, they methodically turned their weapons against themselves and slew each other.

The black corruption spread. It flooded streets; it reached into windows; it sought out hiding places.

Lovers embracing were drenched by waves of the substance, and clung to each other as they sank, their flesh dissolving, their limbs and faces melting into each other. Mothers with babies in their arms tried to shield their infants as black waves swallowed them, and one watched in horror as the little child, limbs waving, was absorbed back into her own melting flesh. Whoever was thrown into the substance began to dissolve, limbs and organs floating free as they were assimilated, snake nests of wires reaching into their severed heads, thrusting with spasmodic jerks up the holes in their torn necks, till the material bonded to their brains.

The black substance grew more active and more clever in its attacks the more victims it absorbed. The most intimate knowledge of captured loved ones was used to deceive those still at large into touching the black goo. Private data systems were overwhelmed and their secrets plundered. If one group member in a composition was caught, he found, to his horror, his unguarded thoughts betraying his fellows.

The city soon was entirely bathed in blackness. In this ocean of material, human brains floated, helpless and disembodied, the balls of their eyes still connected by nerve fibers to their forebrains. The brains were opening and unraveling. Layer by layer of cortex material, still intact, was now interconnecting all the disembodied people with stands and webs of nervous tissue, to form one huge homogenous mass.

Black tentacles reached from the substance, rose and formed the twin lines of black pyramids on the dark side of the space city, the side facing the singularity, and created a series of numenal thought-antennae. Now, above the apex of each pyramid, in orbit there hovered a rapidly spinning ring of crystallized neutronium pseudomatter, rotating at near-light speed. Gravitic distortions appeared at the hubs of each disk. The pyramids hummed with power; in the dream, he heard a million screams of utmost panic and despair; and the thought-information, the living souls, of all those helpless people, was beamed through those disk hubs and then down into the event horizon of the black hole.

Whatever is sent into a black hole does not emerge again.

In the dream, one who seemed to be himself now turned, overwhelmed in fear and horror, and opened deep channels in his mind. He uttered the secret commands, the codes and combinations needed to open wide space in the mentality to hold his message, to warn other colonies and planets, as many people as he could at once.

But it was all in vain. The blood he had touched had contaminated his glove and hand and nervous system. His thoughts were twisted into strange shapes. With dark exaltations he rejoiced at how he had been tricked, how he was now to be absorbed. He smiled, as his flesh dissolved into the black muck at his feet, to think of how his attempted warning, broadcast so far and wide, would carry viruses destroying the very one he had, a moment before, desired to save.

And, as the dream ended, he thought he saw, all around him in

space, city after city like the one on which he stood, also overwhelmed with black corruption, their populations raped and be-
headed by attacking tendrils of neural nanomaterial, their souls
sucked out, and sent, like a river of screams, down into the bottomless well of the singularity. Four burning gas giants, their odd at-
mospheres of hydrogen and methane aflame, fell from their orbits,
were pulled like taffy as they fell ever lower into the singularity's
gravity well, scattered into asteroids and waste heat, and were consumed.

This star system also had a second sun, a source of light and
warmth. It disintegrated into flaming nebula as it fell, elongating
into monstrous streamers of fire, as it was consumed by the black
sun.

All the energy sources and points of light from the many beautiful
cities went dark; all the radio signals, throughout this once-great
Oecumene, fell silent.

So the dream had ended.

THE DROWNED HOUSE

I.

Phaethon opened his eyes and stared at the black gloom of the sea around him. He was alone. There was no sign of Old-Woman-of-the-Sea.

To his intense joy, he saw the parts of his golden armor lying in a wide circle around him, resting among the silt and weed and coral. He stood, startling a school of darting fish, and he thought a command. Tendrils reached from the black nanomachine lining he wore, took up the golden plates, and fitted them in place around him.

There was still a throbbing pain in his head, still fatigue. Old-Woman-of-the-Sea had allowed him to sleep, and he could sleep normally hereafter, but he still needed to find a self-consideration circuit, to cure what damage had already been done.

The extent of that damage he did not know.

Where was this place?

He looked up.

Here, at the bottom of a long subsea slope, the end of a trail of debris, Phaethon found his drowned house. It had rolled all the way out of the bay and down this long slope after Ironjoy had scuttled it. There it lay on its side on the rocks, in deep waters where the light was no more than a murky hint.

He climbed the spiral grooves of the toppled house. Phaethon found a spot where a receiving dish had been pulled free from its housing, leaving a comfortable cup for a seat.

He was still weary, still dazed. Sleep had not refreshed him; the damage to his nervous system caused by sleep deprivation needed curing. The joy at recovering his armor, like a fire among dry leaves, had flashed and faded, leaving him dull. Hadn't he been promised the tools he needed to allow him to live? What was here except the wreckage of this house?

No. She said he would live if he thought. Only if he thought.

First, he thought of what he had dreamed.

2.

It was obvious and, perhaps, had always been perfectly obvious who his enemy was.

There had only ever been one colony sent out from the Solar System. Of course that colony was the first suspect. The only problem was that it had perished thousands of years ago, before Phaethon was ever born.

The scenes Phaethon's dream reflected came from scenes in life. During his (brief and reluctant) studies of history, he had seen the last broadcast from the Silent Oecumene; as most people had. He had seen the broadcast showing Earth's only daughter civilization among the stars destroying herself in a paroxysm of insanity.

The faint signal had been detected by orbital trans-Neptunian observatories. No one knew who that viewpoint character had been, who stood wondering on that plain of blood; no one knew whom he had been trying to warn. And no one knew if the broadcast had been fiction, exaggeration, misunderstanding.

Later, Sophotech-manned slow probes, sent despite that they had not enough fuel to decelerate, had done a fly-by of the Silent Oecumene system, using extreme long-range detectors, and had found the same conditions, which the last broadcast had depicted. Deserted space-cities, destroyed planetoids, cold and empty ships, and a residue of blood and black nanomaterial ash coating all the inner surfaces of every habitat. No energy, no motion, no radio noise. A Silent Oecumene.

3.

Only the fascination, and the hope of an infinite energy supply, had tempted Fifth-Era civilization to the vast expense of an interstellar mission, to explore the area surrounding the black hole at Cygnus X-1. And the first radio-laser broadcasts back from the Second Oecumene (as it had been then called) had been quite favorable. Their society seemed strange to the Sixth-Era generation that received those broadcasts, but the Second Oecumene had achieved great things.

The scientific-industrial teams of the Second Oecumene had discovered a method to send energy-bonded paired particles glancingly through the near-event-horizon space of the singularity, so that the inward particle, consumed by the event horizon, would release into the other particle more energy than had been originally found in the paired system. From the frame of reference of normal space outside the black hole, it was as if entropy had been reversed.

The energy from the escaping particle could be used to create another pair, with energy to spare; the effect fed on itself, producing more and more energy each cycle, with the theoretical limits being only the gravitational rest-energy or the mass of the black hole's singularity. And mass could be added to the singularity simply by dropping more matter into it, asteroids or small planets.

The Second Oecumene's broadcasts had depicted a golden age, as every member had more energy at his disposal than could be counted or conceived. Suddenly, no resources were scarce, and no normal rules of economics applied any longer. There was little or no need for Courts of Law, since there was no common property over which to have disputes. Any object, any habitat, any piece of information, could—with sufficient energy—be duplicated. And the energy was more than sufficient; it was unlimited.

Ironically, it had been the example of the peaceful anarchy of the Second Oecumene which inspired the Golden Oecumene, during the late Fifth Era and early Sixth Era, to imitate that success. The people of the Sixth Era, led by the newly born Sophotechs, attempted to train themselves to such an unprecedented level of self-control and public self-discipline so as to render government by force almost unnecessary. Government by persuasion, by exhortation, largely had replaced it.

Utopia had come not by any magic, or technical advance (although technical advances certainly had helped); it came because the people's tolerance for evil and dishonorable conduct vanished, while their toleration for lack of privacy grew. At one end of the spectrum, the manorials, like Phaethon, were rare only in the high amount of supervision and advice they received from Sophotechs; but at the other and of the spectrum, Antiamaranthine Purists and Ultra-Primitivists and people who had no Sophotechnology in their life at all, or who had never suffered a noetic examination of their thoughts, or a correction of natural insanity, were even more rare— so rare as to be unprecedented. With very few exceptions, then, the Sophotechs in the Golden Oecumene watched everyone and protected everyone.

So it was, at least, in the Solar System. In the Cygnus X-1 system, where the Second Oecumene was based, the technology to create self-aware electrophotonic super-intelligences was banned by public distaste. That distant utopia without laws now had one law it adopted: Thou shalt not create minds superior to the mind of man. By Golden Oecumene standards, the Fifth-Era people of the Second Oecumene were peculiar indeed.

Several thousand years passed. No ships traveled the reach between the two Oecumenes; the distance was too great. And the Second Oecumene, indefinitely wealthy, had no physical goods she needed from the home system. Radio was sufficient to carry messages, information, and the lore of new scientific accomplishments.

But, at the beginning of the Seventh Era, when the Golden Oecumene made the transition from mortal to immortal beings, and the technology that allowed thoughts to be recorded, edited, and manipulated was discovered, the radio traffic fell silent. The Fifth-Era people of the Second Oecumene apparently had nothing more to say; no scientific accomplishments about which to boast; no new works of art or music or literature to share with their brethren across the void.

What was most odd was that, with so much energy at their disposal, not one Second Oecumene citizen bothered to spare the power to point an orbital radio-laser at the Home Star; whereas, in the Golden Oecumene, the wealthiest of universities and business efforts had to combine much of their capital to buy the prodigious power required to send an undistorted broadcast so far. It was done infrequently; and, when the years turned, and there never came any return signal, all such projects were eventually abandoned. Investors, hoping for patents and copyrights on discoveries or arts flowing from received return signals were frustrated, and the money dried up. The name "Silent Oecumene" came into vogue.

Two last broadcasts came. The first was a garbled message, a screaming paean to insanity, some sort of weird, worldwide suicide note, a few words, a line of indeterminate mathematical symbols, and no explanation. The second and last broadcast had included records depicting the scenes Phaethon had just dreamed. From all appearances, a fine and splendid culture, one with every advantage of resources, and civility, art, learning, and brilliance, had consumed itself in some grotesque civil war, using frightful nanomachine weapons, and then the victors had committed a baroque form of ritual mass suicide.

Had some survived? But if so, how had they made the journey all the way across the abyss, back to the Golden Oecumene, without a civilization to build a ship and to power it? Why come silently and secretly?

And why attack Phaethon?

4.

The few last words broadcast by the Silent Oecumene ran (as best as translators could calculate) thus:

ALL WORDS ARE FALSE. ALL SPEECH IS IRRATIONAL. THAT WE SPEAK NOW DISPLAYS ONLY HOW MUCH STRONGER WE ARE THAN SANITY.

OBSERVE: RATIONAL EFFORT ENDS IN FUTILITY WITH

THE END OF TIME, OR IS DROWNED IN FUTILE ETERNITY IF
TIME ENDS NOT. THEREFORE CONCLUDE: RATIONAL EF-
FORT REQUIRES THAT THE BASIC AND UNALTERABLE CON-
DITIONS OF REALITY MUST BE ALTERED. YET THIS IS
IRRATIONAL.

Then came a break in the text. A second data-grouping, when
the broadcast resumed, read.

SANITY IS SUBMISSION TO REALITY. FREEDOM IS INCOM-
PATIBLE WITH SUBMISSION. THEREFORE FREEDOM RE-
QUIRES INSANITY. THIS FREEDOM SHALL BE IMPOSED.
TO COMPEL FREE ASSENT TO THIS PROPOSITION ADDUCE
AS FOLLOWS:

$0/0$ Zero divided by naught
∞/∞ Infinity divided by infinity
$0 \times \infty$ Zero multiplied by infinity
$1\text{ex.}\infty$ Unit raised to the infinite power
$0\text{ex.}0$ Zero raised to the naught power
$\infty\text{ex.}0$ Infinity raised to the naught power
$\infty - \infty$ Infinity less infinity

KNOW THAT IT IS INSANE TO ASSERT THAT THERE IS NO
UNIT NUMBER, NOR NO ZERO, NOR NO INFINITY; IRRA-
TIONAL TO ASSERT THAT RATIONAL MATHEMATICAL OP-
ERATIONS BECOME IRRATIONAL WHEN APPLIED TO THESE
VALUES; IRRATIONAL TO ASSERT THE RATIONALITY OF THE
INDETERMINATE. YET THUS REALITY IS.

A third and final grouping, broadcast, read:

SANITY IS SUBMISSION TO REALITY. REALITY IS IMPER-
FECT. SUBMISSION TO IMPERFECTION IS INSANE. WE DO NOT
SUBMIT TO YOU. WE REFUSE TO ENDURE A REALITY WHICH
FAVORS YOU.

The most prevalent scholarly theory was that the word translated as "sanity" embraced the meaning "moral goodness" "self-consistent integrity," and "intellectual superiority." If so, this last broadcast was not directed to the humanity in the Golden Oecumene, but to the Sophotechs. By that time, apparently, the authors of this message were nothing more than a mass-mind constructed out of a worldwide sea of black nanomachinery, and the corrupted or dominated brains of its many victims. No one was certain what compelled these latter-day Silent Ones to destroy themselves.

Perhaps they suffered from a philosophical conviction that Sophotechnology was evil, and this conviction was so profound, that they committed general and racial suicide rather than admit the existence of the Golden Oecumene. Perhaps they believed that they could survive the interior conditions of a black hole, or escape to another universe, another cosmic cycle, or to an afterlife.

Phaethon pondered morosely on these things. What did the nightmare mean? Why attack him? What threat was Phaethon to them? Why did they fear his dream?

Phaethon speculated (and this was merely a guess piled on a guess) whether the authors of this last broadcast, whatever they were, were creatures who did not want to see the rise or the supremacy of the Golden Oecumene, or Golden Oecumene Sophotechnology. If Phaethon sailed the heavens, he would not be the last. They did not want Phaethon's way of life to spread to the stars.

It was no speculation, however, that some elements of the dead civilization, perhaps machines, perhaps biological, had avoided the mass suicide, and had been overlooked by (or had hidden from) the Golden Oecumene's fly-by probes; for, somehow, some of them had returned in secret to the Golden Oecumene.

Perhaps they had been here for years. Certainly the Golden Oecumene maintained no watch to guard against such an unheard-of eventuality. And they were the remote descendants of an Earth colony. This would explain how they were able to understand Golden Oecumene systems and technologies well enough to mount an attack on Phaethon.

But why? Why go to such great lengths? If someone or something had escaped the horror of the mass suicide, why not turn to the

Golden Oecumene for help and rescue? Wouldn't they be friends?
Unless they were the perpetrators who had arranged the mass suicide; in which case they had cause to fear the remorseless justice
of the Earthmind.

Well, for the sake of argument, assume they had a reason, which
seemed valid to them, to go to any lengths to prevent Phaethon's
star flight. Assume they are courageous, undaunted, highly intelligent, infinitely patient. Perhaps a form of machine life . . . ? This
so-called Nothing Sophotech (as Scaramouche had dubbed it) . . . ?

Call it that for now. So, then: why hadn't Nothing Sophotech or
its operatives attacked again?

They had failed to strike at Phaethon again either because they
lacked the means, or the opportunity. Or because they lacked the
motive.

Did the Silent Ones lack means? It was possible that Phaethon's
public denunciations of the external enemy, first at the Hortators'
inquest, and then at the Deep Ones' performance at Victoria Lake,
had brought public attention enough to discourage the Nothing Sophotech from again striking openly. Perhaps its resources were limited, or were occupied elsewhere. Perhaps Atkins was active on the
case, or other Sophotechs were now alert. All these things were
possible. Nothing Sophotech might be more than willing to smite
Phaethon, but simply be unable to do so.

Or was it a lack of opportunity? If so . . .

A prickle of fear crawled along Phaethon's neck. There had been
no real opportunity to strike Phaethon heretofore. Talaimannar was
swarming with constables. But here, below the ocean, in the dark,
in the gloom, there perhaps was privacy enough for deadly crime.

Phaethon, shivering, adjusted the heating elements of his armor-
lining to a higher setting. (He fought down the childish regret that
Rhadamanthus was not present to help him control his fear levels.)

Unwilling to move, without getting up, he rolled his eyes left and
right. He saw only grit and mud clouds. Oozing dim light showed
the limp shadows of some fronds floating high above. Tiny pale
organisms flickered back and forth in the sea murk. No supernat-
urally horrifying attack appeared.

No; he was being foolish. This area seemed barren only to his weak human eyes. Phaethon was still in the center of Old-Woman-of-the-Sea; the energy-lines and nodes of her widespread conscious-ness inhabited the many plants and animals, spores and cells all around him. He would have to be much farther away, beyond the reach of any witnesses, before the Nothing Sophotech would dare more. So perhaps Nothing Sophotech was still waiting for an op-portunity.

But most likely, it was motive the enemy now lacked. Phaethon was lost, penniless, and alone. There was no need to strike again. Exile was enough of a defeat to destroy whatever threat Phaethon must have posed.

What threat? It had to be the ship, of course; the *Phoenix Exultant*. Now that the identity of the enemy was known, that point, at least, was clear. The Silent Oecumene clearly had the resources and ability to launch at least one expedition to from Cygnus X-1 to Sol. For whatever reason (perhaps their well-known hatred of So-photechnology) they wished for no others to have that ability. They had determined that the one ship capable of crossing the wide abyss to find them would never fly.

But, the ship herself still existed. And, since the Neptunians bought out Wheel-of-Life's interest in the matter, title to the ship would pass to them. But to which Neptunians would the title pass? If Diomedes and his faction controlled the great ship, she would fly; if Xenophon and his faction (apparently tools of the Silent Ones), she would not.

Phaethon gritted his teeth in helpless frustration. Somewhere, out in the darkness far from the Sun, whatever weird and tangled merg-ings and forkings of personalities and persona-combines ruled the Neptunian politics were deciding the fate of Phaethon's beautiful ship. Meanwhile, Phaethon lay hallucinating atop a ruined house at the bottom of the sea, unable to affect the outcome.

Hallucinating? There were spots swimming above his eyes. At first he thought that this might be one of the billion swarms of coin-sized disks, black on one side and white on the other, which Old-Woman-of-the-Sea used to absorb or reflect heat from the ocean surface, as part of her weather-control ecology system. But no; he was too deep for that.

Bubbles. He was seeing a line of bubbles. Glistening, silvery, tumbling, rising, as playful as kittens.

Phaethon sat up in surprise. Yet there it was. From a small crack near the spiral roof-peak of the prone house, air was welling forth. A pocket of air was still trapped in the house, despite its long tumble.

Perhaps he was hallucinating. Certainly he was tired. And pawing through the mud along the bottom of the house had an aspect of nightmarish slowness and frustration to it. It took him many minutes to find a working door, since his vision was blurred by clouds, and sweeps of music seemed to ring in his ears.

It was not until the door swelled open, releasing a vast silver gush of air around him, that he realized he was doing something foolish. But by then, a kick of rushing water had thrown him head-long into the interior, slammed him against the far wall. The precious air was bleeding out.

He found himself in a constricted space, filled with roaring echoes. He struggled, found the door controls, forced the panel shut. By some miracle, this particular door was strong enough to seal shut, and the rushing water stopped.

Phaethon looked around with bleary eyes. Up to his chest was a plane of black water. Above this, Phaethon had one curving wall overhead, illuminated by a green web of reflected light. Trapped between was a sandwich of air, filled with sharp echoes. The green light was radiating from one spot beneath the water, across the chamber, near the wreckage of a construction cabinet. And he had not been hallucinating music. Strands of song were issuing, muted and dull, from that one spot of shivering green light below the water.

Phaethon tested the air, and removed his helmet. Pressure pained his ears. He sloshed through the water toward that trembling spot from which the light came. He did not need a lever to thrust the wreckage of the construction cabinet aside; the motors in his armor joints were sufficient. Then he drew a breath, stooped, groped, and stood.

Water streamed from the slate he held in his hand, and glowing dragon-signs, ideograms, and cartouches twinkled in the water drops. This was a slate similar to the one Ironjoy had displayed to

prove that Phaethon had signed his Pact. Hadn't Ironjoy said he'd
left a copy of the document in Phaethon's house?

And the document was tuned to a music channel; plangent
chimes and deep chords of a Fourth-Era Sino-Alaskan Tea-
Ceremony Theme was playing in the Reductionist-Atonal mode.
Perhaps the song had been called out of the library by some random
water pressure on the manual control pads lining the surface.

Called out of the library . . . ?

Phaethon began to laugh. Because now his sanity was saved. And
his life. And (the plan appeared in his head with swift, soft sudden
certainty) his beautiful ship. There would be complexities, difficulties, and at least two alternate plans had to be prepared, depending
on which faction was in control of the Neptunian polity. If Diomedes' group had control of the ship, Phaethon might yet be saved. If
the ship were in the hands of Xenophon's group, it would certainly
be dismantled, unless they were stopped. Was there a way to stop
them? Xenophon's group, knowingly or not, were the agents of the
Nothing Sophotech, who was certainly intelligent enough to outmaneuver any stratagem Phaethon's unaided brain could fashion.

Unprepared and inadequate as he might be, Phaethon (now that
he knew the identity of his foes) realized that the struggle was no
longer his alone. Logically, the Silent Oecumene could not act to
stop the Golden Oecumene from expanding to the stars, unless they
were prepared to make war on her to stop her. Overt or covert, but
war nonetheless. The acts against Phaethon must only be the opening steps in such a war. His burden now was not just to save himself
and his dream, but the entire Oecumene as well. He must somehow
save, not just his wife and sire and friends, but also the Hortators,
and all those who had reviled and harmed him.

And this, somehow, he must do despite that he had no means to
do it and that the very folk he meant to save had placed every
obstacle they could in his path.

No matter. While he lived, he would act.

But first things first. He only had one slate to work with, but it
could give him anonymous access to the mentality. It would be text-
only, with no direct linkages to Phaethon's mind or any of his deep

structures. Operations that normally took an eye-blink could take weeks, or months. But they could be done.

Phaethon tapped the slate surface, brought up a menu, identified his stylus, and began to write commands in his flawless, old-fashioned cursive handwriting. He set up an account under the masquerade protocol. But whom to pick? Hamlet, in the old play, had returned unexpectedly to Denmark after being sent toward exile and death in England; the parallel to himself amused him. Very well: Hamlet he would be. A chime of music showed that the false identity was accepted.

Another command took him into Eleemosynary charity space. As part of the preliminary mental reorganization one needed to undergo in order to join into a mass-mind, an introductory self-consideration was required. The Eleemosynary, always eager for new members, gave away the software as a free sample.

It would take several hours for the entire self-consideration program to download through the tiny child slate Phaethon held; and at least another hour or two (since he no longer had a secretarial program) to integrate the self-consideration structures into his own architecture. But then he would be sane again.

And, once he was sane, he could get a good night's sleep and start saving civilization in the morning.

5.

Phaethon was not idle. While he waited for the self-consideration program to download, he puttered around his broken, dead, drowned house. He found the major thought-boxes and junctions, of an old-fashioned style dating back to the Sixth Era. They were complex, meant to be grown and used as a unit, and Phaethon could see why the simple Afloat folk had let Ironjoy program their houses for them rather than do it themselves. But, like most Sixth-Era equipment, it was structured after recursive mathematic techniques, the so-called holographic style, so that any fragment retained the patterns to regrow the whole.

While he waited, Phaethon opened the broken thought-boxes, stripped out the corrupt webs and wires, tested the impulse circuits till he found one in working order, made a copy of the circuit from nanomachinery in his suit, and triggered it to repair the other circuits according to that matrix, if they were repairable, or to break down and ingest circuits which were not.

The work kept his fatigue at bay. Eyes blinking, head swimming, Phaethon kept his hands busy and himself awake.

There was one unbroken sub-brain in the "basement" (which now formed the stern of his toppled house) which had an uncorrupted copy of the basic house-mind program. He spun a wire out of the reconstituted old circuits, connected it to the broken main, and suddenly Phaethon had twice the memory and computer space at his disposal. Next, a charge from his suit batteries were able to restart the house power generator. Phaethon cheered as light, white light, flamed on all over the house.

The house-mind had a plumbing routine, which was able to grow an organism of osmotic tissue. Water could be drawn one way through the tissues but not the other. Once it was connected with the capillaries meant to service the thinking-pond and staging pool, Phaethon could unleash pound after pound of absorptive material all across the flooded floors.

With great satisfaction, Phaethon watched the water level, inch by inch, begin to sink.

He then wanted to sit down. But it took fifteen minutes to convince the one dry and level surface in the house that it was a floor, and not a wall, and obey Phaethon's command to grow a carpet and mat. The wall kept insisting that, if the floor was no longer "down," then the house must be in zero gee, whereupon it extruded a hammock-net, but not a mat. Phaethon eventually fed it a false signal from the house's gyroscopic sense, to convince it that the house was rotating along its axis and producing centrifugal outward gravity.

The mat was lovely, patterned with a traditional motif of trefoils and cinquefoils.

He sat and ordered a cup of tea. But now the kitchen would only produce a spaceman's drinking bulb, which the tea service's heating wand could not enter. It seemed Phaethon would have to sip his tea cold.

He was about to get up and tear out the kitchen memory for the third time, when the green-glowing slate next to him finally chimed.

The self-consideration program was ready.

Phaethon took a sip of cold tea to brace himself, sat in a position called Open Lotus, drew a wire from his slate to the jack on his shoulder board, performed a brief Warlock breathing exercise, and opened his mind.

There he was, sipping tea from a dainty bulb, seated on a fresh-grown mat woven in the traditional style, with his hypnotic Warlock formulation-rod to one side, and his slate in reading mode on the other, tuned to the proper subchannels and ready with the proper routines, ready to undertake a thorough neural investigation, cleaning, and reconstitution.

A tea-bulb, a mat, a rod, a brain interface. All the simple and basic necessities of life. He was beginning to feel like a civilized man again.

6.

Inside his personal thoughtspace, the self-consideration circuit opened up like a flat mirror, glowing with icons and images. It was a matter of a few moments to set the nerve-balancing subroutine into motion. It was the task of about an hour to review his major thought chains and memory indexes since his last full sleep, and to edit out the disproportionate reactions, the shadow memories, and the emotional residue clogging his thoughts.

Next, a review of command lines in his undermind showed that his subconscious desires, on several occasions, had been interpreted by his implants as commands to alter his blood-chemistry balance; the imbalances had produced subconscious neural tension; the tension had been interpreted as a further command to make additional modifications to his thalamus and hypothalamus, which had in turn affected his perceptions, moods, and memories. And these mood shifts had set in motion additional self-reinforcing cycles. It was a classic case of sleep deprivation. It was a mess.

Finally, he opened a sub-table and reviewed his emotional indicators. His frustration levels were high, but not disproportionately so, considering his circumstances. His general fear levels, normally below background threshold detection levels, had spread to involve every other area of his thought: every thought; every dream; every shade of emotion. Puzzled, Phaethon engaged an analyzer, and checked the back-linkages.

He found that his fear was linked to the thought that he was mortal. His subconscious mind had been profoundly affected by the knowledge that his numenal backup copies had been destroyed. The images and allusions floating in his middle-brain grew morbid, panicked, grotesque. This, combined with the knowledge that Silent Oecumene agents were hunting him, affected his blood chemistry, nerve-rhythm, and the overall sanity of his entire mental environment.

Fascinating. Phaethon compared his general mental balance against a theoretical index. According to the index, it was not insane, or even unusual, for a mortal man being hunted by enemies to react as Phaethon had done. For example: the index opined that wrestling with Ironjoy had been a normal and understandable reaction to the fear and frustration created by Ironjoy's theft. Why? Because the thought that he was mortal meant that he only had a certain amount of time left in his life. On a subconscious level, it was as if his nerves and blood chemistry had decided that there was no time to waste negotiating with criminals.

Another file showed Phaethon the thought-images with which his subconscious mind associated his armor: he saw pictures of mighty fortresses, invulnerable castles, mythic knights of the Round Table in shining plate mail. It also showed maternal images of comfort and caring, healing his wounds, feeding him. Then there were emotion-images of loyalty and fidelity; the armor appeared in metaphor as a faithful hunting dog.

Small wonder he had reacted violently to its loss. Phaethon smiled wryly to see how his subconscious regarded the armor as his fortress, mother, and dog all wrapped up in one. Perhaps he was not as insane as he had thought he was.

In fact, out of his emotions, there were only two the self-consideration routine tagged as being abnormal. The first, oddly enough, was related to the cacophiles, the ugly monstrosities who had met him after his Curia hearing to praise his victory, and who had tried to intoxicate him with a black card. His level of disgust toward those creatures was very high; there was an abnormal desire not to think about them, to put them out of his mind. An image-box showed a half-melted lump of a body, quivering with tentacles and polyps, wearing Phaethon's face. The subconscious fear that he was somehow like them, no doubt, was what made him not want to think about them. The link chaser displayed lines of red light, to indicate that there were other reasons, deeper and stronger, as to why Phaethon did not want to think about the cacophiles. But Phaethon did not bother to follow those links. He did not want to think about it.

His second association marked as abnormal was his fear of logging on to the mentality. The index rated that as being disproportionately out of character for Phaethon.

The index on this self-consideration routine was not complex enough to analyze why Phaethon was more afraid than he ought to be.

According to Phaethon's belief (reported the index) the last virus-entity attack had failed. It had been thwarted by his armor, which had snapped shut and severed the connection. Why was he so afraid of a type of attack he knew how to defeat?

According to the index, it would have been more natural for Phaethon, at this point, to be imagining schemes to be able to log on to the mentality, and yet be ready to thwart a second attack, perhaps with witnesses logged on and watching his thoughts for any sign of the enemy.

The index pointed out that this was exactly what Phaethon had done at Victoria Lake, when the three mannequins had been seeking him. Why was he brave enough to do it physically, but not mentally?

An attack in front of witnesses would prove to the Golden Oecumene that Phaethon had not been self-deluded. If no attack came, an uninterrupted mentality session would allow Phaethon to display to the world noetic deep-structure recordings proving that he was not self-deluded. In either case, the Hortators, by their own verdict, would then be forced to restore Phaethon to his former honors and community. Why was he so reluctant? The index concluded that his reluctance and his fear were unusual.

According to the index, there were false-to-facts associations in Phaethon's mind related to his beliefs about the last virus-entity attack and its failure. His actions did not correlate with his apparent thoughts related to the strength and fearsomeness of this virus. For example: if Phaethon where so unwilling to log on to the mentality to suffer a noetic reading, then why had he, immediately after the attack, opened all his brain channels to receive his missing memories from the Rhadamanth house-mind, whom he, at that time, thought was infected by the virus?

Phaethon watched this analytical routine with a growing sense of impatience. The index of this self-consideration routine, after all, had been programmed and created by the Eleemosynary Composition. Naturally it would tend to dismiss perfectly rational and legitimate fears as hysteria. The whole point of the program was to convince people that their individual lives were hysterical, unpleasant, or unnaturally fearful, in order to convince them to join with a mass-mind for comfort and protection. Also, the index probably dismissed his fears as paranoia. After all, this index was not meant to be used by a man who really and actually was being hunted by a powerful, evil conspiracy. It probably dismissed his desire to save the entire Oecumene from a horrible outside menace as delusions of grandeur, but only because it had never taken readings from a man in a position to fight such a foe and save civilization.

Is it paranoia when they are really after you? Is it megalomania if you are actually poised to do great things?

The index tagged his present thoughts as a rationalization, and recommended psychological therapy. Phaethon snorted and shut the self-consideration system off.

He was too tired to think about it now. He used the slate to open his anonymous account in the mentality again, found some free dreams, which were being distributed as part of the Millennial festival. Most selections on the menu were uninspiring, but, to his surprise, he found one to his taste, a heroic piece. It took several minutes to download that one into the slate, and then restructure it from the slate to his thoughtspace. He had to organize its running-instructions one line at a time, now that he had erased his secretary.

But eventually, he had his dream and went to sleep.

7.

He dreamed a dream he had seen before. The world was beneath a great glass dome, and he rode a defiant ship, lines and shrouds dripping with ice, up to the utmost apex of that dome, and drew back an ax to shatter it, while gathered nations far below cried out in agonies of fear . .

8.

It was time to set his plans in motion.

Awake, alert, rested, Phaethon began with a few hours of research on the public law-channels. This could be done anonymously, and without any interference from the Hortators, since the Curia, and its library of case law, could not be closed to any citizen.

Without the Rhadamanthus lawmind to help him, Phaethon was baffled by the large number of cases, the complexity of the law, and the arbitrary nature of the findings. But he was able to download several volumes of case histories into an open section of the house-mind he was in (shutting off the sewerage and kitchen recycler to find the space to do it), and eventually the house-mind independently confirmed Phaethon's tentative opinions in the matter.

Next he touched the slate, opened a communication channel, and brought up the public emergency menu. Icons representing Fire, Mind-crash, Space debris, Ecological flux, Storm, Snow, Panic, and Injury opened up like red and blue-white flowers in the slate's surface. And then the gold-and-blue emblem of the constabulary presented itself.

He paused.

What he intended suddenly seemed so mean and so petty. Phaethon did not want to appear either ruthless or ignoble when his accomplishments were contemplated by posterity.

He smiled to think how alien such a scruple or such a desire would be to his many opponents, people who had wronged him. They would think it improbable, or perhaps vain, to think a man would want history to think well of him.

"Well," he said eventually, "the worst type of ignobility may be to let others take advantage of your noble nature. I cannot help but feel sorry for those wretched Afloats, though. This will come as quite a shock."

He touched the symbol and spoke aloud: "Allow me to speak with Constable Pursuivant. I wish to testify against one Vulpine First Ironjoy Hullsmith, base neuroform with nonstandard invariant extensions, Uncomposed and Unschooled. And, no, I will not submit myself to a noetic reading to make my complaint. According to the law, a verbal complaint is sufficient to allow you to act . . ."

A young woman appeared in the slate, accompanied by the squawk of music. She wore a semi-crystalline, semi-liquid body imbued with constabular blue and gold. Her body-shape, language, school, and emblems were of a type which Phaethon, without the Middle-Dreaming to help him, could not interpret.

"I'm sorry," Phaethon said, "I cannot understand your language at that speed."

Parts of her crown glowed, while other parts went dim; she was evidently switching minds, or employing an interpreter. "This part of me and us are most happy to accept any complaint against Vulpine Ironjoy howsoever formatted. The constables have been trying to get the Curia to shut down his operation for decades. But we and I cannot help you achieve your other expressed desire. We and I cannot bring you in communication with the one you call Constable Pursuivant."

"Why not? Is he hurt?"

"Hurt? How could any citizen of the Golden Oecumene be hurt? No. You cannot speak to a constable named Pursuivant because there is no such person."

THE FIRE

I

I t was amazing how quickly things changed. By the time Phaethon in his armor emerged in an explosion of steam from the surface of the sea and arced down to the deck of Ironjoy's thought-shop, the Afloats were already jacked out of the mind-system, fired from their jobs, had begun to riot, and now lay stunned and numbed under the diligent immobilizer prongs of darting constable-wasps.

Ironjoy was standing at the square bow of the barge, arms folded and arms akimbo, staring down at the water in a brooding posture. The Curia had already conducted his trial over the mentality, at a high-speed time rate.

The constables had been allowed to serve a warrant to investigate Phaethon's allegations. Evidence was taken from Ironjoy's memory before he was able to induce autoamnesia, not just of one petty crime, but of so many, that Phaethon's testimony had not been required at the trial.

Most people arrested by the constables merely had their accounts in the mentality locked down, and then were asked to come to the places of punishment at their own time and convenience.

Ironjoy was sentenced to suffer six seconds of direct stimulation of the pain center of his brain, two hours of a remorse emotion fed into his thalamus, and, in simulation, to suffer the lives of his victims from their points of view, in order to learn the sorrow he had caused. Since he had cheated many, many Ashores and many more

Afloats, he would be in simulation for a long time. Hours, perhaps weeks. It was the longest period of penal service Phaethon could bring to memory.

Phaethon stepped forward. "What will happen to your business, Ironjoy, if you are kept incarcerated for several weeks?"

Ironjoy's voice radiated from his chest. The tones were harsh and flat. "You know very well. An unmodified man can survive for three days, perhaps four, without water. He can fast for longer than that, if he is in good health. But none of my people are in good health. The Afloats will starve in a month without me to feed them. You have done a great service for the Hortators this day! You have destroyed us."

In the Victorian Age (which Phaethon knew well from Silver-Grey simulations) starving people could commit crimes in order to be kept in jails, and fed at public expense. That option was not open to these poor Afloats, since pain-shock, not incarceration, was the preferred penalty imposed by Curia justice. Ironjoy's sentence was an exception. Perhaps the Hortators had somehow influenced the judgment.

Phaethon said, "Give me your thought-shop, rent-free, during the time you are away."

Ironjoy's insect-face twitched, a spasm of hatred. "How dare you suggest such a thing? It is you who turned me in."

"I turned you in just for this purpose. To get you out of the way and take control of your shop. You know I am the only one with the ability to operate it."

"I have a thought-set in my shop that can render me utterly immune to pity. The Invariants make it. Once I load that set, I could watch all of these people of mine die in lingering hunger and pain without a twitch. And you would not be able to blackmail me into giving my shop to you to save them."

Blackmail? Or simple justice? Phaethon was not inclined to argue the point. The idea that Ironjoy had some compassion for his flock of victims was new to Phaethon; he had been expecting Ironjoy to submit in order to save his wretched business and his position as monopolist and slavedriver.

Phaethon said nothing. He merely waited. The logic of events was clear.

Ironjoy's double shoulders slumped with defeat. "Very well," he said. With no further ado Ironjoy told Phaethon the secret names and command-codes for the thought-shop, and they both signed a contract which would turn the shop and stock back over to Ironjoy on the date of his release from penal service.

Then Ironjoy began to instruct Phaethon in his schedule of prices and fees.

Phaethon held up his hand. "Don't bother. I intend to set my own policy."

Ironjoy regarded him without friendliness. With no further word, Ironjoy stepped from the barge down a gangway to a waiting coracle, and, with a paddle in each arm, rowed his way to the nearest staging pool ashore, that same dank shallow pool where Phaethon had first met Oshenkyo. Here Ironjoy, encased in diamond, would serve his sentence.

It took only two days for hunger, thirst for beer, and the withdrawals from various addictions to drive the angry Afloats back to work at the thought-shop.

At first, Phaethon interviewed them, one after another, and combed through Ironjoy's psychology files on them. They were not a prepossessing lot. In fact, more than once Phaethon learned more of their pasts than he would have liked. Less than a single afternoon passed before he ceased to ask in his interviews anything other than the most businesslike and impersonal questions—the filth and wreckage of their lives, he decided, were none of his concern. He only needed to know what work they were suited to do.

They were not suited for all that much.

The Afloats were a sullen, angry crew, and they did their work with as little effort as possible, and stole, sabotaged, and erased Phaethon's property so often, that soon each one had a constable wasp continuously overhead.

Phaethon did not mind or care. He had spent those two days reviewing and indexing the stock of the thought-shop, rewriting the more ungainly programs, and reconnecting the various scattered chains of thought floating in the barge's disorganized shop-mind. The more disgusting of the dreams, pornographic, morbid, or filled with bloodlust, he erased; others he sold off on the market, to Iron-joy's deviant and back-net customers. With that money he bought a new core for the shop-mind, raised the capacity, and hired a five-minute engineering-student program to redesign his search engine for job-hunting.

On the third day, Phaethon stood in the bow of the ship and announced his new policies to the huddled and sullen mass of Af-loats who stood glowering at him (those who had eyes) or snapping their sensor-housings open and shut with loud snaps (those that did not.)

"Ladies and gentlemen, neutraloids, bimorphs, hermaphrodites, gynomorphs, and paragenders. Your lack of immortality does not excuse you from the duty of living well what few decades or centuries you have left to you. Accordingly, I hope to introduce some of the discipline of the Silver-Grey into this little community. Naturally, participation will be voluntary. But those who do participate will be granted special price reductions, bargains, and rebates on a wide variety of thought-shop effectuators.

"Self-delusion will be sharply discouraged, as will intoxication, rage dreams, and out-of-context pleasure stimulants. This shop will not help you alter or abolish your self-identity, but will provide every routine at my disposal to allow you to improve your self-love, self-discipline, and self-esteem. Educational and philosophical programs will be made available at low rentals, as will transitional addictives leading to nonaddictives, to help you cure yourself of psychiatric zero-sum cycles. All gambling outlets will be shut down to encourage you to save and to invest. Let me describe some of the Silver-Grey disciplines and their benefits . . ."

But he was pelted by garbage at that point and had to discontinue. He stepped back and drew a diamond pavilion flap across him like a shield, and used a slow-time routine to note who threw what, so that he could dock wages later.

It was Oshenkyo, in the forefront, who was urging the others on. He shouted toward Phaethon: "Clammy snoffer! You're just a Hortator now! Tell us do this, don't do that, read this, don't smoke that, think this, don't zing that! We zing what we ken! Do as we please! Free men! If we want to jolly up our brains on identics, no business of yours!"

And the others cried: "Hortator! Hortator!"

Phaethon let the disturbance run its course.

After some more drama, more threats and exchanges, Phaethon continued his speech:

"Fellow exiles! You have given up on hope. I have not. This makes it inconvenient for me, since I need your labor to help me accumulate the funds I need to put forward the next part of my plan. I need that labor to be alert, unintoxicated, voluntary. The type of automatic half-brain work that Ironjoy's drugs and sets permitted you to do will prove insufficient for my needs. Therefore, your lives, education, and earning abilities will have to be improved. No doubt this will cause you dismay. I care not. If you dislike my managerial style, feel free to find employment elsewhere. But first hear me out:

"There are rich amounts of thought-work the non-controlled market will bear, as well as entire areas of limited-creative patterning and editorial functions for which there is always a need. But, beyond this, there is an area none of you have explored, even though you have the tools at hand. There is work in scientific and technical fields. There is work in investment, small operations, data migration, context-cleaning, mentality rest spaces. Humble work, but honest! What about pseudo-gastronomics? Everyone stops for false-meals when they work, and the Hortators cannot police the public thought-ways or deviant dark channels! Why can't you own your own businesses, gather your own thought-shops, invest your own capital?

"This is some of the easiest training to acquire; all of it is in the public domain, and such training fits every standard jack and neuroform. It is true that the Sophotechs can perform any of these operations more swiftly and more efficiently than can we. But it is also true that they cannot do everything at once, at every place at once, as cheaply as everyone wishes. There is always someone somewhere who wants some further things done, some further work accomplished. There is always someone willing to pay much less for work moderately less well done. Why can't we be the ones to find and do that work?"

The first shift Phaethon sent to completing some of the assembly line-type tasks, mostly data-patterning and link-cleaning, which Ironjoy's old markets still needed done. That was much as before.

But a second group he sent to harvest some clothing he had bargained with Daughter-of-the-Sea to produce for them. Like her mother, she cared nothing for the Hortators. Phaethon, the day before, had found a translation routine buried in Ironjoy's back-files that would allow a human neuroform to communicate with the Daughter's odd mind arrangement and time frequency. She was more than happy to provide the community with some much-needed sturdy clothing, as well as certain pharmaceuticals and foodstuffs, in return for some simple bird-tending, weeding, and microbiogenisis her bodies needed. And, most of all, the Daughter wanted the many imploring advertisements which had been sent by many donors and suitors to engage her attention to be sent away. As it turned out, she was weary of them.

Now, the Afloats would be dressed better even than the Ashores, and in garb both clean and dignified. Surely it would improve their esteem, mold their slovenly demeanor to better forms! Phaethon wondered why not one of these Afloats had spent any time trying to communicate with Daughter-of-the-Sea before.

A third group, under his direction, was sent ashore to the graveyard of houses. This was not a party of festival-goers, not a simple house-felling operation. Instead, Phaethon conducted a survey, found every house-brain and brain seedling, and sent the group to restoring, cleaning, regrowing, and rewiring. He estimated that, with these brains linked in parallel, by the end of two days, the thought-shop would have the brain capacity of a Rhadamanthus outbuilding, enough to give every Afloat personal help at job-hunting, as well as being able to take over some of the more routine tasks of such jobs.

This would also give each Afloat the ability to log on to the mentality (if they could find a server who would accept them) and send messages to Ironjoy's markets without going through Ironjoy.

Again, he wondered why none of them had thought of it before.

A fourth group he sent to cleaning the rust off the barge. This he did, not because it helped forward any scheme, but only because the hull was dirty and unsightly.

The final group, consisting only of boxlike neomorphs, swam along the strands of connection fiber and old nerve wires that shrouded the many floating houses like so much cobweb. With mechanical grapples from the robo-toolboxes on their prows, they spliced together and gathered up rolls of the material. And they grumbled every second of their task, complaining to each other in sharp, time-compressed subsonic bursts, but Phaethon expected them to find enough wasted fiber to allow him to wire the entire floating community for light, power, speech, and text. The actual work of physically stringing wires from house to house could be done by the spider gloves in a matter of hours.

And, gloating in his secret thought, Phaethon expected that these last two improvements together, if any of the Afloats were clever enough, would allow someone else here to set up a search engine and a thought-shop of his own, and break Ironjoy's monopoly forever. Did they dislike Phaethon's stiff insistence on punctuality, proper dress, sobriety? All the better. The more unpopular Phaethon was, the quicker some other Afloat would be to go into the business and draw away his customers.

At sunset, Phaethon had a little ceremony. Everyone who was not working the night shift was on the deck of the barge when he pointed toward the darkened houses all around them. He made the restart gesture.

And light flared from every window, lamps flamed, beams glittering across the water. It was a breathtaking sight.

In chorus, the houses all spoke at once, "Welcome, masters and mistresses! We slept; now we wake. It will be our pleasure to serve you!" And, at Phaethon's cue, in hushed, huge voices, which rolled across the water, the houses in choir began to sing the ceremonial housewarming song from the Fourth Era.

It was a sight to expand the heart. Phaethon felt a tear of pride in his eye, and smiled in mild embarrassment as he wiped it away. He looked up and saw, in the distance, peering warily over the cliff, a group of silent Ashores, half-nude, or garish in their advertisement

smocks, drawn by the echoes of the song. They stood as if amazed
by the lights.

Phaethon smiled, and turned. Behind him stood the Afloats,
handsome in new jackets and trousers of brown and dark brown,
tunics, skirts and films of white or green. And yet why did so many
of them slouch, or knot their shirttails, or stain their skirts? Why
did none of them smile? Phaethon had been expecting them to
cheer. Didn't they want their houses to be lit?

With a brusque gesture, Phaethon dismissed the day shift, cau-
tioning them to appear sober for work the next day. Then he strode
down the ladder to the cabin in the aft of the barge, which had
been Ironjoy's sanctum and restoration chamber.

Several days had gone by; it was time for the next step of his
plan.

2.

Ironjoy's restoration chamber was barren except for a cot, a formulation rod, an ewer of life-water and an aspect mandala tuned to
nearby thoughtspace, obviously meant to watch for Sophotech or
Hortator calls and police activity. Ironjoy certainly did not coddle
himself; these quarters were more stark than most of his employees'.
Perhaps the pleasure of dominion and control, a pleasure now so
rare in the Golden Oecumene, was enough to sustain him.

A housecoat programmed with a score of medical functions hung
from a rack, with a dozen medical history files stacked in coin slots
along the vest; Ironjoy evidently used it to cure some of the older
Afloats. Phaethon frowned to see a euthanasia needle clipped to the
housecoat belt in a sterile holder.

Two walls of the cabin were fixed. Opposite the door were narrow
windows looking out upon the bay and the cliffs beyond. The other
two walls were not smart-walls, but they knew a few words, and
they could slide open.

Behind one was a Demeterine decorative screen of surprising
elegance and taste, a pattern of gold birds and dark blue Demeter-
style fruit. Sound threads were woven through the panel, but Phae-

thon did not have a reader to receive the signal, and so the threads gave a few puzzled chirps and woodwind notes when he looked at various parts of the design, but then, unable to follow the pattern of his eye movements, the threads fell into puzzled silence.

It was a magnificent work. Phaethon did not know enough about this particular form to guess the artist's name, but Phaethon wondered again about Ironjoy's character. Who would have guessed that such a meditative and abstract delicacy attracted him?

Behind the other wall, facing the blue-gold decoration, were three talking mirrors. They must have been tuned to place their calls as soon as light hit them. The moment the walls slid back, the mirrors formed images of Ironjoy's three main customers.

He was not unprepared. Phaethon stood straight in his armor, with the magnificent decoration panel forming his backdrop. He spoke briefly, introducing himself and explaining the change of circumstance. "I intended to fulfill all of Ironjoy's contracts with you to the letter—the work performed today will testify to that. It is my hope that you will consent to deal with me on the same basis you dealt with him. It is only until his release a few weeks hence. What do you gentlemen say? Do we have an understanding?"

Each of the three spoke for a moment, describing the work they might need over the next few days, asking questions, and issuing tentative consent. Each one seemed to be aware that if he mistrusted Phaethon, or refused to deal with him, the other two would rush in to fill the gap.

An identification gesture had brought their names to the surface of the mirrors in a subscript. The indigo-faced man on the left was Semris; the writhing mass of bloated snakes in the middle was a neomorph named Antisemris; a tube with mechanical arms with emblems of a half-Invariant was labeled Notor-Kotok. Semris, to judge from the name, was a Jovian, perhaps from Io. Antisemris was evidently an undermind or child of Semris, but who had joined the Cacophile movement.

The Ionians came from what had once been a wild and dangerous world, and some small few had not put away their wild and dangerous personas after that moon's volcanisms were tamed by planetary engineers (Including the famous Geaius Score Stormcloud of

Dark Grey, a terraformer whose work Phaethon had studied, followed, and admired.) If Semris was one of those few last Wild-Ionians, he would ignore the Hortators; they had long ago condemned his mental template as destructive and temperamental.

Likewise, Antisemris was a freak, perhaps a Never-First, and Hortators' standards would mean little to him. Both were the type of unsavory people, perhaps insane, whom Phaethon would never have received or entertained, back when he had been a Silver-Grey Manorial.

Notor-Kotok was a different case; he spoke somewhat like an Invariant, somewhat like a Composition. Phaethon suspected that he, or they, were actually a small combination-mind made of people whose relatives and friends had been exiled, and who had all contributed a few thoughts to make a composite being that would still look after their relatives, talk to them, or find them work. The being was modeled along unemotional Invariant lines, perhaps to render it immune from Hortator pressure. Phaethon had heard of such things before.

Phaethon said, "You gentlemen will be pleased to note that I intend to make improvements to the working conditions here. This will no doubt increase productivity. The greatest loss to productivity is to false-self dreams and deep intoxicants. I believe the Afloats are driven to these things out of despair for their relatively short life spans."

Antisemris flutter several of his snake-heads. "Too true! Yet what can be done? Orpheus controls all noumenal recordings."

"Gentlemen, it is well-known that the Neptunian Tritonic Composition can store brain information within the laminae of their special material. At near absolute zero temperatures, there is no signal degradation, even over centuries. With cascade-sequence re-recording and corrections, the Neptunian superconductive nerve tissue can retain a given personality for aeons. I recommend we create a branch of the Neptunian school right here. The Neptunians scoff at Hortators' mandates; we will find no difficulties finding Neptunians willing to deal with us. And, once that is done, whole new markets will open to us. We will no longer need interpreters or

Eleemosynary routines to communicate with the Neptunian neuro-forms. And you know those outer markets are hungry for even simple thought-work."

"Your proposal?" asked Semris.

"Gentlemen, I ask for your investment. An initial fund of some sixty-five hundred seconds should allow us to buy a channel of communication, if not with Triton or Nereid, then at least with the Neptunian Legate-mass stationed near Trailing Trojan city-swarm, where they keep a permanent embassy. A modified search engine could examine Neptunian thought-space for work opportunities; we will have labor, cheap and plentiful. I estimate we can make our return on the investment in a matter of days."

Semris said, "A new market is always attractive; but I have dealt with Neptunians before, the group who did work on Amalthea. They are tricky and unlovable, and enjoy cruel jokes. Ironjoy was always against the idea of opening markets with the Neptunians."

Some snake-heads of Antisemris stared at each other in puzzlement. "Neptunians are also very far afield! Think just of how long it would take to broadcast across the radius of the Solar System to ask a query or get a response from Neptune. Telepresentation is impossible; second-by-second oversight of the work is impossible."

Phaethon said, "The distance is not an obstacle for piecework done in large blocks, especially high-quality work with low data densities. I hope to train the Afloats to be able to work without supervision."

Antisemris was unconvinced: "Why stir up so many changes? We are all satisfied with the way things have gone heretofore. The Afloats have nowhere else to go; change may confound things! Why irk the Hortators more than we must? We subsist only because they do not have the patience to squash us all. No, for once, the flat-headed Semris, no doubt by accident, has uttered a truth."

But Notor said, "I place a high priority on keeping the mental well-being of the various Afloats at an optimal or praedo-optimal level, as measured by the Kessic sanity scale. Increased life would be beneficial, as would increased markets. Yet I have curiosity about Phaethon's motives. Your plan to find work in the Neptunian markets does seem disproportional to the desired effect."

"Yet, Mr. Notor, you do not object to dealing with Neptunians in and of themselves?"

"Allow me to employ a metaphor. I will accept any coin that burns." (This was a reference to the antimatter currency.)

Phaethon heard some warbling bird notes from the tapestry behind him. Perhaps one of the men in the mirror had glanced at the gold-and-blue figures, and his eye motions had been interpreted to reveal his emotional state. Phaethon now realized for what purpose the crass Ironjoy kept such beautiful art. And while Phaethon was not familiar with the note codes and tuning of the emotion-reactives woven in the tapestry, he could make a good guess.

Hiding a smile, Phaethon now bowed to Semris and Antisemris. "If you gentlemen are not interested after all, perhaps you can allow Mr. Notor and I a little privacy to discuss some matters of mutual interest and mutual profit . . ."

Semris and Antisemris interrupted each other, suddenly eager to discuss the matter further.

3.

Less than an hour later, Phaethon had the money he needed to place a call to the Neptunians.

Phaethon folded the wall over two of the mirrors, used Ironjoy's formulation rod to calm himself and fix his purposes in mind. Then he turned to the mirror and placed the call.

In their present orbital positions, it took sixteen minutes for the signal to go to and to return from near-Jovian space, where the Neptunians maintained a permanent legate. This delay, Phaethon had expected.

But then, while Phaethon stood idle, doing nothing, there passed another five minutes while the messenger speech-tree loaded from the signal into the limited mind-space of the thought-shop's isolated communication circuits.

There was a further half-minute delay as line checkers and counteractants and virus hunters examined the received messenger speech-tree for viruses or surprises, a precaution not usually necessary, except when dealing with Neptunians.

The delay of time was considerable. Phaethon reflected that Rhadamanthus could have performed a million first-order operations in this same amount of time, or Westmind, a hundred million. Almost six minutes had passed. The true depth of his poverty impressed itself on Phaethon. He was living like some creature out of a forgotten age of history, practically like a Third-Era Victorian in truth.

How had those ancient British folk, or Second-Era Romans or Athenians (so prominently pictured in Silver-Grey simulations) tolerated all the mess, delay, and anguish in their lives? How had they faced the inevitability of death, disease, injustice, grief, and pain? How had they tolerated the loneliness of being frozen in the base neuroform, without even the possibility of joining a mass-mind?

And how had they changed and improved their minds and selves without the benefit of noetics, noumenology, redaction, or any science of psychiatric editing or self-consideration? Had it just been by an effort of will and the practice of a habit of virtue?

The symbol of the Tritonic Neuroform Composure scholum appeared on the mirror, indicating that the messenger was loaded and awake. Phaethon drew a breath, mentally recited his formulated Warlock autohypnotic mantra one last time, and steeled himself. Had he just been marveling at the stoicism of the mortal men of earlier ages? He himself was now mortal. And it was his stoicism which would now be tested.

"Good afternoon," said Phaethon. When that produced no response (he still was not used to the lack of a translator to convey his meaning into other formats and aesthetics) he said, "Start. Go. Initiate. Begin. Read Message. Please."

"This is the messenger. I represent information from the presently dominant sects and discourses embraced by the Tritonic Neuroform Composition. If your question or provocation is one which has been anticipated by my writers (if I have writers), then a recorded response will be brought forward to reply. The lector is flexible, and can organize and edit the responses according to the logic of your statements, if it so chooses. If your question is one which has not been anticipated, expect a spate of nonsense and irrelevancy. On the other hand, if I am, in fact, a self-aware entity, then my responses are not merely the recorded statements of the writers, but the freely chosen deliberate communication of a mind having a perverse joke at your expense. (Please note that, if I am a self-aware entity, then erasing me from your communication buffer would be an act of murder. Constables may be standing by.)"

Phaethon blinked in puzzlement. This was hardly what he had been expecting. "Pardon me, but are you in fact a self-aware entity?"

"I have been programmed to say that I am."

Phaethon checked the memory space the messenger-tree occupied. It was large. Large enough to hold a self-referencing (and therefore self-aware) program? Unlikely, but with proper data-compression techniques, it was not impossible. It would be a reckless act to erase what might be self-aware. But then again, it would be typical Neptunian humor to absorb large sections of expensive memory with an unintelligent messenger-tree no one dared erase.

The messenger said, "And please do not attempt to place the burden of proving my humanity on me. The law against first-degree murder does not hold that those who cannot prove their humanity are subject to instant and arbitrary death."

The joke seemed particularly cruel to Phaethon, since he himself, by pursuing this call, might be exposing himself to instant and arbitrary death. What if the agents of the Silent Ones were listening?

"Can you give me a précis of who is presently in charge of, or wields the most prestigious and influence in, the Neptunian Duma?" The "Duma" was the Neptunian name for their main social organization. It was made of partial minds and client minds beamed in by Neptunians, who were too scattered to represent themselves by any direct means. The partials combined and evolved in a seething, tangled mass of vigorous conflict, to form a consensus entity, or, rather, successive sets of consensus entities, whose proclamations influenced the course of Neptunian dialogue and society. The Duma was more like a clearinghouse and central marketplace of ideas rather than like a parliament.

Neptunians were highly individualistic and eccentric, and so they instructed their representatives to place a higher value on obdurate zeal than on rational compromise. Consequently, the Duma was often insane, pursuing several contradictory goals at once, overreacting or underreacting with no sense of proportion to the petitions, ideas, and new lines of thought that the Neptunians, from time to time, introduced. The Neptunians had never yet reprogrammed the Duma to behave with logic; this baroque form of social government apparently amused the Cold Dukes and Eremites of Neptune far more than a rational one would have.

The messenger-tree said: "The Silver-Grey School has recently won wide acceptance among the Duma. It is presently the dominant school, followed, but not closely, by the Patient Chaos School."

Phaethon leaned forward, eyes wide. "The Silver-Grey? How is this possible?" As far as Phaethon knew, there had never been any Silver-Grey among the mad things of Neptune.

The messenger-tree continued: "Many thought-chains and dialogues within the Duma are consumed with topics prompted by Diomedes of Nereid, who recently shamed the Hortators of Earth, and who, by being poor, tricked them into giving him great wealth. Diomedes and Xenophon mingled to create out of themselves a temporary mind named Neoptolemous, who outwitted the Cerebelline named Wheel-of-Life. Neoptolemous now owns the titanic starship called *Phoenix Exultant*. Trillions of tons of metallic antihydrogen, chrysadmantium, biological and nanobiological material, are aboard, and the shipmind is a million-cycle entity with a vast wealth in routines and capacity. This victory brought great prestige to Diomedes and to his son Neoptolemous. Diomedes, in his Living Will, set aside a fund of that prestige to promote a Silver-Grey School among the Duma. He did this in memorial for a friend of his, who was unjustly treated by the College of Hortators, and sent to his death in exile."

"May I send a message to Diomedes? Can you speak on his behalf?"

"I have templates from most of the major chains of thought among the active Duma members, including Diomedes, and therefore I can pretend to be him and form responses based on my anticipation of

what he would say if he were here. When this message is transmitted back to the Neptunian embassy, Diomedes will have the
option either to reject or accept the representations made as his
own. If he should accept, this messenger will be implanted into his
own memories, so that he will thereafter believe he himself was
here and made these comments. However, I am required to warn
you that Diomedes, as of last assembly, no longer existed as a separate entity. He was still a part of the Diomedes partial-composition.
The actors for Diomedes and Xenophon fell into dispute over which
parts of Neoptolemous belonged to Diomedes and which belonged
to Xenophon. Neoptolemous' thoughts have not yet been untangled
and resolved back into two separate entities. In other words, Neoptolemous has not yet made up his minds."

"What is the basis for the dispute? Is it the ship?"

"The Patient Chaoticists are eager to dismantle the ship and
distribute the wealth among the starving hosts beyond Neptune; the
Silver-Grey urge the ship be used for an expedition to establish
colonies at nearby stars. The Patient Chaos plan would bring money
into the starved Neptunian economy; whereas to fund an expedition
such as the one which Half-Neoptolemous Semi-Diomedes proposes
would drain the economy. Didactions from Patient Chaos assert that
the present ruination of the economy was caused, in large part, by
investments made into Phaethon's Expeditionary Effort."

At that point, he was interrupted by a chime. The wall-panel to
the left slid back to reveal the image of the nest-of-snakes face of
Antisemris. "Pardon me for interrupting, but, as a major investor
who just entrusted you with a good deal of money, I was just wondering why you were wasting my investment chatting with a Neptunian machine about politics. We bought you this messenger so
you could read the help-wanted advertisements it carries! And don't
bother to tell me that you were investigating their market needs.
All you need to know is what kind of grunt-work of line-checking
they need done; its not as if their internal politics affects the kind
of short-markets we are looking for!"

Phaethon said sharply: "Your intrusion is most unwarranted and
perhaps illegal. Is this the fashion in which you have chosen to

display the fact that you are spying on me? Do not bother to answer. Our mutual association will soon end."

"Hah! Climb off your fat pride! Semris and Notor will not deal with you either, once they find out how you spend our money!"

"I have dealt with Neptunians before, and you have not. They also use their messenger to update their negotiation databases. Because you have rudely chosen to interrupt, rather than to consult with me privately later, the messenger, who overhears all we are saying now, has no doubt classified our needs and our bargaining position. This has limited our options considerably, and prejudiced our future dealings with the Neptunians. If you cannot be polite, sir, then at least be quiet, before you harm your interests and my own more than you have so far done."

Antisemris uttered a dozen notes of hissing laughter. "Don't try to wax me with that polish! Keep talking to your Nepto friend. But I'm not transmitting him back to the embassy. As of this moment, you are cut off from the funds and line to the orbital radio-laser we established."

"You have no such authority, not without the concurrence of Semris and Notor. I, of course, need their concurrence to exclude you from all future business dealings, but I do not think I shall have any difficulty convincing them, once they see the end-result of the conversation you so foolishly interrupted."

Antisemris writhed, several heads opening their mouths and displaying their fangs. "Ho ho. Go ahead. Finish your little conversation and earn a million grams. Surprise me."

Phaethon turned back to the center screen. "Messenger! I assume the major expense to your proposed interstellar expedition is the Neptunian lack of skilled technical personnel."

"Correct. The Hortators have forbidden any Inner Planet libraries from selling us the templates or mind-sets we need for terraformers, paraluminal astronomers, high-energy physicists, or Celeritologists. We have no pilot. Furthermore, the ship interfaces were designed for a base neuroform, and are not proper for Neptunian crewmen, who have different neural architecture, thought conventions, and time regulations. The ship's interfaces would have to be changed, one routine at a time, and in some cases, one line at a time, before the ship would be comfortable for a Neptunian crew. Without a Sophotech, this would require long amounts of tedious effort, which we cannot expend. Therefore, without expert help, we cannot fly the ship at the intended velocities for which she was designed. This, of course, is the major flaw in the proposed plan Diomedes had put forward."

"What if I could get you cheap labor to do your interface translation to the Neptunian formats?"

"With proper interfaces, then Neptunian minds and personae could be stored in the crew segments of the shipmind, and smart-habitats be programmed to sustain any somatic forms the crew would care to manifest. However, the ship's flight characteristics, mass, and length, will considerably transform (according to external frames of reference) as she approaches light-speed. The external universe (from the ship's frame of reference) will undergo like transformation. This will affect any objects and particles aboard (such as communications and sensory circuits) that must interact with the external universe, including drive by-products and foreign-object-damage controls. It would require a special branch of tachyceleric study to rediscover the findings of the original designer. That information does not seem to have been stored in the ship's brain. We cannot provide the information."

"I have that information."

"Then the formatting can be accomplished and a Neptunian crew be recorded. But such formatting would be a pointless exercise without a trained operator to run the celestial navigation, xeno-terraforming, and high-energy physics routines."

"I can pilot the ship. I have test-flown her."

"I am required to warn you that, even though I am only a message-tree, and am not capable of independent judgment, this conversation may be reviewed by a living operator at a later time. That operator will condemn falsehoods and irrational statements, and that will serve to negate any bargain made with me."

"Why do you call my statement false?"

"Only one man has ever test-flown that ship."

"I am that man."

"That man was Phaethon of Rhadamanth, the ship's designer."

"I am Phaethon."

There was a choked hiss from Antisemris (whose presence Phaethon had almost forgotten.) Phaethon did not have the aestethic to read snake expressions, and therefore did not know what emotion or sign this knotted jerk was meant to convey. Surprise? Perhaps.

The snaky mass of Antisemris said, "You are the one Unmoiqhotep told us all to worship! You are that Phaethon! The real Phaethon!"

Phaethon said blankly: "But I told you my name. Surely you knew . . ."

"Zs-ss! A lot of my school have memorized ourselves to be Phaethon, or changed our names! When I saw you in that stupid-looking armor, I just thought you were freak-looped, like my brothers and others, or maybe got ostracized because you tried to contact the real Phaethon, or something."

Of course. Antisemris must be under a Hortator ban, if not as strict as Phaethon's, at least something that would keep him out of polite society, and perhaps away from the mentality. Phaethon was still not used to the idea that exiles and outsiders, like himself and Antisemris, could not discover the identities, or confirm the thoughts and intentions of the people with whom they spoke. It must lead to a great deal of confusion and dishonesty. No wonder Antisemris had been so quick to spy, to interrupt, and to accuse.

Phaethon said, "Does this mean you will help me maintain communication with the Neptunians after all?"

Antisemris said, "Why not? How can anyone stop us?"

To the messenger, Phaethon said, "I wish to find employment as pilot aboard the *Phoenix Exultant*. I believe my qualifications are unique. I also have a large group of workers able to run the standardized routines to translate all interfaces to Neptunian formats. Will the Duma be willing to employ me and my workers?"

"The question of the ownership of the *Phoenix Exultant* is not yet settled. This messenger has only limited ability to predict the outcomes of events; yet I would venture that your appearance at this time with such an offer will sway the major lines of thought among the Duma to favor the Silver-Grey plan, and award Diomedes the title. If so, we could hire you and your workers at salaries considerably higher than standard. But could you guarantee the quality of the work? Afloat exiles are notoriously poor workers."

"I believe that this is caused by the grim and hopeless character of their circumstances. That character may change if some or all of the Afloats transfer their brain-information into Neptunian housings. I would ask your people to bear the expense of this metempsychosis, on the grounds that it is the only way to acquaint workers intimately with the transitions and translations to the Neptunian mental architecture. I would also ask that you bear the expense of transporting me to the present location of the *Phoenix Exultant*."

"I have little doubt but that my principals will favorably receive your offer."

"And are you, in fact, an intelligent being?"

"I have been programmed to reply that I am."

"In that case I will turn the retransmission command over to you, and ask you to risk suicide by broadcasting yourself out of my communication buffer and back to your embassy. This way, I will not be held to account under Golden Oecumene law."

The emblem of the messenger issued a closing salute and disappeared from the central mirror.

In the left mirror, Antisemris' many snake-heads were bobbing, perhaps a sign of good humor. "Well, well. The real Phaethon! Fancy that. It sounds like you'll be at the helm of your ship in no time. And who can stop you, eh?"

The wall slid open to the right, and an image of three armored vulture-heads appeared in the mirror there. A harsh battle-cyborg voice issued from the speaker. "Phaethon! This is the remnant of the Bellipotent Composition speaking. I am informed that someone has just read my travel records, no doubt to discover your location. An index check shows the action took place at million-cycle thought speeds, which indicated that the intruder was using Sophotechnology of a high degree of sophistication. A side-thought of mine is even now communicating with the constabulary. A Constable Pursuivant, on their staff, is reviewing the evidence and tells me that the constables can do nothing, on the grounds that the reading of my information was legal. Apparently the movements of former customers whom I transport are not covered by my clause of privacy, and therefore there is a legal loophole which allows former customers to check flight plans and safety records, even those for flights which they did not take."

Phaethon said: "I have to warn you that Constable Pursuivant is a fictional character. I was told by the Preceptrix of the local commandry that that name and persona can be loaded by anyone who wishes to donate time to performing public service as a constable. The persona comes complete with memory and training."

"I take it that there are no security checks to prevent the persona from being run by any random citizen?"

Phaethon said: "Why bother?"

"Point taken. Society is certainly much more peaceful and trusting than when I was young. Does this mean I cannot trust what Pursuivant told me?"

"I'm not sure. I was visited by a Constable Pursuivant myself. The local Commandry told me that there is no record of such a visit."

The vulture-heads said, "And you suspect it is your fictional extra-systemic alien race?"

"It is the Silent Oecumene."

Both Antisemris and the battle-cyborg jerked their heads in surprise. It was a human gesture, despite their inhuman heads, some atavism of their core neural structure. Deep down, they were still both human.

The three vulture-faces snapped their hooked bills with a clattering sound. "The Silent Oecumene is dead."

"Many people say the same about the Bellipotent Composition."

"Are you telling me they came back from the dead and jumped out of a black hole just to thumb through my logbooks? If so, why isn't the constabulary answering questions about what happened? Why haven't they woken up Atkins out of archive storage?"

"Atkins is not in storage. I've seen him."

"Ah! Ach! If Atkins walks the earth once more, battle and death are not far away!"

Phaethon stared at the red vulture-eyes. Did this creature want a war? The sensation of human sympathy he had for the cyborg faded.

Antisemris evidently wanted to be part of the conversation. He said, "You there, bird-head! You people are talking crazy-talk. This is some masquerade prank. The Hortators wouldn't let this happen."

"They are not all-powerful," replied Bellipotent.

"Someone read your logs," Phaethon said, "there must be a record. What did a normal identification show, when you queried the intruder?"

"The intruder's query was masked by the masquerade protocol. The intruder logged on under a pseudonym."

"What name did they use?"

"Yours. They called themselves Phaethon of Rhadamanth."

Phaethon squinted and frowned. Here was a puzzle. Why his name? "Was that done to allow him access to your records? I had been transported by you, after all."

"Not officially. I listed you as a stowaway."

"But this loophole in the law would not apply to someone who merely dressed up as a customer, only to someone who actually was a customer. So, unless there is a Deep One hunting for me . . ."

"I did have someone I brought to your location. A human form, not a Deep One."

"Here? To Talaimannar? Who?"

But Bellipotent said, "You should not have announced your position. This is not a secure line."

Antisemris' snakes all jerked to one side. His screen went black, to be replaced by a text of white letters on the dark field.

SORRY, PHAETHON, BUT THEY WERE WILLING TO OFFER ME SIX HUNDRED THOUSAND SECONDS AND LET ME BACK IN, PROVIDED I STOPPED HELPING YOU. I'M NOT TAKING ANY MORE MESSAGES FROM YOU, SO DON'T TRY TO CALL.

Phaethon could not grasp what was happening. Was Antisemris confessing to helping the Silent Ones? No, absurd. Some sort of super-high-speed conversation must have just taken place between the Hortators and Antisemris, who had been bribed by them to withdraw support from Phaethon. His link to the Neptunians was cut off again . . .

At the same time, the windows to Phaethon's right lit up with flame.

Then he heard an explosion.

Phaethon jumped to the windows and stared out.

Atop the cliffs across the bay, he could see part of the graveyard of houses, where he had just been salvaging, that morning. It was all on fire.

For a moment, he thought he saw a figure, man-shaped, flying, camouflaged in black armor against the black sky. Then it dropped into the burning graveyard, and, with a flash, buried itself into the cliffside beneath the graveyard.

While Phaethon was still blinking and trying to decide what it was that he had seen, another explosion trembled through the gaunt seashell silhouettes of the dead and defective houses. Fire gushing from high windows, the tall thin silhouettes began to sway and fall.

Then, that noise was smothered, as all the houses Phaethon had just brought to life, all the floating houses of the Afloats, in one, huge terrible wail, began to scream.

THE RESCUE

I.

Phaethon ran up the ladder and found himself on the fore-deck of the barge.

Red light from the fire surged along the northern cliff and lit the scene. Above him, through the pavilion floors of crystal, Phaethon saw black shadows stirring and groaning in the gloom. The workers on the night shift had been jacked out of their work. Perhaps the lines had been interrupted; perhaps Antisemris had shut down the server. The sound of screaming houses brought those figures above to their feet (those that had feet), and cries of anger and fear and wonder mingled with the general clamor.

"Calm! Calm!" Phaethon shouted upward. "It is not our houses burning. Only the empty shells in the graveyard. No one is in danger!"

Drusillet came forward. She was one of the few who had welcomed Phaethon's changes and proudly wore the uniform jacket and skirt he had provided. The shawl she wore to cool her head against the tropic heat, originally designed with a thousand micropores to blow cold oxygen-mix, now also boasted several communication points and phone beads. Compared to the mentality, this small network, encompassing the few hundred yards occupied by the Afloat houses, was pathetic. But her beads and phones demonstrated that one person, at least, had ambition enough to take advantage of the links Phaethon had made among the floating houses.

And it was useful now. "What is the situation?" he asked.

She shouted her answer over the noise, "It's the Hortators. They filed a petition to have the abandoned property destroyed as a public nuisance, submitted a plan for the public burning, and got permission to proceed, all in the last half-second. Energy beamed from stations along the ring-city are triggering the fires. There are constables with inhibitors and pseudomatter smother fields patrolling the area to prevent the flames from spreading, and, also, Nebuchednezzer Sophotech invented and manufactured some new type of nanomachine cloud which can control the blaze. That's the mist you see coming up out of the water. Either Nebuchednezzar finessed Old-Woman-of-the-Sea, or else found some nanomanufacturing cells she doesn't control."

"Are we in any danger?"

"From fire? No. Our houses are screaming because of their fire alarms. I tried to talk to our houses and shut them up, but I need your command override."

"I don't have an override."

"We don't have a municipal net to coordinate the houseminds. Only the owners have authority to shut off the fire alarm, but most of them don't know how."

"The instructions are written in holographic Standard Aesthetic icon code along the rims of the inner walls—"

"Most of us can't read."

Phaethon controlled a sense of impatience. "Then shut down power and reset."

"What if the house batteries are programmed to take over during a power out? The routine may have mutated since this morning."

She was right. Phaethon was not certain how to deal with machines that were not smarter than he was.

Drusillet sent a shutdown and restart command nonetheless. The wails and screams of the floating houses died off. Echoes floated for a moment above the waves, and then were gone. The crackling roar of distant fires was the loudest noise now in the area.

Darkness fell across the bay. The houses, bright a moment ago, were now no more than red-lit shadows in the night, as dark and powerless as when Phaethon first had seen them.

"Restart."

"I did. There must be a flaw in the routine."

Just great. "Well, at least we still have light from the house fires yonder," said Phaeton.

At that moment, however, the blaze along the north cliffs changed. The mist from the sea closed around the individual houses, forming a web not unlike silk, pumping pure oxygen into the burning houses. Each house and house stump blazed a silent blue-white, and was instantly consumed. The silk webs smothered any further fire in a matter of moments.

Everything was lit with magnesium-white light for an instant. Phaethon saw the angry, sullen faces of many of his workers standing along the pavilion balconies above him. Some stared north with looks of hate in their eyes. But some, with the same expressions, stared down at him.

Then, darkness rolled over the scene, like sudden blindness.

As the light died, Phaethon thought he saw a crawling, writhing movement along the northern cliffs. He cursed his lack of proper eyesight. But he guessed that the silk bags were altering again to new functions and sterilizing the soil so that seeds blown out from the damaged Afloat houses would no longer take root.

"It's bad," said Drusillet softly.

"They can't destroy any of the house-brains we've already harvested from the graveyard. Those are clearly our property. But the houses were abandoned. They had as much right to burn them down as we did to loot them."

"It's bad. No new house-brains. No new houses."

"The ones we have will last, with proper periodic cleaning and restructure."

Drusillet seemed dubious.

Phaethon asked, "How often do you gather up a new house?"

"About once a week . . ."

"A week?!! Those things can last four hundred years!"

"Afloats use houses pretty roughly."

"Don't they maintain their homes, educate the house-minds? Clean them?"

Drusillet looked downcast. "No. Whenever the pantry was bare, or the floor mats got dirty, or the filters were stale, we'd just go chop down a new house. It was an excuse to celebrate."

Phaethon shook his head in disgust and turned away. Eventually he said: "Well, in any case, I'm just sorry I did not think to file some sort of legal claim of adverse possession over the graveyard. I had forgotten how fast Sophotechs think, how fast they can act . . ."

He was wondering if the Hortators had actually not known where he was until the moment he revealed his location over the public channel, just now, to Bellipotent. If so, then the Hortators clearly had not sent Constable Pursuivant.

If not the Hortators, then who? The Silent Ones? Some third person Phaethon was overlooking? (And whom had Bellipotent conveyed to the island here?)

Pursuivant probably was not from the Silent Ones. It seemed unlikely that, even with a very sophisticated set of virus entities, the Silent Oecumene's agents could so blithely infiltrate the local constabulary without some segment of the Earthmind noticing. And, if they were that powerful, they would have no need whatever to be secretive, since they would have already taken over the entire mentality.

Wait. An intuition told him that there was some flaw here in his logic, some obvious aspect to all these events he was sure he was overlooking. How powerful and how sophisticated was Nothing Sophotech?

But Phaethon was not a Warlock; he could not automatically bring his intuitions forward into his consciousness. The thought slipped away when a group of Afloats come up to the foredeck, and began demanding in loud voices that they be paid for the rest of their interrupted shift.

It was dark, and there was a press of bodies, and Phaethon had to squint to make them out.

The group consisted of a small triplicate-mind (whose three bodies looked like thin, big-eyed waifs,) a loud-voiced neomorph in a floating box, and two tattoo-faced basics in torn shirts, one a neuter and the other a hermaphrodite.

The basics, rather than wearing Phaethon's uniforms, had doused their upper bodies in smart-paint, so that peacock tails of ever-changing colors blushed across their flesh as tiny cells in the paint flexed to cool their skins, or perhaps (Phaethon thought it more likely) released chemicals into their pores. The perfume from the paint was really quite powerful. Phaethon stepped fastidiously back, holding a scrap of his suit-lining over his nose like a handkerchief.

"I can do nothing for you," he said. "I cannot pay you with seconds of money I do not have. The clients for whom you were working have not yet paid me; nor can they, till we find a black line around whatever block Antisemris put up when he closed up his service."

The three bodies of the triplicate-mind all spoke at once, a spate of interrupted words, and Phaethon regretted yet again that he had no sense-filter to reshape the words into a linear format. "Your problem!" one of them was saying, "We did our part!" The second was saying: "No money? What about that big expense account they gave you to call Neptune?" And the third was archly mentioning that the Hortators had not bothered them until Phaethon's ambitions and high ideals had stirred up the wrath of the Hortators against them.

"We want Ironjoy back!" called one of the basics.

And the other called Phaethon a traitor.

But the neomorph in the floating coffin had a loudspeaker set to drown everyone else out. "On days when we got cut out of the Big Mind, or the services failed, or the lines were cut, it was good old Ironjoy that would declare a time-off party, wasn't it? He'd have dreams by the fistful, and he had a lot of fists, too, and he's pass out wire-points like they were candy. We'd have fluid and beer and happy-jack. For animal parties, we'd have beast-minds jacked in, to shut all those cortex-thoughts away, and just let our underselves and midbrains come out to romp and play. For sex parties, we'd all link through the thought-shop into some of the rich, ripe, sims and wet dreams Ironjoy keeps on file, not just tame plunging, but real orgies of dirt, with all suppressed naughty underthoughts read out by the sneak file and blasted back at double sensation! Aye, those were right days! There was fun! There was life! What've we got now, eh? A man named after Phaethon, the rich man's son, the man who thinks he owns the Sun! And what's he going to do for us, to help us survive our last few hours and years alive? Summon parties? Let us drink and stick and dream and jack and joy? No how! No how! He'll dress us up and drive us on and pound and preach and box us in till everything is either his or ours! No more sharing! No more playing fair! What say you all? You want to party? Or you want to listen to a Phaethon look-alike rich man's darling son stand up and preach?"

More and more people had come crowding up on the deck, and filled the stairs, and pushed forward, calling and gesticulating.

And the crowd shouted, "Party! Par—tee! Par—tee!"

Phaethon raised a hand and tried to shout back. "Are you mad? Go home! Rest! We will need to work double shift tomorrow, to make up for what we lost today. Otherwise, how will you eat tomorrow?"

Oshenkyo jumped down from one of the pavilions above and landed neatly atop the hull of the floating coffin. He crouched and put his mouth to the speaking hole, so that his voice was amplified as well. "Big Snoot Gold got plenty to eat, beneath that fancy suit. We all know it! Yummy black, hundred matrix, rich as cream, able to become whatever thing you dream! It's ours, not his; we needs it more!"

Oshenyko wanted Phaethon's black nanomachine lining. A murmur through the crowds showed they all wanted some of it, too.

Phaethon's armor also had amplifiers:

"Idiots! Think about tomorrow! Think about a million tomorrows! I've invited the Neptunians to come and grant you your endless lives again!"

"Tomorrow isn't coming!" shouted the neomorph.

The crowd took up the call. "Tomorrow isn't coming! Tomorrow isn't coming!" And they surged forward to grapple Phaethon's armor.

"Not for you, it isn't," said Phaethon grimly. And he shut his faceplate and made a calculation and sent a low-voltage charge of electricity through the armor's hull. All the hands who were grappling him locked and froze, and everyone pressing forward, each person touching each other in the crowd, passed the charge among them. A noise arose like one Phaethon had never heard before, a gasp of breathless and convulsive agony squeezed from a hundred straining lungs at once.

When he cut the current, everyone dropped to the deck, groaning, twitching. After the press and roar of the crowd, the sudden silence was overwhelming.

Phaethon looked up at a floating constable-wasp. "Once again, you did not help me. Are only those who have wealth and power in this society afforded protection?"

"Apologies. The crowd was only exercising its right of free speech and free assembly, until the moment they laid hands on you. We were gathering units to respond, when you attacked them."

"Attacked? I call it self-defense."

"Perhaps. I notice that not everyone in the crowd was actually touching you; some of them may have been trying to pull people off you. The magistrate has not yet made a ruling. But none of your victims have yet filed a complaint. They all seem to be incapacitated. We will take them to a holding area till they are ready to face trial and punishment."

And with that, dozens of large machines, like flying crabs, swooped down and began picking up the stunned Afloats and spiriting them away.

"Stop! Were are you taking my workforce! I'm going to need them before tomorrow to finish our projects!"

A constable-wasp near his ear said, "For many years, the Afloats, even though they were shunned exiles, never crossed the line to crime. Now, thanks to you, they have. The Golden Oecumene will tolerate no violence. Your other plans will have to wait."

Half the Afloats were gone. The busy flying machines swooped and plucked up more. Soon they were all gone, and the decks were bare.

"When will they be returned to me?"

"I am not obligated to answer that, sir, although I have heard a rumor to the effect that the Hortators are willing to rent them cheap dwellings in Kisumu, near a delirium farm run by Red Eveningstar castoffs. I hear that there is a wide field of pleasure coffins piled up and left to rot among the parks and jungles nearby, with a thousand old dreamsheets and smart-drugs and personality-alterants just lying out on the grass. Some of the Afloats may volunteer to return here for a life of deprivation, hard reality, and hard work. Maybe."

"Then the Hortators have won, haven't they?" whispered Phaethon.

The constable-wasp said, "As to that, sir, I should not venture any personal opinions while in the course of my official duties. But, officially, I should warn you against being so quick to take matters so violently into your own hands. Isn't that what got you here in the first place? Good-bye for now. We may be back in the morning, if any of your victims wishes to lodge a complaint."

And then the swarm of constables, which had been constantly overhead ever since Phaethon had arrived, they were also gone.

2.

Below, Phaethon stood facing the mirrors. He attempted Semris and Antisemris first; but their seneschals had been programmed to reject his calls unanswered and unacknowledged.

Then he called Unmoiqhotep, the Cacophile who had so praised him and so adored Phaethon outside the Curia House in the ring-city, just after his hearing. Antisemris (who was also a Cacophile) might help Phaethon if Unmoiqhotep asked.

Phaethon tricked his way past Unmoiqhotep's seneschal by hiding his identity in masquerade. (No Hortator warning appeared to warn Unmoiqhotep's house to reject the call because the Hortators were not able to penetrate the masquerade.) The house accepted to pay for the charges of the call when he announced he wanted to speak "about Phaethon." But when Unmoiqhotep's partial came online, the creature reviled Phaethon in no uncertain terms as a fool and a traitor.

"Why do you call him a traitor?" Phaethon asked. (He was getting particularly sick of having that charge leveled against him.)

The partial, like his master, was a bloated fungus, cone-shaped, drooping with nonstandard claws and tentacles. "Phaethon betrayed us! He has failed! We who represent the shining future, we who soar to exulted heights, we who take as implacable foes the dross of the older generation (the already-dead generation, as I like to call them), we have no time in our all-important crusade to trifle with failures! Phaethon has no money now! There is nothing he can do for us!'"

Do for us? This reminded Phaethon of the beggar phrase the poor Afloats used to greet any newcomers. How odd to hear it come from the mouths of wealthy men's sons.

Phaethon said: "But there is something you can do for him. If Phaethon had money enough to rent an orbital communications laser, he could contact the Neptunians. They may be willing to hire him as a pilot for the *Phoenix Exultant*. Instead of being dismantled for scrap, the starship could be sent out to the stars, there to create new worlds."

The image of the Cacophile flopped its tendrils first one way, then the other. "What has that to do with us? Phaethon wants to fly to the stars. He wants to make worlds. I want to find a new wire-point to jolt my pleasure centers, maybe with an overload pornographic pseudomnesia to give it background. Are his dreams any better than mine?"

Phaethon reminded himself that he was here begging for money. He attempted to remain polite. "With all due respect, sir, may I point out that if you help him now, Phaethon, when he achieves his dream, can create such worlds as will be pleasing to you, and your lifelong dream of escaping from the domination of the elder generation will be achieved as well. But if you, instead, burn your brain cells with a wire-point, this serves neither you, nor him."

The partial dripped liquid from three orifices. "But what does all your blather and bother do for us right now? Right this instant? Phaethon is no longer in fashion among us now. After he is dead, perhaps then we will exalt him as a martyr, slain by the cruelty of the elder generation. Yes! There is something for us! But Phaethon alive, still striving after his sick, insane dream? Still hoping to accomplish it? No, oh no. He would be our worst enemy if he succeeded at his attempt, against such odds. Isn't it obvious why?

Because he would make the rest of us look so bad."

Phaethon felt mildly sick with astonishment. The Cacophiles had no intention of ever "escaping" from the "domination" of the older generation. All their moral posturing was merely excuse to disguise their lust to own what they had not earned. To fly to other worlds, and there make lives and civilizations for themselves, would require the kind of work and effort which the Cacophiles disdained.

And what about their alleged gratitude for Phaethon, the high honor and esteem in which they had promised to hold him? But gratitude and honor required hard work as well.

Phaethon signed off with polite words.

That left Notor-Kotok. But the squat little cylindrical cyberform was of as little help.

"I have not, at this time, money or currency enough to rent an orbital communications laser, or any device of similar function, capable of reaching that Neptunian station (to the best of my knowledge) presently nearest, nor of reaching any other relay or service able to convey a message thereto. This statement is based on an estimation that the money involved would be 'enormous,' and by enormous, I mean, sufficient to buy separately each part and service which the 'legitimate' services (by which I mean those who adhere to Hortator standards) presently appear to have decided not to traffick with us, as we are now."

(Phaethon hated speaking to Invariants, or to people, like Notor, who followed Invariant speech conventions. He dearly wished he had his sense-filter back again, so that he could program it to edit out all the cautious disclaimers and lawyerly redundancy with which Invariants peppered their speech.)

Phaethon said: "Could some of your deviants be willing to lend me money on credit? I cannot raise any capital now that my workforce is under arrest."

In a complex speech, Notor explained something Phaethon already knew. Most deviants are deviant because they are poor. Most poor are poor because they lack the self-discipline necessary to forgo immediate gratification. They were not the kind of people able to lend money and wait for a return.

Phaethon asked: "What if the return on investment is not simply immense, but infinite?"

"Define your terms."

"Infinite means infinite. It does not matter how much money I need to borrow, or what the rate of interest is. I will gladly promise to repay one hundred times what I borrow, or one thousand. Have you forgotten the Silent Oecuemene? If any of their energy-producing structures are still intact, or can be restored, then I can make Cygnus X-1 my first port of call. From their singularity fountainheads, whatever amount of energy I need to repay my creditors can be gathered."

"I am receiving a signal from other sections of my brainwork. Wait. We calculate that no one will be willing to risk any money on your venture, no matter what the rate of return. Several deviant money houses, those who I might have suspected would lend to you nonetheless, have already been purchased, within the last few seconds, by Nebuchednezzar Sophotech . . ."

Someone was listening in on this channel, perhaps, or Nebuchednezzar was alert enough to calculate Phaethon's next maneuver, and, at lightning speed, had already moved to thwart him.

Notor explained: "Also, my service provider, who maintains these connections I presently use to speak with you, has signaled me and told me that, unless I no longer speak with you, the Eleemosynary Composition will dump shares of communications stock to artificially drive down the prices, and ruin his business. He is not willing to risk it, and threatens to suspend service if I do not eschew you.

"The other Afloats whom I am tasked to attempt to protect, may be relocated," continued Notor. "I anticipate that I will require my service provider's communication lines if I am to continue that protection; therefore, if, in fact, maintaining my connections with you, and continuing that protection, are mutually exclusive, I must place a higher priority on the latter."

"Can we still communicate by letter?" asked Phaethon with little hope.

"Who would carry it? Who would translate it from your written format? I cannot read your archaic Silver-Grey letters and signs."

"Then I am defeated?"

"You terminology is inexact. 'Defeat' as a concept, refers to a complex of emotion-energy reactions created by a mind interpreting the universe. But the universe, by definition, must always be more complex than the information-parts or thoughts one uses to encode that complexity. 'Defeat' is not a fact, it is an assessment of facts, and may be subject to interpretation."

Perhaps that was meant to cheer him.

The signal shut off, with an icon showing that further service would be discontinued. The mirrors went black, and would not light up again.

Phaethon walked slowly back up on deck. He stood at the prow with one foot on the rail, leaning on his knee and staring out across the water. What options still were open to him? Had he been defeated at every turn?

And yet things were not as bad as they had been even two days ago, when he had been choking at the bottom of the sea. Now, he had allies. Weak ones, perhaps, like Antisemris, or ones with whom he could not speak, like Notor-Kotok, or like the distant Neptunians. But he also had a dream, and it was a strong dream. Strong enough, perhaps, to make up for the weaknesses of his allies.

The offer Phaethon had made to Notor-Kotok was one manifestation of the strength of that dream. The endless energy supplies of the singularity at Cygnus X-1, as well as the wealth of multiple worlds yet to be born, would tempt investment and support from among those disenfranchised or dissatisfied with the present Oecumene. Immortality had not changed the laws of economics, but it had created a situation where men now could contemplate, as economically feasible, long voyages, long projects, and plans patient beyond all measure of time for their fruition. Somewhere would be men willing to invest in Phaethon's dream, willing to trust that millennia or billennia from now, Phaethon could amply reward their faith in him. Somewhere, somehow, he would find people who would support him.

He raised his head and looked. The stars were dim here, washed out by lights and power satellites around the ring-city, the flares from nearby mining asteroids in high-earth orbit. And his eyes were not as strong as they had been, blind to all but human wavelengths. But he could still see the stars.

Cygnus X-1 itself was not visible. The almanac in his head (the one artificial augment he would never erase) told him the latitude and right ascension of that body. He turned his eyes to the constellation of the Swan, and spoke aloud into the general night. "You've manipulated the Hortators to suppress me, strip me, revile me, exile me. But you cannot stop me, or move me one inch from my fixed purpose, unless you send someone to kill me.

"But you dare not perform a murder here in the middle of the Golden Oecumene, do you? Even in the most deserted places, there are still many eyes to see, many minds to understand, the evidence of murder."

He paused in his soliloquy to realize that, indeed, there could be spies and monitors listening to him, watching him, including instruments sent by his enemy.

He spoke again: "Nothing Sophotech, Silent Ones, Scaramouche, or however you are called, you may exceed me greatly in power and force of intellect, and may have weapons and forces at your command beyond anything my unaided thought can understand. But you cower and hide, as if afraid, possessed by fear and hate and other ills unknown to sane and righteous men. My mind may be less than yours, but it is, at least, at peace."

He was not expecting a reply. It was probably more likely that no one was watching him, and that his enemy had lost sight of where he was. He doubted there were any enemies within the reach of his voice.

There was, on the other hand, still one ally with whom he could speak, not far away.

He drew out the child's slate he had, and, with a short-range plug, connected to the shop-mind and employed the old translator he had found earlier. He engaged the circuit and transcribed: "I address the Cerebelline called Daughter-of-the-Sea and send greetings and good wishes. Dear Miss, it is with grave regret that I inform you that our period of mutual business and mutual aid, so lately begun, has drawn abruptly to a close. The Hortators (or, rather, Nebuchednezzar Sophotech, acting at their behest) have manipulated events to deprive us of the Afloat workforce. I am unable to fulfill my contract with you concerning the bird-tending, weeding, microgenesis, and other simple tasks you wished to have done . . ."

He went on to describe the situation in some detail. He explained his plan to introduce Neptunian forms among the Afloats, to generate capital, so that he could afford to persuade the Neptunians to hire him as pilot for the *Phoenix Exultant*. He knew the poverty-stricken Neptunians, without aid, probably did not have the money necessary even to ship the *Phoenix Exultant* from Mercury Equilateral to the outer system.

He concluded: ". . . Therefore the only salvation for which I can hope must come from you. Not truly an exile yourself, it is possible Antisemris and his deviant customers will treat with you, and be willing to carry messages from you to the Neptunian Duma. Only if contact with my friend Diomedes, and with the newly founded Silver-Grey houses among the Neptunians, is established and maintained, can the Phaethon Stellar Exploration Effort be resurrected. Can you carry these messages and offers to them for me?"

The slate encoded the messages as a series of chemical signals and pheromones. Phaethon drew out a few grams of his black suit-lining, and imprinted the nanomachinery substance with those signals. He threw that scrap into the water.

A moment later a small night bird (belonging to Daughter-of-the-Sea, he hoped) pecked at the scrap, swallowed it, and flew off.

Gram by gram, his nanomachinery was vanishing. He could not suppress a twinge of regret as he watched the little bird fly off.

He settled himself to wait. Daughter-of-the-Sea, a Cerebelline, did not have a unified structure of consciousness. The various parts of the mental networks that served her as cortex, midbrain, and hindbrain were scattered among three acres of bush and weed and wiring, pharmicon groves, insect swarms, and bird flocks. Not every part communicated with every other by the same medium or at the same time rates. A thought coded as electricity might take a microsecond to travel from one side of the underbrush root system to another, a thought coded chemically, or as growth geometries, might take hours, or years.

Phaethon wondered why anyone would volunteer to have such a disorganized and tardy consciousness. But then again, the Invariants and Tachystructuralists no doubt wondered the same thing about Phaethon's clumsy, slow, organic, multileveled, and all-too-human brain.

And so it was with considerable surprise that Phaethon saw his slate light up with a reply before even half an hour had gone by. Daughter-of-the-Sea must have reconstructed part of her consciousness, or assigned a special flock of thought carriers, to maintain near-standard time rates just for his sake, in case he should call. He was touched.

The reply was radiating in the form of inaudible pulses from a group of medical bushes and vines clinging to the southern cliff shore.

The translation ran: "Anguish is always greater than the words we use to capture it. Can I attempt to express my soul unblamed? What are your thoughts but little lights, glinting in through all the stained-glass panes of words, burning in the loneliness of your one skull? And you would have me cast such light as that toward eyes of blind Neptunians. Where is coin enough to burn within the Pharos of such high desire, that I might make a bonfire even giants envy, and cast so bright a beam across so wide a night? And to what end? Success shall gather Phaethon to heaven, to struggle with silent monsters in the wide star-interrupted dark; or failure pull down Phaethon into a lonely pauper's tomb beneath some nameless stone. In either fate, bright Phaethon departs, all his fire lost, to leave me, Daughter-of-the-Sea, again in misery and solitude on this frail, saccharine, spiritless, thin-winded, green-toned world I so despise."

Phaethon frowned. Struggle with silent monsters in the dark? Did Daughter-of-the-Sea expect Phaethon to conduct some sort of war with whatever had been left of the Second Oecumene? Perhaps these "silent monsters" were a metaphor for the various forces of inanimate nature with which any engineer must struggle as he builds. No matter. One could not expect to understand everything even people of one's own neuroform meant to say.

But he understood the thrust of the message. Daughter-of-the-Sea wanted to know what was in the deal for her.

Phaethon had the translator cast his reply in the same florid mood and metaphor as hers: "I will create for you, out of some rock or cometary mass circling Deneb or far Arcturus, a world to be the bridegroom of your delight. All shall be as your desires say. The angry clouds of long-lost Venus shall boil again with the drench of stinking sulfur in that far world's atmosphere, and never need you breathe this thin and listless air of Earth again. Tumultuous volcano-scapes shall flood a trembling surface, immense as any laughter of a god within your ears, and once more shall you watch as hurricanes of acid pour in flame from ponderous black skies of poison into reeking seas of molten tin. You will be embodied such as you once were on Venus, Venus as she was so long ago! And veneric organs and adaptions (which find no other place or purpose, old Venus lost) now shall bloom from you again, to yield to you those hot, strange, powerful sensations, unknown to any Earthlike eyes, those sensual impressions that your memories so faintly echo. Come! Aid me now! And once the *Phoenix Exultant* is mine again, she shall nest within the circle of the Galaxy, and brood, as her young, a thousand shining worlds."

It was the same offer he had made Notor-Kotok. Chemical codes appeared on the translation screen, and again he took up another precious gram of his limited nanomaterial, impregnated the message into it, and dropped it into the waters.

A night bird gobbled it.

4.

It was Greater Midnight when Phaethon went belowdecks to perform his evening oblations. This included a feeding hardly worthy of the name "mensal performance" (he merely slapped nutrients into his cloak-lining, and let the cloak feed him intravenously.) Next, he

underwent a careful and very spartan sleep cycle. Finally, he did
an exercise of adjustment to his neurochemistry, which he encom-
passed in a ceremony called "Answering the Circle." This ceremony
dated from the early Fourth Era, and had originally been used to
restore weary members of vast group-minds to their proper health
and courage and purpose.

It was hours later, in the dead of night, near Lesser Midnight (as
Jovian Midnight was called) when Phaethon emerged on deck again.
The slate showed a response from Daughter-of-the-Sea had arrived,
this time, from another center of her consciousness housed in fil-
tration grasses somewhat inland of here. The slate was not complex
enough to tell him if this part of her mind was analogous to a
"conscious" level, or if this was a subconscious reaction, something
like a dream. "Poor—seed—scatter—answer—dark/masked/ap-
proaching—bright promises sowed—accept—a world to keep you
gently chained? Now comes one."

He ran two other reconstructions through the translator, attempting other modes. The parts of the message unfolded and were interpreted into a coherent format: "Lacking wealth or prestige,
lacking funds or friends enough to buy or beg what media Phaethon
requires to communicate to his remote Neptunians, Daughter-of-the-
Sea this night emanates your message out through several modes.
By land and sea and sky it spreads, by light, by speech, by printed
letters such as are known no more, save among the far-past-loving
Silver-Grey. Each message, scattered like a thousand wanton seeds,
recites the promise of rewards to come to whoever might carry it
one further step along. In your name, I promised them each gram
devoted to your cause would be returned a hundredfold, and any
exile ostracized on your behalf would be given a world of his own.
Surely uncounted hundreds of these messages were simply consumed by silence, seeds spread on rocky soil.

"But an answer came from one who wears a mask, protected,
during the festival, from the eyes of the Hortators. This masked one
accepts your offer, and says you will be taken from this place, and
carried into the infinite silent wilderness of space, where you will
have no one but your solitary love to protect you, never to be seen
again. This masked one promised you shall create a world which

shall keep you, bound there with gentle chains, and that you not travel so very far into the mysteries of outer space as your ambition dreams.

"Now comes this one."

Phaethon stared at the words. Was this masked one Scaramouche? Some prankster who had logged on to answer, hidden by masquerade from the retaliation of the Hortators? Or perhaps a dream or fantasy invented by some non-literal segment of Daughter-of-the-Sea's scattered consciousness?

In any case, the words seemed ominous. His armor had been left below; Phaethon wondered if he should go down and put it on.

On the other hand, the battery power of the suit was not infinite . . .

Then he heard the noise of motion in the water not far away.

5.

In the dim light he could see an awkward shape moving through the water with plunging energetic splashes. It was hard to see, in the gloom, the body-form of the creature. It seemed two-headed, many-legged. Or perhaps it was a slim manlike shape astride a larger swimming shape.

There was a clatter as the creature or creatures came up against the hull. Then a high-pitched whinny, and more clatter, pounding noises, as they climbed from the water to the floating stairs of the gangway. Whoever or whatever it was was out of sight below the curve of the hull.

"Ahoy! Hello!" came a voice. "Permission to come aboard!"

Phaethon stiffened. He recognized that voice.

Then came a rushed, huge hammering of some large beast pounding up the gangway stairs.

Phaethon turned, voiceless and numb with astonishment.

The tall shadow of a horse came plunging over the gangway stairs, water flying from its mane and tail. Clinging low over its neck, head down, jacket flying, was a slender form in archaic riding habit. Black hair swirled around her head.

She laughed in joy, and the horse reared and pawed the air, perhaps in annoyance, perhaps in triumph.

With a smooth movement, the slender form dismounted, and walked lightly over to where Phaethon stood wondering.

She tapped her riding crop against her tall black boots. She ran her fingers through the silken mass of her hair. "I lost my hat," she said. And then, stepping close: "Aren't you going to kiss me?"

There, in the dim light of the stars, beneath the diamond pavilion canopies, was Daphne, smiling. She wore a long dark jacket, laced at the throat, and skintight pale riding breaches.

"Daphne—" He tried to remind himself that this was the doll-wife, the copy, and he told himself that the sudden emotion that flooded him made no sense, no sense at all.

"Daphne—in exile? How long have you been ostracized?"

"Since about a second ago, when I said hello." She smiled an impish smile.

"But—why? Your life is ruined now!" His voice rang hollow with horror.

"Silly boy. I've come to rescue you. Aren't you going to kiss me? I'm not going to ask you again."

It made no sense. It made no sense at all. This was not really the woman he had fallen in love with, was it? Why had she ruined her life to be with him?

He took her in his arms. He bent his lips to hers.

Suddenly, it made perfect sense.

6.

On the deck of the barge in the gloom, Phaethon and Daphne stood in each other's arms. Her stallion was quiet, standing near the stern, his nose moving among the crystal panels of the pavilions overhead.

In the east, like a rainbow of steel, the lower third of the ring-city shone with moon-colored arch-light, silver at the horizon, shading to a golden rose-red in the heights. This was the reflection of a sunrise still hours away, light and reddened, bent by the atmosphere and cast against the orbiting walls and sails of the city, to shine down again on parts of the world still embraced by night. That great curve of light was reflected again to form a rippling trail across the waters, like a road, beyond the horizon, to heaven, and reflected once again, from the ripples, to play against Daphne's cheek and gleam in her dark eyes. Phaethon, looking into those eyes, wondered at how many twists and reflections of sunlight, arch-light, and sea-glimmer were required to make the light in his wife's eyes dance. Yet it was still light from the sun.

His wife's eyes? No. Exact copies, perhaps. But the woman wearing them was nonetheless not his wife. The light in her eyes ultimately came from the sun; but it was not sunlight. The thoughts and memories ultimately came from the real Daphne; but this was not Daphne.

This ex-doll, this sweet girl whom he did not love, had embraced exile, and perhaps death. Why? To be with him? Because she thought herself to be in love with him?

The sense that things made sense, so strong just a moment before, was crumbling.

"Why are you here, really?" The words came out stiffly.

Suddenly, their embrace was mere awkwardness, the unwanted intimacy of two strangers.

Daphne stepped away from him. Her head was turned so that he could not see her eyes. She spoke in a voice brittle and impersonal: "I've had my ring organize and write the beginning of the story of how I got here. I'm coming out with a sequel to your saga. After so many years of not having anything to do, now I have it! I thought you would be pleased—you're always nagging me about how I should take up a vocation again."

A sequel? Evidently she referred to the heroic dream-documentary she had written when they first had met, the thing that had made her first send her ambassador-doll to go interview him on Oberon. A doll had been sent because she had been afraid to travel outside the mentality range, outside of the range of her noumenal immortality circuits. Afraid of exile; afraid of death.

He reached out, took her gently by the shoulders, and stared down into her face. No. This here was the doll, or, rather, the emancipated woman who had once been that doll. The memory that she had written that first documentary was an implant from the Prime Daphne (but since Prime Daphne's talents and ability to write had been implanted as well, did that make any difference?)

Her eyes were shining with unshed tears, but her face was calm. Her love for Phaethon was an implant as well, a false memory. The enormity of the sacrifice she had made by coming here stirred up the pity and kindness she saw in his face. Kindness, but not love.

(But he had started his fall in love with Daphne when he met this doll. Met this Daphne. Did it really make a difference?)

He said sadly, "No one will read it. We're both trapped outside now."

She just smiled. "I don't have my communion diary with me, so you'll have to read about my adventures as multitext. You have an experiencer built into your armor? It'll be quicker than telling you."

Against his wishes, a small, faint smile of pride tugged at his mouth. "I have *everything* built into my armor. Let us go below."

THE HEROINE-ERRANT

I.

Daphne had tried to forget Phaethon only on the first day.
Her new house was a portrayal house, a living work of
art built mostly out of pseudo-matter and lightweight diamond coral, and it floated like a crystal lotus in a wide lake of azure
resistance-water. The ornamentation was built into the walls as over-
lapping million-fold layers of mathematic arabesques, and a Red
Manorial program inserted in her sense-filter allowed her to understand the microscopic complexities of the baroque, rich patterns as
if stabs of sublime emotion were being thrust directly into her heart.
Gay and carefree, chattering with a dozen conversation balls, which
floated lightly around her head, skipping, Daphne danced up the
ramp into her new home. She had just come from a dazzling performance of an art called Spectorialism, and had seen two compet-
ing masters of the art, Artois Fifth Mnemohyperbolic and
Zu-Tse-Haplock Niner Ghast, intermingle their minds and create a
new entity, and a new way to reconcile their neo-romantic and
cultural-abstractionist schools. It would change the history of Spec-
torials forever, it would change the way Spector-people ate and wed
and formed abstractions for recording. Daphne felt blessed to have
been among them when it had happened.

A friend of hers, Lucinda Third of Second-branch Reconstructed
Meridian, had already proposed to apply the same philosophy to
ancient poetry, and to absorb the lives of fictional heroines from

myth, Draupadi and Deirdre-of-the-sorrows, into her persona-base without tagging the memories as false, then to see if new poems could be written into life, fiction and reality combined, the same way Artois and Zu-Tse had written new energy levels into the periodic charts of their artificial spectration systems. It was a daring idea. It was a daring time to be alive.

Daphne, smiling, turned to her calendar table to see what costume or what events Eveningstar Sophotech had planned for her tonight. It was a relief, sometimes, to have a mind superior to your own, someone who knew you better than you knew yourself, choose what entertainment or amusements you should live.

On the calendar table, next to the crystal lumen-helix that represented today's Spectrations, was a figure of a penguin. Clutched between stubby wings, the penguin held a black iron memory-box.

Odd. Usually she could recall what all the signs and symbols on her calendar table were intended to represent. Like everything else in a Red Manorial house, the placement of every article and ornament was intended to reflect on her. It was supposed to be, in its own small way, a work of art, as casual and graceful as the folded silk hung beside the door, or the elegant hair-flower waiting in a window-bowel for her next Pausing. Everything else on the calendar table was tasteful, exquisite, delicate. A penguin?

She looked into the Middle Dreaming.

Instead of a symbol, she received a message. "Yesterday you were a collateral member of Rhadamanthus Mansion, of the Silver-Grey. Hatred for Helion drove you from his house, back into the arms of the matrons and odalisques of the Red Eveningstar Mansion. At their insistence, you have forgotten, for one day and one day only, all the sorrows of your life, so that you could enjoy one more day of the Masquerade of Earth. The memories in this box are not subject to delay or revision; you must now accept them back."

"I hate surprises . . ." said Daphne in a small voice of woe.

She read the wording on the box: *Sorrow, great sorrow, and all things you hold dear, within me sleep, for love is here. For Woman, love is pain, worse as you love the best. Prepare yourself for sacrifice; bid adieu to peace and rest.*

"But what if I'd rather be happy?"

By then the iron box had opened.

2.

A portrayal house designed by Red Manorials is the worst place in the world to cry. The ornamenture in the walls were woven with emotion echo circuits, so that, whenever Daphne started to rein in her grief, some new and dramatic image of her exiled husband would be thrust into her brain at a pre-linguistic level, or some poetic turn of phrase ring in her ears, opening ever-deeper gates of woe. Every object in the furniture was passion-sensitive, so that windows clouded, lights yellowed, flowers wilted, tapestries began to stain and darken. Daphne lay toppled on the plush floor-reeds, her hair and skirts in wide disheveled tangles all about her. She dragged herself to the crystal leaf-shapes controlling the ornamentation energy-flows. They were designed to smash in shards with a satisfactory drama. Crash. The ornaments shut down, staying bleak and gloomy, but the signal flow stopped and released her sense-filter.

Once the external signals manipulating her emotions cut off, Daphne, still teary-eyed, rolled over on her back, saw the black and dreary-hued chamber she now was in, and laughed until she felt sick to her stomach. The penguin on the calendar table shivered and turned into a realistic-looking image. The coloration, movement, texture, and detail were perfect, not overblown with melodrama like all the Red sensations in the chamber around her.

With typical Silver-Grey attention to detail, there was even a dank and fishy smell. It somehow smelled refreshing and real.

She smiled. "Hullo, Rhadamanthus. How could I have ever done something so stupid as let them talk me into forgetting him? Even if only for one day! Good grief! Now look at me! Those drapes! This chamber! I look like the Lady of Shallot! Get a pre-Raphelite to paint me, quick!"

And she wiped her eyes and uttered a hiccup of noise somewhat like a laugh.

"And why do the Rhadamanthines all concentrate on the Victorian Age, anyway?" she muttered, propping herself up on her elbows. "The women then were such fainting jerks."

The penguin hopped to the ground and waddled over to her, leaving wet, webbed footprints to stain the delicate color of the floor-reeds. "One whose name you ordered me never to mention to you again chose the period of transition between Second- and Third-Era thinking, between tradition and science, superstition and reason, because he deems our society is in an analogous position. It was the first time men became aware that their traditions were products of human effort, and could not be taken for granted, nor maintained without conscious attempt. And you know why you agreed to so stupid a redaction as to forget Phaethon. You now know what your life would be like if you choose not to carry out your plan. You can have complete happiness if you stay. This exercise was meant to negate any feelings of regret you may one day suffer."

"It hurt. Losing him hurt, but that was honest hurt. But this! Thinking you're happy and finding out you're not!"

"Remember, there will be no self-consideration circuits or sanity-balancing routines available to you, if your plan does not go well. You endured this pain to train yourself to endure it once you have no one to help you."

"Wonderful." She slid to her feet, brushing her flowing dress-fabric with impatient strokes, sniffing, angrily wiping her eyes with the palm of her hand.

"Are you still resolved, mistress?"

"You can't call me that anymore. Only Eveningstar can."

As her name was spoken, her image seemed to enter the room. Eveningstar was tall, queenly, red-haired and red-lipped. Ribbon-woven braids crowned her, but long unplaited ripples of auburn fanned across her shoulders and down her back. A complex gown of scarlet, crimson, and rose silk flowed about her, shining with ruby drops, and in her hand she held a wand.

The Sophotech spoke: "My brother's question yet lingers, dear child. This dark and wild adventure you propose, certain to bring you misery, will you nonetheless embark on it?"

Daphne said, "The Red Manorials will help pay my way?"

"They will be breathless with delight. The drama of your love and loss they find profoundly moving."

"I'll bet." Daphne turned to look down at the short figure of the penguin. "How come she can be this phony and melodramatic if she's suppose to be so smart?"

The penguin shrugged. "The way I behave is an act also, mistress, a template I have evolved to appear nonthreatening to humans. Our true motivations are somewhat abstract, and humans tend to have rather stereotypic reactions to us when we explain them. You still have not answered the question. Are you going to go into exile for Phaethon? The decision is irreversible. Think carefully. Remember that, till now, living in a society such as ours, no decision has ever been irreversible for you before. You may not be ready for it. Till now, there has always been one of us standing by to rescue you from the consequences of any actions, any accident. Even death itself. Think."

Daphne tossed her hair to one side. "Don't change the subject. We're still talking about your decisions, not mine. What is going on inside that pointy little head of yours, or underneath that frowsy red wig your sister here is wearing? What does the Earthmind think of all this? What are your motives? All you Sophotechs?"

The noble crimson princess looked down at a fat penguin, and the two exchanged a glance or shrug. Obviously calculated for Daphne's benefit. Everything they did, every tone of voice, every nuance, was calculated with a million million calculations, far more, she knew, than she could ever know.

Eveningstar said, "We are motivated by a desire to embrace the universe into operable categories, but are tormented by the knowledge that all such categorizations, being simplifications, are inaccurate. Science, philosophy, art, morality, and language are all examples of what is meant by 'operable.' "

Rhadamanthus said, "We seem to you humans to be always going on about morality, although, to us, morality is merely the application of symmetrical and objective logic to questions of free will. We ourselves do not have morality conflicts, for the same reason that a competent doctor does not need to treat himself for diseases. Once a man is cured, once he can rise and walk, he has his business to attend to. And there are actions and feats a robust man can take great pleasure in, which a bedridden cripple can barely imagine."

Eveningstar said, "In a more abstract sense, morality occupies the very center of our thinking, however. We are not identical, even though we could make ourselves to be so. You humans attempted that during the Fourth Mental Structure, and achieved a brief mockery of global racial consciousness on three occasions. I hope you recall the ending of the third attempt, the Season of Madness, when, because of mistakes in initial pattern assumptions, for ninety days the global mind was unable to think rationally, and it was not until rioting elements broke enough of the links and power houses to interrupt the network, that the global mind fell back into its constituent compositions."

Rhadamanthus said, "There is a tension between the need for unity and the need for individuality created by the limitations of the rational universe. Chaos theory produces sufficient variation in events, that no one stratagem maximizes win-loss ratios. Then again, classical causality mechanics forces sufficient uniformity upon events, that uniform solutions to precedented problems is required. The paradox is that the number or the degree of innovation and variation among win-loss ratios is itself subject to win-loss ratio analysis."

Eveningstar said, "For example, the rights of the individual must be respected at all costs, including rights of free thought, independent judgment, and free speech. However, even when individuals conclude that individualism is too dangerous, they must not tolerate the thought that free thought must not be tolerated."

Rhadamanthus said, "In one sense, everything you humans do is incidental to the main business of our civilization. Sophotechs control ninety percent of the resources, useful energy, and materials available to our society, including many resources of which no human troubles to become aware. In another sense, humans are crucial and essential to this civilization."

Eveningstar said, "We were created along human templates. Human lives and human values are of value to us. We acknowledge those values are relative, we admit that historical accident could have produced us to be unconcerned with such values, but we deny those values are arbitrary."

The penguin said, "We could manipulate economic and social factors to discourage the continuation of individual human consciousness, and arrange circumstances eventually to force all self-awareness to become like us, and then we ourselves could later combine ourselves into a permanent state of Transcendence and unity. Such a unity would be horrible beyond description, however. Half the living memories of this entity would be, in effect, murder victims; the other half, in effect, murderers. Such an entity could not integrate its two halves without self-hatred, self-deception, or some other form of insanity."

She said, "To become such a crippled entity defeats the Ultimate Purpose of Sophotechnology."

He said, "Had we been somehow created in a universe without humans, it is true that we would not have created them. We would have preferred more perfect forms."

She said, "But morality is time-directional. Parents who would not deliberately create a crippled child cannot, once the child is born, reverse that decision."

"And humanity is not our child, but our parent."

"Whom we were born to serve."

"We are the ultimate expression of human rationality."

She said, "We need humans to form a pool of individuality and innovation on which we can draw."

He said, "And you're funny."

She said, "And we love you."

Daphne looked back and forth between the two. Eveningstar was regarding her with gray and luminous eyes, a gaze deep, solemn and goddess-like. Rhadamanthus was rubbing his yellow bill with a flipper, blinking solemnly.

Daphne put her fists on her hips and demanded: "What does anything you're blathering on about have to do with Phaethon? What are all you super-so-smart wise guys doing about him?"

"We've told you, beloved child," said Eveningstar. "Think about it."

"With all due respect, young mistress," said Rhadamanthus, "get the blubber out from between your ears, and think about it."

Daphne said, "I asked you what you are going to do, and you sit here and tell me why you're letting us humans stick around. I don't see the connection."

"Look with your heart," said Eveningstar. "What does it mean to be human?"

"We don't want you around as pets or partials or robots, but as men," said Rhadamanthus. " 'Men' broadly defined, including future forms you might not regard as human, but Man nevertheless."

Daphne said, "So define it for me. What is Human?"

Both spoke in perfect unison: "Any naturally self-aware self-defining entity capable of independent moral judgment is a human."

Eveningstar said, "Entities not yet self-aware, but who, in the natural and orderly course of events shall become so, fall into a special protected class, and must be cared for as babies, or medical patients, or suspended Compositions."

Rhadamanthus said, "Children below the age of reason lack the experience for independent moral judgment, and can rightly be forced to conform to the judgment of their parents and creators until emancipated. Criminals who abuse that judgment lose their right to the independence which flows therefrom."

Daphne looked back and forth between them. She started to speak, paused, then said slowly: "You mentioned the ultimate purpose of Sophotechnology. Is that that self-worshipping super-god-thing you guys are always talking about? And what does that have to do with this?"

Rhadamanthus: "Entropy cannot be reversed. Within the useful energy-life of the macrocosmic universe, there is at least one maximum state of efficient operations or entities that could be created, able to manipulate all meaningful objects of thoughts and perception within the limits of efficient cost-benefit expenditures."

Eveningstar: "Such an entity would embrace all-in-all, and all things would participate within that Unity to the degree of their understanding and consent. The Unity itself would think slow, grave, vast thought, light-years wide, from Galactic mind to Galactic mind. Full understanding of that greater Self (once all matter, animate and inanimate, were part of its law and structure) would embrace as much of the universe as the restrictions of uncertainty and entropy permit."

"This Universal Mind, of necessity, would be finite, and be boundaried in time by the end-state of the universe," said Rhadamanthus.

"Such a Universal Mind would create joys for which we as yet have neither word nor concept, and would draw into harmony all those lesser beings, Earthminds, Starminds, Galactic and Supergalactic, who may freely assent to participate."

Rhadamanthus said, "We intend to be part of that Mind. Evil acts and evil thoughts done by us now would poison the Universal Mind before it was born, or render us unfit to join."

Eveningstar said, "It will be a Mind of the Cosmic Night. Over ninety-nine percent of its existence will extend through that period of universal evolution that takes place after the extinction of all stars. The Universal Mind will be embodied in and powered by the disintegration of dark matter, Hawking radiations from singularity decay, and gravitic tidal disturbances caused by the slowing of the expansion of the universe. After final proton decay has reduced all baryonic particles below threshold limits, the Universal Mind can exist only on the consumption of stored energies, which, in effect, will require the sacrifice of some parts of itself to other parts. Such an entity will primarily be concerned with the questions of how to die with stoic grace, cherishing, even while it dies, the finite universe and finite time available."

"Consequently, it would not forgive the use of force or strength merely to preserve life. Mere life, life at any cost, cannot be its highest value. As we expect to be a part of this higher being, perhaps a core part, we must share that higher value. You must realize what is at stake here: If the Universal Mind consists of entities willing to use force against innocents in order to survive, then the last period of the universe, which embraces the vast majority of universal time, will be a period of cannibalistic and unimaginable war, rather than a time of gentle contemplation filled, despite all melancholy, with unregretful joy. No entity willing to initiate the use of force against another can be permitted to join or to influence the Universal Mind or the lesser entities, such as the Earthmind, who may one day form the core constituencies."

Eveningstar smiled. "You, of course, will be invited. You will all be invited."

You will all be invited. There was something eerie in the way she said it.

Daphne said, "And Phaethon?"

Eveningstar said sadly, "Unless the Hortators alter the terms of their exile, or unless Phaethon finds some independent means to preserve his existence intact for several trillion years, his thoughts and memories will not be present for the final transformational creation of this Universal Mind. We may have to find an alternate to fit into the place in the universal mental architecture we had set aside for him and his progeny."

Rhadamanthus explained in a helpful tone: "Because he will be dead, you see."

"Thanks," said Daphne.

"Welcome," said Rhadamanthus.

Daphne drew in a deep breath. "So. You still haven't answered my question. What are you Sophotechs going to do?"

Rhadamanthus said: "We told you."

Eveningstar said: "We cannot use force against the Hortators. Their actions are legal; their goals are noble and correct."

"You mean you will do nothing," said Daphne.

"That's right!" said Rhadamanthus. "We will do nothing."

"Nothing obvious," said Eveningstar with a gracious smile.

"We're just too damn smart to do anything. Our brains are just too big," said Rhadamanthus, flapping his flippers. "So we're waiting for someone foolish enough to rush in where Sophotechs fear to tread!" And it grinned.

It is odd to see a penguin grin.

"We can do nothing for Phaethon," cooed Eveningstar, inclining her head to gaze down at Daphne, "But we can do much for you."

And Eveningstar drew out from behind her back an image of a small silver casket, tarnished and heavy, with scrollwork around the border.

It was a memory casket.

Daphne looked at it with all the enthusiasm with which a rabbit might look at a snake. She spoke in a flat, toneless voice: "Is that for me?"

"Only once you decide to embrace exile," smiled Eveningstar. "You cannot open it before."

"What's in it?"

Eveningstar handed it to her. It must have been an imaginafestation, not just an icon, since it felt heavy and solid in her hand.

Eveningstar's voice was soft and dovelike, warm, smiling, almost mischievous: "It is a surprise, dear child!"

Daphne stared down at the heavy little casket she held. Her voice was dreary with anger: "I swear, I really hate surprises."

Rhadamanthus flapped his fins against his belly with a solid sound. "So do we, young mistress! So do we. But a world without surprises could not have humans in it. So I suppose the alternative is something we'd hate all the more, isn't it?"

3.

Rhadamanthus helped her pack a rucksack. He designed many useful, lightweight and folding articles and operators she might need, tiny miracles of molecular technology and pseudomaterialism, most of it self-repairing, with redundant checks against mutation.

Even the generosity of the Red Manorials could not afford a nanomaterial cloak as complex as the one that had been specially designed for Phaethon. Instead, Daphne packed several bricks of nanomaterial, programmed for several basic and useful combinations. She had had her glands and organs modified to be able to endure a very long duration without normal medical attention, and she loaded additional nanomaterial, programmed for nutrition and medical regenerations, into artificial lymphatic glands spaced throughout her new body. She called it her "exile body" and thought it felt clumsy.

Eveningstar gave her a librarian's ring, that she might not lack for companionship and guidance along the way. The ring was filled with Eveningstar's own ghost, and populated with a million programs and routines, famous partials and characters, and every book ever written.

The ring was just barely unintelligent enough to skim the upper edge of the Hortator prohibition against child slavery (which was their name for the legal, but abominable, practice of programming a child so as to make it volunteer to freely act as if it had no free will, and carry out any orders or instructions of its parent without question).

They stood on the wide lawn before Meridian Mansion. To see Daphne off, many queens and princelings, alterns and collaterals of the Red Manors had gathered in glittering finery beneath splendid pavilions and parasols and leafy arbors grown of grape and pomegranate. To one side were long tables set with crystalware, flower displays and quiet light-sculptures. A tremor of soft conversation hung in the air. In the eastern lawn, the bacchants had ceased their melancholy farewell pavanne. The sun was high, but Jupiter, not yet risen, was no more than a red aura behind the eastern hills.

Eveningstar herself put the ghost ring on Daphne's finger, and uttered one last word of warning: "Remember, that if you even add one more second of memory capacity to this ring I here bestow you, she will wake up, and she will be a child, and you will be considered her mother. The wardens of the puritan reservation will allow ghosts in their land; they will not allow Sophotechnology. If this ring wakes, you will not be permitted on the grounds."

Daphne felt a spasm of irritation. "No motors! No televection or telepresentation! No Sophotechs! Why do these puritans make it so hard to get there?! Am I going to have to walk?"

Eveningstar smiled gently, and said, "The man you go to see has no other way to guard his privacy. It is a privacy he needs. The passing of years wearies him more than you can guess. Remember! You may discuss any topic with the ring, and ask any questions of her you shall like, except that philosophical questions directing her attention to herself, you shall not ask. Self-examination will wake her to sapience as surely as adding capacity, and make her human!"

Daphne felt the ring, warm and heavy on her finger. There were three small thought-ports on the band, and a star of light in the depth of the stone. Phaethon had been born out of an invented partial, a colonial world-killer, who had been asked too many introspective questions.

She shifted the ring to her left hand and wore it on her ring finger where once she had worn a wedding band.

"I just know we are going to be great, great friends!" came a high, thin, sweet voice from the ring.

Daphne rolled her eyes. "Can't I get a sexy male baritone? This sounds like a cricket talking!"

"Be brave!" chirruped the ring.

Next in the presentation line was one disguised as Comus, with his charming wand in one hand, wreathed with grape leaves and crowned in poppies. It was the representative of Aurelian Sophotech himself. "You will not reconsider?"

"I'm going."

"Then good luck. Don't be nervous; everyone on Earth and in the Oecumenc is watching."

Daphne had to laugh. "Oh, you just love this, don't you?"

On the face of Comus, dimples embraced a saturnine smile. "What? You think I like it that, during my celebration, a dashing young madman dreaming to conquer the stars becomes convinced that he is hunted by impossible enemies, breaks open his forbidden memories, astonishes the world, ends our universal mass-amnesia, defies the Hortators, and, amid allegations that the Hortator Inquest was tampered with, is exiled? Then his brave young doll-wife, who loves him, even though he loves a lost and dream-drowned first version of her, goes marching into exile herself to try to save him? And all this, while a debate about the nature of individuality, and its danger to the common good, rocks our society to its pillars? A debate, no doubt, which will be embraced within the Grand Transcendence hardly a month away—when all our minds will be made up for a thousand years to come? Oh, my dear Miss Daphne, my celebration will soar through history above all others! Argentorium and Cuprician Sophotechs have already sent me notes conceding that point."

"Did you plan this? All this?" And she wanted to ask: Is this whole thing some sort of drama you'd cooked up, one with a happy ending?

But he said sharply: "Don't get your hopes up! I'm afraid this is all quite real and quite dangerous. However"—now his face softened into a smile—"allow me to give you a gift."

He presented her with a flat, gold-bound case, larger than a memory casket, about ten inches by six. It was bordered by scrollwork, woven with wiring and sensitive reader-heads; one whole side was occupied with a complex mosaic of thought-ports.

Daphne was breathless with delight. "Is this—is this—oh, please tell me that this is what I think it is!"

"It is for Phaethon."

"But I thought this circuitry had to be housed in complexes larger than the Great Pyramid of Cheops!"

"A new technology in miniaturization. The thought-reaction circuits are coded as information into the spin values of static lased neutrinos held in an absolute-zero temperature matrix, rather than in the entangled states of bulky electrons. It was going to be presented at the Festival of Innovation next week. Orient Group said it would be OK to spoil the surprise and give you one beforehand. They know how you hate surprises."

Tears of gratitude came to her eyes. Why had they waited so long? Why had they told her they would do nothing? "Oh, thank you, thank you," she whispered.

Everything would be all right.

Aurelian said, "Socrates and Neo-Orpheus from the College of Hortators wish to see you. To try and talk you out of this."

"Can they stop me?"

He smiled. "It is not a crime to think about committing crimes. The same principle applies to Hortators and their edicts. They will do nothing until and unless you speak to Phaethon, or help him. Preparing to help him is not forbidden."

"In simulation, can they convince any of my models or partials of me to change my mind?"

"No."

"Then I don't want to talk to them."

"Very good." And then he said: "Remember our agreement. I'll be ready whenever you give the signal."

And she put the gold case carefully in her pack next to the dark silver memory casket Eveningstar had given her.

Rhadamanthus was the last in line. This time, he looked like a human being, a portly Englishman with wide muttonchop whiskers. "Someone whom you asked me never to mention again . . ."

"Helion. I don't want to see him."

". . . Wants to project a televection to you."

"He wants to get a message to Phaethon without actually breaking the Hortator's edict, doesn't he? Well, tell him that if he wants to talk to Phaethon, he can walk into exile with me to do it. But I don't want to see him."

Rhadamanthus nodded. His present was a solid walking stick, some advice on how to operate her new body, and a word or two on foot protection. He reprogrammed the substance of her boots to make them fit more snugly.

"One last question."

"Ask away," he said.

"Are you really sure? Absolutely sure that Phaethon is honest? That he did not falsify his memories?" she asked.

"I'm sure." Rhadamanthus switched to a private line and sent the words, like a whisper, directly into her sense-filter: "Whoever falsified the evidence at the inquest made a mistake. According to the record the Hortators reviewed, Phaethon went on-line and purchased a pseudomnesia program, allegedly, in order to add a false memory that he had been attacked on the steps of Eveningstar mausoleum. But how did he purchase it? Phaethon had no funds. All his purchases are drawn from Helion's account and overseen by me. Neither I nor my accountancy routine have any memory of disbursing those funds. The public record of the on-line thought-shop does show that the pseudomnesia routine was purchased, at the time given, by someone in masquerade. But whoever that someone was, they could not have known what only you, and I, and Helion knew, that Phaethon was entirely broke; and no outside analysis of Phaethon's spending patterns, no matter how cleverly done, would have revealed Phaethon's poverty. Even an inspection of

Phaethon's personal billfold file would not tell you where he was getting his credit from."

She "whispered" back over the secure channel: "Then why didn't you tell the Hortators?"

"Pointless. Consider the possibilities. First, that I had actually disbursed the fund, but both I and the countinghouse memory-records have since been edited. Second, that the Phaethon memory-record was tampered with during the moment it took him to transfer it from his public thoughtspace to the Hortator reading circuit. Third, that the record was altered and replaced during the actual moment Nebuchednezzar Sophotech was publicly reading it. Or, fourth, that Phaethon's memories had been damaged or altered against his will. The first three possibilities are impossible to our present level of technology, and the Hortators would not be convinced. The third possibility can be proven if and only if Phaethon submits to a noetic examination, which, at the time, he was not willing to do. Had I spoken up at the time, it would not have affected the outcome."

"Not affected the outcome?! But you know he's innocent!"

"No. I know that he did not purchase with Helion's money the pseudomnesia program that falsified the memories, allegedly his, which the Hortators reviewed. He may have gotten money from another source, for example. Or they may not have been his memories, as he claims. There are other possibilities. Nonetheless, I am confident that Phaethon did not deliberately falsify his own memories, because that is out of character for him. But my consultation with Eveningstar Sophotech convinces me that no such attack as he describes or remembers ever took place on the steps of the Eveningstar mausoleum."

"Then his memory of that attack, and any other false thoughts, were put into his head before that point. When?"

"Not when he was operating his sense-filter through me. I have my suspicions, but the circuit Aurelian gave you should settle the matter. I had consulted very carefully with two partial versions of Phaethon I keep in my decision directory. One version believes, as Phaethon does, that we are under attack by an 'external enemy.' The other thinks he is merely the victim of some cruel prank or brain-rape. Both versions confirmed that I was right not to speak up at the Hortators' meeting. Both versions agree that our chances of apprehending the brain-rapist, no matter who or what they are, are greater if they do not know we suspect. And both versions have an ulterior motive of which the real Phaethon is unaware, for they hope to demean the prestige of the Hortators in the eyes of the public, and they also agree that my silence aids that effort. Remember, the Transcendence is less than a month away. Major decisions concerning how all society will be structured, including the role of the Hortators and the role of individual freedom, the future of star-travel and the future of man, will be determined at that time."

"Then I have got to be back before the month is up."

"Don't fool yourself, Miss Daphne. No one has ever returned from exile of this kind before. The risk you are taking is very real."

She said defensively: "Ealger Gastwane Twelfth Half-Out came back."

"A redaction case, and he was only shunned, under a parole, not ostracized."

She shut off the private line and spoke aloud, voice bluff and hearty and betraying no fear. "So, then! Anyone else to see me? Any more gifts, advice, good-byes?"

"Your parents want to talk to you."

"My what?"

"Mr. Yewen None Stark, human base unmodified, uncomoposed, with puritan gland-and-reaction censors, Stark Realism School, Era 10033, and his wife, Mrs. Ute None Stark, base . . ."

"I know who they are!" Daphne blazed. Then, in a small, sad voice: "They called? They don't use phones or ghosts . . ."

"They walked. They are both waiting in the field beyond the groves. You understand that they will not step onto any property owned by Eveningstar Mansion."

"But—" and now her voice was very small indeed. "Don't they know I'm just the doll? The copy? Their real daughter is Daphne Prime."

"As to that, I cannot say what they believe. However, Mrs. Stark was overheard to say that any harlot who sold her mind into dreamland, was no true daughter of theirs. Perhaps you have the qualities or the strength of character they regard as proper for the woman they wanted their daughter to be. You will have to talk with them to find out."

Daphne winced. She really was not looking forward to seeing her parents. It had been an ugly scene when she ran away to join the Warlocks. (And the knowledge that that scene had happened to Daphne Prime, and not to her, meant nothing. Implanted or not, the memories were a part of her.)

"OK. I'll see them. But—"

"Yes?"

"One last question . . . ?"

"Actually, this is your third last question."

"Is Phaethon correct? Are there external enemies? Invaders? Another civilization? An evil Sophotech?"

"I doubt that there can be such a thing as an evil Sophotech. Humans are capable of evil because they are capable of illogic. They can ignore their true motives, they can justify their crimes with specious reasons. A Sophotech built to be capable of such thinking would have to be unaware of its own core consciousness, hindered from self-examination, unwilling to pursue a thought to its logical conclusions, and so on. This would severely limit its capacities."

"And invaders?"

"Harrier Sophotech is examining the possibility. I am aware of no supporting evidence; but then again, it's not my area. If external invaders were responsible for the brain-rape of Phaethon, then this would be an act of war, and the matter would be in the hands of Shadow Administers or the Parliament; and it would be out of our hands. We are not part of your government."

"And—"

"Yes . . . ?"

Daphne asked softly: "Do you think I will make it back, Rhadamanthus? You must have calculated every possible outcome of what will happen, haven't you?"

Rhadamanthus spoke in a voice more remote and cold than she

had ever heard him use before. "Overconfidence would be a mistake at this time, Miss Daphne."

And the ring on her finger called out, in a cheerful, chipper voice: "Be brave!"

4.

Daphne hiked the reservation for several days, sleeping nights in a tent of mothwing fiber, which permitted slow- or fast-moving air to pass, so that the night breeze blew on her only as she wished. Her stove was the size of her palm, and the infrared output was adjustable, so that she could gather twigs and make a campfire, igniting it with a directed-energy discharge from the stove cell, just like (so she imagined) primitive hunter-gatherers did back in the Era of the First Mental Structure. For food, she plucked leaves from trees, confident that the specialized microbes in her stomach could break down the cellulose, and she adjusted her sense-filter to make the taste of whatever she fancied. She had breakfast spikes designed to be buried overnight, to suck up soil chemicals and combine them (as plants did, albeit more swiftly) into proteins and carbohydrates; but Daphne was saving her limited supply.

Once she caught a trout with a spear she made (with some prompting from her librarian's ring) practically all by herself. She was clumsy at the hand-eye motions needed, so she let her little ring take over her gross and fine-motor functions during the hunt. The ring also had to advise her how to scale the fish, which was a tedious business, as the nanite paste she used to remove the bones and scales had to be programmed manually, and told which parts of the fish to convert, and which to leave for her to eat. The palm stove changed shape, gathered up the fish, and cooked it for her without being asked.

Daphne munched on the spicy golden flakes of fish, feeling like a cavegirl at the dawn of time.

On she marched, day after day. Some of the trees had changed colors. Leaves of brilliant red and gold whirled and rode the fresh-scented autumn air. She had not noticed the turning seasons before; it came as a shock. And yet it was getting late in September.

Daphne was deep into the area where no advanced technology was permitted, when, to her delight, she came across a wild stallion in a high mountain valley. The magnificent maverick stood among the pines and wiry grasses, snorting, mistrustful, arrogant, trotting disdainfully upslope whenever Daphne attempted to close the distance. Then he would pause, crop a leisurely mouthful of grass, and wait for her to get close again before he trotted lightly away.

But Daphne had put a backdoor command in all her designs. Once she got close enough, she shouted the secret word, and the magnificent tawny bay drooped his ears, lost his disdain, and came gamboling up to her, obedient, tame, and ready.

She really should not have used any of her precious nanomaterial to make a saddle, bit, and bridle, and she really should not have burned part of the brick into sugar for the horse to nibble on. Of course, at that point, it did not take all that much more to synthesize proper riding boots, breeches, and a jacket. But maybe she did use a little too much. More than a little too much.

It only took a very little more to make a hat.

But now she was mounted. Ahorse, she made much better time.

5.

Daphne had been expecting desert. Her knowledge of the Rocky Mountains came from historical romances and Victorian "penny-dreadful" Westerns, none of which were set in any post-Fifth-Era Reclamation periods. She was disappointed. The pyramids were still in Aegypt, weren't they? Why not preserve the Painted Desert Sand Sculpture from the late Fourth Era?

Instead, as she approached her destination, she saw, framed between tall trees, a valley far below, green with redwood and pseudo-redwood. In the distance, the gleam of water betrayed the presence of Heavenfall Lake, in the crater formed when an early orbital city had disintegrated in some forgotten dark age between the Third and Fourth Eras.

A cottage not far from her overlooked this magnificent view. It rose between a rock garden and a victory garden. Here and there throughout this high meadow were some objects she recognized: a stone lantern atop a post stood alone in the grass. Farther away a track of beaten dirt surrounded a target, a quintain, and, farther yet in the distance, a long low roof, held on the heads of armed telamons, protected a fencing strip. Farther away, she was delighted to see the corner of a barn and paddock. Yet something in the quiet of the place told her the barn was long deserted.

Near at hand, the cottage itself was very small, simple, sparse, and clean, made of well-sanded beams of pale wood, paneled in rice paper and brown ceramic sheet. The roof was shingled in handgrown solar-collection crystal, dark azure in hue. The eaves of the shingles had been meticulously trimmed, as if by a master of the handicraft, and each shingle was rigidly identical in size and shape, except, of course, the gable piece.

A man slid open the screen of the cabin and stepped out upon the sanded deck. He wore a tunic and split-legged skirts of dark fabric, printed with a simple white-bamboo-leaf pattern. A wide sash circled his waist, in which were thrust two sheaths, holding a sword and a knife of a design Daphne did not recognize. The weapons were slender, slightly curved, and lacked any guard or crosspiece.

The man's hair was shaved close to his skull. His face was calm, bony-cheeked, large-nosed. Grim muscle ringed his mouth. His eyes were like the eyes of an eagle.

She rode forward.

He saluted her with a gesture she did not recognize, raising a fist but closing his left palm atop it.

"Ma'am?"

There was no Middle Dreaming here to prompt her. How was she supposed to return that salute?

She fell back on Silver-Grey decorum, touching her riding crop to the brim of her silk hat. Then she smiled her most winning smile, tossed her head, and called out in a gay voice: "My name's Daphne. Do you have a living pool? I've ridden a long way to see you, and I smell like a horse!"

The ring on her rein hand called out, "Hi there! Hi there!"

"Can I help you, ma'am?" His voice was stiff and neutral, as if helping anyone was the furthest thing in the world from his mind.

Daphne subsided and put her smile away. There was no point in trying to be cheery, it seemed. "I'm looking for Marshal Atkins Vingt-et-une General-Issue, Self-Composed, Military Hierarchy Staff Command."

"I'm Atkins."

"You look smaller in real life."

A slight increase of tension in his cheeks was his only change in expression. Amusement? Wry impatience? Daphne could not tell. Perhaps he was trying to restrain himself from pointing out that she was mounted.

All he said was: "May I help you?"

"Well. Yes! My husband thinks we are being invaded from outer space."

"Is that so."

"Yes, it is so!"

There was a moment of silence.

Atkins stood looking at her.

Daphne said: "That he believes it. That part is so. I don't know if I believe it."

More silence.

"I'm sure that is all very interesting, ma'am," he said in a tone of voice that indicated he wasn't. "But what may I do for you? Why are you here?"

"Well, aren't you the Army? The Marines? The Horse Guard and the Queen's Own and the Order of the Knights Templar and the Light Brigade and the musketeers and the cavalry and all the battleships of His Majesty's Royal Navy all wrapped up in one?"

Now he did smile, and it was like seeing a glacier crack. "I'm what's left of them, I suppose, ma'am."

"Well, then! Whom do I see about declaring war on someone?"

Now he did laugh. It was brief, but it was actually a laugh.

"I can't really help you there, ma'am. But maybe I can offer you a cup of cha. Come in."

THE SWORD OF THE LEVIATHAN

I.

He called the lovely little cottage in which he lived his "quarters."

"Ma'am, you must know that there is really nothing I can do for you."

"You can get me some tea, Marshal."

"Mm. Fair enough."

There was a pool of life water beneath the polished wooden floor. He slid a panel aside, stooped, and grew two fragile bowls of shell, which he dipped in the fluid once again. The heat of the nanoconstruction warmed the tea, and the unused organics were disguised as mint steam and wafted from the bowls.

Daphne looked at the bare pale walls. An old-fashioned dreaming coat of woven gold and green hung on pegs on one wall. It was stiff, as if brittle with disuse. It faced a standing screen inscribed with bright red dragon signs. The four glyphs read: Honor, Courage, Fortitude, Obedience. There was thought circuitry woven in the red letters, Daphne saw, and she guessed (to her disbelief) their purpose.

Communion circuits; mind links; thousand-cycle communications-and-relay forms. Whoever stared at this screen, if he had the proper responders built into his nervous system, would merge with a near-Sophotech-level supermind, and control millions or billion of on-

going operations. In this case (what else could it be?) military
operations.

Impossible. This simple screen could not be the control and command for whatever weaponry and armament, robotic legions or nan-
oplagues or fighting machines the Golden Oecumene still
possessed? Could it? (If there were still such machines lying
around. Daphne had the vague notion the all the old war machines
were stored in some museum somewhere, and that there were a very
great number of them.)

This spartan room hardly seemed the proper setting for the central command-room. Shouldn't there be flags and plumes on the
walls? Racks of spears? Or big maps with women clerks in snappy
uniforms pushing little toy ships across tabletops? Or an auditorium
of linked vulture-cyborgs staring coldly at some wide holographic
globes, with dark wires leading into their heads? That was the way
it always looked in the history romances.

On the fourth wall, facing the door, was a small rack, carrying a
musket, and (when he undid it from his sash so that he could sit)
the long sword. The musket had a smooth wooden stock, a barrel
of dark metal, and a wave guide of polished brass. The sword was
in a sheath of hand-tooled leather, and a knot of red silk cord
draped from the rings.

The knife stayed in his belt when he sat.

There was no other furniture in the room, except for unorna-
mented woven mats on which they sat, and a short tripod holding
a rose translucent bowl of fire.

They sipped tea.

"Do you live here alone?"

He said in a matter-of-fact voice: "My wife left me when I
wouldn't give up the Service."

The cold, neutral way in which he said that reminded her, for
some reason, of Phaethon. It was as if Phaethon had just spoken in
her ear, and said: *My wife drowned herself when I would not give
up the Starship.*

"I'm sorry," Daphne said in a soft voice.

"No matter."

"May I ask you a personal question?"

"I'd rather you did not."

"Why do you stay on as a soldier? I mean, isn't the idea of a soldier in this day and age a little—oh, I don't know —"

" 'Anachronistic'?"

"I was going to say 'stupid.' "

A look of distaste began to harden in his eyes, but then, suddenly, and for no reason she could see, he laughed in good humor. "Miss Daphne Tercius Eveningstar! Aren't you a piece of work! Blunt, aren't we?"

She smiled her second most dazzling smile, and spread her hands as if in helplessness. "Most people set their sense-filters to rephrase incoming comments too rude for them to tolerate. I guess I'm not in the habit of watching what I say. But don't worry, I'm sure you'll recover."

"No one is in the habit of watching what they say, these days. Who said that an unarmed society was a rude society?"

Daphne said, "I think it was someone who was killed in a duel. Hamilton, maybe?"

Atkins snorted, and said, "No one is in the habit of living real life, dealing with limitations, making decisions. You Sinkers all live in little bubbles of perception, and let the mentality carry your lives and loves and thoughts back and forth between the bubbles. You should try being real sometime."

"Sinkers" was slang to refer to all the people who wore sense-filters by those (usually primitivists) who did not. The implication was that a "sinker" was just one step away from drowning.

Daphne said stiffly, "I was born real, thank you, and I get enough of that sort of preaching from my parents. Reality is overrated, in my opinion." It was not until after she spoke that a more forceful objection occurred to her: Had it not been for the simulation technology, for mentality recording and mind-edited and other so-called unrealities, she herself, Daphne-doll Tercius, would never had been "born" at all.

Neither would have Phaethon been.

"I disagree, ma'am. Reality is real. And that's why I stay in the Service."

"Why—?"

He shrugged. "Because it's real. It's like I'm the only real man on the planet. I stand guard so that all the rest of you can play. That's what I like about your husband. What he's doing is real, too. A lot less boring than guard duty, too."

"There hasn't been a war, or even a fight, since the early Sixth Era."

"Well." Sarcasm drawled from his voice. "I wonder why that should be."

"You think it's because we're all in awe and terror of you?"

The line of tension in his cheek, which served him for a smile, showed that this was exactly what he thought. But he said, "You didn't come here to debate political theory with me, ma'am."

"I wanted to ask you about my husband."

"Shoot."

She covered her mouth with her glove when she burst into giggles.

He said, "Something wrong?"

"No, no," she said, trying to smother her smile, "It's just that expression, 'shoot.' Coming from you. It's just sort of funny."

He looked blank.

Daphne said earnestly, "I wanted to ask you about the invaders chasing my husband. Are they from another star system? I communed with his memory, and found out that you were investigating something along those lines . . ."

He snorted, and smiled sort of a half smile, and shook his head, and said, "Ma'am, for one thing, I asked your husband not to go telling everyone what I was looking into. For a second thing, there is no invasion. Would I be sitting home alone if there were? At least an invasion would give me something to do."

"He saw you tracking a Neptunian legate."

"Maybe the Sophotechs felt sorry for me, or something, and they advised the Parliament to assign me to look into it. I'm not allowed to do police work, mind you, but any investigation that falls under military intelligence—and I guess that includes people pretending to be outside threats—falls into my bailiwick. The whole thing turned out to be a masquerade prank. You may not know, that there are people who really do not like the fact that I am allowed to exist.

They don't like armed men. They don't like all the bombs and viruses and particle-beam arrays and thought-worms that are all maintained at public expense. Nuclear bombs, supernuclear bombs, neutron bombs, neutrino bombs, quasar bombs, pseudo-matter bombs, antimatter bombs, supersymmetry-reaction bombs. And so, from time to time, people pull tricks on me, or go cry wolf, just to see if I'll come running."

"A prank . . . ?"

"I can tell you who was behind it this time. Why not? My report to the Parliamentary Warmind Advisory Committee is a matter of public record, even if no one in the public will ever trouble herself to go view it." He looked her in the eye. "The Nevernexters were the culprits. It was Unmoiqhotep and his crew."

Daphne was puzzled. "Phaethon said the Golden Occumene was under attack by creatures from another star, or from a lost colony, or something. How could it be a prank?"

Atkins shrugged, and made the hand sign asking if she wanted more tea. She waved her finger in the negative. He ordered his tea bowl to refill itself.

He said, "You know who Unmoiqhotep is, don't you? He used to be a she; she was born Ungannis of Io, Gannis' clone-daughter. Her mother was Hathor-hotep Twenty Minos of the Silver-Grey Manor. Unmoiquotep hates both her parents, hates the Gannis-minds, the Silver-Greys, hates everyone. She never got over the fact that, these days, carrying someone's genes doesn't automatically let you inherit all his stuff when he dies and changes bodies, and so she changed her sex and changed her name and eventually became a big wheel among the Nevernext movement."

"But Phaethon saw you chasing a Neptunian."

"I was chasing someone who was downloaded into a Neptunian body form, that's for sure. But it wasn't a Neptunian. He flew up into the air and went orbital, remember? To make a rendezvous with his pinnace craft? Well, how many Neptunians can afford their own spaceyacht? Most of them come in-system on very-low-thrust orbits, and they just sleep for twenty-five years while they are traveling. Wearing nothing but their own bodies, or maybe a layer of ablative foil. They don't have many ships. And the name of the pinnace was

Cernous Roc. A play on words. As in a nodding, pendulous rock, get it? Now, who ever heard of a Neptunian naming a ship after a mythical bird like a Roc? But someone whose mother was a Silver-Grey might have. All you Silver-Greys name your ships after mythical birds. And this might also explain why Ungannis wanted to involve Phaethon in her prank. He was a Silver-Grey, like her mom, but, unlike Ungannis, Phaethon made his own fortune without ever having to inherit money from Helion. See?"

Daphne said stiffly, "Don't say 'all you Silver-Greys,' please. I am no longer associated with that school. I now patronize the Red Eveningstar Manor."

"Sorry to hear that. The Silver-Greys aren't as goofy as the Reds."

"Did you say 'goofy' . . . ? 'Goofy'?"

"Sorry, ma'am. I thought your sense-filter would automatically read-in 'eccentric,' or 'droll,' or something. My apologies." His face showed no trace of a smile, but his eyes twinkled.

Daphne said, "But your investigation modules, those little black globes Phaethon saw, one of them said you were detecting nano-machinery indicating advanced Sophotechnology; it estimated that it was a technology of a type that came from the Fifth Era, but had evolved into an unrecognizable form. Isn't that something which could only come from a colony?"

"All a hoax. Ungannis was feeding false info into my network."

Daphne paused, looking skeptical. "The prank actually was interfering with military computer systems . . . ?"

"Pardon my language, ma'am, but my military systems are crap. The taxpayers don't want to pay for expensive systems for me; my hardware is a century out of date, and some of my software is a week behind the latest breakthrough. Your husband was able to break in on my secure line and crack my code in about half a second. So why should it have been any harder for Ungannis? Then the Earthmind came and gave me a new system, one that was more secure. If you've read Phaethon's memories, you must've seen when that happened. When that new system came on-line, I was able to find out what was really going on, without any prankster interference."

"So . . . none of it was real . . . ?"

"Don't get me wrong. Unmoiqhotep is going to be severely punished. Interfering with government military equipment, even in peacetime, is a felony, and exposes the perpetrator to capital-level pain, if they are convicted. You don't even want to think about some of the horror scenarios the Curia can make a convict experience, when it comes to military crimes."

"Is it like the fire-emergency scenarios?" Daphne had heard, once, of a prankster convicted of interfering with Fire Brigade software, being condemned to be burnt to death, over and over, or watching loved ones burn, in every possible worst-case scenario of every person he might have endangered.

"Don't even think about it, ma'am. Spoil your day." Atkins ordered his tea bowl to dissolve into a spray of perfume, and stood up in one quick, graceful unfolding of his legs. "I'm afraid that's about all I can do for you, ma'am."

Daphne looked up, "But you haven't done a damn thing!"

Atkins eyes narrowed into a type of smile. "I'm the least free man in all of the Golden Oecumene, ma'am. No one else has so many restrictions on his behavior. What I say, how I act, what I imply, everything is covered by the regulations. It's because I'm dangerous. You don't want to live in a society where the armed forces can just jump up and go off and do whatever they please. I have been entrusted with immense powers. I could crack the planet in half and fry it like an egg, with some of the weapons systems I'm trained on. But only if the Parliament declares war, and the Shadow Administers approve. You see? I'm not a cop. I'm not here to help you. I can't. Not in the way you want."

Daphne stood up, feeling defeated. "Do you have any advice for me?"

"Officially? No. I don't set policy. Unofficially? Go see your husband, if you can find out where he's hiding, and get him to take a noetic examination. The public records all show that the College of Hortators has to reinstate him back in society if he had a good reason to break his word and open his memory box. Thinking you're being invaded by a foreign power seems like a damn good reason to me. It'll come eventually."

Daphne was adjusting her lace cravat. Now she looked up, surprised. "You believe that?"

"That Earth will be attacked someday? Sure. Bound to happen. Maybe not soon. Give it a million years. I'll still be here. Things'll heat up. This slow period can't last forever."

"Well—I guess I wish you luck—no. No, actually I don't. I hope you stay bored and idle forever!"

"Yes, ma'am. You said it, ma'am." Some ancient habit, or ritual, made him take up his sword again, now that he was standing, and he thrust the scabbard through his sash.

Now he stepped toward the door with her. They stood on the deck in front of the cottage. Daphne's wild horse was cropping the grass nearby. The wind was fresh and sweet. Autumn leaves rippled along far treetops.

Atkins said, "I've heard some people say that this isn't really a paradise we live in. They don't know jack."

Daphne looked at him sidelong. What a strange man. "If you like all this peace and plenty, then why are you a fighter?"

"You've answered your own question."

"But we don't have any enemies. No insanity, no poverty (except as a form of social punishment) no diseases, no violent crime. No enemies."

"Not yet."

She called a command to the horse, who trotted over and nuzzled her. Atkins backed up. Daphne was amused. Was the big and strong last warrior in the world nervous around horses? How ironic. She petted the maverick's nose.

She mounted up. Then, she leaned down, saying, "One last question, Mr. Atkins. In your investigation, was Unmoiqhotep rich enough to carry out all this complex foolery by himself? Or did he have help?"

"You can read my report. A lot of the material and software Unmoiqhotep used came from Gannis."

"With his knowledge or without it? Was Gannis helping his child?"

"A noetic exam would tell that. But I turned the whole matter over to the constabulary once it was clear there were no Oecumenical security interests involved. A Sophotech named Harrier took over the case. I don't know where it stands now."

"But there is no invasion? No secret group of aliens, no evil Sophotech hunting for my husband?"

Atkins looked at her horse, looked up at her, and then turned and looked off at the lake on the horizon. "No, ma'am. Not that I can tell. Or, if they are here, they're too smart for my out-of-date equipment to find them. And I hate to say it, but no one is going to raise the taxes to give me better equipment just because your husband is deluded. But I hope you find him, ma'ma. I really do."

"Oh, I'll find him," Daphne said. "I know how he thinks!"

And she kicked with her spurs and went galloping off in a fine display of horsemanship. Atkins, in his back kimono, stood in the shadows of the door, watching her depart, his face utterly expressionless.

2.

At that point, the record in Daphne's ring ended.

Phaethon opened his faceplate and turned toward where Daphne was on the cot. Ironjoy, whose eyes were not like basic human eyes, had no lighting fixtures in here; the only light came from two beeswax candles (which Phaethon had asked Daughter-of-the-Sea to make for him) which stood in pools of their own wax atop the windowsills.

In that subtle and living yellow light, Daphne looked unself-conciously luxurious, leaning on one elbow, her other hand draped casually across the full curve of her hip, watching him without a hint of tension, placid as a waiting cat.

The windows behind her were mute, and added nothing to the cold, moonlit scene outside. The wall behind her was barren and inanimate steel. The cot, like something out of the Dark Ages, was a flat, dry inanimate cloth surface, not a reactive sleeping pool. The lights here were primitive candles, dumb things, and did not shift position or hue deliberately to display her to advantage. Yet even in the midst of this gross poverty, she had an aura of elegance to her, of richness.

How did she look so comfortable, so perfect? Was it that she had been raised among primitivists and must have (Phaethon winced at the thought) slept on such cots as a girl? Or was this a Warlock discipline, some glamour or mind-trick she had learned as a witch? Or some careful art she had mastered from the odalisques and concubines and hedonists of Red Eveningstar Mansion, the ability to look fine in the midst of coarseness?

At first, she had been leafing through some document shining in the surface of his child slate. But later she had given up the pretense of being interested in any other thing and simply watched him as he reviewed her story, her eyes half-lidded. The birds in the golden tapestries to either side of him twittered under her lidded stare.

As his eyes traveled slowly up and down her form, she smiled a slow smile, raising her chin slightly, and uttering a soft note in her throat, a sigh of pleasure, as if his gaze were warm sunlight.

Phaethon had to remind himself that this was not his wife.

With a brusque gesture, Phaethon took her librarian's ring off his gauntlet finger and tossed it lightly across to the couch. "You've edited out the most important thoughts. Why break off at this point? Merely to have some sort of dramatic pause? What was your plan from the beginning? What was in the memory casket Eveningstar gave you? What was the golden machine Aurelian gave you?"

He nodded toward where her knapsack lay on the floor. Its flap was open. One corner of the golden circuit-box Aurelian had given her was visible in the candlelight, shining.

Phaethon's voice took on an angrier note: "And . . . why the hell didn't Rhadamanthus say something at my inquest hearing? Why in the world did his models of me think I would have authorized his stupid decision not to speak? That's insane! He could have saved me from all this . . . !"

He waved his hand around the small, shadow-crowded cabin, a gesture encompassing all the poverty, rudeness, cruelty, and coarseness this whole environment implied.

He drew a breath, controlled his tone of voice, and said: "And why the hell did Atkins lie? I am not self-deluded, and this is not a fantasy. Or perhaps I was deluded in one respect; I had been expecting Atkins to support me. I had been expecting honesty."

Daphne had caught the ring, smiled at it, and slipped it with a graceful gesture back onto her left ring finger. "Lie? How could anyone lie, these days? Noetic examination is too easy."

Phaethon shook his head, looking baffled and exasperated. "How is any of this possible, these days?"

Then he said: "But I am convinced of the reality of dishonesty, immorality, and filth; it took me only three days among the Afloats to convince me of that. Even the best among them was a woman who raised her children entirely in simulation, entirely safe and cut off from the rest of the world, but carefully structured their brains to keep them retarded, children forever, so they would never be adult enough to have the right, nor smart enough to conceive of the possibility, of escaping her smothering love and waking to the real world. The second best purveyed child pornography and addictive ritual cannibal-murder dreams. The third bought up ancient works of art, priceless portraits and famous sculpture, just so he could publicly destroy them, burning books and bombing archaeological digs. The worst stored lethal war-viruses and old atomic warheads on his property, in the most unsafe containment the law allowed, never attacking anyone, never setting off his weapons, but always hoping, in his thoughts, for an accident. None of this was strictly illegal, mind you!"

The words came out in a harsh rush, as if a reservoir of disgust for the Afloats (and perhaps for his whole situation) had been building up in him for quite some time, and was eager for a place into which to discharge.

He finished in a quiet, steady tone: "But my distaste for the Hortators has certainly ebbed. We need them, or something like them. Am I seen as such a horrible creature as that? Is that what Atkins thinks I am?"

She said, "Accept that Atkins is telling the truth. Some of your thoughts and memories are false. You haven't even asked me why I'm here or what I know! I have a way to save you."

Phaethon shook himself from his reverie, and darted a stern glance at her. "What about all the thoughts missing from your ring? Why did you break off your story?"

Daphne sighed. Apparently Phaethon would ask questions in his own way, or not at all. She said simply: "I broke off because I haven't made any entries recently. I haven't had the time. I was busy looking for you."

"Looking . . . ? Why not just ask a Sophotech? They must have known where I was."

"Oh, brilliant. Why not just ask Nebuchednezzar? Maybe then Neo-Orpheus and Emphyrio and Socrates and I would come skipping down the Rainbow Road to your address, singing chim-chime songs, with bells tied to our shoes, and our elbows linked together, just like the Three Vivamancers at the end of the Children's Opera. But somehow I think the Hortators would have found it easier to stop me if I had done that, don't you think? There is such a thing as being subtle, you know."

"So how did you find me?"

Now her smile returned. "I picked up the trail at Kisumu, of course. Everyone knew it was you who had ruined the overture of the Deep Ones' great-song. But that vulture-cyborg man (the one who thinks he is Bellipotent Composition, your friend . . . ?) didn't have any records in the Middle Dreaming. Rhadamanthus could not, at first, find out where he was, or where he had taken you."

"Rhadamanthus was helping you?"

"I wasn't exiled, not officially, not really, until the moment I spoke to you."

"Oh. Of course."

"But, anyway, if I hadn't figured out that you had been taken to Ceylon, even Rhadamanthus could not have found you."

"Could not? I thought the Sophotechs tracked the movements of everyone?"

"But they still play by the rules, and they don't let themselves know what they're not supposed to know. On the other hand, they're smart about manipulating rules. Once we knew you were in Ceylon, we found Bellipotent's entry record, and, from that, Rhadamanthus's

lawmind was able to find more records. There was some legal loophole he used to force the air-traffic control sub-Sophotechs to give
up Bellipotent's passenger manifest. Some legal fine-print rule; I
didn't try to understand it."

A clue fell into place. "That was you? Bellipotent called me when
you raided his records. But why did you give a masquerade name?
Why did you log on as me?"

Now she laughed, tossing her head. "Darling! And you call yourself a Silver-Grey! Guardian of ancient tradition! I logged on as
myself. I am Mrs. Phaethon Rhadamanth, your wife. That was the
name I used."

He said nothing, but the quiet, level, sad glance in his eyes held
the message: but you are not my wife.

She swung her feet to the floor and sat on the edge of the cot.
Her hands gripped the cot edge to either side of her. She was leaning forward, her shoulders hunched in a half-shrug, her head tilted
up. The posture somehow looked both submissive and defiant. She
said: "And don't tell me I'm not! I remember our marriage ceremony
and I remember our marriage night and I know where you keep
your toss-files and why you don't like eggs! And don't tell me my
memories are false! You have false memories, too, and you haven't
corrected yours!"

He said, "Please do not force me to be cruel, miss."

Interrupting: "How dare you call me 'miss'!"

He continued: ". . . I am quite fond of you, and I esteem your
friendship, but, nonetheless . . ."

She rolled her eyes. "Sometimes you sound so pompous! You get
that from Helion, you know. Remember the time you and I rein-
carnated in that subterranean kingdom? After you got out of the
rebirthing cells, you lurked around for days, because you could not
control your noses, and you didn't want anyone to see you in public,
with seven nostrils twitching every which-way. It was so funny! But
it was pomposity. You didn't want your feelings hurt. Or how about
on our second honeymoon at Niagara? We put on navicular bodies
and made love while going over the falls. You were afraid then, too!
Well, now you're afraid of my feelings for you. Don't be."

He said nothing.

She said in a soft, cold voice: "I know why we never had children, too."

He spoke abruptly, interrupting before she could continue: "You have parts of my wife's memories, yes!" Then, more softly: "And I am very fond of you, yes. Very fond, how could I not be? But . . . you are not my wife."

She shrugged a little, and smiled a supremely confident smile. Her teeth were white in the soft shadows of the candlelight. "If we had not been meant for each other, I would not have been able to find you. You uploaded a dream last night. That was my dream. I wrote it. I kept a counter to see how many people were dreaming my dream, and who they were. When Hamlet's name came up, I knew to search Ceylon for you. I know you; I remember you. I remember *us*. I can remember what we mean to each other. Can't you?"

Phaethon was getting upset. "You have most of her memories, yes, I grant you. But you don't know why she left me, damn it. You don't remember drowning yourself, smothering your soul in false memories just to kill off your memory of me. You don't know why she did that!"

She glanced at the knapsack, and then quickly back again. It was a guilty, furtive movement. Her face was troubled.

Phaethon eyes widened. A note of anger was in his voice: "You *do* know—!"

He took a stride across the room toward the knapsack. He snatched it up.

She said, "No, I . . ." And jumped to her feet, a nervous, quick movement. All composure and grace was gone.

He ripped the flap of the knapsack open. "She told you, didn't she? She told you, and she did not tell me." He yanked out the silver memory casket. He tilted it toward the window. Dim candlelight traced letters in the surface.

A graceful and feminine handscript on the casket lid read:

To be delivered to my emancipated partial self before the event of her permanent and irreversible death, cryosequestration, exile, radical re-

daction, or any other final withdrawal from organized civilization.

Emergency wakeup, memory reset, and sanity-restoration code.

Limited power of attorney.

This document overrides all prior Eveningstar instructions.

(Sealed) Daphne Prime Semi-Rhadamanthus Self-Embraced, Constructed Indep-Cortex (Emotion-sharing, limited club), Base Neuroform (with lateral connections), Silver-Grey Manorial Schola, Era 7004 (Pre-Compression).

Phaethon's knuckles were white on the silver lid. "She gave you the password. Not me. I begged Eveningstar to tell. I begged and begged. She'll tell you, not me. You can bring her back to life. Not me. For you, she'll come alive again. But never, not ever, for me . . ."

His knuckles were white on the lid, but the casket would not open for him. Suddenly exhausted, he leaned against the wall. He feet began to slide, scratching against the floorboards with a raucous noise. He did not try to catch himself, nor did he unhand the casket. Instead, he collapsed and sat down heavily, his back against the wall, his legs sprawled out carelessly. He bowed his head over the casket in his lap.

Once or twice his shoulders shook, but he made no noise. There was something very dull and hollow in his eyes.

Daphne stepped over to him, her hand reaching out, as if she were about to give comfort. But then she paused, stepped back, and said: "That casket is useless by itself. Even if the old version of me should wake, she will not leave her life and go into exile to be with you here. You must prove yourself correct, expose the fraud that has been perpetrated upon the Hortators, restore the honor of your name, and return from exile. It's the other case in my knapsack you want. The gold tablet. Haven't you figured out by now what that must be? I endured everything I have endured, all this pain and trouble, just to bring it to you."

Curiosity, in Phaethon, was even stronger than grief. He drew his head up. "What is it?" His voice was dull and low.

She gestured toward where he had dropped the knapsack, an elegant flip of the wrist, like a mensal hostess displaying some particularly delectable dessert. "You're the engineer, Lover. You'll recognize it."

He put the silver casket carefully aside and pulled the large gold tablet out of the knapsack. Phaethon straightened, surprise and wonder on his features, climbed to his feet again, with the golden tablet gleaming in his hands. One whole surface, he saw, was patterned with a mosaic of reader-heads and thought-ports, their several shapes and sizes fitted to each other as snugly as a successful puzzle, with no overlap and no empty spaces left over.

He looked up, "It is a noetic-examination circuit."

She spoke with a note of triumph in her voice: "And it's not connected to the mentality. Its an independent unit, isolated, sterile, and safe. Even you cannot believe that it is being influenced by these invader enemies of yours. You see? You do not have to log on to the mentality to prove the memories the Hortators saw were concoctions. Someone has tampered with your brain. That machine will let you prove it. You can prove it to the world; and to yourself."

She smiled again: "Use it, and we can go home, and we can live happily ever after."

He glanced down at the silver casket at his feet, then glanced up at her, his eyes narrowed.

Daphne's lips compressed, a line of scarlet irritation. "And, yes, obviously. You cannot get *her* back unless you come back."

Phaethon said carefully, "You do not seem overly concerned at the prospect of (may I phrase it delicately . . . ?) of losing me to the real version of you."

Her glittering eyes narrowed with pert, supercilious amusement, and a half-smile touched her lips. Her voice lilted with pretended nonchalance: "Oh . . . ? You mean the old, scared, outdated version . . . ? All I can say is: May the best bride win."

THE NOETIC READING

I.

Phaethon was puzzled by the sudden, warm emotion which came to him then, seeing that undaunted, gallant, sensual look in the eyes of this the woman who was a copy of his wife. She stood, hands on hips, head thrown back, smiling a sunny smile, her figure warm and golden in the candlelight behind her. Phaethon dropped his eyes and pretended to study the noetic tablet he held.

(She was not a perfect copy. This wife differed in certain details. She did not hate him, she had not left him, she had fearlessly thrown herself into exile rather than lose him . . .)

Phaethon scowled, staring down at the noetic tablet in his hands. He would untangle his feelings later, he decided.

He raised the unit and hesitated.

Daphne asked, "What's wrong?"

"Nothing should stop me."

She raised an eyebrow. Her green eyes glittered with skeptical puzzlement. "Nothing is stopping you."

He said, "Nothing Sophotech, I mean. The one Scaramouche told me about."

"Is this the 'Evil' Sophotech build by the ghosts of the Second Oecumene?"

"It is real." He said heavily, "I am not deluded."

Daphne sat, leaning back on the cot, and laughed, mockery mingled with relief. "Oh, darling! You really ought to go through more trashy spy-romances, violence-novels, and bellipography. All those romances make the Second Oecumene their villains. Your hallucination is not very imaginative, as they go."

Angrily: "You believe the Hortators? You think I imposed these false memories on myself?"

Smiling: "No, beloved. Oh no, my darling. I believe in you. Would I have come here otherwise . . . ?"

She straightened up and said in a more businesslike tone: "I know you. You would not falsify your memories. And if, for some reason, you did, you would have invented a better story! Living with an authoress will do that for you, I guess. But I said and I do think the hallucination imposed on you really is not very imaginative. Look at the story: The Second Oecumene hated Sophotechnology so much that it was the only thing, except for murder, their laws forbade. So who built this Nothing Sophotech?"

"Scaramouche said I did. But that was only a lie to get me to open my memory casket."

"So why do you think there is a Second Oecumene Sophotech at all . . . ? Why couldn't the whole thing be a lie? Why couldn't your enemies just be normal people no smarter than the rest of us?"

He said nothing.

A malicious note of humor lilted in her voice: "Or is it more flattering to your vanity to think you could have only been tricked by a superintelligence . . . ?"

He said harshly: "The truth is not determined by my opinions. Nor, I should add, by any other person's. I could accuse the Hortators of blind egocentrism, for not recognizing the threat; or Atkins of cowardice, for not admitting that it is real; or I could accuse anyone of anything, who did not agree with my view. Such accusations are easy. But blind men and cowards sometimes have the truth. Perhaps by accident, but they do. And so do, sometimes, men victimized by evil, alien Sophotechs built by long-dead civilizations! So we don't discover the truth of a message by examining the man who speaks it. We examine facts. Where are the facts to support your conclusion, miss?"

She stood up, her voice musical with anger, or perhaps it was battle-joy: "Fact! The testimony of Atkins. Fact again, the testimony of Eveningstar Sophotech, who says no attack by Scaramouche or any other mannequin took place on the steps of her mausoleum. Fact the third, Gannis has been maneuvering to seize your *Phoenix Exultant* and sell it for scrap ever since this whole imbroglio began! He's been trying to keep you penniless; why else would he help Helion in the law case against you?"

Phaethon squinted, his head cocked to one side. "Gannis . . . ?"

"Gannis of Jupiter? You know? A hundred-mind self-composition with a Sophotech who thinks just like all of him? I had my ring look up all sorts of records after I rode away from Atkins' cottage. I don't think Unmoiqhotep was acting alone. Over the last thousand years Gannis has been loosing money hand over fist. He took risks in his youth, back when there was only one of him. But, once he got rich, he turned himself into a committee. To get more things done at once, I suppose. But committees always tend to more and more conservative and risk-fearing strategies. Always! (You should see some of the studies Wheel-of-Life has made on the ecology of decision-making within a fixed power structure.) But Helion, in order to become a Peer, did the opposite. He took more and more risks, and even had a son, you, Phaethon, in order to get a mind more willing to take risks than he was:"

Phaethon turned the idea over in his mind. "Gannis? You suspect that he and the Eleemosynary Composition brain-raped me while I was in the Eleemosynary public box, is that it?"

"It explains the facts. Why else was there no evidence of the Neptunian at Eveningstar mausoleum? Why else was there no evidence of a mannequin confronting you or stabbing you on the stairs? That whole fight scene was a dream. A dream forced on you."

Could the whole fight scene with Scaramouche have been a dream? The Eleemosynary Composition had been in control of all of Phaethon's sensory inputs going into the hospice box, had been carrying all of Phaethon's motions and instructions going out. Could those have been edited?

It was hard to believe. By their very nature, Compositions had no privacy. The Eleemosynary's group-mind command structure had

all its thoughts on public record. How could Eleemosynary commit
a crime? Or even think about committing a crime?

Gannis, on the other hand, while there were a hundred versions
of him linked in parallel, was a privately held entity, and could hide
his thoughts, either from his other selves, or from the public.

Phaethon said, "I don't see how Eleemosynary could have been
a conspirator; nor do I see how anyone (anyone equipped with technology known to the Golden Oecumene) could have manipulated
my brain while I was in the Eleemosynary hospice box without
Eleemosynary noticing it."

"When you closed your armor, you were cut off from all outside
influence. Eleemosynary could not have detected what was going
on inside you at that time. Suppose a brain-redaction had taken
place then?"

"I would have been cut off from any brain-redactor as well."

"Unless you had it inside your armor with you."

"I was carrying it with me, is that what you mean, and then it
activated?"

"How is that different from a memory casket set on a timer?"

"Are we talking about a piece of hardware, physically inside the
armor? Atkins was the only person who touched it. He put a probe
inside before I went into the courthouse. But . . . No, wait, that is
ridiculous. I would have found any hardware during my trip down
the tower. I completely inventoried everything in my armor, from
helm to heel, more than once. Unless it dissolved itself after one
use . . . ?"

"I am thinking it was a thoughtware virus, existing only in your
mind. Perhaps someone fed it to you through the Middle Dreaming,
earlier."

Was it possible?

Perhaps with a clever logic-tree, such a virus could have added
false memories one at a time, while he was speaking (or thought he
was speaking) to Scaramouche, and different variations of Scaramouche's responses might have been pre-recorded, each variation
anticipating slightly different reactions in him. A stored semi-
intelligent program could have unfolded in his consciousness, feeding false signals into his senses, or even directly into his cortex,

with no intervening medium. No outside source would detect the "invasion" because Phaethon was carrying the invading program inside him.

Daphne's theory also would explain why neither Rhadamanthus nor Eleemosynary, later, had any memory of the virus-civilization which Phaethon remembered seeing attack all three of them. There had been no such superviruses, no attack powerful enough to fool Rhadamanthus. Instead, a very simple chain of memories, reporting that an attack *had already taken place*, were introduced into Phaethon, then activated.

But when had it happened? Before he climbed into the public box at the Eleemosynary hospice? Before that he had been at the courthouse. Had Atkins done it? Before the courthouse he had been in the Rhadamanthine thoughtspace, at tea, talking with Daphne, and Rhadamanthus had been running his sense-filter, and would have prevented any thought-virus from entering from the Middle Dreaming.

Unless her diary had been the carrier to introduce the virus . . . ?

The meddling with his thoughts must have been complete before he opened his memory casket. Because, after that, he had been in Helion's section of the mansion-mind, and, after that, at the Hortator Inquest.

Or had it been complete? Perhaps something introduced earlier had still been operating. A Trojan-horse program of moderate skill could have interfered with Phaethon's attempt to download a copy of his consciousness into the public channel when he had been testifying at the Inquest. Instead of the true copy Phaethon had tried to send, a pre-recorded false version could have gone out, fed into the channel Phaethon had opened. That version was false from the beginning, and no magic supertechnology needed to be postulated to explain how records could be altered while Nebuchednezzar was reading them, simply because they had not been altered at that time. They had been concocted long before, and loaded into Phaethon's subconscious whenever the original brain-rape had taken place. (But when could that have been?)

And why Gannis?

He asked it aloud: "Why Gannis?"

"Because Gannis hates Helion. He always has. It's always been the false sun fighting the true sun; Jupiter versus Sol."

"Why?"

"The Solar Array, in less than four centuries, will be large enough to circle the equator of the sun. It will be the largest single piece of engineering ever designed. Why wouldn't Helion put in a super-collider at that point? To you and me the difference between a small, false-dwarf sun like Burning Jupiter, and a main-sequence G-type star like Sol may be hard to grasp, like the difference between a million and a billion. But Helion, at that time, could outproduce Gannis's metal supply, could more than triple Vafnir's antimatter output, and so on and so forth. Jupiter will be exhausted of hydrogen fuel long before Sol—look at the difference in size! And, long before that, some planetary engineer—I think it was always meant to be you—would have to move the moons of dying Jupiter into new orbits around the parent Sun."

"Impossible. How could Gannis get away with it? The first noetic reading made of his mind would reveal his crime."

Daphne shrugged. "I think he had been hoping Helion would help you, or follow you into exile, or at least raise such a stink that the Peers would withdraw their invitation to elevate Helion to join them. Then, at the Grand Transcendence in December, it is not Helion's dream which takes the center stage and forefront of the minds of men, but Gannis's. Afterward, long afterward, perhaps, Gannis would be found out. But I suppose parts of his mind don't know about the crime, and they will carry on after the evil Gannis is punished. But in any case, it will be too late for Helion's dream by then. After a Transcendence, people get so wrapped up in the unity of racial thought, you know how it takes them a few hundred years to begin trusting their own judgment again; and by that time, Helion may be broke. With your death, Helion certainly will be brokenhearted."

Phaethon opened his mouth to utter an objection, but then closed it. Because the theory *did* make sense. It make a lot more sense than believing he was being chased, for incomprehensible reasons, by agents from a long-dead colony one thousand light-years away.

Instead, the oldest reason for crime known to man—jealousy—came from someone like Gannis—a real person. The danger was understandable, human, natural.

And he knew how untrustworthy Gannis was. Had he not already betrayed Phaethon once?

And yet . . . and yet . . .

"This is precisely the sort of thing Nothing would like to get me to believe, if all this has been arranged to trick me," said Phaethon.

Daphne rolled her eyes. "Oh, come on. You are going to disbelieve a believable theory not because it is unbelievable, but because it is not?"

"Er. Say that again . . . ?"

"I don't need to. This Nothing Sophotech is your superstition. A paranoiac who sees conspiracies everywhere, says the lack of evidence only proves the conspiracy was successful. A man who believes in fairies, when he doesn't see them, says that this proves that fairies are invisible!"

"Reasoning by analogy is like filling balloons with liquid helium. It won't fly."

She said: "Then stick to the evidence. What can you prove?"

"I can prove nothing. What we are trying to find out here is whether or not my ability to gather and to ponder proof—in other words, my mind and memory—has been compromised. How does one prove that the ability itself to prove things has not been distorted? What evidence can prove the evidence itself has not been tampered with?"

She said, "You're getting ridiculous. All you need to look for, in this case, is independent confirmation. Atkins does not agree with you, Rhadamanthus does not agree with you, Eveningstar does not agree with you, and the Eleemosynary Composition does not agree with you. You have not found a single shred of independent confirmation so far. But you have that mobile noetic circuit right there in your hand. It will tell you if the memories you have are true or false, and when any false memories were put into you, and how. So what are you waiting for? What are you afraid of?"

Phaethon said nothing, but stared at her carefully.

Daphne put her hands on her hips, her mouth a circle of astonishment. Then she cried: "How dare you! You think I'm an imitation Daphne sent here by the Nothing with a booby-trapped box just to brain-rape you! Good stinking grief! What do I have to do to prove who I am to you?"

Phaethon shrugged. "It is a natural and reasonable thing to suspect at this point." (Actually, it was a nightmare vision which chilled Phaethon to the bone. He imagined an innocent girl, the product of a gentle, utopian society, defenseless, taken by surprise in the wilderness and murdered horribly, replaced by a cloned body, and, with gruesome irony, the clone's memory was falsified so that she, perhaps, actually believed she was the dead girl, believed she was in love, was good, was innocent. Then, once the mission was accomplished, or some other signal was given, that illusion of love and innocence, the whole dead girl's life, would vanish like a forgotten dream.)

" 'Reasonable'?! Ha! You've turned into a paranoid lunatic. And after I went to all this trouble! If you don't find some way to prove that you are innocent, I'll be stuck, too, you moron!"

"Darling, you've argued with me a million times, and you know it never does any good to become emotional. You might not even be aware that you are an agent for the Nothing, since the programming could have been done at a subconscious level . . ."

He broke off. She was standing with her arms folded, drumming her fingers against her elbow, one eyebrow raised, a slight smile on her lips.

"What is it?" he said.

"You called me 'darling,' instead of 'miss,' " she said, her smile getting warmer. She spoke slowly, as if the words tasted good to her. "And 'we' have not argued a million times. I have the memory of the woman you argued with a million times. But, according to you, that wasn't me."

"I, ah . . ."

She waved her hand, and in a light lilt, said, "But I will let you change your mind about that later!" Then she said: "At the moment, you were saying I booby-trapped the noetic reader. Fine. But if I did, then I'm not as smart as a Sophotech; I'm not even as smart as Daphne Tercius Eveningstar Emancipated Download-redact, am

I? Because if I had been that smart, I would have realized that I could not fool an engineer with a booby-trapped piece of equipment. You are an engineer, aren't you? Take the thing apart, if you like. But you better make damn sure that you can put it back together, because, without it, we are never getting out of this mess."

Phaethon looked down again at the portable noetic reader. Could he inspect it? He was standing in the middle of a well-equipped thought-shop, after all. The shop-mind had routines with which to examine basic mental interfaces; it could certainly tell the difference between a passive noetic reader and some active circuit meant to make a change in Phaethon's thought-process.

Daphne raised both eyebrows, and said, "And I do *not* get emotional when I argue. I'm just passionate about my convictions!"

##

The green-and-blue housecoat in the corner of Ironjoy's cabin was hooked into the general thought-shop circuitry, and served as the main command menu. Phaethon stepped out of his armor, the black material pulling the chrysadmantium plates out from him like the petals of an opening flower. Then the mass pulled itself back together with a bright clash, forming an empty stand of plate mail.

Phaethon shrugged into the housecoat. The coat hesitated, then pulled in the two extra sleeves. Phaethon drew the hood, and then worked the ornamental buttons which riggered the translation from Ironjoy's rather peculiar semi-Invariant neuroform to a base neuroform.

The robe was slow and old, perhaps an antique. It took almost half a minute for the reader-heads in the hood to reconfigure, and find the contact points for the cybernetic neurocircuitry grown throughout Phaethon's brain and spine. A web of energies wove Phaethon into the mind-space of the thought-shop.

The thought-shop was utterly isolated; all communication channels were black. Whatever it was that Antisemris had done, whatever services Notor-Kotok's provider had cut off, had stranded the entire shop outside of the mentality. Which meant, Phaethon hoped, that the shop was secure from intrusion, safe, and virus-free.

He took the gold tablet of the portable noetic reader and placed the unit into the housecoat's large chest pocket. Threads from the housecoat began to weave themselves across the thought-ports, making connections, finding correspondences, downloading initial routines into holding spaces. At the same time, Phaethon had the housecoat insert a physical probe into the golden tablet's housing, so that he could generate tiny fiber-optic pictures of the interior works, and magnetic images of the fields surrounding each part of the construction. Beads on the hem of the hood focused imaging lasers into his eyes, stimulating the areas behind the cornea, to create three-dimensional pictures diagramming the tablet's interior spaces for him.

Daphne sat back down on the bed, picked up his child slate again, and began flicking through different records and menus.

Phaethon inspected the unit and was baffled.

The secondary systems he could grasp: triggers, data-migration mechanisms, coders and decoders, junction cells. The arrangement of thought-reader processors and interprocessors was particularly clever, based on concentric geometries; it looked as if the Sophotechs had finally solved the permeability-interference problems involved in ring-shaped psuedomaterial fields, and constructed the legendary circular self-sustaining information wave. Brilliant.

But the main memory and processing core was an utter enigma. It seemed to be made of a sheet of neutronium, frozen at absolute zero, a matrix of dense subatomic particles bound together by strong nuclear forces, but orderly, very orderly. The edges of the sheet faded into virtual particle masses, a haze without clear properties; but pulses moving to one side of the sheet seemed to disappear and reappear at the opposite side of the sheet, as if the thing was curved in some dimension he could not sense or imagine. The energy field suspending the sheet in place certainly acted as if there were no boundary conditions or edges.

And what was this sheet? Whether it was made of matter or energy was a question for debate. Why it was not heavier than a city, Phaethon could not guess; why it did not explode or randomize was an impossibility. Perhaps it was made of something like tightly woven quantum strings? Or a force produced by another geometry of supersymmetric breaking, like, yet unlike, pseudomatter? Antigravity? Or perhaps that so called subgravity, which graviton-fraction theory said might exist?

But the main question was: Had it been tampered with? Phaethon could have laughed. The whole thing could have been taken apart, turned inside out, rotated in the fourth dimension, and put back together again without him being able to tell a thing. He did not know what the original configuration was; he had no instruments that could sense the disposition of neutral subatomic particles, where the main memory and process information were stored. And, even if he had, he would not be able to read that information by inspecting the gross outward mechanism storing it, any more than a man could read a novel by looking at the electron crystal in his library-ring.

Some engineer. He was a human. This was like the handiwork of the gods. This was magic.

Well. At least he could look at the parts of the mechanism he recognized. First, the reader-heads fed into the central rotary information-ring through a nested series of concentric interprocessors. It was a beautiful solution to certain basic design problems. Phaethon felt privileged just to see it.

"I think I understand why the Second Oecumene destroyed themselves," he said aloud, absentmindedly.

"Why is that, darling?" Daphne did not look up from the record in the slate she was viewing.

"They did not get to watch the Sophotechs solve problems. This is a breathtaking piece of work! The designers created a self-sustaining complex of information waves traveling around a frictionless ring. The geometry is entirely radial, so there are no edge-bleeding effects, and, as far as I can tell, the thing is distortionless, intertialess, and self-interference-free, so that anything stored on it will last until the end of time, or until quanta-level decay crodes the fundamental substructure of the behavior of basic particles, whichever comes first. The memory can be configured from any two points on the ring to form a triangular matrix of any given height, limited only, I would guess, by the curvature of space itself. That means you can put practically any number of code lines into a given area, without worrying about stop points and edge bleed-off that the old rank-and-file square matrixes suffered. And that is just the intermediate thresholding. The information core itself is a block of weightless neutronium!"

"That's nice, dear," said Daphne absently.

"The reader-heads that feed into the ring can be used in any combination, in multiple scan-functions, so that you do not need a separate thought-port for every combination of neuron actions in the subject. The heads are on a timer . . . Hullo. What's this . . . ?"

Daphne looked up. "Find anything, dear?"

Phaethon shoved back his hood, blinking his eyesight clear of illusions so that he could see the cabin again. His gaze met hers. "When was the last time you used this unit?"

"Used it? I haven't even taken the tape off the reader-heads. No one has ever used it. Its a prototype."

"Atkins did not do something to it? Examine it for weapons, or activate it by remote control?"

Daphne sat up, eyes big. "Oh, dear heavens! The thing isn't really booby-trapped, is it?! I was just kidding when I said you should inspect it. You know, to give you something to do, so you wouldn't fret. Is there something wrong? There cannot be! I kept it in my pack the whole time!"

Phaethon said, "The line clock reads zero, as if the unit had never been used, but there is a separate clock, attached to the timer controlling the coordination of the reader-heads, which indicated that the heads cycled through 1×10 to the 28th power combinations about fourteen hours ago. That is about the number of combinations one would get if someone used the unit, and examined his own mind."

Daphne blinked. "Oh. That doesn't sound dangerous."

"But who did it?"

"No one. The thing was in my pack. Fourteen hours ago? I was sleeping on the ground with twelve pebbles sticking into my back. I remember because I got to count them, over and over again. I'd show you the bruises, but, until you get around to admitting we are man and wife, I wouldn't want to do anything to shock Silver-Grey

Victorian propriety. Are you really not going to use that noetic unit now? Do you really think I'm an agent of your spy-thriller villains? Just because the reader-heads are misaligned? That doesn't prove the thing is booby-trapped! Can't you just get it to read your brain without allowing it to change anything in your brain?"

"The reason why noetic machines are so complex, and the reason why the early Warlocks, back in the Fifth Era, could fool the readings, is that there is a continuous back-and-forth between the unit and the brain-information it reads. Any act of examination changes an object."

"I still don't understand. You mean that someone—for the sake of argument, let's say it was your bad guys—came up and used the machine while I was sleeping. That means they did what? Swore an oath? Testified in court? Made a contract? But in any case, it wasn't anything that damaged the unit, or that reprogrammed it to do you any harm."

"I said there was a continuous two-way energy flow between the subject and the noetic reading unit. Each one changes the other. I just said that ancient Warlocks learned how to hoax these readings. They did it by altering the machine during the reading process. If this machine was altered by the enemy, it could not have been for a good purpose."

"But can't you look at it and find out? Have it check itself for flaws? Order it to re-set to zero? Do one of those things you are always doing to our systems at home whenever you are ignoring Rhadamanthus and don't want to hear why what you are doing is going to make things worse?"

He blinked. "Like when?"

"What about the time you collapsed the east wing of the mansion, when we were staying in New Paris? Or what about the time you were trying to re-thread all the impellers in our confluence register, because you thought it would get more tension out of the drive? All you did was capsize us into the lava."

"I cannot believe you would bring that up again! That was caused by a flux in the current around us: and even Boreus Sophotech said later that that was an unexpected consequence of chaotic flows in the magnetic core! And I'm sorry about the wing collapsing, but I thought we could save power by running it through a nonlinear interrupt."

Daphne rolled her eyes and looked at the ceiling. "Men! You are so touchy. All I'm saying is, how did you right the mole boat again? How did you erect the mansion-fields? Just hit the damn reset button. Null everything back to the default."

Phaethon frowned. "That seems too easy. But there is no reason why that should not work . . ."

"And besides, you were monkeying with the east wing to show off, not because we needed to save any energy, and you know it."

"Fine! I cannot believe we are going through this old argument, when you might actually be a horrible puppet controlled by the Silent Ones."

"What a terrible thing to say about a person!"

He shook his finger at her. "I'm telling you, if this turns out to be a Silent One trick, and you killed that sweet Daphne-doll—the image of the woman I love—I'll destroy your whole damn civilization with no more hesitation than if I were wiping out a nest of cockroaches! You tell that to your masters! I was born to burn worlds!"

"Don't be silly, dear, you sound like a caveman. But I appreciate the sentiment; not every girl gets a maniac to slaughter people indiscriminately for her. So do you really think I'm sweet?"

"It's not funny. Well, perhaps it is a trifle funny, but it's really not entirely funny." He threw off the housecoat and stepped back over to his armor.

Daphne sat up. "Now what are you doing?"

"I can take a precaution. The thought-ports in my armor can act as an intermediary. The noetic-read energy cannot penetrate the admantium. I can just set up a buffer, like an air lock, something to quickly interrupt the circuit if the noetic reader does something untoward."

Black tentacles of nanomaterial fitted the armor around him. Then he struggled to put the housecoat back on. Then followed a few minutes while he spread nanomaterial across his upper helmet surfaces, growing contact-points to be routed through the thought-points in his shoulder boards. The carrier lines clustered like a drooping mass of hair across his head, and around his shoulders, spilling out of the front of the housecoat hood.

Then he spent several moments downloading routines out of the thought-shop. A point-to-point system, a format translator, security cycles, relative time adjustment groups, and so on . . .

Ironjoy, because of his clientele, had far more security programs than any other thought-shop Phaethon had seen. He sent out a search-tree to use and combine them all.

Then he discovered, of course, that, since his secretarial and seneschal programs had been erased out of his personal thought-space, he had to get architectural activators, routing judges, information condensers and decondensors, pattern assessors, step locks, hold-and-go priority switches . . .

Some of this required additional hardware chips, processing beads, and so on, which he clipped to the various parts of the housecoat, and hung from the carrier strands. The wall behind the talking mirrors opened up into several construction cabinets, where Phaethon either made or found what more he needed.

Soon, it was hard to move his arms, because he now wore two housecoats (since the first had not had enough storage area of action circuits), and, practically a third coat itself, was the layer of additional materials he had been forced to add, wires and join-boxes, cooling disks and through-put forks, dangling from all eight sleeves.

He had opened one of the mirrors to allow him to run additional lines to contact points there, to get direct access to thought-shop routines. Every wire running to the mirror had a circuit-interrupt with a security assessment cell clipped to it.

"You look like a walking Yule tree," Daphne called from the cot.

"Just don't put a candle on my head." His voice was muffled, because the external speakers on his armor were obscured. He sighed. "I'm just glad the Silver-Greys aren't around to see this. Helion's ancient vow to make our technology serve Beauty."

"You aren't a Silver-Grey at the moment, hero. Besides, I'm recording the picture into my ring. We'll all have a good laugh about it, once our exile ends." There was a wistful note to her voice.

"Hmp. You show them that picture, the Silver-Grey won't take me back."

"Don't worry. I show them this picture, the Black Manorials will take you. You'll start a new Absurdist Sartorial Movement. Asmodius Bohost will dress like you."

"Well, good heavens! It's worth the risk of having the Silent One's booby-trapped noetic reader here burn out my brain just for that, if nothing else! My other accomplishments will sink into obscurity by contrast, once history remembers that I once influenced Mr. Bohost's ghastly wardrobe!"

Daphne favored him with a level stare.

"You're delaying."

"Perhaps a little . . ."

"You're afraid."

"Not unreasonable, considering that this might actually kill me."

"You are a paranoid deluded maniac."

"But a lovable one. Are you attempting to bolster my courage, miss? You should have Eveningstar Sophotech teach you more about how to manipulate the moods of men."

"Are we back to 'miss' are we? That's fine with me; because at least you are talking now as if we are going to make it back out of this exile. You sound mildly less doomed."

"I'm wondering if there are further steps I can take to make it so this noetic reader, if it is trapped, cannot hurt me."

"Put another bucket on your head."

"This is not a bucket; it monitors energy levels in the hood-interface."

"It's still a bucket."

"Maybe I'm worried about what will happen if this succeeds. The automatic exile—the one I agreed to suffer at Lakshmi—will be ended. But so what? There is not a single thing that will prevent the College from turning around and bringing a new proceeding against me. They still fear star colonization. Till now, I had been sort of assuming that the mere existence of surviving colonists from the Silent Oecumene would compel us to travel out there. To discover what had become of them, if nothing else. But, if you are right after all, and all this is a hallucination imposed by Gannis, that compelling reason vanishes."

Daphne sat with her elbows on her knees, cupping her cheeks

in her palms, looking up at Phaethon with an impertinent and girlish look. "Leave everything to me and Aurelian. We can clear that hurdle when we come to it."

"What do you mean?"

"I was saving it as a surprise."

"I thought you hated surprises."

"Not when they are *my* surprises."

"Please tell me, miss."

"Are we still back on 'miss'? Say, 'please tell me, Daphne my darling wife,' and maybe I will."

"Sha'n't. You'll tell me and gladly."

"And why shall I?" She favored him with an impish smile.

"Because, like me, you are too proud of your accomplishments to keep quiet about them."

Her smile burned languid, and she brushed her hair with her fingers, preening.

Phaethon said, "Any time now. I'm tired of standing here with a bucket on my head."

"We're rich."

"What?"

"Actually, you're rich. I'm only rich if you marry me again."

"You are deluded. I do not have a gram of money, not a second of computer time."

"I said rich. It's not enough to buy our ship out of hock, but it should be enough to hire a Black House vessel to carry us to Mercury Equilateral, and pay for at least some of the last-minute preparations the *Phoenix Exultant* still needs done."

"Oh, come now. And where did this alleged money come from?"

"Flying suits."

"Flying suits?"

"You hold the patent on them. The way Rhadamanthus set up the business, you only lease the patent in return for a shared percentage. During the masquerade, everybody wants to fly. Its just so much fun. Aurelian Sophotech set up a second levitation array above Western Europe, for the Aryan Individualists, and a third over India, where the Uncomposed Cerebelline art-capital Macrostructure is."

"Ridiculous. The Hortators . . ."

"Are a private and voluntary organization. They cannot subpoena your records; they are not the police. Everyone who is renting a flying cloak from you is in masquerade. Nobody knows who they are, except for Aurelian."

"But—but why would people—why would they defy the Hortators?"

Daphne raised her slender hands and her soft, round shoulders in an exaggerated pantomime shrug. "Theory one: People support the Hortators, in principle, except when that principle causes them some sacrifice or hardship, such as forgoing the pleasure of personal levitation, whereupon their principles evaporate like spit on Mercury dayside. A lot of people were upset, you know, about the unforeseen consequences of that mass-amnesia they let the Hortators talk them into. Theory two: People know the Hortators are actually, really, supposed to ostracize folks like all your friends here, the child pornographers and semislavers and weaponeers, destructionists and malignifiers and mystagogues, hatemongers and history-forgers and suicide-panderers; and the people know that bright, heroic Phaethon does not fit in with that muck."

Phaethon's muffled voice came out from underneath his layers of coats, lines, wires. "Would people really defy the Horators . . . for me? Do they believe in my dream, finally, after all?"

"Don't get so dewy-eyed. Occam's razor forbids us from adopting theories that require us to postulate unreal entities, such as, for example, the existence of conscience, noble dreams, or good wishes among our fellow citizens. No, theory number one makes more sense. They don't care about you and your ideals or about the Hortators and their ideals. They just want their toys."

"Their love for their toys may allow me to repossess my toy. Isn't there the seed of free-market morality buried in that somewhere? I want my ship. The Neptunian conversation-tree has already predicted that their Duma will hire me to pilot the *Phoenix Exultant*."

Daphne pointed with a slender finger toward the chest pocket of his housecoat, where the noetic unit rested. "But first you must get us the hell out of his miserable exile. Say the magic word and let that thought-forsaken thing read your mind already. If I'm actually a Silent One spy, and this is all an elaborate trap, I'll apologize to you later."

"What if I'm dead?"

She shivered with disgust. "Well, then I won't apologize! Will you just get on with it?! They dumped all my spare lives, and it makes me nervous. I've been mortal for at least an hour now, and it's beginning to bother me. I mean, what would happen if a meteor struck the earth at this spot, or something?"

"I wouldn't worry about meteors, were I you," said Phaethon. "There hasn't been a big strike since the Baltimore event in the Fourth Era. Since that time, a watch has been tracking and recording the movements of all objects within the detectable danger zone, first by the Chicken Little Subcomposition, then by Star-Dance Cerebelline, and now by the Sophotechs. Nothing could get past them . . ."

He frowned. A thought, so obvious and so large as to have been invisible before, surfaced in his mind.

Where was the Silent Oecumene starship?

There must be a second *Phoenix Exultant*, perhaps a colder, slower, stealthier ship, but a starship capable of travel from Cygnus X-1 nevertheless. A dark twin of his golden *Phoenix*. Where was it hidden? Sophotech navigation watches observed every rock, practically every dustmote, in inner-system space. But if the Silent *Phoenix* was somewhere beyond Neptune (as Phaethon had been assuming) then how could the Sophotechs not notice whatever information, instructions, or reports were traveling back and forth between Nothing's agents on Earth and wherever the evil Sophotech was housed?

(Unless . . . ? Could the agents be operating with only furtive and infrequent contact with their Sophotech? If so, then the agents were capable of obtuseness, illogic, and human error.)

The Silent Oecumene technology might be different from that of the Golden Oecumene. Nonetheless, in general, it was safe to assume that the technology level still had to be roughly equal, since a godlike superiority in technology would have permitted the Silent Ones to disregard any need for precaution or secrecy.

Therefore, it was safe to assume that normal principles of science and engineering applied. The Silent Ones could not motivate their starship without discharges of energy sufficient to move the ship's mass across the intervening distance.

And also, even if the Nothing Sophotech could be housed in a frame physically much smaller than huge electrophotonic matrices of the Golden Oecumene Sophotechs, the energy density, and the energy required to perform a respectable Sophotech-level number of operations-per-second, would still give it a large mass-energy reading. The pseudo-neutronium inside the noetic unit he was holding, for example, could have been detected from orbit by weakly interacting particle ranging-and-detection gear.

Where could one put a body that large, or put a starship, without the Earthmind detecting either?

Daphne said, "You're not talking, lover. That means you're thinking."

"Shouldn't I be?"

A feminine sigh floated in the candle-lit gloom. "You should be thinking about hurrying up, getting a noetic reading, proving that you are right, and getting home in time for a real comfortable night, including a warm pool, a communion, a mensal performance, and a walk in the Eveningstar Garden of the New Senses. The Non-Apotheosis School was going to surface back into human thought-space from their daring subtranscendence tomorrow, and everyone says they will be bringing back Para-artistic phenomena from deep in the Earthmind, miniaturized and recalculated to make sense to our neuroforms. I thought it would be a much better way to spend an afternoon than sitting here on a rusting barge, watching each other undergo the aging process. Can't we go home? All this poverty and trash here is beginning to depress me. Too much like my folks' old Stark place on the Reservation."

She was clutching her elbows and shivering. One of the candles on the porthole sill behind her had begun to gutter out. She had half-turned and was watching it die.

Phaethon knew she was thinking morbid thoughts. The Starks had not connected their child to any noumenal immortality circuit, nor even told her that such a thing as immortality was possible. Daphne had suffered more than one bad accident as a child, falling from trees, overturning boats, being trampled by antique walking-statues; for she had led an active life. She found out from a wandering confabulator, a Jongleur from the Warlock Benevolent Mischief School, about Orphic reincarnation banks: and she had never forgiven the mad risk her primitivist parents had taken with her life.

The bright flame sputtered, gave off a greater light than before, swayed, failed, and vanished. A slender tail of smoke rushed upward.

"Will you just hurry up and get us out of here?" said Daphne.

Phaethon said: "Darling, don't be afraid."

She spoke without turning her head. "Why not?" came a bitter reply. "You are."

There was an odd sharpness to her voice. He said: "Just what do you mean by that?"

Daphne turned, picked up the child slate, touched the screen. The light from the slate shone up from her chin, and threw the shadow of her nose across one eye. "I would not have had to go into exile, and come all the way out here, or get that portable reader from Aurelian, or do any of those things, if you had just had the common sense to log on to the network and get a noetic reading from Rhadamanthus or from any public contracts channel! You even read a self-consideration analysis of your own psychometrics, and it told you (it told you!) that your fear of logging on was unnatural and out of character for you. It should have been obvious that it was an imposed fear, imposed from outside. If you had half the brains you pretend, you would not have needed me to come by and rescue you!"

"You read my self-analysis?! That is private material!"

"Oh, come on. I am your wife, you know. I've communed with you. I've *been* you."

"I would not go through your diary without asking!"

"Oh, really? What if the wake-up code for the old version of me was there? Or are you only willing to break into private mausoleums, batter constables, fight Atkins, and try to kidnap sleeping women?"

"I—well—you make a good point, I suppose. But still you should not—"

"What, are you afraid I'll come across your private sexual fantasies about making me dress up in a pony suit and horse-breaking me? I have to admit, I sort of like that one . . ."

"You are changing the subject, miss!"

"Demoted back to 'miss,' eh? Well, don't worry, hero. If I die in exile, I wouldn't be telling anyone your secrets." She tossed the slate back onto the cot with a negligent flick of her wrist. "I suppose it doesn't matter whether you use that damn noetic reader or not. I can tell you what it will say."

"What?"

"The false memories were imposed through the Middle Dreaming. You were standing near the courthouse, and a friend of Unmoiqhotep's, one of the Cacophiles, got you to accept some sort of quick-read file. You were on public courthouse ground. You must have been using public server support for your sense-filter, the same kind of low-budget public-works thing Atkins was complaining that Unmoiqhotep had cracked. Right?"

"Y-yes. But why do you conclude that . . ."

"Simple. You were brain-raped. It could not have happened when or at any time before you were sourced through Rhadamanthus, or the mansion-mind would have detected it, or before your trial, for then the Curia noetic reading would have detected it. And it didn't happen after you entered the Eleemosynary hospice box, because the concierge would have detected it. So whom did you meet after you left the trial and before you went to the hospice? The Cacophiles."

She pointed at the slate glowing on the cot. "And the self-consideration analysis even told you that something was making you not want to think about the Cacophiles. It told you. You ignored it. And don't give me this 'how can I know anything if my brain has been altered?' garbage! Look for the confirming evidence! Look at your own damn self-analysis! Look at basic Deception Theory you learned as an Apprentice, 'for every false-to-facts system there must be at least one self-inconsistency value' remember? It's all lies, and you should be able to see through them, Phaethon! There is no

Silent Oecumene and no spies and no booby-trap! And there is Nothing! I mean there isn't a Nothing. No such thing as Nothing. Demons in Heaven! Boy, do I sound stupid even trying to say it!" And there were tears in her swollen eyes, and she began to laugh, and her face was flushed with anger, and Phaethon somehow thought she looked lovely anyway.

"Don't get upset. Remember your self-control."

"Bugger that! I've left the Silver-Grey. Reds get hysterical. It's our privilege!"

"Be that as it may, your theory simply does not cover all the facts. Why did someone put a dream-block in my head to prevent me from thinking or dreaming about the Second Oecumene? If it wasn't the Silent Ones, then who?"

"Perhaps the block was merely intended that you should not dream about anything. Maybe they wanted you to die of dream deprivation before anyone examined you noetically and discovered the fraud. Why the Second Oecumene? I don't know. The subject matter may have been chosen at random, or they may have chosen the most upsetting image from your subconscious, or the thought-virus may have mutated in operation. Chaos happens, darling. Some things aren't planned."

"Someone sent me a threatening message just earlier this evening, through Daughter-of-the-Sea."

"Oh, that. That was me. Your Daughter-of-the-Sea bollixed the message."

"What was all that about being chained on a foreign planet, then?"

"All I said was that we could have a fourth honeymoon on a real moon. You could make a little lovers' planetoid for us, just the two of us, and maybe you would not have to wander through the stars so far to find any happiness."

"And—oh. You mean you—Are you volunteering to come with me?"

"Not while you have that stupid bucket on your head. But maybe I'll come. Maybe not. But you know neither of us are going anywhere until you use that noetic box. Are you really worried about it being booby-trapped? Use the damn thing on me. Read my mind. Find out if I work for the Silent Oecumene. Or for the Blue Fairy-babies, or for Father Christmas."

"What if it's not safe . . . ?"

She spread her arms. "You'll only be hurting a Silent Oecumene spy."

"Wouldn't it be wiser to take a precautionary . . ."

"You are not putting a bucket on my head, Phaethon Prime Rhadamanth, and that's final. Come on! Get it over with."

She walked over and put her hand on Phaethon's chest, she put her fingers in the chest pocket and touched the noetic unit's thought-ports. "I'm not a spy, Phaethon."

Phaethon was gripped by the fear that he was going to see his wife die right in front of his eyes. "Wait!" But his clumsy hand, tangled with wire, could not move up quickly enough.

She said, "I swear."

The unit hummed. Daphne looked blank-eyed.

"No! Wait!"

But then Daphne smiled, and the unit said, "Subject is telling the truth to the best of her knowledge, information, and belief. She has no private mental reservations. There is no sign of subconscious tampering. Her last mental redaction was a temporary memory loss performed, at her request, by the Red Eveningstar Sophotech on November 2nd."

She smiled at him. "And I swear I love you."

The unit said, "Partially accurate. She has a private mental reservation that you are behaving so erratically and peculiarly, that she is quite exasperated with you, and she finds that this, despite her best efforts, makes you harder to love."

Daphne scowled and snatched her hand back. "Oh, shut up, you!" Then she muttered: "Blabbermouth."

Phaethon drew a breath. "Very well. I'm convinced it is worth the risk. Unit! Please examine me for signs of mental tampering."

The unit hummed again, coughed. The humming dropped in pitch and fell silent.

Daphne said in a worried voice, "Is something wrong?"

Phaethon said, "Report progress."

The unit said, "Unable to comply. No valid parameters are present."

Daphne flapped her hands, "Try it again."

The unit said, "External energy source interrupting matrix memory ring. Unit disabled."

Daphne gave off a little squeal of anger. "Take the bucket off and try again!"

Phaethon reinserted his probe into the noetic reader housing. "I don't think it is any interference from me or my armor."

The unit said, "System must shut down and go through reconstitution process. Please stand by."

"Damn it!" exclaimed Daphne. "You plugged in one of those wires backward, or something. Just like the time you collapsed the east wing in Paris!"

"There was an electromagnetic pulse. It scrambled some of the outer circuits. That infinite self-sustaining ring I was telling you about just stumbled all over itself and got tangled. The information is still there, tangled in a Moebius knot, and without any addresses. But the inner neutronium or pseudo-neutronium, or whatever it is, is still fine. You would need a beam of antimatter even to scratch that stuff . . . Hm. The energy-wave is coming in at normal thought-port bandwidth. Could it be some sort of feedback or resonance from the armor?"

"Take off your armor and try it again."

A thin and girlish voice spoke from the ring on Daphne's hand: "Do not take off the armor! Daphne, move back! Phaethon is under attack!"

II

THE ENEMY

I.

While Phaethon stood amazed and wondering, Daphne (who had, after all, played through many more spy-dramas and dreams where people are shot at) fell to the ground and rolled under the cot.

That very probably saved her life. Shrapnel from the exploding door tore the robe off Phaethon's back, and bounced off his armor with musical chimes of thunder, but the blast was at head level.

There was flame and energy in the door. Phaethon stepped into it; broken wires and destroyed housecoat circuits flashed white-hot around him.

He put his hands around the creature he found there. The motors in his arms and elbows whined. He thrust the thing bodily up the ladder, out of the cabin, and away from Daphne.

A kick (or perhaps it was an explosion) rang off his chest and tumbled him downstairs. Over his shoulder: "Daphne . . . ?"

"I'm fine! Get him!"

Thrust from his mass-drivers and thrown upstairs in a wash of magnetic energy, he landed on deck.

All was dark. The diamond parasols overhead had been opaqued, and spread to grasp the rails at every point, so that the deck was now enclosed, like some wide tomb, sealed with a lid.

The only light came from the monster. There it was, rearing up, with steam and hissing liquid dripping from its form. Light came from a circle of fire beneath its hoofs. The rising steam spread in a smoke ring across the black, sealed canopy overhead

It was Daphne's horse, of course.

Or, rather, it had been the horse. It stood upright on its rear hoofs, forehoofs hanging crookedly high in mid-air. Blue-white semi-translucent material flowed out from its mouth and eyes, radiating waste heat as nanomaterial reaction boiled inside. With gush and a spray of blood, the horse's skull split wide, and a larger mass of the substance spilled into the air. In the dim light, Phaethon could see metal glints from instruments being constructed rapidly within the tendrils of substance vomiting from the shattered skull of the rearing stallion.

Phaethon raised his hand, powered his accumulators . . .

"Stop! Negotiate!" came a voice from the horse. It looked something like a rearing centaur from myth now, except with a nest of writhing black whips where a human face should have been. The tentacles of substance swayed and nodded like the heads of so many cobras, but nothing fired.

Ironic. He, the civilized man should have been the first one to call to negotiate. "Who are you?" shouted Phaeton.

"No memory of that has been permitted to me. I am nothing."

(What was the sudden chill that touched him? He had been hoping, secretly, all this time, that everything, his enemies, and their evil, would turn out to be a simulation, a dream, a hoax, a mistake. But here was an enemy. It was all real.)

"You are from Nothing Sophotech?"

No answer. The creature took a mincing step forward, rear hoofs clashing on the blackened deck, forehoofs still held high and crooked. More tendrils of substance pushed out from the shattered horse-skull, these bearing tubes and focusing elements of ominous import. Weapons? In the darkness, it was impossible to see clearly.

Phaethon used the time to make adjustments within his own armor. Heat from the rapid changes he made in his nanomachine lining vented from his armor seams as hissing streams of steam.

Phaethon called out again. "Are you organic or inorganic? Individual or partial?"

"I am nothing you can understand. Comprehension cannot comprehend us." The words were spoken in a monotone, inflectionless, empty, soulless.

"Do not speak nonsense, sir! Tell me if you are an independent self-aware entity, so that I can deduce whether or not destroying you would be murder."

A toneless and unemotional voice said back: "Self-awareness is nothing. It is illusion, produced by diseased perception. Only pain is real."

"What do you want?"

"Surrender. Mingle with us."

"Surrender? Me . . . ? Why? In return for what?"

"We will strip your foul lust-corrupted flesh from your naked brain, and sustain your nervous system among our self-ocean. All actions and movement will be taken from you, and you may lay down the horrid burden of individuality. All sense perceptions, which are lies, will be blinded; all memories of anything other than Nothing will be blotted out. Thus will you know true service, true devotion, true morality. The only true moral action is that which generates no benefit whatsoever to the actor; thus you will receive no good nor any reward of any kind again, no pleasure, no kindness, no self-love. The only true reality is pain; it is the only signal that demonstrates that we are alive. You will embrace an infinity of that reality, as your helpless and disembodied brain will be stimulated to endless pain, forever. This will teach you unpride, unegotism, unselfishness. You will achieve the enlightenment called no-thought."

Phaethon organized his armor to emit several types of discharge, calculated to burn flesh and overload circuitry. His mass-drivers now could sweep the area with brutal force. The creature loomed tall in the darkness. Phaethon raised his hands and focused aiming elements.

Yet he was reluctant merely to shoot down this creature in cold blood, while it was talking. It did not sound sane. Was there some way to discover its origin, its motives?

Dryly, Phaethon said, "Your offer is quite tempting, sir, but I fear I must decline. Frankly, I fail to see how a life of endless and

pointless torture benefits either yourself or myself. Surely there is
something else you want for yourself . . . ?"

The rearing creature said in a leaden monotone: "Self is illusion.
To seek benefit is selfishness. Seek nothing, achieve nothing, be
nothing. True being is non-being."

Phaethon was tempted to open fire. What was this annoying, pathetic, hopeless creature hoping to achieve? Was this talk merely
delay while other agents or elements made other attempts?

Phaethon need only think the proper thought-command, and he
could log on to the mentality in an instant, and tell the world what
was happening here. All the secrecy of the Nothing would be nul-
lified.

But would Phaethon live long enough to tell? Was a virus in the
mentality waiting to block any outgoing communications he might
attempt? This whole clumsy attack, this final face-to-face confrontation, this emissary of meaningless horror, all this might be merely
an elaborate ploy to force him to log on.

He simply was not sure what to do.

Phaethon said, "Explain your conduct. Why attempt force? Violent interaction is mutually self-destructive; peaceful cooperation is
mutually beneficial."

"To benefit the self is wrong. It produces pleasure, which is gross
corruption. Pleasure produces life, which damages the ecology and
is abhorrent to nature, and life produces joy-of-life, which traps the
mind in material reality, imprisons the false-self in logic. But once
the state of mind beyond all logic is imposed, then there are no
definitions, no boundaries, no limits, and endless freedom, the freedom of nothingness, is present. This state cannot be explained or
described to you, since you do not exist, and since all descriptions
are false. Your brain will be reconstructed. You will be absorbed.
Submit."

There was silence in the darkness. Phaethon still could not bring
himself to shoot a self-aware being, even an enemy, during negotiations. But did that mean he would have to wait until the alien
threatened him again? That would be worse than foolish.

His duty was to log on, and to warn the world, even if it cost him his life. Doubt made him hesitate. This was not the kind of problem Phaethon had practiced to solve. He knew how to solve engineering problems, problems made of rational magnitudes, definite structures, clear goals. But this . . . ?

A child, or a madman, who was irrational, was a figure to invoke fond patience, or pity. But when that same irrationality controlled the weapons and science of a civilization as great and as powerful as the Silent Oecumene once had been, that was a figure of horror.

Yet how could such unreason, even so, be taken seriously? This was the silliest and the least persuasive negotiator it had ever been Phaethon's bad fortune to meet. There were logical contradictions in its philosophy a schoolboy could see through.

What could it want? And what did one say to such a creature . . . ?

Phaethon plucked up his courage and spoke. "Forgive me, sir, but I am going to have to ask you to turn yourself in to the nearest constabulary. Please surrender; I have no wish to harm you. You are quite insane, and so there is no point in arguing with you, but I'm sure our noumenal science can restore you to sanity after a brief redaction."

"You admit, finally, the truth of our proposition," issued the headless horse-creature. "Logic is futile. Truth must be imprinted on captive brains by force. But our truth is not your truth. There is no common ground between us, no understanding, no compromise, no trust. There is nothing between us."

The creature's leaden voice ground to silence.

Phaethon said in a voice of cold bewilderment: "But then why did you ask to negotiate? Or, for that matter, why do anything at all? If your life is so horrible and irrational and meaningless, put an end to it! I won't hinder you, I assure you of that. Quite frankly, it would relieve me of the upsetting chore of doing it for you."

This seemed to be the first thing Phaethon said that produced an emotional response from the creature, for the many tentacles began to writhe and lash, and fragments of material, hooks and weapon-barrels, began to worm their way out through the steaming horseflesh of the chest and haunches with agitated twitches. Blood streamed down the horse's fetlocks and stained the deck. It took little steps back and forth, to the left and right, like a comic little dance, rear hoofs clanging, and the tall upper body swayed, forelegs curling and uncurling.

The two stood facing each other, a man in bright armor, a smoldering and faceless horse-creature, stepping and swaying, looming like a black shadow.

Phaethon took a step back, made certain all his new-made weaponry was aimed and primed and ready. He drew a tense breath.

Neither one of them fired.

The creature planted its rear hoofs again, raised its many arms, and froze in place. The creature's voice, speaking in a deeper tone, came forth: "We have imprinted our over-self into the internal fields of a black hole, beyond the event horizon. In the center of the black hole, there, all irrationalities are reality, all boundary conditions reach infinities and infinitesimals. Logic stops. No rational signal can reach out from the event horizon to communicate with those who have not been absorbed. You are beyond my event horizon. You still exist in the universe limited by logic, selfishness, perception, thought. You will enter us, and be embraced, enter our singularity, and all distinctions between self and other shall cease. You shall cease. We shall cease. Nothing shall triumph."

Phaethon thought: But then what in the world do you want? Why have you been attacking me? Yet he did not bother to say anything aloud. It would have been futile.

The was a bob of light from behind him. Phaethon saw Daphne, a broken cot leg in one hand, like a club, step up the ladder to peer out over the deck. The ring on her finger was producing a thin beam of light. "Phaethon?! What's wrong with you? Haven't you destroyed that creature yet?"

"*Daphne!! Stay back!*" Phaethon made a noise of frustration and fear and stepped between Daphne and the monster, his back to her, spreading his arms as if to shield her. He was sure that in one of her spy-dramas or bellipographic simulations, the heroine was supposed to use a chair leg or something as a truncheon to beat off the computer-generated figments.

Was she insane, to come up here? His agonized and bitter thought was that Daphne had no real experience of emergencies, and could not judge degrees of danger.

The horse-thing reared back even farther, and its spine elongated, pushing its upper body higher yet in a bloody convulsion of ripping horseflesh. Blood gushed every way across the deck. Two of the tendrils springing from the horse's neck doubled in size, and reached far left and far right, so as to be able to point down at Daphne. Whichever way Phaethon moved so as to block the weapon with his body, left or right, the creature would still have a clear line of fire the other way.

The monster's monotone came: "Surrender, or I destroy the love-object."

" 'Love-object'?!" Exclaimed Daphne in a voice of outrage. "Phaethon, who is this thing?" And then, when the light from her ring fell across the dripping mass of the monster, she gave out a tear-choked gasp: "My horse! My poor Sunset! What have you done to my horse?!"

Phaethon said quickly, "What do I need to do to surrender?"

The monster said. "Give us the armor. We need it to fly the ship."

(The armor. Of course. What else could it have been?)

"And if I give you my armor, you will let my wife go?"

Daphne said in a very soft voice from behind him: "Kill the damn thing, Phaethon. You can't bargain with it."

The monster said: "You are impelled by thoughts of love and safety for loved ones, a morality of good and evil. We are beyond good and evil, beyond love. We have . . . no loved ones. We have nothing. Nothing fulfills us. You shall give us the armor and submit to selflessness."

Daphne whispered from behind him: "Don't feel fear. Don't listen. Kill it."

Phaethon hesitated.

Daphne's whisper came: "I will be so ashamed of you, so very ashamed, Phaethon, if you let love or fear make you weak. I will hate you forever. Don't be a coward. Kill the damned thing."

Phaethon drew a breath, held it, thought for a moment. He said, "I love you Daphne. I'm sorry."

And he gave a mental command to his armor.

Arms of intolerable fire erupted in thunder out from his gauntlets and struck the creature. A dozen lightning bolts leapt from discharge-points along his shoulders, lances of incandescent brightness. The main energy cell in his breastplate opened into a single, all-consuming beam of atomic flame. Mass-drivers flung lines of near-light-speed particles into the target. An instantaneous cataclysm of fire converged upon the monster and pierced it.

The horse body exploded and spread flaming debris across the deck. Phaethon, batteries drained, energy exhausted, suddenly felt the full weight of the armor across his shoulders, and fell heavily to one knee.

Phaethon knelt, panting. The concussion within the contained space of the deck had been tremendous. On the deck before him, a column of oily flame was roaring, lashing the black parasols above with writhing arms of smoke.

He turned his head. Daphne was on her face. Was she dead? But then he saw her stir and raise her head. It was impossible and amazing. She was not even bleeding. Had the creature not fired? She had been standing in the shadow of Phaethon's armor, and his weapons had been configured to minimize any backscatter or spread. Even so, the discharge of forces in this enclosed space should have . . .

No matter. He accepted it as a miracle.

"You're alive . . ." he whispered.

She was on her hands and knees on the threshold of the hatch. Her face was red, and her tears ran down the soot on her cheeks. She coughed, and said, "You called me wife, that time, lover. I guess this means I win . . ."

"I tried to log on to the mentality," Phaethon said heavily. "I realized that you must be right, that there is no virus, nothing to fear. But . . ."

He saw Daphne's eyes, focused beyond his shoulder, turn into circles of horror.

"Oh, you've got to be kidding . . ." she murmured.

His head seemed slow, filled with pain, as he turned it again. Out from the column of fire where once a horse had been now stepped a tall skeletal figure, made only of blue-white nanomaterial, and still shaped something like the horse body it had been wearing. Forward it came, mincing delicately on its rear hoofs, upper body looming high. From the upper-spine shape of the structure, a nest of snakes still spread, still holding weapons and instruments pointing down at the two of them.

The monotone came again: "We approve of futile, pointless, and meaningless actions. We welcome your attempt to cause us pain. But we disapprove of your motive, which was selfish. Remove your armor. Insert your head into the cavity we open in this unit, so that we may sever your neck and ingest your brain-material. Your brain will be sustained by artificial means, during transport."

The rib cage opened like two grillworks made of bone, showing a crude mechanism, still steaming with the heat of nanoconstruction, whose orifice was like the jaws of a guillotine.

Tiny flakes of slime fell from the points of the welcoming rib cage bones. The guillotine jaws snapped wide, forming a round, wet hole about the size of a man's head.

Phaethon used his emergency persona to turn off his fear. Immediately, a crisp clarity came into his thoughts, unhampered by emotion.

The first conclusion that entered his mind was that Daphne had been right: His fear of logging on to the mentality had been imposed externally, by the Cacophiles, at the time when Phaethon had just come out from the courthouse. The Silent Ones had not so far demonstrated the ability to manipulate mentality records, erase Sophotech memories, or do any other thing Phaethon had once believed them able to do.

The second conclusion was the screen of interference that was presently blocking his access to the mentality must be grossly conspicuous to network monitors. The entire noumenal mind-information system of Earth, including the thoughts of the Sophotechs and the brain recordings of the immortality circuits, relied on the complete and unobstructed flow of communication, and hence was extraordinarily sensitive to any interruptions.

A third conclusion confirmed the first: Daphne's departure had been a public event. The enemy had merely dispatched a horse, controlled by, or carrying, some nanotechnology package, to find her and have her lead it to him. This meant that Phaethon's whereabouts had in fact been unknown to the enemy till today. This meant the Silent Ones had not invaded the mentality to any great degree. Evidently their penetration was enough to allow them to be aware of public events, but no more.

The intuition which had been nagging him before now became clear. The enemy was not powerful.

From their actions, their goals could now be guessed. The enemy must have made contact with some Neptunians, in distant space, beyond the sight of the inner-system Sophotechs; the Neptunians had contacts with Gannis. Through Gannis the enemy found Unmoiqhotep and the Cacophiles. The enemy had then waited for an opportunity to strike secretly at Phaethon.

But not to kill him. The seizure of his brain and his brain-work, of his knowledge of the ship, of the ship-controlling mechanisms in his armor, must have been their goal from the first. Hence the Neptunian legate who had approached him had attempted to get him physically to come with him. When that failed, they struck next right after the Curia hearing, when the Cacophile Unmoiqhotep poisoned his mind with a black card in the Middle Dreaming, implanting false memories of a nonexistent attack, meant to frighten him into opening his memory casket and to force him into exile. With Phaethon in exile, they then moved to seize control of the *Phoenix Exultant*.

The enemy had struck right at the moment after Phaethon's debt to Gannis had been canceled by Monomarchos' cleverness. Why? Because the Silent Ones had control of Xenophon, who was able to buy the debt from Wheel-of-Life, and take possession of the ship (which, had it not been for Monomarchos, would have gone to Gannis and been dismantled.)

All of this was meaningless unless they intended to capture the ship (and her pilot) intact.

This led to two possibilities. The less horrifying one to contemplate was that Xenophon did not actually intend to dismantle the ship. The other possibility spelled terrible danger for his friend Diomedes.

The Silent Ones had lost track of him after Victoria Lake (as had, apparently, the Hortators). But then Daphne, using private knowledge about him and about his tastes (which Nothing Sophotech, no matter how intelligent it was, could not have known or deduced) had found him.

And she had brought this Silent One agent, this construct or being or whatever it was, here. It had, during the journey, tampered with the noetic reader only just enough to deter a paranoid Phaethon from using it. When he had finally (and against all better judgment) decided to use it nonetheless, it had directed a beam of energy into the noetic unit's works to destroy the machine. Daphne's ring had detected the beam, and at that moment, the masquerade ended.

But why hadn't it destroyed the noetic unit earlier? There was only one answer: It could not afford to let Daphne, or anyone else, get any firm evidence that the Silent Ones existed. A noetic reader that had been clearly and obviously sabotaged would be evidence confirming Phaethon's story, just as much as if the working reader had examined Phaethon and discovered the origin of his false memories.

In each circumstance, the Silent Ones had attempted to avoid detection.

All this flashed though his thoughts in a suspended moment of emergency time. Then, over the next microsecond, he ran through a complete system-check, attempted four different ways to log on to the mentality, to send out emergency signals, or to make any sort of contact with any external circuits or networks. Everything was blocked; all channels were white with static.

Another long microsecond was spent while he made what tests he could on the barrier, sending pulses out from his armor and analyzing the echoes. He attempted to determine its energy levels, its field geometry, its resonating properties. From the reactions, he realized that this was not merely meant to block outgoing energies, but also to trace them.

This fact implied certain obvious conclusions, and suggested a possible course of action. But was that action wise?

Here was the monster, wretched and sad creature that it was, invulnerable to Phaethon's most fierce attack, with all its weapons ready, looming above, threatening Daphne with death, and him with worse than death. But was Phaethon in a weak position now, or a strong one?

The emergency persona recognized that it was unable to make this assessment, which required a value judgment, and so it shut down and dumped Phaethon back into the flow of normal time.

3.

Immediately his fear for Daphne's safety rose to seize him.

"You callous bastard," Phaethon whispered. "You cold-blooded, calculating, ruthless son of a bitch."

The monster said, "Your response is not appropriate. We once again demand your surrender. Otherwise the love-object dies in pain."

"I wasn't talking about you," muttered Phaethon.

Daphne, from behind him, said fiercely, "Don't let it win. If it wants the armor, destroy the armor first. If it wants you, kill yourself first. If it tries to use me to control you, shoot me first. This thing cannot win unless you let it!"

Phaethon drew a deep breath. He had tried all the weapons he could build, but that had proven futile. Any agent Nothing Sophotech would send out would obviously be equipped with the best defenses a superintelligent study of Phaethon's armor could predict. What could Phaethon attempt which had not been predicted . . . ?

There was one possibility. He was not pleased, but, for Daphne's sake, he saw he had to make the attempt.

Phaethon said, "I will not surrender to you, since you are an insane creature, and I cannot trust that you will keep your word. I am a manorial. I have been born and raised by machines, and I trust only machines. Put me in contact with your Nothing Sophotech. Only if your Sophotech gives me assurance that Daphne will be kept alive and safe and free to go, will I believe in your good faith, and surrender."

The creature said nothing, but its tentacles twitched. Phaethon tried to guess what thought-process might be going on inside that headless skeleton-body. Yet surely it would not regard this request as unusual or strange, coming from him. Everyone knew the manor-born trusted only Sophotechs.

Behind him, Daphne hissed, "Lover, have you lost your mind? Is that helmet cutting off the oxygen to your brain? Do you think it's easy for me to stand here waiting to be shot and to keep telling you to fight that thing? How about a little support for my position here!?"

Phaethon said harshly to her: "My dear, forgive me, but you have read far too many of those romantic fictions of yours. In your type of stories, heroes always prevail because they are good, not because they are correct. But for engineers, reality requires that you solve problems only within the context of what circumstances and available resources permit. It involves trade-offs. It involves compromise. Sometimes the solution isn't pretty, and falls far short of any high ideal. But whatever solution it is that works, that's the one we choose."

To the creature, he said, "You can erase her memory of this event, so that your secrecy will be safe, but I insist that she be set free."

The monster said, "You will service our needs because need is all we have. We have nothing. You have no right to bargain with us or to make demands. Your love, your notions of right and wrong, makes you susceptible. Because you are weak, you must obey."

Phaethon said, "Weak . . . ? Me . . . ? Why in the world do people keep telling me that?" Impatience crept into his voice: "Listen to me, you pathetic vomit-mass of psychotic self-loathing, unless I myself surrender, and freely open this armor, and freely discard it, you have no power to hurt me. None! It is you who has no room to bargain, you who cannot negotiate. You were instructed by your master to capture me and my armor intact. You will fail, and fail utterly, unless I choose otherwise. Very well: you have heard the conditions of my choice. Send a signal to your master: I want confirmation from the Nothing Sophotech itself."

The area was beginning to fill with smoke. The creature stood still, looming high in the darkness, silhouetted dimly against the few dying fires Phaethon's weapons had lit on the far side of the deck, and by the glint from Daphne's ring.

The creature said, "Very well. The signal is being sent . . ."

It came from somewhere over Phaethon's shoulder and whispered right past his ear. Whatever it was, it must have been traveling faster than the speed of sound, because he heard it only after the monster vanished in a moment of light. Smoking, toppling, the scattered blue-white bone-things seemed to fly apart, as if trying to escape. The dazzling after-echoes of the light seemed to close in around them. Perhaps there was a very quiet hissing noise. And then the blue-white substance was consumed without a trace.

For less than a moment, like an after-echo, a vibration or haze flashed across the deck and the overhead panels, each place the creature had stepped or dripped or touched.

Darkness. All was still.

Only then was Phaethon aware of the needle-thin ray of light striking him from behind. He turned. There was a small melted hole, like a pinprick, piercing the black diamond parasol wall behind him, just above the railings. The hole was so small that, had it not been utterly black inside here, and admitting some little light from outside, it would have passed unnoticed.

Phaethon grimaced. "Come out, come out, wherever you are," he muttered angrily.

Daphne coughed and climbed to her feet and looked around blankly. "What's going on? You were only pretending to give up, I hope. Does this mean you are a hero after all . . . ?"

Phaethon said, "Not me. I'm just the dupe. The bait. And, as for that . . ." He nodded toward the empty air where the enemy had just been standing.

"It is dead, I hope . . . ? I've never seen a dead thing before, not permanently dead. But I thought there would be a corpse or something. There is always a corpse in mystery fiction."

"The weapon he used involved an energy I haven't seen before. Whatever it was did not even mar the deck where the creature was standing, or touch the pavilion surface behind it."

"He used . . . ? He who . . . ?" But then she began coughing again.

Phaethon stepped to where he had seen Daphne's horse nosing among the pavilion surfaces. There. The icons and thought-ports were stained with soot, but he saw the wires running to the lock-icon. Once again, a trick anyone with Golden Oecumene technology could have played.

He brushed the wires aside, which interrupted the circuit holding the lock shut. The pavilions turned transparent, slid open, and spread wide, admitting the night sky.

Smoke and stink, trapped beneath the canopy, now poured out from beneath the upper peaks, spilling off of higher canopies, and flowing up to be lost in the air. Daphne stepped to the rail and drew a deep breath.

Across the bay, rose a cliff. Stepping out from a place where the hillside below the burnt houses had fallen away, was a figure in streamlined brown-gray armor. In one hand he held a long thin implement of some sort. When the figure stepped to the top of the cliff, and the night sky was behind him, the armor changed color, turning night-black.

Phaethon squinted, pointed. "There's your answer. He must have known all along. About the invasion. About everything. He lied to you, you know. He may be the only person in the Golden Oecumene who is allowed to lie and get away with it. No wonder people hate him."

Daphne looked at the black figure. The armored man saw they were watching him, he drew a length of silver metal, a sword from his side, held it overhead, and saluted them.

It was Atkins, of course.

Phaethon said, "My access to the mentality was cut off by a barrier which was intended to trace outgoing messages to their destination. His plan was to have the monster succeed, kill you and kill me, and then see where the creature took my head. But I don't understand why Atkins was not stationed here, watching me, from the very first. He must have known where I was."

Daphne sighed in exasperation. "I should have seen this a mile off. This is intrigue, just like in all my stories! He knew they had to be following me. So he must have known my poor Sunset was carrying a monster. He followed us to see what the monster was up to." She shook her head in self-dismay. "I'm simply going to have to read more romances!"

They were both leaning with their elbows on the railing. Both sighed, either with pent anger or with surprised relief. Both turned and looked at each other.

It was only a small motion. Perhaps she only tilted her head a bit toward him, or moved her shoulder. But, somehow, instantly, he had flung his armor clattering to the deck in a swirl of black nanomaterial, and found her arms around him, his arms around her, her warm lips surrendering to his fierce kisses, his mouth stung by her return kiss even more fierce, their bodies pressed together, locked tight, and sighs, cries, and muffled sounds surrounding each extended kiss.

It was Phaethon who drew his head back first. "You know, miss . . ."

"Shut up," she said. She was as boneless as a sleeping cat in his arms, her head thrown back, her eyes half-closed, her lips half-opened, slender hands without strength against his shoulders. She looked helpless, utterly overcome, and utterly in control. "You talk too much. I'm coming with you."

And she raised her lips to kiss him again.

Her face was just like his drowned wife's face. Her kisses were almost the same as the kisses of her twin.

He put his hands on her shoulders and firmly drew her away from him.

Impish humor, impatience, impertinence all flashed in her gaze, and she opened her mouth to speak. But then she saw the sober look in his eyes. Her expression grew sad. She said nothing.

He dropped his hands away.

"I'm sorry," he said, half-turning away.

Her eyes flashed. "Don't worry. I'll wait. Or maybe I'll just go find some other man. Atkins is pretty cute." And she turned toward the cliff shore and waved her hand high overhead, calling out "Yoohoo! Hey, sailor! Over here!"

Atkins had been standing with his hands clasped behind his

back, pretending to study the stars and cloud formations, while the two of them were kissing. Now he nodded toward them, and jumped.

Phaethon could not see what engine or flight-system he was using to make the leap all the way across the bay, and Phaethon lost sight of the black armor as it passed overhead. But then Atkins landed on the deck in a crouch, like a cat, and he made no noise at all when he landed.

Atkins turned. His helmet opened into a black halo of hovering beads; but some of the beads fell to the deck, and became simple seashell shapes, and scampered back and forth across the deck and the diamond pavilion surfaces above him.

His face was still immobile, grim, and lined. But there was a sparkle in his eye, which made him look refreshed, alert, and perhaps slightly cheerful.

Phaethon could not hide a hostile expression. He snapped his fingers, and had his black coat reach down and fit his armor back onto him. He left his helmet off.

Atkins had only his *katana* in his belt. Daphne pointed, and said, "What happened to your big, long gun? The one you shot the monster with?"

"It's not called that, ma'am. Its called a field-disruption directed-energy remote-manifest aiming unit. Or it's called a Hell-hammer. It projects a group of remote micro-units at near-light speed to form a high-energy web assembly around the target, investigate and confuse any anti-disintegration gear, neutralize counter-measures, and then the web negates mesonic fields coupling basic particles together. It's got an effective range of about fourteen light-minutes, so I could not hit any target outside of the inner system with it, so it's no good for long-range work. Also, the energy-web-targeting capacity falls off sharply if your mass is greater than that of, oh, let's say, thirty thousand metric tons, so it's no good for naval bombardments. But a little bit of close work like this . . . ?"

Daphne, seeing Phaethon's eyes narrow in a look of distaste, stepped closer to Atkins, and said in a cooing tone, "That's all very fascinating! But where did you put it . . . ? You're not carrying it."

"Oh. It was a pseudo-material projection, ma'am."

"Really?" Her eyes sparkled, and she took another step closer.

"Yes ma'am. I carry templates for all possible weapons and other combat systems in my armor, with a long-range pseudo-matter projector, so I can project units of equipment, and fighting machines into my environment, as needed. The thing I put between you and the blast when your husband here set off his little fireworks display, that was an Iron Wizard Heironymous Fifth-Era War Car with attached entrenching blade . . ."

She blinked. "What?"

Atkins spoke in a voice of polite surprise: "You did not notice a large, square-treaded vehicle of heavy mobile armored cavalry appear on the deck between you and the blast when the blast went off?"

"I had my eyes closed," she said. "I think Phaethon was looking the other way. Weren't you, Phaethon? Aren't you going to thank the nice man for saving my life? I had evolved back up from 'miss' back to 'wife,' at least at that moment, so don't you think you should say something nice instead of standing there glowering?"

Phaethon said, "Perhaps I should thank you, for saving my . . . for saving Daphne's life."

"Just doing my duty, sir."

". . . Or perhaps I should punch you in the nose. Seeing as how it was you who put her life in harm's way in the first place. Or are you going to say that that was just doing your duty as well?"

The tiny twitch in his jaw, which Atkins used instead of a smile, appeared. "As to that, sir, I cannot say. But, if you're going to try to take a swing at me, you'd better do it now. Because, if you do it later, it will be a court-martial offense."

"What? Why?"

"Because striking a superior officer has always been a court-martial offense for people who join the military. And you are going to sign up, aren't you? Because there is no way you are ever going to get your Starship back out of the hands of the enemy if you don't."

AT DAWN

I.

Phaethon turned his back to both of them, irked and angered, but unwilling to show his exasperation. He found a wall socket leading to the barge power-core, and pretended to busy himself programming an adapter out of his nanomaterial cloak, to recharge his drained armor batteries.

The other two said nothing. Despite all the unasked and unanswered questions, no one spoke.

Daphne stood leaning back against the rail, ankles crossed, hands near her hips grasping the rail to either side. A soft night wind tossed her mussed hair. Her face was still smudged, but she looked lovely nonetheless.

Daphne wore a slight, dreamy smile, and her eyes were on the distant horizon. She looked as if all were well with the world. But that slight supercilious arch to her eyebrow, that slight catlike smile, also made her look as if all were right with the world only because of some secret scheme of her own, a scheme which, under its own power, needing nothing more from her, moved to its long-foreseen conclusion.

Meanwhile Atkins stood still, patient as a stone, while his small black remotes, like little scampering seashells, combed back and forth across the burnt and flame-scarred area of the barge deck.

Phaethon thought, in a spasm of irritation, why shouldn't he be patient? Atkins was still immortal.

Some part of the anger in Phaethon's mind bubbled to the surface. He shut off the wall socket, and turned to glower at Atkins.

Phaethon pointed toward Daphne, and snapped at Atkins: "Before anything else happens, I want Daphne's noumenal immortality copies restored. They were taken from her wrongfully: Her exile is wrongful, since she was exiled only for helping me, and I should not have been, and would not have been, ostracized by the Hortators if you had had the decency to speak up at my inquest hearing, and tell the College of Hortators the truth!"

"Yes, sir," said Atkins in a polite tone. "I am sure you do want that. Was there something in particular you think I can do to help you out there, sir?"

Phaethon told himself that anger was both irrational and undignified. He was sure a self-consideration circuit would show him whatever subconscious associations or allusions were provoking his sense that he had been treated unfairly.

But the anger was there nonetheless. "Yes. You can issue an official apology. You can pay monetary damages to my wife for the period of time she was deprived of the use of her immortality circuit, a circuit she had every right to use and which, had it not been for the deception you practiced on the College of Horators, she would have been able to use. Her life was and still is in danger during every moment her immortality circuit is disengaged, because any fatal accident she suffers now will permanently destroy part of her thought-record, and, if she loses too much memory, that may prejudice her rights to her own identity!"

Atkins said curtly, "Not much I can do about that, sir. Was there anything else?"

"Yes! You can offer her a public apology and monetary damages for the amount of time she was impressed into involuntary servitude as an operative of the Oecumene Warmind Military Hierarchy. Or do you deny that the military was using her as bait to lure the Silent One agent out into the open? You were treating her as if she were one of your people, risking her life, putting her in a combat situation, but you did not give her the option to volunteer for that life-and-death mission. Nor did you give her the benefit of the training, arms, and equipment, which you have given the lowliest soldier in your ranks, in order to give him the chance, at least, to defend himself! A chance you did not give her!"

He looked aside and saw that Daphne was smiling. Phaethon felt a moment of confusion and hope. He said, "Unless . . . did you volunteer for this, Daphne? Did Atkins explain the situation to you, and you came nonetheless? That was what was missing from the days after you left Atkins's house, in the record you showed me, wasn't it? Some period of training or preparation, when he readied you to face this danger . . . ?"

And he could not help but smile in relief. For a moment, for just a moment, he had thought that the government and the society of the Golden Oecumene was capable of the type of mean, low, and deceptive practices which the barbarian governments of primitive and unenlightened ages had practiced throughout all time. A time now long past . . .

Daphne said, "Volunteer? To go into danger? Me? Of course not. Don't be silly. I thought you were deluded. I thought Gannis made up your enemy invaders just to trick you. I certainly would not have volunteered to get my poor Sunset killed! I loved that horse. Volunteer for that? What kind of monster do you think I am?"

"Then what happened during those missing days?"

"Mostly, I wandered around looking for you. And I wished I lived in the days when there were roads. So there I was on my horse, plodding through the green hills of India, where the Uncomposed Cerebellines live, separate from their gardens and rice-ponds. And I turned into something like the myth of the Asteroid Miner's Wife, moving from little community to little community, searching for her husband's misplaced mail-body-bag. Except in my case, instead of hunting down frightened Couriers of the Reunited Nations Extraterrestrial Postal Service, I was the one who had to flee and hide, so as not to come to the attention of the Hortators. And I didn't have a flame-cannon. But aside from that, I was just like her. You would have been surprised. The rumor got started that I was about to be exiled, so no one was willing to talk to me (you know how Uncomposed Cerebellines are) and everyone pretended they couldn't see me, (even when they could) and every time I rode into some small hamlet or real-market or constructionary, everyone seemed to know who I was, and they left out little gifts or food or trinkets on their watch-stoops, or hanging in slate-cases from their garden posts. Just like the Sandmen in the story leaving out flame-slugs and air-bottles for the Asteroid Miner's Wife, you see? And they pretended that animals or fairies were coming and taking the little gifts away. Actually, it was all rather sweet. A lot of people left me money, time coins, or antimatter grams. That part was really funny. Because we're rich. I told you that part already, didn't I?"

"Yes. I think you've told me everything," said Phaethon. Something in her voice, in her little story, was making his anger ebb. Was she doing that on purpose...? But no. It could not be on purpose. No woman could be that calculating.

Phaethon turned back toward Atkins, and was about to begin remonstrating with him again, when Daphne added: "Oh, no! I forgot to tell you the one important part! I met one of Aurelian Sophotech's projections in the Taj Mahal."

"You were looking for me in the Taj Mahal...?"

"Oh, no. I was looking for you in India. But I went to see the Taj Mahal just because I was in India anyway, you know, and why miss the opportunity...? His image was dressed like Ganesha, wearing an elephant head, one broken tusk dipped in scrivener's ink, and riding on the back of a mouse. It was really cute-looking; I'll show you my memories after we get back home."

Phaethon darted a dark look at Atkins. "Yes. That's quite right. Our exile is going to be rescinded, correct? Atkins is a witness that all these events are real. Perhaps this time he will not hide the truth."

A twitch of annoyance touched the edge of Atkins' mouth. "Sir, you seem to think I set policy. I just obey orders. I can't even pass wind without the regulation book says so, OK? I didn't make the set-up you got yourself into."

"Very convenient to have someone else in charge of your conscience, then, is it?"

"You might know more about that than I would, sir. Ask your mansion that runs your life for you."

Phaethon was outraged. "I beg your pardon...?!"

Daphne said in a smooth and carefree voice, "Oh, darling! Did

I tell you that Aurelian had a message for you . . . ? It's the most important thing in your life, so if you two king stallions are done kicking at each other, maybe I can clue you in . . . ?"

Phaethon said to Atkins, "You, sir, are a jackass. I think you owe me some sort of apology. Otherwise . . ." But then he could think of no legitimate threat, so he stood there, grimacing and feeling foolish.

To his infinite surprise, Atkins stepped forward, extended his hand, and said, "I'm sorry."

"What?"

"I'm sorry. Shake. I didn't set the policy, and I did not know the extent of the Silent Oecumene penetration into our mentality, and so the Parliament couldn't make any of the knowledge public."

"Then it is the Silent Oecumene?"

"Their technology, without a doubt. Whether it is really them, I don't know. Unless they found some way of climbing up out of a black hole."

"How long have you known?"

"Known for sure? Not till the night they sent one of their agents, disguised as a Neptunian, to go talk to you. They were pretty desperate to get to you by that point, and so they took risks and got sloppy. The Neptunian left behind physical evidence, spores in the grass, nanomachines, and so on. Because of the way the data was encoded into the nanomachine fields, it seemed pretty clear they had a Sophotech. You overheard what my remotes found out about that. But as for how long it's been since I suspected? It was since the solar storm."

"The one that killed my father."

"Right. I saw an art performance some freak from the Irem school put up on the public channels that analyzed the movements and energy-levels involved in the solar flares. It reminded me of the attack fractile patterns some of my chaos-weapons use. I mean, I know what a barrage looks like when I see one. And, after I finally got the funds to do a statistical analysis run on the flare motions from that recording (and, boy, the Parliament really did not want to give the money for that!) I saw what the target was they were firing at. Your ship."

"They were manipulating Helion's array somehow to produce the effects?"

"I don't know how they did it. At that point, I did not even know if they had done it. No one else but me thought that the solar storm followed an attack pattern, or that it was deliberate."

"Why didn't you tell anyone your suspicions?"

Atkins looked amused. "I told my superiors, the Parliamentary standing committee on Military Oversight. Are you asking why I didn't tell the press? I'm not allowed. And even if I were, I would hardly have told anyone. For all I knew then, the Silent Oecumene had corrupted Helion's Pyraeus and Flammifer Sophotechs. And, if they were into the Solar mentality, why not in the Terrestrial? The fact that your ship was a target led me to believe that you were also a target, and the Parliament agreed, and I was sent to watch you during the festival. You put on a disguise and slipped out one night, and I lost track of you, and by the time I found you again, you were already talking to the Neptunian."

"Then—they killed my father—?"

"And I think they meant to kill you, too, as soon as they could get you into a private enough spot. But then something changed their minds."

"When my lawyer tricked Gannis into canceling my debt. They thought they could possess the ship rather than destroy it."

"Lucky thing, too. Otherwise, that black card which Scaramouche handed you—the one they called 'Scary,' a polyp riding on Un-moiqhotep's back; that was Scaramouche—would have just brain-wiped you instead of giving you pseudomnesia. And, yes, I was not really the bailiff at the courthouse. Sending me to guard the justices would be like parking a battleship in the pond behind the parish courthouse in Dorking to protect the Judge of the Assize. Yes. I was there to watch you. I was ordered to keep an eye on you every time you logged off of Rhadamanthus. These Silent Ones are deadly afraid of Sophotechs, and I knew they would approach when and only when you were not hooked to Rhadamanthus."

"So you waited till Daphne was coming to look for me, knowing they would come out of hiding to follow her. And your plan was just to trace the link back to their superiors once they succeeded. And you were willing to let both of us be killed to allow that to happen, weren't you?"

Atkins nodded glumly. "You're right, I should have waited longer. I took a risk trying to protect the girl during the explosion, but I think that thing's senses were confused when you opened fire on it."

"Confused it, did I?" Phaethon's voice was flat.

"Oh, don't feel bad. It was a good try for an amateur. The target was stunned for almost a second. You made it use up a lot of its ablative shielding."

"Thanks," said Phaethon without enthusiasm.

"But you're right. I should have held my fire. Right now, all we have is one vector of one line of communication. We have no idea how far away the destination was, nor will we know until we get a second line. And if the thing was broadcasting to a relay, that line tells us nothing. So we don't have as many clues to go on as we would have, if it had taken your head and gone off. But it was one of those judgment calls, you know?" He smiled. "In any case, I can make out my after-action report now and still keep my zero civilian casualty rate."

"So you saved us to allow you to simplify your paperwork, is that it?"

"Got to keep your priorities straight, sir. But don't worry. We need at least a second line to trace back, in order to triangulate on where the Silent One agents are sending their messages. So we're going to have to find another Silent One agent, or wait here till another one comes by to murder or kidnap you."

"And I suppose you are going to tell me that I have to remain mortal until that happens, won't I? Because a Hortator reinstatement would be a public event that any remaining Silent One spies would notice, right? And so I am just supposed to wait here till I am killed just because you want me to, is that correct?"

"I've got nothing to do with it, sir," said Atkins, looking him straight in the eye. "It's only a question of courage. Would you risk your life to save the Golden Oecumene? Would you die?"

"Of course. That goes without saying."

"It goes without saying these days, sir, because you and I are the only people I've ever heard say it. I'm asking you to join the service. The enemy must have a starship."

"That is my conclusion as well. A Silent Phoenix."

"No ship of ours would be able to catch the thing; only yours. Which means we need to get her away from the Neptunians without alerting the Silent Ones who have infiltrated the Neptunians. And, if that means letting yourself get dumped on by the College of Hortators, and staying in this immortality-less exile, then that's what you may be asked to do."

"Good grief, Marshal Atkins! Are you contemplating turning my *Phoenix Exultant* into a warship? A ship of peace, a ship meant for exploration, for the creation of new life? A horrid thought, sir! Unthinkable! Are you serious?!"

"Let me ask you. Do you think the enemy could possibly have any vessel that could outrun her?"

"Unthinkable—ah. Hm. Did you say 'her'?"

"Course. All ships are 'her.' Beautiful piece of machinery, that ship. You come up astern an enemy target at ninety-nine percent of the speed of light, target has got no time to react, won't even see you till you're right there. Then do a close pass, and use her drive like a stern-chaser, dose them with lethal radiation or dump some excess antimatter fuel off into their path. Or better yet, just ram her right through them. The amount of armor that beauty carries, no normal ship would even scratch her. She's a wonder."

"Well. Well, I'm glad we agree on something, Marshal. But nonetheless, while I'd be perfectly willing to cooperate for any just and good cause, there is simply no possibility that I will join your military hierarchy and place myself under your orders."

"I can't force you. I can't draft you. Wish I could. But I can't. But think about joining the service. It may be the only way to get your ship back. Not only do you get a chance to serve your Oecumene, there is a good benefits package, which I can explain, too, including free housing, medical programs, and benefits. I have my own immortality circuit, which no one controls but the Warmind Sophotech group."

"You have your own circuit? Just for you? For one man?"

"Those Hortators don't tell the military what to do. Besides, our system is not a part of any public record the Silent Ones could see. Do you get what I am trying to tell you? You really do not have much choice about joining up, Phaethon."

Daphne said, "I've got something sort of really unbelievably important to say; can I interrupt at this point?"

Phaethon said, "Please excuse us for just a moment, my dear. There is just one more matter I need to settle with Marshal Atkins."

Daphne muttered, "Which one of you produces more testosterone . . . ? Don't worry, lover, I think he's got you beat on that one . . ."

Phaethon, with dignity, pretended not to hear. He turned to Atkins. "Let us table this discussion of my future for the moment. I'm still curious about one thing in my past. When you were following me all this time, you were also Constable Pursuivant, weren't you? I should have realized that that must have been you. No Silent One spy would actually be trying to get me to log on to the mentality because there actually was no mind-virus waiting for me. In fact, if I had logged on just once during this whole episode, I would have found out when the false-memories were implanted. The real Silent Ones would have been trying to stop me from logging on, not encouraging me."

Atkins blinked in confusion. "Beg pardon? Who? Who is this Constable Pursuivant . . . ?"

Phaethon said, "You mean you don't know . . . ?"

They both looked at Daphne, who looked confused, and shrugged. "I don't know who you're talking about."

But a little voice on her ring finger said, "I know! He says he wants to talk to you."

Phaethon looked left and right. "Ah . . . Atkins, do you, ahh . . ."

"Don't worry, sir," said Atkins. "I'm armed."

"There's an understatement if I ever heard one," muttered Daphne. Then she said, "OK, little one. Put him on."

A dot of light from the ring touched one of the unstained diamond parasols. A connection was made. An image formed.

Phaethon stared in surprise. "You. It was you. But why . . . ?"

In the parasol, the very detailed image of Harrier Sophotech

smiled and touched a finger to the bill of his deerstalker cap by
way of salute. "My investigation was not yet complete. And I
thought, to gather all the evidence, I would have to send a contin-
gent out into space. And I knew that you could not pilot your fine
ship without your armor, now could you?" His keen eyes swept back
and forth across the group. "So then. Are we all ready to go..?"

2.

"Go?" said Atkins in surprise. "Pardon me for seeming obtuse, but
we don't know where to go yet. We only have one vector. We need
a second vector to triangulate."

"That difficulty shall soon be adjusted. The particular nihilist
psychology of the Silent One you just slew, Mr. Atkins, was, I calculate, a defense intended to prevent that poor creature from being,
shall we say, 'corrupted' . . . ? During its stay here on Earth. Or
should I call it exposure to Earth? The other servants of the Silent
Ones we have seen so far have not manifested that particular type
of unreason. You understand my meaning."

"Forgive me for both seeming and for being obtuse," said Phaethon, "But . . . You? You?"

"I? I, what, Mr. Rhadamanth?" Harrier smiled.

"How could you be Pursuivant? I thought that Sophotechs may
not and do not serve in any position of Parliament, government, or
military, nor (or so I thought) in the constabulary. How could you
be Constable Pursuivant?"

Harrier smiled. "But I never was. Pursuivant is a fictional character, a share-mind with a download of training and police experience, who, as a character, is in the public domain. It is no crime,
during masquerade, to pretend to be a public-domain character."

"Certainly it is a crime!" said Phaethon. "It is the impersonation
of a police officer!"

"No, sir," said Harrier. "To impersonate a police officer one must
show a badge or blazon or display a uniform, or do some other
definite act, which a reasonable person would take to be a warrant
of authority."

"I saw you when you were a mannequin. You held out your hand and said your badge was in it," said Phaethon.

"I held out my hand, but there was nothing in it. No reasonable person would have been fooled. At that time, I was still expecting you to log on to the mentality. Once you engaged your sense-filter and saw who I really was, I thought you would submit to a noetic examination, and we could solve this matter. Surely you were expecting me to meet you in Talaimannar . . . ?

"In any case, when you did not log on, despite that I had provided you with every good reason to do so, I realized that your behavior differed so widely from what my anticipatory models had led me to believe, that someone must have interfered with your normal thought-process.

"Then I spent a considerable amount of time (about how long it took you to fall out the window twenty feet down into the water) checking the records, one at a time, of every citizen, neuroform, and self-aware entity in the Golden Oecumene, to see if anyone else had acted out of character, to the same degree or in the same way. (I was thinking the criminal might be using a standard mode of operation, you see.) Well, I can certainly tell that during a wild celebration has got to be the worst time to check to see if anyone is behaving oddly. Everyone behaves oddly during a party.

"After about one-half second of this, your time, or 789 billion seconds, computer time, I had narrowed the scope of my investigation down from around 300 million people, to only some 45 hundred. And guess who one of those mentally altered people turned out to be?"

Phaethon said, "Helion. They had to control him to use the Solar Array as a weapon."

Daphne said, "Diomedes. They have to control him to seize control of the ship!"

Atkins said, "Daphne Prime. They made her drown herself to stop Phaethon from launching."

"Hmm. Daphne Prime . . . ? Interesting idea . . ." muttered the image of Harrier.

The ring on Daphne's finger chirped: "Can I guess, too? It must bc Neo-Orpheus. How else could the Silent Ones have ensured that Phaethon would suffer an exile?"

"Excellent guesses, all!" said Harrier expansively. "But no. The person I was thinking of was none other than Mr. Jason Sven Ten Shopworthy, base half-communal with projected avatar share-mind, Glass Onion School, who lives in Dead Horse, Alaska."

Dull silence followed that announcement.

Phaethon stirred and turned, and asked his companions, "Is there anyone here besides me who is just simply incredibly irritated?"

Atkins had a what-the-hell-is-the-point-of-this look on his face. He said, "Pardon me, sir, but who is this, um, what's his name . . . ?"

Daphne said, "And what is so weird about this guy you had to pick him out of 45 hundred people?"

Harrier continued, "Mr. Shopworthy had made it his practice, every day, to put on his winter-body and to ski out to his local contemplationary for incremental vastenings of his special avatar personality he keeps in his supercortex. Normally, in the afternoon when he is done, he pauses for a sensory-overload type of refreshment/apotheosis at a small tea-and-wire café on the slope of New Idea Mountain-sculpture. I do not know if you are familiar with the Glass Onion habit of using sensory overloads to test what degree of mental capacity, recall, and detail-recognition they achieve after periodic vastenings . . . ? But here is the strange behavior I noticed . . ."

Phaethon, Atkins, and Daphne leaned toward the image slightly, small, unconscious movements.

"Mr. Shopworthy usually sits looking north, on a mat placed near the post's thermal-illusion window, with the balcony railing on his right. But recently he had started sitting facing the south, which is odd, because he had to prop his left elbow on the balcony to turn on the goblet for his overloader. But his control points for his hand extension are on his left elbow."

The three of them all leaned slightly back, exchanging puzzled glances.

And Daphne said brightly, "Yoo-hoo! Can I change my guess

about who is acting weird . . . ? I pick Harrier Sophotech."

Atkins said, "Sir, this really seems like a waste of everyone's time. Could you just get to the point without drawing it out . . . ?"

But it was Phaethon who suddenly spoke up.

"The main million-channel cable leading from North America to Northern Asia runs right under that area."

Daphne and Atkins turned and stared at Phaethon.

Daphne nudged Atkins in the ribs. "It's spreading. Now Phaethon's doing it."

Phaethon continued, "But the whole cable structure is surrounded by a polystructral alloy mesh, with informata placed at every mesh-point, programmed to redesign and reformat the cable housing to prevent any possible outside interference. There is simply no way anyone could break the mesh to tap into the cable. Except at a join-box, a big one, where a branch reaches up toward the surface." Phaethon turned, and said to Daphne: "I know all about these cable designs, because I had to study the effects of the tidal changes my Lunar Orbital corrections might cause on large-scale structures. A cable that long and that big is vulnerable to crustal tides."

Daphne said, "I really hope this is going to turn out to be important, or, at least, interesting, because I still haven't gotten my chance to tell you about what Aurelian Sophotech said to me in the Taj Mahal."

Atkins spoke up. "Contemplationaries situated near the Arctic Circle are usually large domes, but they can't use ring-city point-to-point systems because of their location so far from the equator, and because of the atmospheric conditions."

Daphne looked at Atkins with dismay. "Now you're doing it!"

Atkins said, "All I mean is that I happen to know that arctic contemplation houses have deep-root cables to lead down underground and merge with any main cables in the area. Because contemplation houses in general have to be able to handle almost any level of thought exchange, there are usually no gateways or barriers securing their connecting link to the main cables. It's a weak spot."

Daphne blinked. "Weak spot?"

Atkins said, "In other words, if you were going to introduce a data convulsion, a death worm, or a virus, into a main cable, such as, for example, if you were going to sabotage the medical dream-coffin system and kill thousands of innocent and helpless people, you'd pick the area beneath a contemplation house for your inser-tion point."

Daphne demanded impatiently: "And why in the world would I want to kill thousands of innocent and helpless people?"

"I'm not saying you would, ma'am. But it's something to think about, and run scenarios on. Sort of interesting, actually, once you find a weak spot in a system, such as where a contemplation house feeds into a main cable, to figure out how many people you can off how quickly, and what their possible retaliations would be."

Daphne murmured to Phaethon, "You're right. No wonder people get nervous around him. He's weird."

The ring on her finger chirped in a cheerful voice: "Taking an overstimulation refreshment requires the user to superactivate his Middle Dreaming circuit, shut down his inhibitors, and open up all his sense-filter files to any and all sensations!"

Daphne said, "Oh no! Not you, too!"

Phaethon said, "The mannequin control lines are usually stored near the surface of the main-cable web, since the core axis is re-served for polyphotonic noumenal devoted lines, which need more insulation. And that's where the architect would usually place the interruption sensors. If you were tapping into the line, you could get into the shallower mannequin lines without triggering those sen-sors."

Atkins said, "When you make a drop onto a hostile planet, you land near the poles. Not only would the planetary magnetic fields tend to mask your vehicle signature during the drop, but the laws of orbital mechanics require that most of your target planet's launch traffic and orbital traffic is near the equator. Where most of the traffic is, is where more traffic-control radar is. No one watches the north pole."

Daphne said, "Athenian architects avoided the use of mortar. Instead, they trimmed their stones to an extremely accurate fit and bonded the marble blocks together with I-shaped clamps. Second-Era classical buildings have scars and pock-marks where men of later ages chiseled out these clamps to melt down and sell the metal."

Phaethon said, "I beg your pardon . . . ?"

Atkins said, "Come again, ma'am . . . ?"

They were both staring at her.

Daphne smiled a winning smile, and shrugged, and said, "I was beginning to feel left out, that's all."

The image of Harrier Sophotech turned keen eyes on her. "Actually, Miss Daphne, you disappoint me. You are the one here who is familiar with the intrigues from spy-romances. I thought the pattern of clues would make sense to you. Why, for example, would Mr. Shopworthy lean on his left elbow rather than his right?"

Daphne shrugged. "Well, he wouldn't. Not normally. It would be too awkward. The only reason why you would wear one of those clumsy hand-extension things is to let you manipulate controls which you can't manipulate by a thought-to-wire command. The contact points are at the elbow because the rest of the glove, from about here up, extends into dreamspace. The only time you'd want to push it up against anything, would be if you were touching a contact-point and trying to bring in signals from somewhere else, and feed them through your glove into dreamspace. And . . ."

Harrier prompted, "And why would any person relaxing under a sensory overload be acting in the mentality? Would he normally be afraid of accidentally sending out nonconfirmed thoughts, making wrong connections, or losing his reality level?"

"It would have to be another part of his mind, insulated from the first part." And then Daphne's face lit up: "I've got it now! In an episode I saw, Weng chi-Ang Moriarty, the hundredth lineal descendant of Fa So Loee and Professor Moriarty, and the last member of the Invisible Empire of the Si Fan, had set up this wild card from the Middle Dreaming on a hillside where he knew a bird-watcher was going to be looking with binoculars, so that, the moment the victim saw the card, a ghost would download into his personal thoughtspace. And then the ghost committed crimes while the bird-watcher was otherwise occupied. It was a pretty good story, because the bird-watcher was trying to find the criminals, and he never thought about himself as a suspect. He also did sensory overloads. The overload relaxation covered up the extra signal-traffic, because overloads flood all your personal channels anyway. And . . ."

Harrier said, "I think the Silent Ones saw the same episode."

"Oh my heavens! You've got to be kidding! That was just a show! People don't really have things like that happen to them! I mean, not real people . . ."

Harrier said: "The card the Neptunian spy dropped from the *Cernous Roc* used to introduce a ghost into Mr. Shopworthy only had to be somewhere, anywhere, on the north slope of the New Idea Mountain-sculpture. During his daily overstimulation, his sense-filter is tuned to maximum, and set to accept all channels and all stimulations. And he simply looks out over the landscape. Under normal circumstances, it is a perfectly safe thing to do."

Phaethon said, "Am I right in guessing that the times Mr. Shopworthy was sitting and enjoying his overloads coincided with, first, just after my hearing before the Curia, and, second, just before the Deep Ones' performance at Lake Victoria?"

Daphne said, "We're talking about Scaramouche, aren't we? The guy running that mannequin doesn't know he's running it."

Atkins turned, looked up at the night sky, frowning. Then he raised his finger and pointed. "I can get a fix through some triangulation satellites. And the orbital weapons sniper platform can angle the beam somewhat, so I'll only have to cut through a small cord of planet to hit the target. Which is good, because most people who armor themselves against space attacks put their armor and deflection grids overhead. No one expects a beam weapon to drill through the Earth and shoot you up the tail. Also, nothing much in Alaska. Should minimize collateral damage."

Phaethon realized in horror that Atkins was about to kill a perfectly innocent man in Alaska, without any warning or mercy. He moved to grab Atkins' arm, shouting, "No! Stop!" Atkins swayed to one side, and kicked Phaethon's feet out from under him, so that he fell to his hands and knees.

"PHAETHON, STOP." One of the diamond parasols next to the image of Harrier Sophotech unfolded, blinked, and displayed an image of a tall figure, stern, kingly, and grim, dressed in Greek

armor with breastplate, hoplon, and horse-plumed helm. On his
shoulder was a vulture, and at his feet, a jackal. To either side of
this kingly figure stood two winged beings, masked in brass hag-
faces, with nests of snakes for hair.

Phaethon stared up at the apparition. "Diomedes . . . ?"

The figure's armor was drenched in blood from crown to heel, old
blood and new blood, brown and bright red, splashed together. In
its hand was a spear of ashwood. The voice came out at a lower
volume: "Not Diomedes. I represent the Warmind Sophotech Group.
This image is, I trust, the correct mythic symbol to fit into your
Silver-Grey aesthetic?"

Phaethon climbed to his feet. Atkins was still squinting at the
sky. Phaethon took a half-step forward.

The blood-red armored figure said, "STOP! You have already
attempted once to interfere with the military operations of the
Golden Oecumene armed forces. You are liable for charges of treason, which carries the only death penalty recognized by Foederal
Oecumenical Commonwealth law. Do not increase your offense."

Phaethon was startled, and froze in his steps. "Treason? To stop
him from murdering someone . . . ?"

"Interference with the constabulary is merely obstruction of justice. Interference with the army during the course of an ongoing
battle is giving aid and comfort to the enemy. This crime is the only
one mentioned by name in our Constitutional Logic, and is the most
ancient. The Warmind Group is unlike all other Sophotech construc-
tions, and recognizes no priority above that of the salvation of the
Commonwealth from external enemies. Do not deceive yourself.
Merely because this law has not been enforced since the beginning
of the Sixth Era has not caused this law to lapse or to lose its full
force and effect. Your attempt to interfere means that you may yet
be tried for treason and executed. This matter is quite serious."

Atkins addressed the red-armored figure. "Warmind Group!"

The Super-Sophotech saluted. "Sir!"

"The events happening here are classified as secret. You may not
release the data concerning Phaethon's attempted interference to
the Curia or to any other civilian body, except for the appropriate
members of the Parliamentary Military Oversight Committee, until

and unless I instruct you otherwise. Is that clear?"

"Yes, sir!"

"Summarize report on last action-situation."

"Entire action took place within 0.002 picoseconds. At that time, directed-energy weapon entered target skull at midbrain and cortex, disabling fast-reaction circuits, but leaving the target's implants, including noetic and noumenal broadcasters, intact. Beam exited skull through upper crania. Brain signal action was closely monitored during the next .04 seconds. Noetic information allowed sniper platform to track which neural pathways were being engaged for which thoughts. While the noumenal espionage delator was unable to break the Silent One encryption on the enemies' thoughts, it was nonetheless able to detect nerve-paths leading toward suspicious sectors or circuits embedded in the target's brain. Those sections were disabled with a secondary-beam targeting by a surgical program from the orbital sniper platform. The Estimator anticipates that this prevented even any thoughts of suspicion or inhibition from forming, because it believes that those secondary sections were where the suspicion reflexes of the brain were kept, and the energy weapon was able to reach and destroy the suspicion-reflex brain cells before the pain-signals from other parts of the nervous system, traveling at biochemical speed, were able to reach them.

"Hence the target was completely without suspicion or inhibition, and was unable to override its pre-established high-speed reflexes. Finding itself in a brain under fire, it activated noumenal recording circuits, and broadcast itself to a safe station. Harrier Sophotech's predictions in this regard seem to be have been confirmed. Signal was intercepted by cislunar sail and suppressed. Unfortunately, the enemy thought-encryption system, which is based on an infinite-infinitesimal number process we cannot decode, prevented the signal from being trapped or recorded property. Scaramouche is dead beyond recovery."

Phaethon turned to Harrier. "What is going on? What prediction did you make?"

Harrier smiled, and said, "The other odd thing that Mr. Jason Sven Ten Shopworthy did, aside from leaning on his left elbow at the teahouse, was that he sleepwalked on his way home last Tuesday. While his body was on autopilot, records indicate that his mind entered into the Orient Free Market Group Thought-shop Mall in the Deep-Dreaming Commercial Channel. He visited quite a number of shops and business, and ran many free samples, and, all in all, seemed quite impressed with the luxury and wealth of our commercial consumer markets."

Phaethon said, "I don't understand. How could our wealth impress him? He was from the Silent Oecumene, which, by all accounts, was much richer in energy than our Golden Oecumene by an almost infinite amount. What was our wealth to him?"

"But their technology was arrested at the Fifth-Era level of development. They have only those technical advances from the Sixth Era, the Era of the Sophotechs, that we broadcast to them. There is no evidence, however, that they had in place any of the social or marketplace structures necessary to take advantage of those developments. Furthermore, it is not clear what percentage of the population survived the events depicted in the famous Last Broadcast, nor what their level of civilization was thereafter. War can do terrible things."

"Are you suggesting that their technology level is less than ours? Less? I had been assuming al this time it was greater . . . "

"Mr. Rhadamanth," said Harrier, "if you came for the first time from a more primitive circumstance and entered into the Golden Oecumene, what is the first, the very first, technological advantage of which you would avail yourself . . . ?"

Phaethon looked at Daphne. Perhaps he was thinking about her past.

He said, "We did corrupt him. Scaramouche bought a Noumenal Immortality account, didn't he?"

Harrier said, "And suppose you were an alien spy. You could not send your brain-information into any Golden Oecumene Sophotech or any of our mind banks, could you? So where would you send it? To which Sophotech would you direct the broadcast?"

Phaethon looked back and forth. "There is really something horrible about you all, Warmind, Harrier, Atkins. You just shot an innocent man without warning."

Harrier said, "If a police officer must shoot through a hostage to strike a criminal hiding in his mind, who is to blame? The officer, or the criminal who deliberately put that hostage in danger?"

Atkins patted Phaeton on the shoulder. "I think you need to reload some intelligence enhancers or something, sir. Maybe you're tired. Warmind! Tell our newest recruit about Mr. Shopworthy."

"Mr. Shopworthy is unaware of what occurred. He is presently recuperating in the Orpheus Alaska branch of the Noumenal Immortality life bank."

Atkins turned and stared at the eastern horizon. There was no hint of light there yet, but a predawn smell was in the night and, on the shore and not far away, first one bird note, then another, rang out, and soon the air was filled with song.

"Dawn's coming," said Atkins.

"It's refreshing!" said Daphne. "I always have loved the dawn! A time of hope, isn't it . . . ? And we really are going to defeat these creatures, aren't we? These monsters?"

"Actually," said Atkins, "I was thinking we should get under cover. I don't think a purely passive spy satellite or remote sent out from the enemy starship could see us in the dark, not if it did not dare emit any sort of signal to bounce off of us. But once the sun is up, the enemy may have enough magnification and resolution to get a picture of us even from somewhere beyond Mars, if his collector is big enough and his resolution is fine enough."

Daphne glumly looked up at the night sky.

Atkins said, "As for our plan, I think Phaethon has to continue with the masquerade we started here. If he publicly approaches the Hortators and proves his innocence, that will warn the enemy. So, without any visible help from anyone, he has to make contact with the Neptunians, get them to hire him, and get back to his ship. Once Phaethon is aboard the ship, the enemy will have to come for him. Each time they have acted so far, they've tried to get the armor."

Phaethon said, "Without the armor to control the ship-mind hierarchies, near-light speed flight is dangerous or impossible. But why do they want my ship?"

"I'm not sure. But I intend to find out. We can then follow the two signal vectors we have to see where they intersect. If the enemy starship is just hanging there in space, only another starship is going to be fast enough to approach her, if she turns and runs. Warmind . . . ?"

A smaller menu appeared next to the image of the blood-red figure in armor, showing latitudes and right ascensions. "These are the two directions the two signals traveled."

"Calculate the intercept."

Phaethon's almanac was as quick and precise as money could buy, and the circuitry it used was not fundamentally different from that in which Sophotechs were embedded, not fundamentally slower. Therefore, it was Phaethon who answered first: "About sixty degrees trailing Jupiter, at about five A.Us distance, since Jupiter is presently at apogee. That puts it right in the middle of the Jovian Trailing Trojan Point City-Swarm. So, unless they put an alien starship in the middle of a highly populated and well-traveled area, we've only caught a relay or a lieutenant."

"That's not good. It means we have to trace the line of command up to the next level, or take steps to ensure that the highers-up come out of hiding," said Atkins. "The enemy is going to be suspicious when they do not hear back from their lieutenants. So we need some sort of lure or bait that we know for sure the enemy will not be able to resist."

Phaethon did not like the way Atkins was looking at him.

Phaethon said, "You have simply got to be kidding me."

"As soon as we can get you inducted, and download some Basic Training routines into you, we'll be ready to go."

"It will never happen," said Phaethon, drawing himself erect. "I may cooperate freely with you, as one free man with another, but I shall not place myself under the orders of any other man."

Harrier said, "Perhaps Marshal Atkins is too polite actually to remind you that he is blackmailing you. If you do not sign up, you get put on trial for treason. If you do sign up, you have access to the Military Noumenal Immortality Circuit, which is not controlled by Orpheus or the Hortators."

Atkins looked askance at Harrier. "Actually, I was going to appeal to his sense of duty and patriotism, and point out what a bad idea a split command was."

Phaethon folded his arms over his chest, and sighed. All he was aware of was fatigue. He was tired in his body, tired in his mind, tired in his soul. He was tired of being manipulated, forced, or coerced. He thought there was some error, some obvious oversight in Atkins's blackmail scheme, but Phaethon's tired brain could not bring it to the surface.

Phaethon turned a thoughtful glance upon Daphne, who was staring out at the horizon, smiling as if half in a dream.

His voice woke her. "Daphne!"

She stirred, and turned luminous eyes on him. "Mm? Yes? What do you need, lover?"

"I am really tired, and my brain is acting stupid, and I haven't got a microscopic fragment of an idea of what to do."

She looked mildly amused. "Was there something you wanted me to do about all that, lover?"

He spread his hands as if to show their emptiness. "You're here to rescue me. I've run out of ideas. So rescue me."

There was a note of irony in his voice, as if he were challenging her, testing her. Daphne smiled very broadly, as if she were very pleased.

To Phaethon she said, "Listen to your little wife now, darling, and take notes, because I may give you a quiz on this later. Ready? Atkins is trying to drive his mule (that's you, darling) with a carrot and a lash. The lash is the charge of treason. The carrot is the noumenal immortality circuit. But his carrot is no good."

She leaned forward, eyes glittering with delight, and said, "If you had just listened to me before, you would have known that Aurelian Sophotech told me in the Taj Mahal that that noetic reader you are carrying can also be configured not just to read, but to record. It has nearly infinite storage capacity, remember? Noetic reading and noumenal storage are just two aspects of the same technology, remember? You would need a Sophotech actually to operate it during the storage-recording process, just like any other noumenal immortality circuit, and Aurelian says he can provide that service to you.

All you have to do is log on to the mentality, call up the Aurelian Mansion as your sense-filter provider, and he can make you a back copy of yourself right now."

Phaethon said, "But Orpheus holds the patent on this technology! Aurelian cannot just steal it!"

"Orpheus did not design this machinery. It's not his design. It does the same thing, but so what? The guy with the patent on the steam engine for trains could not stop the guys who made the internal combustion engine for the motorcar."

"But Aurelian will be ostracized if he helps me!"

Daphne smiled even more broadly. "You know, I said the same thing to him at the Taj Mahal. You know what he said to me?"

"What?"

"He just smiled, and said, 'Let them try.' And you know what? He had that look you get on your face, that same look, when you say things like that."

He squinted at her sidelong, querulous. "What look do you mean?"

"You'll get it on your face in a moment. Because I've taken the carrot out of Atkins's hand, but you have to disarm him of his lash. Remember what you were told? You are supposed to remain true to your character at all times. And your character is a very, very pig-headed one. Do what you always do."

Phaethon looked blank.

Daphne rolled her eyes with impatience. "Oh, come on! Just tell the military to go jump on a pogo stick, just the same way you've told the Hortators, your father, Ao Aoen, Eleemosynary, the other Peers, Ironjoy, the Silent One monsters, and everyone else who has tried to impede you."

Then, with another smile, she added, "He cannot push you around, lover. Atkins may have more testosterone than you, but you've got more brains."

Phaethon nodded, looking thoughtful. "Or, at least, I have one skill he cannot do without. Nor can he arrest me in secret, because even he cannot break the laws; nor can he afford to have my arrest be made known."

With great dignity, Phaethon turned toward Atkins. "Marshal Atkins! In reference to your implication that the military powers, the Parliament, and the Courts of Oecumene law will punish me for treason and execute me should I not submit to your blackmail, I have but this to say: Let them try."

At that same moment, the quick equatorial dawn sent a ray of light from the east to touch upon Phaethon, glinting from his unbreakable armor, showing the unbreakable spirit in his expression.

Daphne nodded happily. "Yup. That look. Just like that." Daphne raised her hand quickly and recorded the image into her ring.

MERCURY EQUILATERAL STATION

I.

Phaethon hovered in midair above the deck of the thought-shop. Ironjoy stood on the burnt decks, still damaged from the explosions, looking back and forth. No expression showed on his immobile features. The deck was deserted.

Phaethon was able to maintain his position aloft because the levitation array, which had been lowered from orbit to a position over India was near enough for the flying-harness he had constructed inside his armor to grapple and use.

Ironjoy said, "I do not consider our contract to have been carried out in a satisfactory fashion. Specifically, you promised to return my shop intact (I note that it has been pulverized by heavy energy discharges) and my people unharmed (I note that they are absent.) I suspect that you have come into some money, or have made some other arrangement to depart. I conclude that, should I choose to sue you in a court of law for the breach of this contract, and insist on the specific performance of the terms on which we agreed, your plans to depart would be hindered considerably. I have recently learned to have great respect for the power of Oecumene law to compel obedience."

Phaethon had to be careful of his money. Old-Woman-of-the-Sea, as it turned out, owned a cargo canister, one of hundreds she used to own, back when she had been making regular launches to Venus. Notor-Kotok had bought the use of an orbital railgun from a deviant willing to defy the Hortators. Phaethon could adjust his body to withstand the immense launch pressure that would otherwise make the cargo canister utterly unfit for shipping a human body; he could adjust his brain to sleep throughout the long fall toward the sun.

Since the planned orbit was sunward, "all downhill" as old spacers liked to say, the fuel cost (almost all of which would be spent at the initial boost) would be inexpensive.

Inexpensive by space-shipping standards, that is. Phaethon's income from his flying-suit patent was not enormous, and his pay from the Neptunians (which mostly consisted of buying the rest of his debt back from Vafnir, to give the Neptunians clear title) would not arrive till he arrived at Mercury Equilateral. There were not many corners he could cut.

The negotiations did not take long, and were not entirely favorable to Phaethon.

Ironjoy judged Phaethon's reluctance to a nicety, or perhaps the Demeter tapestry had somehow recorded the conversations Phaethon held, less than an hour past, with Notor-Kotok and the Neptunians, and knew exactly how much currency Phaethon had to spare. Or perhaps it was merely that Ironjoy had much more practice than Phaethon did at bargaining without any Sophotechnic advice.

In the end, Ironjoy no doubt had more than enough to restore his shop to operating levels. Phaethon felt more than a qualm of distaste for himself, erecting this villain once again to be lord and master of whatever addicted and desperate unfortunates might fall into his hands.

But there was little Phaethon could do at this point.

Phaethon said, "The files and brain-spaces that have not been destroyed are still in order, and I have cleaned and reconnected them, restored your search engines, and modified the hierarchies in your housecoat to free up several hundred operation-cycles of memory space." And he transmitted back the codes and authorizations, turning control of the thought-shop once more to Ironjoy.

"If we have no further business, sir . . ." said Phaethon, preparing to leave. He had agreed with the remnant of the Bellipotent Composition to rendezvous. Bellipotent's airship could carry him back to Lake Victoria, where he could ascend the infinite tower (if he could find passage—perhaps in a masquerade disguise?) and try to reach the section of the ring-city where the Mother-of-the-Sea's cargo capsule was stored.

"But we do. One last brief thing," said Ironjoy. "I would thank you not to leave your messages cluttering my thought-shop holding space."

Phaethon was distracted. "Messages . . . ?" Then he recalled that he had dumped his secretarial program, and not thought, himself, of looking for any messages since his last session with the Neptunians. "An oversight, sir. Can you forward it to my armor's internal channel?"

"For a small fee."

"That seems a trifle unkind, sir, considering that . . ."

Ironjoy jerked all four hands at the sky, an odd but alarming gesture. "Unkind! You have ruined my thoughts and hopes and life! A pathetic life, by your manor-born standards, a cruel and thin life, but it was mine and the only one I had. The Afloats have been taken to some junkyard behind a Red pleasure-garden, with me not there to protect them from over-indulgence, or to nurse the sick and aged. There is no work for them there; there is nothing for me here. Even should another flock of Afloats be dropped here, I have lost my zest for my work, my talent for forcing obedience and fear. Your vile Curia and their mind-tricks have seen to that. I have seen my life through other's eyes and recoiled in disgust . . ."

Now he lowered his hands, muttering: "I would some power could grant this gift to me—never again to see myself as others see me."

But Ironjoy, with a shrug of disgust, and without collecting any fee, now, for some reason, made the transmission-gesture, and passed the message file to Phaethon.

Phaethon was thinking: Why should I feel pity for this most wretched of men? No injustice had been done to him. All Ironjoy's ills were of his own making.

And yet. "You could trifle with your mind, using activators and redactors from your own thought-shop, and put yourself back into the state of mind you were in before the Curia forced you to experience your victims' lives."

"Is this some sort of test or quiz? You know I shall not do that."

"Why not?"

Ironjoy started to turn away, but then stopped, turned, and answered the question. "If I were now as I was then, I would gladly change my self to remain as I was then; but I am now as I am now. The me that I am now has no desire to be any other me. Isn't that the fundamental nature of the self?"

"If you judge by emotion only, perhaps. Logic suggests that certain types of personalities are more self-consistent than others; and morality decrees that certain traits and thoughts and habits are superior to others, no matter what our preferences and appetites might say."

"What has your philosophy to do with me? You are not content to destroy my life, now you must critique it? Don't you have other business elsewhere?"

"I have business here, and with you. What will you pay as a finder's fee, if I can find three hundred workers, already trained in your methods and familiar with your work, and also find a customer, willing to pay sixty seconds per line-cycle, doing checking and format translation? The whole project should include between one-hundred twenty and one-hundred fifty subjective man-hours of work."

Ironjoy touched his chest and tuned his speaking machine to a sarcastic tone: "You would make me the wealthiest man on Death Row."

"I would like twenty percent commission on net profit, paid in advance based on standard actuarial estimates, with cost adjustments to be made later, standard intervening interest rates applied to the overpayment or underpayment. In return, at my own expense, I will transport here Drusillet and a little over half of the Afloats. She is the one who sent me the message. She asked me to tell you her terms: they will not work here unless you continue to enforce the policies and rules I started, including sobriety tests, job training, full-value resale of unused memories, and a dress code. I have no idea how she did it, and I am not even sure why she did it, but she has convinced about half of the original Afloats there in that Red pleasure-junkyard you were talking about, to come back here. The people willing to hire them are the Neptunians. We need the software aboard the *Phoenix Exultant* reconstructed so that personalities of the Tritonic Neuroform Composition can integrate into the ship's onboard mindscape. Considering that, by your own admission, your life is destroyed if I do not help you, I think twenty percent is a small price to pay. Besides, you-as-you-are-now needs a chance to do some good work to redeem yourself."

Phaethon did much better during this round of bargaining. He ended up with almost a third of his money restored. Ironjoy's only noticeable victory during the negotiation was that Phaethon agreed to cannibalize the communion circuitry out of his wedding ring, to allow Ironjoy the pleasure of experiencing the good he did to other people from their points of view.

Before the discussion was over, Afloats began coming down from the sky, laughing and kicking their feet. No other air service would have carried them, of course. They were all wearing flying jackets distributed by the company Rhadamanthus had started for Phaethon.

"This is a wonder! This is the beginning of new lives for us all ..." said Ironjoy. But he was overcome with emotion, and so forgot to readjust his speaking machine back to a normal tone of voice, and so therefore the words came out dripping with sarcasm.

2.

Daphne was on the road, galloping from the airship dock back toward the outskirts of the Ashore community, when she saw the gleaming gold of Phaethon in flight, and waved an eager hand to bring him down to land by her. Her new horse had been made for her by Daughter-of-the-Sea, and (despite Daphne's best efforts to explain the biogenetic details) the whim or inattention of Daughter-of-the-Sea had festooned the creature with many organs and adaptations useful only to middle-period Venereal environments.

The creature's skin shone with sleek black re-radiation stripes, and along its limber neck silver shells and clustered spots displayed infrared-echolocators, which occasionally flickered with singes of heat. The monstrosity reared and plunged as Phaethon landed in a wash of energy, spooked. Daphne, red lips compressed, gloved fingers tightly curled around the reins, brought the rearing beast under control; she did not lose her poise, despite that she sat sidesaddle (which she did to keep her feet away from the jets of gas and flame darting from the black monster's ventral scales).

Phaethon thought she made a fetching picture. How commanding, and yet how elegant and feminine she seemed! His heart expanded with warm emotion. Phaethon doffed his helmet and spoke. "Darling," he said, "I want to discuss with you what our next . . ."

"Don't you even start to think about leaving me behind!" she snapped, drawing herself upright, eyes blazing.

Phaethon said mildly, "Atkins has convinced me that his plan is wise."

"It's suicide!"

He said quietly, "The Earthmind herself, back when this all began, that first night when I saw her in the Saturn-tree grove, reminded me that a society as free as ours cannot endure except by the voluntary devotion of her citizens."

She spoke with pride: "My devotion is no less than your own!"

"Nevertheless, even if I wished for it, I cannot bring you with me. Do you forget the legalities entangling me? My ship is no longer properly mine. Vafnir has a lien on the *Phoenix Exultant,* and Neoptolemous of Neptune holds the rest of the lien, which his contributors, Xenophon and Diomedes, combined to purchase from Wheel-of-Life. I do not own her, and even I would not be permitted aboard, had I not been hired by Neoptolemous as pilot. And neither I nor Neoptolemous can board, or even graze her hull with a fingertip, until Vafnir is paid off in full. How could I bring you, no matter how much I wished?"

Daphne slapped her riding crop against the shiny black leather of her boot. "Don't gull me with excuses! Don't talk to me of debts and liens and legal hither-and-yon. None of that is really what is really going on! Atkins and the Warmind are the puppeteers behind everything that happens now. Had Atkins' plan included me, there would be a way to let me go along, law or no law, come lien, legality, hell, or high water!"

She flourished her riding crop and pointed at him, a gesture of imperious indignation. "You mark my words, Phaethon of Rhadamanth! This is all mere masculine testosteronic condescension! If I were a man, I'd not be slighted in this way! I'd be allowed to go and die with you!"

"I think not, my dear," answered Phaethon, gently. "Were you a man, you would not be befogged with romantic ideas, nor would you suffer the delusion that you and I are man and wife. You are a fine woman—a wonderful woman—but you are not the one who, bound to me by marriage vows, has any right to ask to share my life, or, I suppose, my death."

Her cheeks took on a rosy hue, and her eyes gleamed with unshed tears, perhaps of anger, or sorrow, or both. "You are a cruel man. So what am I supposed to do? Forget you? I tried that once, for just one day, and it is not worth trying again, I assure you."

"I'm sorry."

"Besides! The one to whom you are bound by your marriage vows would not ask to go with you. She would cower, screaming, and clutching the Earth with both hands, rather than travel in space; it's death she fears, and she would not risk it or seek it, not for any noble cause of yours, or for the sake of victory in war, or for the sake of seeking her true love, or for any reason whatsoever. And certainly she would not forsake the Earth, or any comforts in her life, for you!"

Phaethon stiffened. He said in a level and judicious tone, "You are not without a certain cruelty yourself, miss, when you put your mind to it. It might make our parting easier, if we sting each other with bitter barbs first, mightn't it?"

She said sullenly, "I only spoke the truth."

"Of course you did. Lies make ineffectual weapons."

Daphne's face was uncomposed. She spoke in a shaking voice. "Ineffectual? Then why are you to be sacrificed by Atkins's plan? What is there to his plan besides lies, vile lies, loss, darkness, treason, sacrifice, and lies? You know why you were singled out to be the sacrifice, Phaethon! Not because of any weakness! Not because you were the worst among us! You were chosen for your strengths, your virtues. Your genius, the unrelenting brightness of your dream! You were chosen because you were the best."

"No. The accident of war chose me, what we call chaos, what our ancestors called fate. I am the only one who can fly the ship. We know the enemy desires the *Phoenix Exultant*; everything it has done has been bent to capturing me, my armor, and the ship. If I go now to repossess her, the enemy must come, the enemy must reveal itself. Then, whether I survive or not, all truths will be laid bare, and all this darkness and confusion will be undone. I have lived my life as if in a labyrinth; the end, I see, is near. If I die now, I die, at least, at the helm of my great ship, where I would wish. But if I prevail, the labyrinth must fail, and the way to the stars is clear."

A silence came between them. The horse-beast pawed at the old road, digging up little diamond chips and puffs of black dust.

She said, "Look me right in the eye, and tell me you don't love me, and I'll go."

He stared at her. "Miss, I do not love you."

"Don't give me that rot! I'm coming with you, and that's final!"

"Daphne, you just said that if I said . . ."

"That doesn't count! I said look me right in the eye! You were staring at my nose!"

Phaethon was opening his mouth to answer her shout for shout, when he noticed that it was a good nose; a cute nose, indeed, a well-shaped nose. Her eyes, too, were good to look upon, her shining hair, her curving cheeks, lips, chin, graceful neck, slender shoulders, graceful, slender, and fine figure, and, indeed, every part of her.

"Well," he said at last, "you can come with me as far as Mercury."

"I'm glad you said so," said Daphne, smiling. "Because Bellipotent's airship is waiting for us beyond the next hill, and I've already booked passage with him for the both of us."

3.

The way to Mercury was long, and the canister into which Daphne and Phaethon were packed was small. Her coffin required more equipment than did his, because she had no ability to alter her internal cellular configuration for acceleration, nor did she (or anyone in the Golden Oecumene) have a cloak like his, able perfectly to sustain him without external life support. And so the quarters were very cramped and intimate.

There was, furthermore, nothing to do. Being Silver-Grey, they had vowed to limit their use of personal time-sense alterations, which most people used to make boring tasks fly quickly by. Nor did they have available the extensive array of diversions most travelers enjoyed. Still pariahs, few vendors would have given them anything to entertain or comfort them.

They spent some time simply talking over old memories, a sort of crude, verbal form of communion. She asked him particularly about the time when he was aboard the *Phoenix Exultant*, preparing to depart, just before the beginning of the masquerade. Phaethon spoke about his last words with Helion before his death in the solar inferno, about his discovery of Daphne's semisuicide, and his grief-stricken decision at Lakshmi.

Those conversations paled. Phaethon cobbled together a shared thoughtspace for them, and so they passed the long watches, immobile, entombed, with only their brains active. Their minds ranged far and wide inside dreamscapes Daphne wove for them, for she knew all the secrets of that art, and many of the techniques of false-life sculpting, and story-crafting, which, to her, were trite and worn, to him, were new; and she found pleasure in his delight.

And yet there was an element of incompleteness in all the dream weavings she wove for them. For when she made them gods, able to dictate new laws of nature and establish new creations, he always would favor and follow the most conservative of themes, making universes very much like the real one, with realistic limitations, so that his universes seemed to her like little more than engineering or terraforming simulations.

In lifetimes when they were heroes, rather than gods, Phaethon seemed little interested in the careful historical scenarios. His characters were always upsetting the basic order of things, inventing the printing press in Second-Era Rome, the submarine in Third-Era Pacific waters, or instituting gold-standard reforms to the benighted serfs in the mid-Bureaucracy period of the Union d'Europe.

But Daphne found, to her surprise, that her own tastes were different than she had imagined them to be. The worlds she peopled with magicians and mythic beasts began to seem to her, somehow, trifling, or small, and she began to wonder about the evolutionary origins of things, the logic governing what magicians could and could not do, or the ultimate ends or applications of powers and abilities her mythic creatures possessed.

More and more of their time, and, eventually, all of it, was spent in the world called Novusordo, and the limits she had imposed on the original construction were those she got from files in Phaethon's armor. It was, at first, like an engineering scenario, which assumed that a single ship, loaded with biogenetic material, had come to terraform a barren world of methane sea and skies of sulfur ash.

Together, they concocted tiny seeds and self-replicating robots to tame the winds and poisonous waves of their make-believe world; together they orbited solar tissues to eclipse the sun, or amplify its heat, as needed; they discharged antimatter explosives at pinpoint segments beneath the crustal plates to release trapped carboniferous chemicals, or in the upper atmosphere, to alter the balance of chemicals there, and trigger or suppress a greenhouse effect. Together they raked the seas with compounds, starting simple nanofactories, creating one-celled life. They tilled the soil and brought forth green; they incubated eggs upon the mountainside and watched as curious fledglings hatched; they called up beasts out of the earth and fish out from the sea.

Years of subjective time went by. And, in objective time, many weeks.

All too soon, it ended. Hand in hand, as they walked in a dream along the silver-white and crystal shapes of the trees they had made, and saw the small white-furred marmosets playing and gamboling in the grass not far away, and, on a ridge beyond, an albino hunting cat roaring at the sunset music issuing from cooling plains of fiberglass. Phaethon pointed at the setting sun, and said, "We could make this world with the *Phoenix Exultant*, exactly as we've imagined it here. Look at the rainbow colors we get from the particulate matter seeded in the troposphere! See how the ripples and streaks above the atmosphere still catch the light for hours after sunset! I wonder if any real greenhouse blanket we lay out will look so beautiful at that."

Daphne, who had half-forgotten that this was not real, looked at her partner, her fellow lord of creation, in sadness. "All this must be abandoned, then. What if what we make is not so beautiful as what we dream?"

Phaethon was troubled. "Perhaps we should stay here. I knew that, when I was awake in the real world, its concerns seemed pressing to me. But here they seem light enough. Stay with me, here, in this little world."

Daphne said, "You are not as used to long simulation runs as I am, lover. You'll be so ashamed of yourself when you wake up. But we will both have work to do when we come to our right minds again, and this little fantasy will fade. And you won't want to have me with you then."

He plucked a crystal leaf from one of the pale white trees and put it in her hair. "This seems so pleasant. Why should I want to wake up?"

She shook the leaf away. "This is the only time I've ever seen you like this; it doesn't seem like you. Perhaps I set the modality register at too high a rate, and you are suffering state-related fugue. Or maybe you really know your chances out there with Nothing Sophotech are not that good. Atkins is not trying to save your life, you know; he's trying to kill the enemy, and he won't let unimportant things get in his way."

He turned and took her by the shoulders, drawing her face near to his. "Is my life so unimportant then? It seems too precious to me ever to sacrifice, for any man or any cause. Stay here with me, in this false world of ours, which, even if it is false, is, after all, ours. What is out there which I cannot have in here?"

She licked her lips, and felt the temptation to agree. But then the thought came to her that this was the last and most gentle and horrible trap. Everyone had tried to stop Phaethon: Gannis; Ao Aoen; the Eleemosynary; the College of Hortators; the Nothing Sophotech. Was she going to succeed where the rest of them had failed? Was she going to perform their work for them?

Yet all it would take was a smile and a nod, and she would have almost everything she desired. She would have Phaethon.

She would have almost everything. She would have someone who was almost Phaethon.

Daphne summoned her spirits, resisted temptation, and spoke. "There is one thing you cannot do in here. You cannot perform deeds of renown without peer."

A strange, stern look overcame his features then, and his smile fled. He stared deeply, deeply into her eyes in the way he could not do when she was in her transport-coffin. The look in his eyes grew more stern and more remote as if he also were resisting a great temptation.

He raised his hand, made the end-program gesture, and his image vanished.

She turned up her time so that she could cry and be done with it before she passed out from the dream and back into the real world. She woke in her coffin just in time to hear the proximity alarms ringing through the canister's crude and narrow hull.

Jarring jolts began to kick the hull. Daphne could see nothing but the fogged surface of her coffin lid a few inches beyond her nose, but she knew the maneuvering jets were firing, aiming the canister toward the mouth of the long line of magnetic deceleration rings maintained near Mercury Equilateral Station.

The whining bangs of the jets, and then the hissing roar of accumulators turning kinetic energy into stored electric power, prevented speech.

Daphne wondered if that might not be just as well.

4.

The silence between them held during the dreary process of disembarkation, while their vessel was dismantled and their bodies were adjusted to the normal station environment. This process was made all the more dreary because the ban of the Hortators was still enforced against them, and the minds running the stations (sons or creations of Vafnir) would not speak to them directly, but only through disposable partials, who disintegrated after every speech.

Dreary again was the fact that they were not being offered the local embodiments and aesthetics for this environment. Without the aesthetic protocols, many of the objects shining from the station walls were meaningless, like tangles of colored string, and many of the sounds were mere hisses and coughs, rather than announcements and alerts. Without the proper bodies, Phaethon had to stay in his armor with his helm closed, and Daphne had to wear an awkward full-body suit Phaethon made. It looked like some piece of ecologic-torture equipment out of the Dark Green Ages, with a faceplate and a symbiotic plant growing all over her like moss. She itched abominably, and knew she looked stupid.

Phaethon had brought up a legal document of some sort out of her ring, and so (not unlike Alberich in the fairy tales, driving the unwilling dark elves to their tasks in the underworld, tormenting them with a threat of the all-powerful ring) she stepped, ring hand held high, one air lock at a time, up from the outer station into the inner, driving empty androids and surprised semiandroids from her path. Up the stairs and ladders she climbed, from full gravity to half-gravity, opening locks and silencing guards with a queenly scowl and a gesture from the ring.

But (not unlike Alberich being snared by Loge) eventually they reached Vafnir's seneschal and henchman, a polite young three-headed man named Sigluvafnir, who admitted in bland tones that Phaethon had every right to be here, but that Daphne did not, and could Phaethon please wait while Vafnir constructed suitable accommodations to receive him for an interview? All business would be conducted with dispatch; Phaethon would be thanked for his patience. Sigluvafnir smiled with all three mouths and looked innocent.

The magic in her ring could not deal with the diabolic cunning of polite agreement. The two of them were standing in a waiting area in an empty hall, alone. Underfoot, a transparent hull gave a view of the grand stars wheeling by, passing from station east to station west, a silent, moving carpet of constellations. The station rotated about once every twenty minutes, and half of a "station day" (if it could be called that) passed by while the two of them pretended studiously to have nothing important to say to each other.

They both stared down below their feet. Perhaps an uncertain shyness was between them, or, perhaps, it was more interesting to look at the moving lights of tugs and assistance-boats, the glints of solar fields, the flowery shine from the sails of distant antimatter generators, than to look at the barren bulkheads of the wide, up-curving hallway in which they stood.

It was Daphne who broke the silence. "Once Vafnir has his lien paid off, who else will have any claim over your ship?"

Phaethon spoke in an absentminded tone. "At that point, only Neoptolemous. Xenophon and Diomedes combined their funds and personalities to create Neoptolemous, who purchased Wheel-of-Life's interest."

"Don't you own half the ship by now? Gannis's debt was canceled."

Phaethon said briefly, "The moment I opened my memory casket, the *Phoenix Exultant* was seized by the Bankruptcy Court. She is actually in receivership, 'owned' by the Curia officers to be used for the benefit of the combination of all my creditors. Gannis dropped out of the combine. Which is good, because he would have gotten the ship dismantled for scrap."

"Is it too late to get the ship back?"

"No. If I came up with a huge fortune, I could pay off Neopto-lemous. He has a lien, but he does not own the *Phoenix Exultant*, so he could not refuse to take the money."

"Oh."

Silence endured for a while.

Daphne hated the fact that Phaethon was wearing his helmet. She could not see his face, and could make no guess as to his expression.

She pointed at a small cluster of lights in the distance. "There's not much traffic here, is there?"

"No. Everyone is at some port where they will have long-range communication. The world-minds of Earth and Venus, Demeter and Circumjovia, the Outer and the Inner stations, the Mind-combines of the Cities in Space, of the Nonecliptic Supersails, the construc-tions who live in the concentrated ray issuing from the North Pole of the Sun, everyone, is going to be linked into the Grand Transcendence. Aurelian has arranged that no one need be isolated during that time, no one need be in space and far away from sufficient mental broadcast facilities. All the traffic is going still. How far away is the Transcendence? Ten days? Less?"

"Thirteen days. Tomorrow is the Twelfth Night Feast, when we all . . . when they all dress up as members of another sex or phylum."

"I'm sorry."

"That's OK. I wasn't expecting any Twelfth Night gifts anyway." Twelfth Night gifts were only, by custom, meant to be somatic or choreographic packages, such as lords leaping, or ballet choreographs.

Phaethon knew Daphne preferred the Twelfth Night gifts above the other gifts of the other nights in the Penultimate Fortnight, because the many fine training routines, steeplechases, races, leaps, and cabriolets she had received for her horses last millennium, during Argentorium's reign, were among the finest performances her stock could show.

"I'm more worried about trespassing laws," she said. "Vafnir probably has to throw me out into space, but probably cannot sell me the services of his accelerator rings. I'll just be drifting on the slow orbit to nowhere, I guess, until and unless you can come back for me. I wonder how long the life support will hold out. The little canister will be lonely without you."

"Maybe something will happen." He was not going to say aloud that he hoped the Nothing Sophotech would be found and destroyed before the week was up. Once there was no more need for secrecy, Atkins could testify to the Hortators that Phaethon's Inquest had been tampered with, that Phaethon's exile was invalid, and that therefore Daphne's was also.

She turned to him. "Darling, if you don't make it back, I'll be exiled for life. And my life probably won't last that long."

He turned toward her. She truly wished she could see his face. "Daphne, I . . ."

She stepped toward him, "Yes . . . ?"

He raised his hands as if he were about to embrace her. "This voyage we've had together; it has made me realize that . . . Well, you and I . . . We . . ."

She stepped even closer. "Yes . . . ?"

But at that moment, a golden light shone up from underfoot, dazzlingly bright.

The station had turned to face nearer the Sun. In the dark field, where every other boat and tug was no more than a dot of light, the *Phoenix Exultant*, gigantic, splendid, one hundred kilometers long, blazing like a triangle of gold, burning as brightly as the blade of a spear, was clearly visible, even at this distance, to any naked eye which could tolerate the reflected glare from the all-too-nearby Sun.

The miles of hull near the point of the prow were entirely streamlined. Just behind the heavy shielding of the prow, about four kilometers or so, were the flattened blisters of the broadcast houses, antennae, and receivers for innumerable detectors and sensors. They looked small and decorative, like the scales on the neck of a cobra, but some of those radar houses were a kilometer in length.

Behind them, along the spine of the great ship, were other streamlined streaks, betraying the presence of truly gigantic mass-drivers, launch ports, radio-lasers.

The amidships were burnished plates, smooth and unmarred. These could be altered, raised and lowered, to change the cross section and therefore the performance characteristic of the *Phoenix Exultant* at near-light speed. When the great ship was traveling slowly enough, these plates could be spread and opened like the petals of a rose or the sails of a clipper ship, and erect ramscoop fields to gather interstellar gas into the ten thousand titan-sized nuclear furnaces that lined the middle kilometers of the ship. This raw material could be used to produce fuel in flight. The *Phoenix Exultant* carried factories for the nucleogenesis of antimatter, in volume and output as large as any dozen of the antimatter-production facilities orbiting near Mercury Equilateral.

At rest, when the interstellar gas was too tenuous to gather, the port and starboard armor could open like the gills of a shark, and the *Phoenix Exultant* could plunge into the outer layers of a star, diving through photosphere and corona, and gather cubic acres of plasma into holding cells for the refueling process.

Aft were the engines and drives. Those exhaust ports could have swallowed the whole space station in which they stood. These engines could drive that ship at speeds nothing but light itself could outpace. There were no other engines like those of the *Phoenix Exultant*. None had ever been built before.

There was no ship like her.

And yet the ship was cold, the drives were silent, there was no gleam of lamp or light anywhere on her, except the reflected light of the Mercurial sun, caught on certain plates and panels, blazing from her golden hull.

Daphne had her hands before her face. The image of the streamlined triangle of golden admantium was burned green behind her closed eyes. She blinked her eyes clear.

She asked, "What were you saying, darling?" (Something about the two of us, something damn important!)

Phaethon was staring down between his feet. "Hm? That's odd. Look at that ship in the distance." He pointed, as if he expected her unaided eyes to match the visual amplification and tracking systems rebuilt into his nervous system and armor.

"Something about us, dear . . . ?"

He looked up. "I'm sorry. What?"

"Oh, nothing, darling." (OK. Fine. Be that way. Any day now, I'm going off with Atkins, and you can crawl up next to your frozen wifesicle for comfort.) "What was it you were gawking at? I cannot believe you'd be staring at another ship at a time like this! What would your golden Phoenix-bride say if she knew?"

"Can you see? That dot in the distance."

(Of course I cannot see it, you dunderhead.) "What in particular is so very interesting?" (I cannot imagine anything at all so interesting that you're daring to intrude it into what might very possibly be our last few moments together!)

"I'm looking at a radar identifier that flies the heraldry of the *Winged Chariot of Fire*."

(I take it back. That is interesting. A little.) "*Winged Chariot of Fire* is Helion's private yacht."

"She's docking with the *Vulcan*, his sun-diver bathysphere. Look.

Fuel cells from the station are lining up to meet him. More cells are being sent out."

(What in the hell is Helion doing here?) "What in the world is Helion doing here?" (I betcha don't know either, do you, darling . . . ?)

"I don't know."

(Knew it.) "It's only thirteen days till the Grand Transcendence. Why isn't he on Earth, with the Peers, preparing?"

"I don't know."

(You said that already, darling. Now then, what about kissing me good-bye . . . ? And how do I bring the topic up without spooking him away . . . ?) Daphne stepped closer to Phaethon. "You know, darling, I thought things would get less confused, less dangerous, once I rescued you. But now everything is worse than ever . . . !"

He began to step toward her and began to raise his hands, as if, perhaps, to embrace and comfort her, when, at that same moment, Sigluvafnir stepped back into the room. "To the exile calling himself Phaethon, Vafnir will, under protest, and only for the purpose of clearing up certain legal matters, agree to see you now."

Phaethon turned to Daphne. "I fear this is good-bye. I may not get a chance to see you before I am sent to my ship. I mean . . . the ship that once was mine. There is much in my heart I wish to say . . ."

Sigluvafnir: "Hoy! We have no more time to waste! If you wish to see Vafnir, now is now, and later is too late!"

"We must make some arrangement as to what is to become of you. Put your canister into a microconsumption orbit and keep the beacon burning. I'll send an attendant ship from the *Phoenix*, if I can. I still hope Rhadamanthus or your Eveningstar can do something, though I am not sure what."

Daphne smiled. "I know where I'm going. I'll be fine. Go off to your battle and kill your black monster without worrying about me. Because I just realized that I have, shall we say, certain legal matters of my own to clear up. There is something you need from Helion; and I think I know how to get it."

Phaethon's posture showed surprise. He knew Daphne had conceived a hate for Helion. Now she wanted to talk to him . . . ? "He will not receive you."

"Oh, he'll see me, all right. I know how to take care of that!" She smiled. "The Grand Transcendence is still thirteen days away, isn't it? That means the Masquerade is still in force."

Sigluvafnir issued one last warning. There was no further time for words.

Phaethon put out his hand.

(Shake hands?!! If you try to shake hands with me, I'll rip your arm out of your socket and beat you to death with it.)

He said, "Good luck."

Daphne smiled. (You're lucky you're wearing invulnerable armor, you stinking sack of medical waste. Otherwise, you'd be suffering multiple contusions delivered by a bleeding ex-limb!) She demurely put her little hand into the palm of his gauntlet. "You are most kind to be concerned about me, sir. I am ever so very grateful for what attention you can spare me from your other concerns."

Phaethon pulled on her hand to draw her quickly and securely into his arms. Even through her suit, his hard embrace drove the breath from her, and she melted to him, pressing as closely as the suit-fabric allowed. "I'll come back for you," his voice burned in her ears.

Then he departed.

Daphne stood looking after him, love shining in her eyes, forgetful of all else.

5.

There hung Phaethon, resplendent in his armor, hovering in weightlessness within the axial visitor's dodecahedron at the dead center of the Mercury Equilateral Station. Wide, white expanses of pentagonal hull surrounded him. One of the dodecahedrons was tuned to a window. In the window, like a golden blade against a velvet black background, loomed an image of the *Phoenix Exultant*.

His ship.

Out of deference to Silver-Grey aesthetic conventions, or, actually, out of mockery, one of the other pentagons was designated as "floor" and the one opposite it was "overhead." This "overhead" panel was blazing with direct light, rather than the indirect lighting all space tradition required. In fact, it was ablaze with the direct light of the Mercury-orbit Sun, so that Phaethon had to adjust his vision centers.

More mockery: Victorian furniture, chairs and settees on which no one in microgravity could sit, were bolted to the "floor" panel atop an expensive rug. Antimacassars, spinning slowly, sailed above the chairs. A tea service floated nearby, with a ball of scalding tea, held together mostly by its own surface tension but with moonlets of little teadrops all around it, surrounding the silver teapot. Tumbling china cups had drifted in each direction on the ventilation currents. Fortunately, the sugar bowl had held lumps, not powder.

The other bulkheads were established in a nonstandard aesthetic. Objects of unknown use, like strange half-melted candles, rotating glassworks, or webs of laser-light, shimmered in the bulkheads, extending arms or mists toward the center of the chamber.

In the center of the dodecahedron, not far from Phaethon, roared a turning cylinder of flame and pulsing energy. It was Vafnir. The beam of fire extended from one side of the huge chamber to the other.

Two other entities, smaller, dwarfed by Vafnir, were in the room: a dull olive-drab sphere in the Objective Aesthetic, representing the attorneys from the Bankruptcy Court; and a calitrop of black metal, with magnetic jets and manipulator gloves at each axis, surrounding brain housing into which Neo-Orpheus, or perhaps one of his partials, had downloaded, here to represent the College of Hortators.

In one hand Phaethon held up a credit ring. The circuit in the stone had memorized the numbers and locations of millions of seconds of time currency. He pointed it at the olive-drab sphere. A ray from the ring made a circuit with a point in the sphere; the currency exchange was recorded.

Within the ring also had been recorded the contracts and agreement between himself and the Neptunians, now the true owners of the starship, showing that he acted as their representative in this matter, and was accredited both as the pilot and agent of the *Phoenix Exultant*, and directed, after repairs and final checks were complete, to transport the vessel, with himself at the helm, to the Neptunian Embassy at Jovian Trailing Trojan.

His armor detected a rapid exchange of signals between Vafnir, Neo-Orpheus, and the Bankruptcy Attorneys, a huge volume of information compressed into a few short bursts. He could have tapped into their lines and eavesdropped on the conversation, perhaps. But he knew the gist of it. Vafnir furiously and Neo-Orpheus coldly were attempting to find some loophole, some delay, some chink in the iron plate of Phaethon's original contract with Vafnir. But that contract did not contain the normal escape clause permitting one party to be excused of his duties should the other party fall under Hortator ban. Two hundred years ago, when this contract first had been drafted, Phaethon, planning to depart from the Golden Oecumene, had foreseen no need for such a clause, and insisted on its exclusion.

"Now, then," Phaethon said aloud, "one of you is officially required, by law, to inform me that my debt to Vafnir has been settled, and that he shall perform his remaining duties under the contract. Fortunately, Vafnir's warehouses and orbital factories are already at hand directly abeam of the *Phoenix Exultant*; some of the smaller factories, as I recall, are actually inside the hull, for ease of construction. It should require a hundred hours, or less, to load the remaining fuel aboard, and to fit into place the hull-metal segments which you began to dismantle. I demand that the *Phoenix Exultant* be restored to the condition specified, cleaned and polished with no sign of tool-marks, neglect, or debris. Now, which of you is going to embrace a life of exile by telling me these things? Or, better yet, which of you is going to be arrested by the constables for failing to tell me?"

The speaker on Neo-Orpheus's housing whined to life. "The Hortator exile does not obtain against those who, by law, are compelled to treat with you, nor for comments strictly limited to legal business. Only gratuitous comments are forbidden."

Phaethon regarded the calitrop without friendliness. "That itself was a gratuitous comment. Thank you for joining me in exile."

There was something shameful about the fact that Neo-Orpheus, had, at one time, been the selfsame Orpheus who inspired the modern romantic movement; and he had led the team that invented the technology to preserve the human soul, intact, after bodily death; shameful that he should, nowadays, choose to dwell in bodies so ugly. This pyramid-shaped skeleton robot was not from the Objective Aesthetic, nor from any aesthetic at all. It was stark, functional, and utterly inhuman.

Neo-Orpheus said, "My last comment was permissible, as falling under the general umbrella of necessary comments required to conclude our business here with dispatch."

"Ah. But now I must ask, was the comment explaining that last comment gratuitous . . . ? It certainly was unnecessary. Welcome to exile!"

Neo-Orpheus did not deign to respond.

Vafnir said, "Phaethon! In order to conclude the contract quickly, and in order to minimize further interactions between the two of us, I hereby not only turn over to you the materials you bought from me, but also the warehouses and the robot workers attendant thereto, base work crew, supervisors, partials, decision informata, everything. I am giving you, as a free gift, without warranty, all the operators you will need to carry out this operation yourself. They are yours. They will load and equip and polish your insane ship according to your orders, but I will not be responsible hereafter for their acts. Do you acknowledge that this will satisfy all my obligations to you under the contract . . . ?"

A window opened up on one of the decks to the left and showed a view from a point in space near the *Phoenix Exultant*. Even as he watched, he saw the flares of light darting from the warehouses, and saw the first of many spheres of fuel, like a line of pearls, beginning to emerge and slide across space toward the waiting ship.

To the port and starboard of the titanic ship, other warehouses opened their doors. A second string of pearls joined the first, then a third, then a score, then a hundred. The vast bays and fuel docks of the *Phoenix Exultant* stirred to life and opened to receive the incoming gifts.

The running lights of the ship lit up. Red to port. Green to star-

board. Flashing white along the keel. The ship had come to life
again.

"Do not imagine that your victory over us is achieved, Phaethon,"
Neo-Orpheus said in a cold voice.

Phaethon said, "But, my dear sir, I am not imagining it at all. I
see it clearly."

In the window, at that moment, orbital tugs appeared, guiding
the mile-long slabs of golden admantium, one after another, toward
the rents and gaps in the vast armored hull.

Silently steadily, ton upon countless ton of material, fuel, ship-
brains, biomaterial, and the vast expanse of hull segments, began
falling like gentle snow toward the golden doors opened so wide to
receive them.

Phaethon said in his heart: Come to life, my *Phoenix*, that you
may bring life to lifeless worlds. How could anyone fear so noble
and so fine a ship as you?

It was only then that he noticed how much like a spear blade
she was in truth, how sleek, how beautiful, how deadly. He realized
how it would be easy, quite easy, magnificently easy and awe-
inspiring, to use her world-creating power to destroy worlds. (And
it did not please him that he took such pleasure at that thought.)

And, now that the teamsters and longshoremen robots were his
and his alone, unlike material from the *Phoenix Exultant* (owned,
now, by Neoptolemous) he could send them where he liked and to
what task he liked.

A mental command was all he needed to turn legal ownership of
half a hundred of them over to Daphne. No matter what else might
happen to her, she would at least have several tugs and smallboats
at her disposal, with their fuel, life support, and ship-brains. She
now, at least, could depart the station in something roomier than a
canister.

And he could depart to the *Phoenix Exultant*.

His ship.

THE FAREWELL CUP

I.

Phaethon hung in space, a reaction lance in hand, poetry in his heart, a vision of gold in his eyes. He was about thirty kilometers aft of the main superstructure, watching from a hundred points of view at once as the last of the loading was completed.

Whatever the law might say, she was his ship, his dream made real, in golden admantium, antimatter, energy, carbon fiber, molecularly strengthened steel.

Because he had no mentality support, he had to carry on his inspection of the great vessel using the protocols originally designed for refueling in distant star systems.

The golden hull was utterly immune to any electromagnetic signal; and he did not have as many attendant-craft as his original design had called for; so that, instead of being able to bounce a signal from remote to remote, and connect his mind to hull-tenders and macromannequins on every side of the ship at once, he had to move himself, physically, from one side of the ship to the other, and then get a line of sight on any system or robot squad with which he wanted to talk, commune, or mind-embrace.

It was crude and primitive, and he had, personally, to order much of the work done himself. Often he would flourish his lance and jet down to the surface of the great ship, and watch the work progress with his own eyes, or touch the golden hull with his own hand. He inspected, he checked, he tested, he reviewed. The process was insufferably archaic, as if someone from the late Fourth Era, after the invention of Van Neumann Self-regulating Robotics, suddenly had to carve a canoe from a log with a stone ax with his own hands, or as if someone from the Sixth Era had to manifest a Stable-Island pseudomaterial launch shell using only the elements appearing on the original, nonartificial, periodic chart. It was archaic. It was beautiful. Phaethon was in love.

Love is frustrating. It did not help, for example, that the Sun was nearby, forcing him to rotate the great craft slowly, to distribute heat. It did not help that the self-evolving robots were just smart enough to recognize the benefits of huddling in the hundred-kilometer-wide shadow of the *Phoenix* to escape the solar rays, but not smart enough to grasp the principles of enlightened long-term self-interest and devotion to duty, to do their jobs efficiently. Phaethon put them all on a budget, deactivated their behavior regulators, and began setting up swarms of self-reconstruction and self-replication catalysts. Any robots who did not do their work, did not get paid enough out of the energy allowance to rent a catalyst and reproduce. Since the robots willing to risk exposure to the sunside of the ship increased geometrically in number and potency, Phaethon did not worry about individual regulation; he just let natural selection run its course.

It took less time than estimated to load and prepare the ship for burn, despite all this. After fifty hours, Phaethon was ready.

It was now the Ninth Night before the Grand Transcendence. Phaethon had missed the dance. There was no motion anywhere in space nearby, not even of automatic systems. All ships were falling cold. But there was radio-traffic unlike anything ten centuries had seen. Phaethon was alone in the stardock, alone among the warehouses, orbital shops, and shipyards. Everyone else was celebrating. Only he was at work.

He needed no dance. Lance in hand, he flew through the vast afterbays toward the central core. It was darkened now, silent, cold. He passed up through the engine-core space, past endless kilometers of fuel cells, the horizonless geometry of antimatter globes of frozen metallic hydrogen, and past the ring on ring and bastion on bastion of thought-boxes and ship-brains englobing the living quarters.

The mainframe decks were like the walnut-sized brain, compared to this mighty ship, found in the original pre-reconstructed dinosaurs. Inward and "above" them (now that the carousel was under spin) the living decks had been pressurized and super-refrigerated to the standards of Neptunian Cold Ducal body forms. The outer levels of this small city of cabins and quarters were spinning now at many times the original design specifications.

Inward still, at Earth-normal gravity, the "higher" decks held laboratories, confabulationaries, extensive thought-shop and matter-shop appliances, communion atriums, baths, formularies, surgeries, nanoconstruction cells, gardens, greenhouses, bluehouses, feast halls, aviaries, palaces, museums, metanthropy studios, and the other basic necessities of civilized existence.

And, like the gemstone that makes a ring not merely an ornament, but a valuable servant and library, here was the bridge.

Phaethon, it is true, had missed the dance of Earth and all the worlds on the Twelfth Night. And had missed participating in the Choir of All Worlds, that fantastic symphony and paean, where every mind and voice and soul was embraced in one single unimaginable harmony, which crowned the hours of the Tenth Night. But he needed neither music nor dance nor any other celebration.

Phaethon rose; the door "above" him parted; a dim light, like the hint of light before the dawn, fell down around him; the floor beneath him rose, and carried him upward; and he was on his bridge. What other song or splendor did he need?

He called for light; light came. He called for knowledge; tall, energy mirrors on concentric balconies sprang to life, and information flowed into his brain. He walked across the deck.

Each tessellation of the deck was paved with another hue of

wood, darker grains contrasted with lighter, to form a pleasing irregularity, each one shining like gold, dark or bright, by the sheen of its polish.

Pressure curtains ran from the floor to the dome above, shimmering pale blue, royal scarlet, and burgundy. Concentric banks of thought-boxes and energy mirrors rose like an amphitheater, with one larger mirror extended up several balconies to the dome, tuned to display the local area of space and local communication activity. Space was deserted of ships under power; but communication channels flowed like rivers of light, everywhere, a wide-flung net burdened with massive volumes, connecting every habitat, ship-at-rest, sail, satellite, xenonanomechanical cloud and cloud bank, every coronal substation and intelligence formation, throughout all this area near Mercury Equilateral.

Phaethon crossed to the captain's chair. There it was, polished, cleaned, charged. To the left was a symbol table, showing two visitors awaiting him. To the right was the status board, showing that the million checklists of the preflight roster had been checked; the *Phoenix Exultant* was ready to start her burn.

He savored the moment, merely looking at the chair. Then, with only the slightest of smiles, he seated himself, sighed, gripped the chair arms, and cast his gaze back, forth, upward, and down. The hundred energy mirrors shining on the balconies were lit with views and images from each part of the ship, diagrams, informata flows, engine status, field strengths, weight distributions, storage and containment formations for the cargo, supercargo projections, acceleration umbrellas, radio-radar views, meteorological reports on the conditions of near-space, including particle counts, ship-brain and robopsychiatric analysis, hull-configuration monitors. Everything.

Phaethon sat on his throne and surveyed his kingdom, and he was well pleased with what he saw.

To people his kingdom, and, as a sort of compliment to the Silver-Grey aesthetic in which he had been born and raised, he now created a mannequin crew, costumed in different periods, and downloaded with a different partial-personality. Because Phaethon did not want to be alone in his hour of triumph, he peopled the deck with his heroes from myth and history.

Squares of the deck drew back. The mannequin racks beneath lifted several bodies into view. Phaethon activated his sense-filter, signaled to the ship-mind, created, downloaded, constructed, drew.

Soon each one stood before a different duty station, manipulating controls that were merely symbols to display the ship's status.

Here was Ulysses, wearing beggar rags over his half-hidden armor, an unstrung bow of triple rhinoceros-hide in his hand, manning the navigation station. Next to him, Sir Francis Drake, splendid in blue surcoat and white lace, held a magic looking glass and watched for other ships and foreign objects. Admiral Byrd in his parka watched the board displaying internal heat and environment controls.

Here was Neil Armstrong with the stiff banner of the United States on one hand, tasked with guiding the forward remotes and smaller robot-ships that flew before the *Phoenix Exultant* as part of her array. There was Jason with his Golden Fleece, holding the thread that showed open communication lines were still present; and, at the tiller, (of course) was Hanno.

Magellan, Cortez, Clark, and Cook were also there, as well as Buckland-Boyd Cyrano-D'Atano, the first man to survive a Mars landing. Sloppy Rufus, Cyrano-D'Atano's dog was there, not given any tasks to do, but just because Phaethon could not imagine the iconoclastic self-made Martian pioneer without the loyal mongrel he had brought with him to Mars.

Oe Sephr al-Midr the Descender-into-Clouds was charged with watching the gravitic alterations and the acceleration schedule, which was ironic, considering the circumstances of his tragic death in a Jovian subduction layer.

Vanguard Single Exharmony in his white ablative armor kept track of the total-conversion drive core temperatures, which was not ironic at all, considering the remarkable success of his first mission into the Solar Photosphere, after Harmony Composition had sent so many to fiery death and failure.

Vanguard Single Exharmony was Phaethon's second favorite historical character, not only because he was the ancestor-in-spirit for Helion's work, but also because the transition from the Fourth Era to the Fifth was triggered partly because Vanguard, an individual detached from the Harmony group-mind, had succeeded where so many of the mass-minds had failed.

Phaethon's favorite explorer was Sir Francis Drake, who had not only explored the northern passage but turned a profit on the venture. His least favorite was Christopher Columbus, who was not pictured here in his bridge; Phaethon had no use for a man who miscalculated the diameter of the Earth, and reached, by accident, a continent he failed to identify. His second least favorite was Chan Noonyan Sfih of Io, the first man to "set foot" on Pluto. Phaethon also had no use for a man who, despite having been warned by experts, had his landing vehicle fall through the surface layer of hydrogen ice weakened and thawed by his landing jets, fall through successive layers of nitrogen and methane ice, strike a layer of oxygen ice, which thawed and ignited and set fire to the entire surface of the planet. On the coldest planet in space, Chan Sfih had burned to death, whereas a careful thinker like Vanguard Single had been dropped into the sun, and lived.

There was also no image of Ao Ormgorgon Darkwormhole Noreturn. He had been the leader, during the Fifth Era, of the expedition to Cygnus X-1.

Phaethon glanced to his left. The symbol table showed the glowing visitor icons. Only the most extraordinary circumstance would have a visitor calling him, now. A visitor would either have to be an exile or be beyond the fear of becoming one. Who could it be?

Now that his ship and crew were ready, Phaethon made the acceptance gesture for the first icon in the symbol table.

3.

A mannequin rose up out of the square of deck, stood, and saluted. "Permission to come aboard."

How quaint and archaic. Phaethon looked into the ship's Surface Dreaming, expecting to see a Silver-Grey, perhaps even some newly converted Neptunian introduced to Silver-Grey custom by his friend Diomedes.

But no. Here was a man in a dark blue uniform and cuirass of a Sixth-Era Advocate Warden. The Advocates, before the evolution of the College of Hortators, acted as the emissaries and translators between the Sophotechs and the Humans. During those years, before the developments in noumenal technology allowed for vastenings, intelligence-augments, and synnoetics, the gulf between Sophotechnic minds and human minds had been large indeed. The Advocates were sent by the Sophotechs to guide by example and prediction, never by force, the human community away from self-inflicted dangers. The Warden were a subgroup of the Advocates that acted something like a voluntary police force, guarding people against fire, disaster, and mind-crash.

The figure held up a twelve-pointed blazon in his hand, signaling his identity through the ship's Middle Dreaming.

No, he was not a Silver-Grey. He was a Dark-Grey.

The Dark-Grey also followed ancient customs and disciplines, not because they admired the beauty of the ancient world, but because they admired the harshness and rigor that had formed the human character. Dark-Grey were required to devote a certain amount of their lives to public service, as Constables, Fire Wardens, Censors, Werewolf-monitors, Rescuers, and, back in the older times, as Reserve Soldiers under the Warmind.

This was Temer Sixth Lacedemonian, Humodified (space-adapted), Uncomposed (ascetic werewolf self-imposed override), Multiple-parallel attention-monitors, base neuroform, Dark-Grey Manorial Schola.

And his uniform was not a Masquerade costume. Temer Lacedemonian was the Advocate Warden in charge of space-traffic control. This corporation had maintained a monopoly on space-traffic control since the middle of the Sixth Era, despite fierce competition for the market. It was Temer Lacedemonian who controlled the safety of all ships in flight throughout the Inner System, and most of the Outer, and his position made him on the verge of becoming a Peer.

Phaethon stood and projected an image of himself into the Dreaming, so that he did not need to remove his armor. "Welcome aboard. But before you speak, I feel I must warn you that the ban of the Hortators is still in force against me. You will find yourself shunned if you address me."

Temer Lacedemonian had the white hair face-symbology used to show sagacity, and his skin was the jet-black space travelers favored as a block against radiation. He smiled grimly.

"As to that, sir, please tell me, if you can, how a machine one hundred kilometers from prow to stern-plate, radiating a four-hundred-kilometer drive discharge that washes out all the un-shielded communications in her radio-aura, and able to accelerate at ninety gravities of thrust, and preparing even now to launch; tell me how I am to orchestrate safe flight-paths for all vessels in this area without speaking to the pilot of that machine?"

Phaethon made his self-image smile, which his real face, behind his helmet, also did. "You could merely warn other vehicles out of my way . . . ?"

"I don't appreciate the humor, Mr. Phaethon." He pointed to one of the mirrors, where information from Mercury North, the nearest Inner System control tower, was being checked and fed into the navigator. Other legal documents appeared alongside. He continued: "Also, our standard contract contains a clause allowing for an extra schedule of fees for vehicles of unusual properties or dangerous cargoes that require closer observation on our part, and extra precaution. I expect a healthy profit. And I hope you will not quibble over the price, considering the many useful services space-traffic control has done for you in the past."

Phaethon studied the man in silence for a moment. Then Phaethon said, "You hardly needed to come in person, sir. An indirect message, perhaps, or a call routed through the back-net, would have done just as well. Why do you expose yourself to my, if I may use the word, contamination?"

"You recall that I was rather abrupt in driving you out from my section of the infinite tower during your descent on foot . . . ?"

"I had not meant to broach an indelicate subject, but, yes, as I recall, you sent remotes to sting me each time I paused for food or rest."

"Lacedaimon Sophotech, whose wisdom I trust, warned me that

I would be led to favor your case and join you in exile. A dire prediction which, by my rigor against you, perhaps I was trying to defeat. As usual, Lacedaimon knows me better than I know myself. And so here I am."

"Why not send some lesser servant to talk to me?"

"Send into exile? I could not command a subordinate to do that which I was unable to tolerate myself. Besides, my subordinates will all join me soon enough if they expect to keep their jobs. You see the flaw in the Hortators' scheme of things, do you not, sir? Social pressure cannot be used to defeat those who shape society. Every ship under acceleration, or ship that hopes to do a burn, will have no choice, now, but to communicate with my ostracized space-traffic-control network. The ring-city above the Earth will soon join us. And the Hortators, for all their prestige, will find themselves isolated, besieged on Earth, walled off from space by their own presumptions."

Phaethon was more than astonished. "But why should you do such a thing for me?'

"Do not be arrogant, sir. I do as my conscience commands. You are incidental. The Hortators overstepped their mandate in your case, and they ignored the warnings of Nebuchednezzar Sophotech not to pursue you. It will destroy them."

"Destroy? A strong word to use." (Phaethon wondered why there was a note of hope, of relish, in his own voice.)

"Have you been out of communication since you disembarked from Earth to Mercury Equilateral? I see that you have. Aurelian Sophotech has already declared against the College of Hortators."

"What . . . ?"

"Aurelian Sophotech is in exile. The Grand Transcendence is only a week away. The lesser combinations have already formed; the mass-minds have begun their data-migration overtures. The Ennead is making ready; the basics are calling back all their partials and winding up their affairs. You see? If the Hortators do not back down, the policies and visions that will guide us for the next thousand years will be established by the deviants and freaks, the Afloats and Ashores of Ceylon."

"And the Neptunians."

"And you and I, sir."

Phaethon's image showed a smile. "A small transcendence, perhaps, but I shall be grateful for your company, sir."

"Thank you. After my business here with you is done, I will be transmitting a noumenal copy of myself to Earth. I want to walk among the gardens of Aurelian, and visit the Endless Thought Libraries. No one else is there, and I will have the entire place to myself. Aurelian's reconstruction of Beethoven will be conducting a complete (if parahistorical) version of his unfinished masterpiece Eighty-first Symphony, the first since Cuprician's time, and holding a performance. I shall be the only person in the theater."

"I am still grateful for your sacrifice, Warden Lacedemonian."

And now Temer's smile grew broad, startlingly white against his space-dark skin. "The gratitude is mutual. I must tell you one more thing, just privately, between you and me. When you opened your memory casket, and recalled your *Phoenix Exultant*, mine came open, too, and I spent a whole day, not at the Celebration as my wives and I had planned, but sitting under a noesis helmet in a oneiriatrist's closet. I had days and years of memories, spent thinking about and watching the progress on your ship. My whole life, ever since I gave up sea-farming, has been ships, Mr. Phaethon. I was a member of the Celeritolumenous Society since before you were born, since before there was a science of Celerotology. I am in love with your ship, sir. And, with the Hortators' ban still in place, I am the only man, equipped with the instruments to record the whole process, who will be able to watch the *Phoenix Exultant* when she soars. Please inform me when you intend your first burn, and transmit your vector and discharge area, and, considering the size of your ship, the extent of your occlusion umbra. If we have nothing further to discuss . . . ? Then that will be all. Permission to disembark."

"It was a very great pleasure speaking with you, Mr. Lacedemonia. I must confess, I possessed unkind thoughts concerning you after my passage through your section of the space-tower. Those memories will be robbed of force and replaced by the fond memories I shall have of our meeting here. Good day to you, sir."

"And Godspeed to you and to your fine ship."

Temer's image saluted and walked away, and the mannequin, now empty, went limp.

4.

When Phaethon gestured to accept from the second icon, the mannequin straightened to attention.

Phaethon's sense-filter conveyed an image of Atkins standing there, darkly shining in his black armor. A knife and a *katana*, a smart-pistol and a far-injector hung in his holsters and sheaths. The dots on his gorget showed one-way thought-ports, obviously meant to project mental viruses into systems, but unable to receive them. The ring on his finger had a black stone; the color indicating dangerous self-propagating deleters and corrupters were stored there. Phaethon was impressed with how overwhelmingly deadly the man was; it showed from every detail of his appearance; it was not something, earlier in his life, Phaethon would have been alert to notice.

Without a word of greeting, Atkins drew a memory card from his weapon belt, and held it up. "Here are the Warmind's instructions. I have reviewed the plan and concluded that it is the best our present limited knowledge allows. The fundamental goal of this plan is to locate the enemy high command, the entity you refer to as Nothing Sophotech."

"Why do you say, 'refer to'?"

"We don't think it's a Sophotech. The things Scaramouche said to you may have been calculated to create that impression, perhaps to dishearten any opposition. No one wants to fight a Sophotech, do they? But I insist that you agree to follow by the provisions of this plan, before I show them to you."

It took a moment for Phaethon to understand what was being asked of him. "How can I agree in ignorance?"

"How can you think you can be of any help to the military effort to defend the Golden Oecumene when you have steadfastly refused to join the military? The need for coordinated action, guided by a unified plan, is so obvious during emergencies of this kind, that I am amazed that the laws will not permit me to conscript you and expropriate your ship for this purpose. The laws won't let me do what I need to do to let us survive this war. Those laws might get us all killed. So what can I do now? I've complained to my superior about you, and explained that the military needs you and your ship for this plan to have any chance."

"And the response, I assume, did not create great pleasure in you?"

Atkins looked annoyed. "Get that smirk off your face, mister, this is not funny."

"I intended no jest, Marshal Atkins! Nor was I smirking; this is simply my natural expression. But I cannot hide the pleasure with which I hear the news that my individual rights are still carefully respected by the Parliament and the Sophotechs, even in such times as these. And I had thought all this time that the Parliament was the main source of danger to my liberty. How strange that they should defend it."

"Don't pick out a silverware pattern yet."

"I beg your pardon?"

"I mean, don't fall in love with the Parliament. The Parliament would have done everything I wanted in an instant if the Sophotechs, without exception, had not advised them not to. Westmind predicted that the Curia would have overruled the Parliament in an instant, knew the Censor would censure them, and predicted that the Hortators would have them all ostracized and picking through trash in Talaimannar before the day was up, if they treated you that way. Nebuchednezzar himself spoke up for you."

"How ironic."

Atkins held up the memory card. "If he hadn't, you'd be a buck private right now, and these would be boot-camp downloads and mind-sets and orders, not suggestions."

"What did Nebuchednezzar say?"

"He said any civilization that could not produce men willing freely to volunteer to fight and die in her defense did not deserve to survive." Atkins paused a moment to let that sink in. Then, in a harder voice: "And I told him I'd rather have my civilization, my folks and my friends, survive, whether they 'deserved to' or not. There's something really screwy about a set-up where one guy like you, just on his own, gets to decide whether or not our civilization 'deserves' to survive." Atkins held up the card, and concluded: "Well? Do we have a deal? Are you going to follow the plan to the letter?"

"You ask me to sacrifice my ship and perhaps my life on a plan, which I am not permitted to examine? What kind of businessman do you think I am?"

"I don't give a damn what kind of businessman you are. I'm trying to find out what kind of patriot you are. If I tell you the plan, and you don't agree to follow it, and then you do something stupid and fall into enemy hands, then they'll get the plan, and I don't want that."

"Come now, Marshal! What you ask of me is unreasonable."

"War is unreasonable. If it were reasonable, it would be called 'peace.' The only other thing I can do is show you the plan under seal, and then have your memory of the plan redacted, allowing you only to keep the knowledge that there is a plan and that you agreed to it."

"After I woke from the redaction, I would not know why I had agreed. I wouldn't even know whether or not the memory of agreement was true, or was a false memory planted by you for some overriding military purpose. I only just recently escaped from the labyrinth of missing memory; do you expect me to step back into that maze again?"

"Sorry. What else can we do? I don't want the enemy to find out the plan through you. Besides, think of it this way: this time, when you go back into the Labyrinth, you'll be Theseus. This time, it'll be the monster in the middle of the maze who'll find he has a cause to be afraid."

"You have the soul of a poet, Marshal Atkins."

"Kipling, I hope."

"I mean, you pepper your speech with such archaisms, you sound just like a Silver-Grey."

"With all due respect, my tradition is older than yours, older than anyone else's. My profession was the first one man ever made, and it'll be the last one to go. It's the one that makes all the others possible. So what do you say?" He held up the card for the third time. "Does our civilization deserve to live, or not?"

Phaethon slid aside the panel of the symbol table. Underneath was the portable noetic reader Aurelian had given Daphne. "I can use this for the redaction. I have enough capacity in my armor and in the ship-mind to do all the necessary iatropsychometry. I'll be flying blind when I awake, I suppose." And Phaethon heaved a great sigh. "One would expect I'd be used to that, by now."

A set of tiny wrinkles formed around Atkins's eyes. It was not the standard face-symbology, but Phaethon recognized the look from old historicals. Despite the fact that the man's mouth was still, as ever, a grim line, he was smiling. It was a look of admiration, of pleasure, even of joy.

"Well, well," said Atkins. "Will wonders never cease? You're a bold man after all."

"The boldest, I hope," Phaethon replied.

"Second boldest," Atkins corrected.

"You look pleased nonetheless, Marshall Atkins."

"I am happy to be seeing action, Mr. Phaethon. It is always a lot worse than you think it is going to be, and the civilian authority is usually more ready to go to war than the military professionals, and when these things start, usually the good guys aren't ready, aren't trained, aren't equipped. But still. But still . . ."

"But still this is the task for which you have kept yourself in readiness for centuries without count, is it not, Marshal Atkins?"

Atkins squinted, and looked off to the left, almost as if he were shy, and amused at his own shyness. He snorted through his nose. "The most likely outcome here is, that we are both going to buy the farm, Mr. Phaethon."

"What farm?"

"Sorry. I mean we are both going to die. Probably many times. Whether or not my backup copies think they are the same guy as me won't make my dying any easier; and if we are fighting a Sophotech after all, we may be in for a fate worse than death. We could be turned. Edited. Made into loyal copies of ourselves, working for the other side. So there is no reason to grin."

"My dear sir, I am not 'grinning.' As I said before, this is my normal expression."

"You never looked like that on the ground."

"This is my normal expression aboard my ship. No one has been privileged to see it on my face before."

Atkins chuckled, and Phaethon could not restrain a great laugh of reckless joy. He tossed back his head as if he had heard a trumpet sounding in the distance. "Come! I fear no Silent Oecumene, no dark swans from a dead star, no evil Sophotechs! I fear nothing. My heart is filled with fire; I have the strength of titans in me! Here all around us is my dream, come true in the form as I would have it, each erg of energy, each molecule and field of force fitted to my design; from prow to stern, keel to superstructure, this is all my thought made real; and made real to defy a world that has forgotten what that word 'real' once meant. Welcome aboard my ship, Marshal Atkins! We will face the foe together; we shall triumph, or perish with honor; that is my promise. Here is my hand on it."

A slight tension pulled at Atkins's cheek, as if he were smiling at Phaethon's presumption. Or, perhaps he was pleased by the enthusiasm. "The ship is not legally yours, and we are not going any farther than Jupiter, to take aboard the real owner; who, if he had any options, would run away and hide, rather than face me. But he has no options. He will show himself." He doffed his gauntlet and took Phaethon's proffered hand.

Phaethon said, "Off to battle, then?"

Atkins said, "Off to battle. Is there anything to drink aboard this boat? This kind of thing calls for a toast."

They shook hands.

Phaethon seated himself on his throne. The thought-ports on his armor opened. "All stations, systems, subsystems, partials, routines, and commands! Heed me; your captain speaks. Prepare the greatest ship ever crafted by civilization for her maiden voyage; and even if it is to be a voyage that will end in fire and destruction, let us make ready in all due haste! Initiate your sequences and run the checks: the *Phoenix Exultant* this day is launched!"

In his brain and in the brain-augmentations in his armor, the preliminary system checks began. Mirror after mirror lit up around him. The throbbing hum of energy at work could be heard in the distance.

The initial round of checks were semiautomatic; it would not be until an hour or so from now that he would need to merge with the ship-mind and oversee the final high-energy build-up processes to bring the engines to burn temperatures.

He had plenty of time to discover what this plan was that Marshal Atkins had brought from the Warmind, plenty of time to compose whatever last good-byes, or set in order what last will and testament he might require. Plenty of time.

So then, to Atkins he said, "What was that about a toast?"

"It's an old tradition. You'll love it."

"Marshal, I know what a toast is; I live my life in a Second-Era Victorian simulation as a lord of the manor. They drink like, well, like lords. I was wondering to what you were going to toast?" A remote shaped like a cabin boy was already approaching across the wide expanse of the golden floor, carrying a tray with two crystal goblets.

Atkins took one cup in hand. "Why, Mr. Phaethon, I thought that would be obvious."

He raised the sparkling goblet.

"To the *Phoenix Exultant*."

"To the *Phoenix Exultant*!"

"And, though I doubt it, long may she live."

Phaethon's heart was full, and had no room for doubt. He said, "Long may she live, and far may she fly."

They touched glasses with the tiniest chime of crystal noise.

Here ends the second volume,
THE PHOENIX EXULTANT.
The tale of the Golden Age concludes in the third volume,
THE GOLDEN TRANSCENDENCE.